Fabulous praise for
Deborah Donnelly's
Wedding Planner Mysteries

May the Best Man Die

"Romantic and bright—an odd atmosphere for a murder mystery. But it works!" —*Every Other Weekly* (Washington)

"Offers droll humor, interesting background, cunning whodunit misdirection, and what amateur-detective cozies so often lack: real detection from fairly presented clues."
—*Ellery Queen Mystery Magazine*

Veiled Threats

"Reminiscent of Donna Andrews's *Murder, With Peacocks*, this zany mystery is a bubbly blend of farcical humor, romance and intrigue. First-time author Donnelly will beguile readers with her keen wit and mint descriptions, but it is her characters that make this a stellar debut."
—*Publishers Weekly*

"Donnelly's fast-moving story and likable sleuth will please readers...." —*Booklist*

"A solid start for what could be an entertaining edition to the cozy ranks. With her charm, intuition and the unpredictability of weddings, Carnegie could find herself a very busy sleuth." —*Mystery Reader*

"A nice mix of romance, suspense and humor...Like Elizabeth Peters, Donnelly offers a solid read, lively and entertaining, with a spunky, independent heroine."
—*BookLoons*

"An exciting and highly entertaining ride through danger and suspense with a dash of sensuality along the way."
—*Romance Reviews Today*

Death Takes a Honeymoon

DEBORAH DONNELLY

A DELL BOOK

DEATH TAKES A HONEYMOON
A Dell Book / May 2005

Published by
Bantam Dell
A Division of Random House, Inc.
New York, New York

This is a work of fiction. Names, characters, places, and incidents either
are the product of the author's imagination or are used fictitiously. Any
resemblance to actual persons, living or dead, events, or locales is
entirely coincidental.

Dell is a registered trademark of Random House, Inc., and the colophon
is a trademark of Random House, inc.

ISBN 0-440-24130-8

Printed in the United States of America
Published simultaneously in Canada

www.bantamdell.com

OPM 10 9 8 7 6 5 4 3 2 1

For Kristina Schnur, who is truly
her father's daughter

Acknowledgments

There is no smoke-jumper base in Ketchum, Idaho. I placed one there for the sake of my story, the way I took a few liberties with the Pioneer Saloon and other landmarks. But there are certainly smoke jumpers in Idaho, several of whom helped me with this book by showing me around the real bases in Boise and McCall. My special appreciation goes to smoke jumper Dave Estey and his wife Flap, as well as to flower wizard John Carpenter and wedding planners Lona Schuster and Glenna Tooman. Many thanks also to Libby Hellmann, Roberta Isleib, Laurel Sercombe, and Gemma Utting for their generous moral support, and to Caitlin Alexander, my excellent editor. Finally, and as ever, my love and gratitude to Steve, who makes it all a honeymoon.

Death Takes a Honeymoon

Chapter One

BE CAREFUL WHAT YOU WISH FOR, THAT'S WHAT THEY SAY. And whoever they are, they were certainly right this time. When I wished for heat, serious heat, I got what I wished for and then some.

It all started in the middle of a Sunday morning in the middle of June, as I stood in my houseboat sulking up a storm. A rainstorm, to be precise. This was Seattle, after all.

Huddled in sweatshirt and jeans, I leaned my forehead against the sliding-glass porch door and glared outside. Beyond my narrow wooden deck, the surface of Lake Union was the color of pewter. Dull, wet, rain-speckled pewter.

In addition to sulking, I was sipping hot strong coffee and yearning for hot strong sunshine. I wanted clear skies and high temperatures, the higher the better. *You call this June?*

Even in Seattle, June should bring at least a hint of summer. An arched eyebrow, a mischievous wink, a suggestive nod in the direction of halter tops and sunscreened shoulders and watermelon leaking pink through paper plates. Was that so much to ask?

This June we had sunscreen, all right: a coffin lid of cloud that screened the sun like an SPF 30 lotion. For weeks now, the temperature had been just high enough for cotton clothing, just low enough to skip the gin and tonics after all. Day after day after day of Mostly Cloudy, Some Chance of Showers, and I was Pissed Off, No Chance of Smiles.

The phone jangled—the business line. On a Sunday? Business wasn't all that good, so I set down my mug and answered briskly.

"Made in Heaven Wedding Design."

"Relax, it's me. Jeez, Muffy, you sound a hundred and three years old."

Please understand, my name is not now, nor has it ever been, Muffy. It's Carnegie Kincaid, and I'm about seventy years shy of a hundred and three. But this wasn't a wrong number. The familiar voice, as raucous as a magpie and as subtle as an elbow in the ribs, was Brenda Jervis, better known as B.J.

B.J. was my high-school buddy from Boise, Idaho, where I grew up and where my mother still taught school. She and I and a third girl, Tracy Kane, had called each other "Muffy" throughout the long, hilarious, hot-blooded college summer that we spent working at the Sun Valley Lodge. Tracy was younger, a tagalong friend, but B.J. and I were bonded for life.

The resort village of Sun Valley is a two-hour drive from Boise, but just ten minutes up the road from the mountain town of Ketchum. Tracy's mother, Cecilia—"Call me Cissy"—lived in Ketchum, and Cissy Kane wanted to give her teenage daughter a little freedom after her graduation from high school. So she kept a tolerant eye on the three of us—blonde Tracy, brunette B.J., and redheaded me—as we shared a cheap apartment and waited tables at the venerable old Sun Valley Lodge.

The Muffy thing was a private joke that summer, to lightly mock the tanned and pampered ladies who played tennis and rode horses and had pedicures at the resort, while the three of us humped platters and flirted with the line cooks and drank too much beer. B.J. and I still used the silly name in our occasional phone calls and e-mails, but I hadn't heard from Tracy, the junior Muffy, in years.

Not until Tracy's wedding invitation arrived, in the soggy April preceding this soggy June. And it was as stiffly impersonal as an invitation could be. On vellum thick as cream, in the curliest of curly engraving, the honor of my presence was requested on Midsummer's Day—this coming Saturday—at the union of Tracy Marie Kane and John Holland Packard III. Someone even dug up my top-secret middle name, Bernice, to address the envelope. But there was no personal note for Muffy.

I had declined the invitation, and that's why B.J. was on the phone. She lived in Ketchum herself now, and she was in cahoots with the mother of the bride.

"Cissy told me you're not coming! What's the matter, Muffy, no date? Did that short guy dump you?"

"He's not short, B.J., he's just shorter than me." Which isn't hard; I'm a six-footer in heels. "Nobody's dumping anybody."

"Not yet, huh?"

"Oh, *B.J.*" How many times had I said her name in precisely that tone of affectionate exasperation?

"Well, you used to rave about this guy and now he's the Invisible Man. You never mention him. Matt and I want to look him over and ask him embarrassing questions."

"I thought Matt was still in Germany."

"He'll be back just in time for Tracy's wedding. Which you *will* be attending, with Shorty or without him, if I have to come over there and drag you."

"His name is Aaron, all right? And we're still seeing each other." I flopped onto the couch and pulled an afghan over my bare feet. "I'm just too busy to make it. I put a note in with my RSVP, but Tracy didn't answer, so that's that. I can't change my mind less than a week before the wedding, it would be rude."

"Tracy never answers anything. And Cissy says there's plenty of room. Half the guests are bringing guests. It's going to be the party to end all parties. You've got to come! Listen to this menu..."

As B.J. regaled me with the lamb chops in phyllo and the roasted pears with pecorino cheese, my thoughts drifted. *Too busy to make it* was a blatant falsehood, and *seeing each other* was hardly an adequate term for my current relationship with Aaron Gold.

Driving each other crazy was more like it. Good crazy—that was the sex. And bad crazy—that was just about everything else.

You see, back on New Year's Eve, at an intimate bistro under a Miami moon, Aaron had gazed into my eyes and presented me with a box. A little velvet box. The kind that might, just might, contain a diamond ring.

Actually, the box was just a thought too large for a ring, but at the time I wasn't thinking any thoughts. I was revved up on romance, and the diamond ring idea zoomed straight from my imagination to my mouth without pausing for a pit stop in my brain.

Major mistake. Because the box contained, of all things, a banged-up steel cigarette lighter. Aaron's chain-smoking had been a problem for me from the day we met, and giving me the lighter was a dramatic way to announce that he meant to quit.

Well, fine. Wonderful. Only by the time I realized that, I was already in mid-blurt.

"Oh! I . . . thought it was a ring."

Major, major mistake. Aaron went instantly to Red Alert, I got mad to cover my embarrassment, and we had one of those ghastly exchanges that make you cringe at the memory.

"A ring! Are you nuts? I just got divorced."

"I know you're divorced, Aaron. You told me right after you casually mentioned that you were married."

"Are we back to this? OK, so I didn't tell you about Barbara right away. I was wrong. How much longer are you going to throw it in my face?"

"I'm not throwing anything. But if you think you'd be nuts to marry me—"

"I didn't say that. I just didn't know you were so eager to plan your own wedding."

"I'm not! Don't be ridiculous. I'm not ready to get married, to you or anyone else. I was joking."

"Really?"

"Of course."

"Oh. OK. You want another piña colada?"

"Of course."

So we went on with our dinner, and then on with our vacation. The sun and sand and exotic birds made an effective distraction, but from that moment forward, everything changed. The ominous M-word had been spoken, and a faint but persistent self-consciousness lingered in the air between us like the acrid smoke of a snuffed candle. Except in bed, and you can't stay in bed forever, can you? Though Aaron certainly gave it a shot.

After the vacation, back home in Seattle, we got busy with jobs and friends and the dailiness of life, but we had to work a little too hard at being casual. We spent most of our time together, but remained deliberately vague about the future. Passionate in what we did, but cautious in what we said.

What bothered me most is that Aaron somehow stopped saying "I love you." And I was damned if I'd say it—or bring up the subject of marriage—until he did. But he didn't, and maybe never would. I had to admit it: we were having Commitment Issues. It was trite and tedious and absurd— and I couldn't stop thinking about it.

On top of that there was the smoking, or absence thereof. Aaron was naturally a high-voltage guy, with an electrical wit and energy to burn. But with no tobacco to burn, he was by turns preoccupied, touchy, and just plain glum. Once in a while he'd fall off the wagon, and though I disliked the smell of cigarettes, I secretly enjoyed what they did for his disposition.

"So?" B.J.'s voice tugged me back to the present. "Have I talked you into coming?"

"Um, not sure. Who's going to be there? Mostly Tracy's TV crowd?"

"Yes, indeed." B.J.'s voice dropped a tone. "I'm hoping for that hunky guy who played the veterinarian in the pilot episode. He's still a Maybe, but lots of other actors are coming for sure. Eye candy, yum, yum."

Tracy, you see, had hit the big time. After the Muffy summer, only two of us finished college. I went on to a public-relations job for a Seattle bank, while B.J., whose thumbs were both green, became assistant manager of a garden center in Ketchum. But Tracy dropped out in her freshman year and went back to waiting tables.

Those tables, however, were in Los Angeles, and between shifts she haunted auditions. Her wide, uptilted blue eyes and sultry purr won her a few TV commercials, then bit parts in the soaps. And then, triumph of triumphs, she landed the lead role in a prime-time comedy about a single, sexy, zany dog walker.

So now, ten years or so later, the Muffies were making their mark. I owned Made in Heaven, B.J. owned High Country Gardens, and Tracy Kane owned the hearts and minds of the Wednesday night audience for *Tails of the City*.

"The guest list is huge," B.J. was saying. "Cissy has been clucking around town like a smug little hen, playing mother of the bride. It's hysterical."

Sam and Cissy Kane, the wily old real-estate developer and his shopaholic wife, were longtime fixtures in Ketchum. Like so many residents of the Wood River area, they lived in California and came to Idaho when they pleased, in winter for the skiing and in summer for the golf. But unlike many, they were born Idahoans. Sam had even run for governor once, or so I'd heard. Even now the Kanes kept a hand in local affairs, chamber of commerce and town planning on Sam's side, arts events and charities on Cissy's.

The arts included opera, an interest that she shared with my mother. Mom called Cissy Kane the silliest woman she'd ever met, but she was fond of her, nevertheless. And everybody who met Sam liked him. Tall and rawboned, Sam ambled along like an animated scarecrow and rarely removed his cowboy hat except for sweeping salutes to the ladies, including his plump little wife. If not the king and queen of Sun Valley, Sam and Cissy were certainly the duke and duchess.

And they were certainly putting on a royal affair. Tracy's vellum envelope had bulged with engraved cards, maps, and RSVP slips for various festivities throughout the wedding weekend, from ice skating to spa treatments to a bachelor baseball game. A destination wedding, as we say in the business, with no expenses spared.

Most of the preliminary events, and the guest accommodations, were at the Sun Valley Lodge, but the ceremony and reception would take place somewhere I'd never heard of, the White Pine Inn. When I asked B.J. about that part, she was scornful.

"You really are out of touch, aren't you?" To B.J., Seattle was just some distant, mildewed city of exile for those who couldn't find honest work in Idaho. "White Pine is Sam's new project up in the mountains. It's not finished yet, but it's going to be a luxury resort."

"Have you seen it?"

"No, but I'm dying to. I hear it's spectacular. You go up a long private road through a canyon, then it's a big complex along the top of a ridge, with incredible views and a hot spring and everything. I can't believe you're missing this just to work! What kind of wedding are you doing? Is it Saturday or Sunday?"

"Well . . ." Old habits die hard. B.J. had always bullied me a little, and I had never been able to lie to her with any success. "It's more that I'm working on weddings that are scheduled for later on."

"And you have to do that on a weekend? Come on, Carnegie, 'fess up. Couldn't you come if you really wanted to?"

"Well . . ."

"Don't you remember our vow? That the Muffies would dance at each other's weddings? You came to mine."

"But Tracy didn't."

"Hey, she was in Belize with that cute producer. I couldn't blame her. Come on, Carnegie. It's not just actors, some old friends of ours will be there. I bet you haven't seen your cousin in ages."

"My cousin?"

"Hel-*lo,* your cousin Brian? He just moved to Ketchum to start smoke jumping."

"Second cousin," I reminded her. "Or maybe it's once removed, I can't remember. Anyway, I never see him, which is fine with me. What does Matt think about your old boyfriend showing up?"

I meant that sarcastically. Matt was B.J.'s husband, a mining engineer and a hunk in his own right, who traveled a lot for his job but treated her like a goddess when he was home. They'd been inseparable during the Muffy summer, except for a brief interlude when Brian Thiel came through town with a firefighting crew. Brian was tall, dark, and devastating, his own biggest fan. A few dates with him and his ego had sent B.J. back to Matt.

"Oh, please," she retorted. "That's ancient history. I just thought you'd like to know you have a smoke jumper in the family now."

Here in misty Seattle we don't think about it much, but across the intermountain West, summertime is the time of fire. Generations of men—and now women—had enlisted in the standing army of wildland firefighters, making full-time careers or just part-time cash working for the Forest Service or the Bureau of Land Management or the National Parks. They're strong and skilled and dedicated, and they seemed very glamorous to a couple of young waitresses.

Actually, they still seemed kind of glamorous, especially the ones who reach their fires from the sky. But it would take more than that to polish Brian Thiel's image in my eyes. I just didn't like the man.

"He's always been a good athlete," I said grudgingly. "But he's still a jerk."

"Bri isn't so bad. Wait a minute! Talk about ancient history! Talk about smoke jumpers! You're avoiding the wedding because of *Jack*. You're skipping out on a Muffy wedding because of what happened that night between you and Jack the Knack."

I sat bolt upright.

"Absolutely not," I lied indignantly. "I haven't thought about Jack Packard in years."

"Bullshit," said my old friend. "Complete and utter bull. I bet you think about Jack every night. I bet you don't dare see him in person because you're afraid you'll steal him away from Tracy just so you can—"

"B.J., I've got someone at the door." I reached out a hand to make a knocking noise on the coffee table. "Sounds urgent. Talk to you later, OK?"

"OK, but promise you'll think about coming. Promise, Muffy?"

"I promise, Muffy. Now good-bye."

I remained on the couch, mummied in my afghan, staring out at the rain once more. The air was so pale and dense with droplets that I could barely see the blue and orange girders of the Fremont drawbridge across the lake, or the lone sailboat tacking across the middle. Must be the SS *Masochist*.

Idaho, I mused, would be hot and sunny and *dry*. I hadn't seen my mother in a while. Tracy the television star might not care about the honor of my presence all that much, but B.J. was always a hoot to be around. Not to mention Sam and Cissy Kane and their legendary hospitality. I could even stay at the lodge, and let the latest crop of waitresses wait on me. Besides, there was that vow the Muffies made, to dance at each other's weddings. . . .

But not with Jack, no way. I drew my hair down over one shoulder and twisted my fingers into the curls as my thoughts went twisting into memories of hot summer nights, parties and laughter, fast cars and slow dances. But most of all, I was remembering Jack the Knack, the here-today, gone-tomorrow smoke jumper who broke every female heart within range. Including mine.

I'd fallen hard for Jack Packard, yearning at him from the edge of his wide and lively circle of friends. Then one fateful night he had asked me to dance. When the music slowed I moved boldly into his arms, and slipped my hands into his back pockets with a show of sophistication that Jack mistook for reality. We ended up in bed, I ended up in tears, and he ended up driving me home in appalled silence. We avoided each other for the rest of the summer, and even now I winced at the thought of that foolish, foolish girl. But even now, as a woman, I sometimes caught myself daydreaming about a rematch with Jack the Knack.

I sighed and shoved my hair aside. *He's probably forgotten all about that night, anyway. I bet he's changed a lot. He's almost forty. Mom said he's retiring from smoke jumping so he can move to California with Tracy, so I'll probably never see him again. Never is a long time. I'd love to see him just once—*

"Hey!" I jumped, startled, as a whiskery kiss landed on the back of my neck.

"Morning, Stretch. Been up long?" Aaron Gold, unkempt and unshaven, rolled lightly over the back of the couch and heavily onto me. He pushed me flat and slid his hands down under the afghan, and then up under my sweatshirt. He wore jeans and nothing else.

"Not long," I said, making a halfhearted attempt to fend him off. "Don't tell me the phone woke you. Nothing ever wakes you."

"Nope. Just having a dream about you, so I thought I'd check out the reality. Mmmm ... reality's pretty dreamy." His hands wandered, then he pulled them free to plant his palms along either side of my head. He did a push-up and held it, looking down into my eyes.

"Tell me something, Stretch."

"What?" I asked brightly, hoping for a query about breakfast, about the weather forecast, about anything in the world except—

"Who's Jack Packard, and why have you been thinking about him?"

"I said I *hadn't*."

"That's not what your voice sounded like."

Sometimes you bluff your way through an awkward moment. Sometimes you kiss your way through.

"Forget Jack," I told Aaron—and myself—as I wound a hand around the back of his neck. I love the back of his neck. "C'mere, you."

No deal. Aaron's a reporter, and once his curiosity is engaged, he's undistractable. "I'll c'mere in a minute. Who was on the phone?"

That was a safer question. "Oh, just B.J., my friend from Idaho. I've told you about her."

"Yeah, I remember." Aaron's eyes narrowed thoughtfully. They were fine eyes, a deep, polished brown, surrounded by laugh lines. He wasn't laughing now. "You were trying awfully hard to get her off the phone."

"She's ... really long-winded." Then to distract him, I

spoke on impulse. Never speak on impulse. "Aaron, let's take a trip next weekend, get some sunshine."

"Now you're talking." He dropped beside me and propped himself on one elbow. "I'm starting to rust around here! Where shall we go? A guy at the *Sentinel* just got back from Puerto Vallarta. He said it was dirt cheap and the snorkeling was incredible."

"Um, I was thinking about Sun Valley."

"Idaho? That's for skiing."

"No, it's great in the summer. In fact, they get more tourists in summer than winter. We could go hiking or kayaking or horseback riding. And Ketchum, that's the main town, is full of restaurants and art galleries."

Aaron cocked his head, considering, and a lock of crow-black hair fell across his eyes. That gets me every time.

"Sounds too much like work," he said. "I'm more in the mood for vegging out on the sand. You could wear that little bathing suit you bought in Florida. Or *not* wear it. This guy says suits are optional down there, if you go to the right beach."

He began to demonstrate that sweatshirts were optional in Seattle, but I stopped him.

"The thing is, Aaron, this other friend of mine is getting married in Sun Valley next weekend. I thought I'd be too busy to go, but I'm not, and I really should be there. That's what B.J. was calling about."

"Oh. A wedding."

"A fancy wedding—the Kanes are quite wealthy. So, gourmet food and live music and a weekend at this private resort in the mountains. It'll be fun, and you can meet B.J. and my other friends—"

"And Jack Packard?"

"Well, sure, he's the groom."

"*Oh.*" Aaron relaxed perceptibly, and I pressed my advantage.

"We can fly into Boise and rent a car. Ketchum's just a couple hours' drive, and we could stay the first night with Mom. She'd like to meet you. Actually, she knows Tracy's mother, Cissy, so she's going to the wedding herself. We could give her a ride. . . ."

In my enthusiasm for the logistics of the trip—I adore logistics—I failed to notice the look on Aaron's face. But then I caught it: the look of a man who's been asked to meet his girlfriend's mother. At a wedding.

"Come to think of it, Stretch," he said, rising and heading for the bedroom, "I don't have a lot of vacation time accrued right now. Maybe later this summer."

I heard a drawer shut, then he reappeared in a Red Sox sweatshirt, car keys in hand.

"I'll get the *New York Times* and the bagels, if you scramble the eggs. Deal?"

I sighed. "Deal."

Chapter Two

A PROMISE IS A PROMISE. ON MONDAY MORNING, HIGH ATOP the global headquarters of Made in Heaven, I held a company-wide staff meeting and gave serious consideration to B.J.'s request.

Which is to say, I leaned back from my secondhand desk in the workroom, one rickety flight upstairs from my kitchen, and said, "Eddie, what if I went to Idaho for a long weekend? Would that be a problem?"

I was hoping for an affirmative, but my half-time, not-too-silent partner just snorted. It's one of his job skills.

"Wouldn't be a problem if you went for a month," he growled. "We've got no damn business till August. I told you we should have taken a booth at that bridal expo in February, but you were too busy playing around with Aaron."

I swiveled to face him. Eddie Breen is white-haired and wiry, an old friend of my late father, retired from both the merchant marine and a career in accounting. He handles the contracts and the money, when there is any, with ferocious precision, and he holds decided opinions about everything. Up to and most certainly including my personal life.

"You used to encourage me to play around with Aaron," I pointed out. "You were his biggest fan."

"He's all right." Eddie glanced up from his computer and

rotated the ever-present cigar from one side of his jaw to the other. *Unlit* cigar; I run a nonsmoking HQ. "You taking him to meet Louise?"

"N-no." Louise was my mother. "No, an old friend of mine is getting married in Sun Valley, but Aaron can't come. Mom will be there, though."

"Hunh. Big wedding?"

I nodded, knowing what was coming.

"Then why in blue blazes shouldn't you go?" he demanded. "See what kind of ideas you can pick up. Maybe pick up some clients. Come to think of it, why didn't this friend hire you in the first place?"

"Tracy and I aren't that close anymore," I said, swiveling back. Both our desks face the lake, by far the best feature of the workroom. The good room out front, where I meet with clients, has a lake view, as well, but also the classy carpet and the adorable wicker furniture. "Besides, I'm not sure I feel like going on a trip by myself."

Eddie didn't reply. But as the raindrops slithered down the windows in long wavering streaks, a thought came to me. I could keep my promise to the Muffies and do my mother some good into the bargain.

Mom had spent Christmas on the Oregon coast with Eddie, and neither one of them had told me about it beforehand. So that meant there was something going on. Something romantic? They'd seen each other only once since then, as far as I knew, but Mom seemed to call Eddie even more often than she did me.

"Here's an idea," I said casually. A light touch was called for. "Why don't we both attend this wedding? I'm welcome to bring a guest, and you could size up the vendor operations while I'm looking over the dresses and the flowers and so forth. Then we could visit Mom for a day or so afterward and compare notes."

Not light enough.

"Listen, sister," said Eddie over his shoulder, as he stabbed at his keyboard. "You know damn well I'm doing this overhaul of our billing system. Why would I want to go gallivanting off to see some friend of yours get married and make small talk with a bunch of strangers? Probably have to wear a tie, for God's sake. If you want to go, then go."

That was the crux of the matter. I didn't want to go, and I didn't like the reason why. I was happy for Tracy, really, but also a little envious. OK, more than a little. Tracy was a bride, B.J. was a contented wife, and I couldn't get a date for a wedding.

Aaron said once that weddings make single women feel extra single, and he was right. Irritating and averse to commitment, but right.

"Never mind," I muttered. "I'll stay here and concentrate on marketing."

"You sure?" asked Eddie. "You don't sound sure."

"But I am. I'm not going to Sun Valley, and that's final."

"All right, then," he said, rummaging in the stacks of paper on his desk. "If you want to think about marketing, think about this."

He tossed a magazine at me, and I caught it in a heavy flutter of glossy pages and pull-out postcards. You can get a real workout hefting bridal magazines. The gown ads alone pump up your biceps something fierce. But it was the cover of this particular rag that Eddie wanted me to see.

The cover was a close-up of a devilishly handsome rogue in his forties, sporting a tuxedo and a sensuous, self-assured smile. He had a full head of lustrous, wavy, run-your-fingers-through-it black hair, and a spark in his bedroom eyes that said if you were lucky, the fingers in question could be yours.

The man was Beau Paliere, international celebrity and wedding planner to the stars, and the headline read "Beau Knows Romance!"

I sighed, a deep, complicated sigh. Those curving lips promised romance, all right, or at least the most exquisitely romantic wedding any bride could desire. But to me they promised only exquisite revenge. Beautiful Beau was my own personal, private Parisian nemesis. Every chance he got, Beau got between me and success.

"It says he's coming through Seattle this summer," said Eddie sourly. "Private party for Bill Gates and then a cruise to Alaska. How many possible clients you think he's gonna turn against us this time?"

"It wasn't my fault, Eddie. He insulted me!"

This past Christmas, after upstaging me royally on a local TV show, Beau had invited himself to a Made in Heaven wedding. During the reception, he'd offered to make me one of his personal assistants—and then demonstrated just how personal my assistance was expected to be. I had not responded well.

"But did you have to knock the man down?" demanded Eddie, not for the first time.

"I didn't knock him down! I keep telling you, he fell. How was I to know he'd lose his t-toupee?" I snickered as I brought the word out. I couldn't help it, the memory was just too funny.

Eddie struggled to remain stern, then gave up and cracked a smile. "Must have been a sight, all right."

"It was priceless!" My snicker burst into laughter. "Can

you imagine what it cost him to keep those pictures out of the tabloids? Not that he'd even notice the money, but—"

"*Kharr-negie!*"

This time Eddie and I both swiveled to look through the good room toward the doorway that led to the houseboat's outside staircase. The door had been flung open by a massive grizzly bear of a man in a dripping rain parka. He had flame-blue eyes and a dark thicket of beard, and he was dangling a long white cardboard box from one shovel-sized hand.

The bear flashed a gleaming grin. "Kharnegie, my friend, you mek me breakfast, *da?*"

Eddie snorted again and returned to his stabbing. Boris the Mad Russian Florist was not his favorite individual. Besides, my partner left the vendor management, along with the bride management, to me. Not a people person, Eddie Breen.

Boris Nevsky, on the other hand, was hugely personal. When I joined him in the good room and shut the connecting door behind me, he deftly shifted the box to one side and swept me into a massive Slavic embrace. I pushed him away, but with a laugh. I'm fond of the Mad Russian.

"Boris, what are you doing here?"

"I deliver centerpieces for leddies' luncheon at Spinnaker's." This was a lakeside restaurant near the houseboat. "My last job before vacation. But door is locked! I call manager, she is coming in one hour. One hour! I myself deliver, special favor to her, and she kips me waiting! So I think, I visit my dear friend, she will mek me breakfast. See, I bring you extra flowers that I take to fill gaps. Manager does not deserve special favors. She deserves gaps."

He thrust the box—the bribe—at me, and as he bent to clear the glass-topped table of wedding magazines and photo albums, I folded back the lid. Stargazer lilies, pink lisianthus, baby's breath...

"These are beautiful, Boris, thank you. But I'm working, I can't just drop everything and—"

"Bah! You are not working too much these days." He dropped himself into the wicker love seat, which moaned in pain, and took the box from me. With surprising delicacy, his broad brown fingers began to shake loose each blossom and set it on the table. "Joe tells me so. He worries for your liddle business. Bring vase."

"Joe gossips too much," I said severely, filling a wide glass cylinder from the sink in the corner where Eddie makes coffee. "He should mind his own business, not mine."

Joe Solveto, Seattle's premier caterer, had offered me a job the previous year. A good offer, and maybe I should have accepted. But being my own boss suited me, and I was determined to stick it out.

I joined Boris on the love seat and began to hand him stems as he demanded them, like a nurse slapping scalpels into a surgeon's palm. The Mad Russian had his quirks, but I loved to watch him make his magic.

"More freesia, the yellow... Now fern, liddle one."

"The market's kind of slow right now," I ventured.

"Not so! Joe is busy. I am busy. More fern."

"If you're so busy, why the vacation?"

He shrugged. "I must take week off because of repairs to my building. My customers will miss me terribly. Terribly! Now lily."

As the arrangement took shape, I pondered my own lack of customers. At a more prosperous time, Beau Paliere's revenge might not have mattered. But with the economy in the doldrums, the majority of middle-class brides were having smaller weddings and doing the planning themselves. A wedding designer had become an expendable luxury.

Meanwhile, luxury-class brides were spending as much if not more than usual, throwing caution to the wind along with rose petals and rice. But now celebrity weddings, bride styles of the rich and famous, were all the rage, and everyone wanted wedding designers with upscale experience. If you had prominent names on your client list, you were booking a year or more ahead.

But I didn't have any, not with Beautiful Beau dropping his poisonous little hints in certain ladies' ears. Made in Heaven was languishing, and so was I. That ill-fated Christmas wedding hadn't yielded any referrals, and my big New Year's wedding had been canceled by the groom. Not that I blamed him for dumping that particular Bridezilla.

In any case, I'd managed some smaller ceremonies since then, along with a few private parties. But if I didn't score a high-profile bride pretty soon, I might as well close the office and sublet the top of the houseboat to tenants. I'd have an easier time paying my rent.

"*Finis!*" announced Boris. His English was uneven, but his French was flawless. "*Les belles fleurs pour ma petite amie. Voilà.*"

He swept the unused flowers into the box, set it aside, and slid the overflowing vase to the precise center of the table. The new creation was perfectly proportioned for its spot, and it subtly echoed the colors of the room, right down to the throw pillows on the love seat and the landscapes on the wall.

"Boris, you're a wonder!"

"*Da,*" he said, a modest man admitting the truth. "Genius

of flowers, one customer calls me. She is correct. Now, break-fast?"

"All right," I laughed. "I guess you've earned it. Let me just tell Eddie."

But Eddie was pushing open the connecting door, his snowy eyebrows drawn together in concern.

"Your friend B.J.'s on the phone, says it's urgent."

"She never gives up! Hang on, Boris." Exasperated, I returned to my desk and lifted the receiver. "B.J., I haven't decided yet, OK? I'll call you tonight and—honey, what's wrong?"

For a moment I heard only sobbing. Then, "Carnegie, I need help."

"Is it Matt?"

"No. No, I just . . . I just need you to . . ."

"What is it, what happened?"

Another harsh sob, then a long, shuddering breath, followed by an audible attempt to get a grip and control the tears. B.J. was always the tough one.

"Couldn't you . . . I mean . . . look, could you possibly come to Ketchum for a couple of days? It would mean a lot to me. You don't have to stay for the wedding if you don't want."

"Of course I will. I can probably get a flight today. But what—?"

"Muffy, Brian is dead."

Chapter Three

THE SEATTLE TIMES SPELLED HIS NAME WRONG.

It was a tiny item anyway, a paltry paper headstone. Brian "Theale," 34, a first-year smoke jumper based in Ketchum, had died Saturday while parachuting to the Boot Creek fire in the Frank Church Wilderness of central Idaho. Details as yet unknown. No other firefighters injured. The fire was now contained. End of story.

Wildland fires are usually named for the nearest landmark, however big or small; I'd never heard of Boot Creek. Tomorrow's paper might bring more details, perhaps a map with a little flame symbol to mark the accident site. Or a blurred snapshot of my cousin's face with a quote from someone or other about how he had died doing what he loved. More likely, the story would be crowded off the page by some new tragedy somewhere else.

I gazed down from my window seat to where the huge snowy island of Mount Rainier shouldered up from a dark green sea of foothills. Plenty of sunshine up here, in the high, wide afternoon. Plenty of time to think.

So I thought about my feelings for Brian Thiel, and found them wanting. I was sorry he had died, of course, but in a distant, abstract way. What I was really feeling, more than any sense of grief or loss over Brian, was curiosity about B.J.

Why was she so upset about this? She'd hung up the phone as soon as I agreed to come, saying she'd explain it all in person.

Well, I'd have the answers soon enough. I read the rest of the paper, just to pass the hour-long flight. The plane droned along above endless wooded slopes, and I didn't glance up again until I heard another passenger's voice.

"Look!"

We all looked. The limpid summer sky was empty of even the smallest cloud. But up ahead of us, huge and alarmingly solid-looking, towered an immense column of smoke. The crown was shaped like a giant cauliflower, the edges of its blinding white billows etched sharply against the sapphire blue. But down below, the column darkened to yellow-gray and smudgy brown.

Forest fire.

As we flew closer, I craned my head to peer down at the base of the column. It formed a dirty gray curtain that followed the rise and fall of the folded land, thinning to a mere veil in some spots, thick and opaque in others, hiding the trees as it consumed them. A ragged line of orange flame crept along one ridge, and helicopters drifted in and out of the smoke like fat black dragonflies.

From my window seat the silent spectacle was fascinating, even beautiful. But down there, in the searing heat and thunderous roar and stinging fumes, crews of people would be working harder than I'd ever worked in my life to try and tame the inferno. This wasn't Brian's fire, but his death made me look at it with new eyes.

And the sight of the fire certainly gave me a different perspective on Brian himself. So what if I remembered him as a childhood bully, or a swaggering adolescent? My cousin had been doing something brave and fine with his life, and now that life was over. Who was I to criticize him?

But moments of insight, however high-minded, are only moments. As the plane slanted toward Boise, the fir-covered mountains gave way to parched brown hills and irrigated river valleys, the smoke tower passed out of sight behind us, and I gazed eagerly down at my hometown.

Boise, Idaho, was once the reverse of Manhattan: a great place to live, but you wouldn't especially want to visit there. These days, though, the city boasted better restaurants and bigger concerts and fancier lifts at the Bogus Basin ski area, only fifteen miles away. Best of all, at least to me, June in Boise looked exactly like June should, as burstingly green and blazingly bright as all the summers of my childhood.

There were changes each time I came home, a new building here, a rerouted street there. But the hills of the Boise Front still defended the north edge of town, tawny hills like the flanks of lions. And closer in, along the bike lanes of the Boise River Greenbelt and the quiet neighborhood streets, the fine old silver maples and prospector elms and broad-limbed sycamores would still be casting their pools of deep, warm, murmuring shade. I love Seattle, but it's always nice to go home.

Not that I'd be in Boise all that long. Mom had offered to meet me at the airport, just to say hello, and we'd visit some more in Ketchum during the wedding weekend. I thought I might stay over in Boise for a few days afterward, too. Eddie didn't need me to rush back, and the way Aaron was acting lately, it might be time to deprive him of my delightful company for a while. Maybe absence would make the guy grow fonder.

We landed with a bump and a whine in the bare, empty

stretch of land south of Boise. Seattle doesn't have a bare empty inch. As the seat-belt sign blinked off, I checked my watch: four-thirty. Plenty of time to drive to Ketchum, pick B.J. up at work, and take her out for dinner and drinks. Dinner optional.

The covered jetway was air-conditioned, but just stepping onto it from the door of the plane, I could feel the hot high-desert air stealing in from outside, with that peculiar and enlivening quality that tells you you're not at sea level anymore. It felt odd yet familiar, and I knew that after being here, my first breath of Seattle air would taste damp and heavy.

At the security gate, I scanned the waiting crowd for a familiar face.

"Carrie, over here!"

"Mom?"

I set down my tote bag to embrace her, then leaned back to stare. Tall and trim, she wore a leaf-green linen dress I'd never seen before, as well as mascara and a touch of perfume. All three were unusual for my mother, but the real shocker was her hair. Short and chic, it framed her long, strong, suntanned face in curving silver feathers.

"What have you done with my mother?"

She smiled demurely and gave me both profiles. "Do you like it, really? I got so tired of all the perming and the coloring and the fussing, I thought, what the hell!"

I laughed aloud. Coming from Louise Kincaid, this was daring language indeed.

"It looks terrific, Mom. You're right, what the hell!"

"Don't you dare tell Timmy, though. I want to surprise him." My younger brother had been called Timmy as a child. Now, married and with a child of his own, he was still Timmy to me.

"My lips are utterly sealed."

Then we both stopped laughing, struck by the guilty realization that our first words should have been about Brian. We spoke at once.

"I was so sorry to hear—"

"It's terrible, such a nice—"

We fell silent and hugged again, holding on to our own bond at the news of our relatives' loss.

"Do you know how it happened?" I asked, but Mom shook her head.

"Only that it was an accident. I called his parents in Chicago, of course, but they didn't have the details yet and I hated to pester them." She sighed. "The funeral will be out there, but I didn't offer to attend. Is that awful of me? Last-minute plane fares are so expensive, and I haven't seen anyone on that side of the family in so long, I'd feel like a bit of a hypocrite."

"I'm sure they understand, Mom."

"I hope so. Well, shall we have coffee here before you go? I need to perk up for my tennis tournament, and I don't want you getting drowsy on your drive. You look so tired, dear. Are you getting enough sleep?"

"I'm fine, Mom." As we walked, I took in the wide hallways and the artful tile work of the new terminal. Boise was coming up in the world. "I'm just fine."

"What a shame Aaron couldn't come and share the driving with you. He's never seen your hometown."

"It's only a two-hour drive, Mom. And Aaron isn't self-employed like I am. He couldn't take the time off."

"Mmm."

I knew that *Mmm.* "Look, I'm fine, and Aaron will come another time. Could we drop it?"

"Irritability is a sign of sleep deprivation, you know. Let's get you your coffee. We'd better fetch your bag first, though, you can never tell who's lurking around. Not that we have anything like the crime rate of Seattle. I saw on the news just last night—"

"Mom, I've been meaning to ask," I countered, fending off our umpteenth conversation about why I should move back to Idaho. "Should you be playing tennis with your arthritis?"

"Don't be silly, dear! Everyone says that exercise is the best thing you can do. Is that yours? You didn't pack very light, did you?"

"Sure I did. Sort of." I yanked my suitcase off the conveyor belt. At the last minute I'd thrown in all my cosmetics and this heavenly little turquoise dress I'd bought in Miami Beach. You never know. "So what's this tournament?"

"Just a little seniors competition. Imagine me being a senior! But it's sixty and over, so I qualify." As we rode the escalator to the airport's coffee shop, she put a hand on my arm. "Give B.J. my best, won't you? Cissy told me that she was a friend of Brian's."

"I will. And you'll probably see her yourself at the wedding."

At the café we took a booth and ordered, coffee for Mom, coffee and pastry for me. Then I clenched my teeth and swore not to comment on what was bound to happen next. Sure enough, my darling mother, normal enough in most respects, dived into her oversized purse and pulled out a big fat plastic jar of Folger's Crystals.

Our server, a young Hispanic woman, set down two steaming cups and stared. "I thought you wanted coffee. Is there something wrong?"

"Not at all, dear," said Mom, blithely unscrewing the jar. "No one ever makes it strong enough, that's all. Would you care for some, Carrie? No, you never do . . ."

As she stirred spoon after spoon of brown powder into her coffee, I smiled tightly at the retreating waitress and bit into my scone. Ah, airport food. So bland and yet so stale.

Mom took a healthy swallow and sighed. "We should be talking about poor Brian, but I don't know what to say. I've hardly set eyes on him since he was a child." Another swallow. "He was a difficult child."

"Difficult! Mom, when he was nine he sat on me and tried to set my hair on fire."

"That's right, he did." She chuckled. "But after all, you did burn all his baseball cards. Goodness, you smelled awful!"

That's the great thing about my mother, she's always ready to laugh. I am, too, and so we did. That changed the mood, and she changed the subject.

"Carrie, I have a wonderful surprise for you. I've been talking to Cissy, and we've had the best idea."

"Oh?" I said warily. Cissy Kane meant well, but ideas were not her strong suit. Shopping and dithering were her strong suit.

"Cissy's been all in a tizzy—you know how she gets—because the wedding planner that Tracy hired can't be there in person after all. Something about an emergency with some other bride, but I don't think that's fair, do you? They sent a substitute, a junior person from New York City, but Cissy and Tracy simply despised the woman right from the start for being so bossy. You're not bossy with your clients, are you, dear?"

"Mom, what's this about?"

"Well, Tracy is off visiting friends in Portland, trying to

relax before the wedding, but when I told Cissy you were coming to Ketchum, we thought of the perfect solution!"

I set down the scone. "Please don't tell me you volunteered my services."

"You guessed!" She beamed at me and sipped some more of her mud. "Honestly, I don't know why Tracy didn't ask you in the first place—"

I was already shaking my head. "That was her choice, Mom, and I can't possibly interfere with it. And anyway, I'm here to take care of B.J., not to work. No way. No."

What part of "No" does my mother not understand? When she wants something, the whole part. She smiled blandly.

"You're just like your father sometimes. So excitable! You won't be working, you'll be helping out a friend in need. Tracy will be so pleased when she hears about it. Cissy's expecting a call from her this afternoon, so by the time you get there—"

"Mom, you set this up without even knowing what I'd say?"

She blinked. Her eyes, like mine, were an undecided hazel, somewhere between brown and green, and just now they looked puzzled and a little hurt.

"But what is there to say? You and Tracy were so close, and here she's having a problem with her wedding and you're an expert at weddings. And you'll be there anyway. You wouldn't stand by and refuse to help her, would you? Not even talk to her about it?"

"Well, of course I'll talk to her, but I'm not going to muscle in on someone else's contract and—"

Mom beamed and reached for her bag. "I'm sure you won't need a contract, dear, not between friends . . ."

Famous last words, I thought with a silent groan.

"...though Cissy might give you a little something in cash, just for old times' sake. Isn't that sweet of her? Now, I really have to rush. It takes forever to walk to the parking garage. The old airport was so nice and small...."

As I walked Mom to her car, I kept protesting and she kept beaming. Then, while she fumbled in her purse for the parking-garage receipt, she played her trump card.

"You know, Carrie, your father always said that you can judge a man by the way he stands by his friends, and of course he meant a woman, too. Isn't Tracy your friend? Here's that silly ticket, right at the bottom. I'm parked down this way...."

Trailing along behind her, thinking about Dad, I caved.

"All right, all right. I'll talk to this New York person and offer my assistance. But tactfully! If she doesn't want me around, I'm not going to push it, OK? And cash under the table from Cissy is completely out of the—what on *earth*?"

For as long as I could remember, my mother had favored medium-brown hair and medium-blue sedans. These were fixed points in my universe. But now this snazzy silver-coiffed woman led me up to a spanking new PT Cruiser in the most astonishing color, a sort of pale fluorescent orange. It was stubby and shiny and adorable, like a cartoon character. Ollie the Orange Automobile or Connie the Coral Car. All it needed was a theme song.

I circled the car with my mouth open. It was Mom's, all right: a decal from North Junior High adorned the rear window, and the bumper bore a sticker that said "Teachers Rule!" Mrs. Kincaid was everyone's favorite English teacher.

"Your kids must be in shock!"

"I call her Tangerine. Isn't she gorgeous? They tried to persuade me to take this blue one that they had on the lot but I said, 'Oohh no, I want what I want and I'll wait as long as I have to.'" She slipped behind the wheel and donned a pair of rock-star wraparound shades. Those were new, too. "You take care driving, now."

"I will. See you Saturday."

I'd considered asking about her relationship with Eddie, but that could wait. Maybe after the wedding we'd have lunch and a heart-to-heart talk—as long as we talked about her heart and not mine. Given her interest in Aaron, that might get tricky. Mom was bound to have questions, and I was short on answers. So for now I just held my peace and began waving good-bye.

But then I waved at her to stop. "Wait a sec! You haven't said which wedding planner Tracy is using. Is it Manhattan Memories?"

That was the top firm in New York, the big time, the major league. Working with them, even temporarily, would add a certain pizzazz to my portfolio. Maybe this wasn't such a bad idea.

"That's the best part." Mom lifted her sunglasses and smiled. "Now, I know you've had a little bit of a problem with him in the past, but seeing you two on television that time, I could just tell how well you'd hit it off if you really tried. And he's *so* good-looking."

"Mom, don't tell me—"

She nodded, her eyes alight with mischief. "Tracy hired that gorgeous Frenchman, Beau Paliere!"

Chapter Four

HALF AN HOUR LATER I WAS IN MY RENTAL CAR, SPEEDING down I-84 South. Speeding and fuming. Beau Paliere! Of all the wedding planners in all the world, why did Tracy have to hire Beautiful Beau? And why did my mother have to railroad me into assisting him?

I could always refuse, of course. I could look my old chum Tracy right in the eye and say... *what? I don't care if it's the most precious day of your life, I won't lift a finger to help?*

OK, I couldn't do that. But maybe Tracy wouldn't even want me to get involved. Maybe this was just my mother and her own chum Cissy doing some ill-advised matchmaking. Maybe—

A glance in the rearview mirror interrupted my musings. The column of smoke I'd seen from the plane still hung in the sky, distant and blurry, beginning to disperse. I wondered if any of Brian's crewmates from Boot Creek had jumped into this new fire.

If so, they might still be there, chopping out underbrush and digging a fire line of clear dirt to starve the flames, too exhausted and endangered themselves to grieve for their dead comrade. By comparison, Monsieur Paliere was just a petty annoyance. I sighed, and returned my gaze to the road ahead.

For the next hour, from Boise to the air force town of Mountain Home, the drive was just as tedious as I remembered. Vast empty miles of sagebrush desert stretched south to the arid Owyhee Mountains and beyond into Utah, with little to vary the monotony except power lines and an occasional freight train in the distance.

I left the interstate behind, and went swooping across the hills of southern Idaho with the sun at my back. I'd put the windows up to keep out the dust and the wind, and two minutes later I'd found the button for the air-conditioning. That was kind of fun. My van in Seattle doesn't even *have* air-conditioning.

As I zoomed along, heat mirages wobbled up from the black asphalt ribbon. To my left, the grassy hills were broken by low basalt outcrops fringed with sagebrush. Behind them the hills rose to forested heights that would eventually rise to mountains, the Sawtooths and the Pioneers and the White Clouds.

To my right, sunflowers popped up among the sage and rabbitbrush, and the creek bottoms were richly green with cottonwoods and willows. Someone once said that you have to blow the dust off Idaho to appreciate its beauty. It's true, but the beauty is there.

Suddenly, out past a yellow OPEN RANGE sign with its black cow silhouette, I caught a rippling flash of movement. Four or five small slender forms, tan-and-cream-colored with delicate horns, were racing along parallel to the road. Antelope are nothing at all like deer, really, just as deer are nothing at all like horses. They don't even run, they seem to float—

Watching the antelope, I almost hit the dog.

It was a huge, tawny, toothy beast, galloping across the

highway trailing a rope leash and barking like a mad thing. I swerved around it, brakes squealing, and saw a convertible slewed across the shoulder up ahead, the driver's door hanging open and no driver in sight. A blown tire? I honked at the dog, trying to scare it off the road to safety, and pulled in front of the other car.

Here in the open hills, grasses burned brown by the sun, stepping out of the AC was like tugging open an oven door. As I crunched along the gravel shoulder, heat hammered down from the sky and welled up from the asphalt, gripping me like muscular hands, squeezing me breathless.

I felt prickles of sweat all over and the staccato beat of my pulse as I approached the convertible, afraid of what I might find. First-aid class was a long time ago, too long...

"Hello?"

The empty car was an old Cadillac with tail fins like a jet plane's, painted and repainted a dull tomato-soup red between the patches of rust. The backseat was full of camping and fishing gear and other junk, and one side was scarred by a long ragged scrape like a lightning bolt. But that was rusty, too, not recent.

Puzzled, I looked around. No sign of a collision, no sign of people, just the hot wind and the vacant road and the distant horizons.

And the dog, now racing toward me at a shocking speed. I stumbled backward in the soft gravel, then braced myself just in time. Broad paws slammed into my chest, massive jaws gaped just inches from my face...

"Off!"

I love dogs, but they have to behave, even in emergencies. I grabbed this one by the front paws—*his* front paws, for he was clearly, not to say obtrusively, male—and held him away from me.

"Off!" I repeated firmly, and thrust him toward the ground. Immediately he leapt again, and again I grabbed his paws. This time I held on for a moment, keeping him balanced on his hind legs just long enough to consider the error of his ways.

When I set him down again he stayed down, grinning up at me and wagging a short, crooked, muscular tail with a scar near the end. He had scars in several places, showing through a short rough pelt the same shade as the desiccated grass. But he certainly didn't seem injured.

"Where's your owner, big guy? Is he all right?"

The dog raced away, hind legs flying out to either side, toward a nearby tumble of boulders shaded by aspen trees. Leading me to the driver, thrown clear of the Caddy?

I made to follow but the dog reappeared, galumphing back toward me with something clamped in his huge jaws. Something that glinted in the sun and trailed a golden stream of liquid behind it.

A beer can, draining rapidly into the dust. My new friend dropped his gift at my feet, spattering my sandals, and barked delightedly. A voice emerged from the rustling bushes.

"Gimme that back, you son of a bitch!"

Soon the owner of the voice, and apparently the dog, emerged, as well. He was a burly, dark-haired, darkly tanned man in his mid-thirties, dressed in a sweat-stained gray T-shirt and a pair of ragged cutoffs.

The puzzle was instantly solved. He was zipping his fly.

"Sorry," I managed to get out. "I didn't mean to . . . Your dog was in the road."

"He's always in the road, aren't you, you son of a bitch? Gimme that!"

The man snatched up the can and then grinned at me, his teeth even bigger and whiter than his companion's. In fact, he resembled his dog, as people sometimes do. The two of them were hearty and muscular, roughed up by life but intensely alive and brazenly sure of themselves. *Lucky you,* their grins seemed to say. *You get to meet me.*

And somehow it worked, for canine and human alike. During the Muffy summer, Tracy and B.J. and I had developed a glossary of men, with categories like Unbearably Cute and Ugly-Sexy and Ugly-Ugly. With his low forehead and battered nose and ropey, black-furred forearms, this man was Ugly-Sexy.

"Thanks for being a good Samaritan," he said. His voice was deep and rough-edged. "Domaso Duarte, pleased to meet you. And this troublemaker"—he ruffled the dog's flopped-over ears—"is named Gorka."

"Carnegie Kincaid," I replied automatically. And then, just for something to say, "What kind of dog is he?"

Domaso shrugged. "No idea. He adopted me, three–four weeks ago. Hey, you must be Louise's daughter."

"You know her?" Hearing Basque names like Domaso and Gorka was no surprise, not in Idaho. From early-day shepherds to present-day ranchers and merchants and mayors, Basques were common enough. But having this character toss off my mother's first name put a bizarre twist on an already odd situation.

He shrugged again. He was good at it, working his face and his shoulders together. "I work for her."

"At the school?"

Domaso stared at me and then laughed, a deep rich chor-
tle that set me smiling and the dog barking in glee. "What,
like a teacher? No! I do odd jobs, small construction. I dry-
walled her study there at the house. She said it used to be
your bedroom. Nice."

His eyes traveled over me as he said it, and I nodded
uneasily. When I was in high school, the hottest boys were
always Basque. Dark-eyed, brooding, fight-starting, loud-
laughing Basque boys. In fact, I knew the name Gorka perfectly well. That was the name of the boy who sat next to me
in algebra and distracted me from polynomial equations. Remembering him after all these years, while Domaso talked
about my bedroom . . .

"So you're the wedding planner," he continued. "You going to Tracy's wedding?"

"Y-yes. You know her, too?"

"Oh yeah." He coughed a little, then poured the last of
the beer down his throat and crumpled the can the way I
crumple paper. "I'm doing some work for her father up at
White Pine. There's two kinds of people in Sun Valley, you
know. The ones with three houses and the ones with three
jobs. Guess which one I am?"

He laughed uproariously at his own joke and added, "I
know the whole family. I'll be at the wedding, too. You can
dance with me."

"Did you know Brian Thiel?" I blurted, without quite
knowing why.

"No." He looked away. "I heard about him, though. Some
kind of relation to your family, huh? Sorry."

"Thanks. We weren't really—"

"Well, you probably got to hit the road." Domaso flicked

the can over his shoulder. "Thanks for checking on me and my friend here."

"You're welcome."

I paused, waiting for him to turn toward the convertible. But he didn't move, so I crunched back to the rental and climbed in, gasping at the touch of the superheated car seat. As I pulled away, I looked back to be sure that Gorka didn't follow. But man and dog stood watching me go, until they disappeared from my mirrors behind a bend in the road.

The highway soon ascended to a viewpoint, where I pulled over to take in the vista of sagebrush and basalt and aspens. Far below me I could make out the now-tiny figure of Domaso Duarte. But instead of returning to the convertible, he was retracing his steps. As I watched, he bent to tie Gorka to a bush, and then vanished into the trees.

Chapter Five

DRIVING UP THE WOOD RIVER VALLEY TOWARD KETCHUM, you pass through the pleasant but unremarkable little town of Bellevue, and then through the larger but still fairly little town of Hailey. Hailey seems unremarkable, too, until you skirt the local airport and notice that the tarmac holds several million bucks' worth of private jets.

Or maybe you notice the name of a Very Famous Actor on the marquee of the local theater—only it's not a movie theater. The actor is starring in a play because he lives in Hailey, at least part of the year. So does his Even More Famous Ex-wife, and the new governor of California, and the richest woman in New York City, and various other celebrities. One minute you're watching the deer and the antelope play, and the next minute you're hip-deep in headliners. You haven't even hit Sun Valley yet, but you and Toto have definitely blown out of Kansas.

Cruising past the Hailey airport with my AC on high, I wondered how many of the Lears and Gulfstreams parked there had transported Tracy's wedding guests. Probably quite a few. Was it worth crossing Beau Paliere's path to get close to these folks? Or would I just be handing Beau another opportunity to do me dirty? I chewed on that the rest of the way to my destination.

Ketchum is an appealing, outdoorsy town of just three thousand residents—and three traffic lights—but its small scale belies its cosmopolitan soul. You can buy a mountain bike that costs more than a car in Ketchum, or an oil painting that costs more than that, not to mention superb sushi and divine French cuisine and the very latest in drop-dead resort styles. All this and the best of Mother Nature, too. The town nestles between Trail Creek on one side and the Big Wood River on the other, with Bald Mountain rising broad and green—not bald at all—in the background.

It was Old Baldy that caught the eye of Averell Harriman, the chairman of Union Pacific, back in the 1930's. Ketchum had boomed and busted with silver mining, then revived a little with sheepherding, but Harriman introduced a third and grander S-word: skiing.

Harriman envisioned a European-style winter resort to lure passengers onto his trains. The valley outside of Ketchum was perfect. In 1937, Sun Valley Resort opened its doors and its ski lifts—an innovation at the time—to the stars of Hollywood and the millionaires of both coasts. Errol Flynn and Claudette Colbert showed up right away, Ernest Hemingway not long after, and Ketchum hasn't busted since.

On the way into town I passed the smoke-jumper base, a small airstrip, a low office building, and the big "ready shack" building where the jumpers maintained their gear and supplies. One end of this main structure was tall and narrow, almost like a barn: the parachute loft. I took such sights for granted. Along with Sun Valley, smoke jumping was a colorful part of Idaho history.

Today, though, I had a more personal history in mind. As I drove, the saffron light of late afternoon played over the brick and sandstone storefronts and the timbered, deep-eaved hotels, and glinted on a sign that said MAIN STREET. It should have said "Memory Lane."

There was the bookstore I used to haunt, and there was the art gallery where I applied for a job once, when waitressing got me down. And over there, near a Starbucks that was new since my time, stood the Pioneer Saloon, which was old when I first arrived. Night after night at the dark and smoky Pio, the three Muffies would camp out in a corner booth and evaluate the guys at the bar. And vice versa, of course. Those were the days. . . .

A few more blocks and I was pulling into High Country Gardens, a hardworking little nursery whose hardworking little owner was out front, stacking sacks of bark chips next to a display of ornamental grasses.

B.J. wore a polo shirt and khaki shorts that stretched across her full breasts and hips, with a baseball cap yanked low on her forehead. I'm not sure what I expected, but it wasn't the faint, uneasy smile she wore as she pushed back the cap and came to hug me. She smelled like the sun.

"Hey, Carnegie. I shouldn't have asked you to come, but it sure is good to see you. I'm sorry if I've messed up your schedule."

"No problem. I could use a vacation, and it'll be nice to see Matt." That sounded heartless, so I tried again. "Is there a memorial service?"

She nodded curtly. "It was this afternoon, while most of the jumpers were still at the base. Oh, damn, I'm sorry. I didn't tell anyone you were coming. Maybe they could have delayed it for you."

"Don't worry about it. Just tell me what's going on. You sounded awful on the phone."

"Yeah." She stripped off her work gloves, avoiding my eye. "I think I was overreacting or something."

"To Brian's death? Do you know the details yet?"

"I'll tell you everything over dinner, OK? Give me a minute with Liz and we'll walk over to the Pio. Liz is my assistant; she knows more about plants than I do. You can leave your car where it is."

After two hours inside my little bubble of air-conditioning, the walk to the Pioneer was a stroll in the Sahara. I flinched behind my sunglasses, feeling the arid heat invade my mouth to suck my breath away.

"Awfully late in the day to be this hot," I said, just to break the silence. "And awfully early in the summer."

"Wimp." B.J. bumped me with her hip. "You've been in Seattle too long."

I bumped her back. "Don't give me that. It must be a hundred degrees!"

"Ninety-five at the most," she said, pulling open the tavern door. "Actually, it is unusual for June. We've been breaking records all week, even at night."

Getting inside was a relief, if only for the shade. The Pio's been around for half a century, and its mode of decor is Early Taxidermy, so we stood adjusting to the dimness under the glassy gaze of various elk, deer, and buffalo.

Turning my own gaze to the humans, I was surprised to see so many tables filled on a Monday evening. The Pio had gone no-smoking, but the crowd had a familiar feel, mostly young, mostly casual, with a few older couples dressed up for dinner elsewhere. Two such couples were just leaving a booth in the corner—the Muffy booth.

"Just like old times," said B.J., laying claim to the spot before someone else snagged it. "Must be our night."

"Must be."

I settled in and took a long, fond look at her. A wealth of dark unruly curls still framed her heart-shaped face, and her eyes, even bloodshot from weeping, were beautiful. They were eyes just made for flirting, huge and velvet purple, with long lashes under winged brows. B.J.'s dimples might be deeper now, and her cheeks a bit fuller than before, but I envied her eyes and her curves both.

My own curves are minimal, to put it mildly—talk about your late bloomer—but at least I have red hair. My late father, a copper-top himself, told me again and again growing up that redheads were special, and I came to believe him. So my hair was my secret solace, just as being flat-chested was my private bane. Tracy used to say that if you added me and B.J. together and divided by two, you'd get a perfect figure. Meaning, of course, hers.

I was still waiting for B.J.'s explanation, but she flapped open her menu. "Think you can manage a humongous hunk of beef like you used to?"

"Why not?"

These days I'm more of a pinot grigio and grilled ahi kind of girl, but these rough-hewn surroundings called for heartier fare. When in Rome . . . We ordered a couple of New York strips, medium rare, and two bottles of Moose Drool Ale, keep 'em coming. I was so parched that my second bottle was half gone before I really noticed. Meanwhile B.J. chattered away, as if to keep me from asking questions.

"Some of the jumpers will probably come in here later. The whole crew that jumped at Boot Creek has been taken off the active list until after the wedding. It's safety protocol. They don't want anyone who's distracted working a fire."

She was definitely stalling. "Do you know many of the guys?"

"Most of them. Actually there's a woman, too, Pari Taichert. They call her the Little Tyke. A real jockette, good buddies with Jack. Most of the crew are friends of his, so they came for the memorial service and then they're sticking around for the wedding." B.J. frowned. "Kind of creepy, isn't it? I know Brian was new on the crew, but still, you'd think Tracy would postpone."

I noticed she blamed Tracy and not Jack. Which was probably accurate, since the bride was the star of this show in more ways than one.

"Be fair," I said. "Big weddings are a nightmare to reschedule, even if you're not a celebrity like Tracy. Vendors get booked up, and there's all the arrangements for out-of-town guests—"

"OK, point taken. Sam's spending a fortune on this one weekend! He spoils Tracy even more than he does Cissy. Wait'll you see her dress—Tracy's, I mean. Although Cissy's outfit is pretty outrageous, too. Pink dress, pink shoes . . ."

I followed B.J.'s lead, and as we sawed at our steaks I told stories about my brides and their gowns. Then I asked for a cup of decaf, but B.J. changed the order to a round of Irish coffee. Apparently, whatever she had to tell me required a lot of liquid courage. Finally, I lost patience.

"Let's hear it, Muffy," I said. "What's going on with you? Why am I here? And what exactly happened to Brian?"

B.J. sipped from her tall glass mug and answered my last question first, using smoke-jumper jargon that she knew I'd understand. Both of us were born and raised in Idaho, and familiar with the basics of wildland firefighting. In fact, there's a smoke-jumper base at the Boise airport, and in junior high I'd had a desperate crush on a boy whose dad worked there, the glamour of the father shedding luster on the son.

So as B.J. sketched out the story of the Boot Creek fire, my imagination filled in the details. Just as it had on the plane this afternoon as I'd looked down into that curtain of smoke and wondered what it was like to leap into hell.

"Brian and the Tyke were first stick..."

A "stick" is a two-person team that jumps in quick succession from the smoke-jumpers' plane, once the spotter by the door gives them the signal. They have to keep clear of each other, but each one watches where the other lands. In puncture-proof Kevlar suits and heavy grilled helmets, they steer their parachutes toward an agreed-upon target, the jump spot, trying to avoid the trees and rocks and snags racing up from the ground like weapons, hungry to crush or stab. Or kill.

"The wind got fluky and Brian blew way off the spot, into a burned-over area on the other side of a ridge. What they call the black zone. The Tyke couldn't see where he landed. The next stick was Todd Gibson and Danny Kane—"

"Tracy's brother?"

"Half brother, yeah. You know him?"

"I met him a few times at Cissy's house." I remembered Danny as a tall, weedy fellow, his eyes small and worried, his dark hair soft and untidy. "He seemed nice."

"I guess so. He's been jumping quite a while now. Sam says it's too dangerous, but you can tell he's proud of him. Only son and all that. Anyway, Todd and Danny and the Tyke headed for the fire, but kept an eye out for Brian. Between the smoke and the rough ground, they got separated..."

That was the part that amazed me. After jumping from an

airplane—scary enough in itself—these people packed up their gear, picked up their chain saws and Pulaskis and meager rations, and tramped through brush and rocks and ravines into a fire. No roads, no trails, just smoking trees and erupting flames and long unrelieved hours of intense physical labor.

I hefted a Pulaski once, on a tour of the smoke-jumper base in Boise. It's a double-headed tool, ax and hoe both on a long wooden handle, and I knew instantly that I couldn't swing one for fifteen minutes, let alone fifteen hours. All wildland firefighters do that kind of backbreaking labor. Smoke jumpers just use different transportation to commute to work.

"The Tyke spotted his parachute in a grove of ponderosa pines. It had hung up in a big snag, so he'd used his letdown rope. You know, that they rappel down with?"

I nodded. Smoke jumpers learn to lower themselves from trees with a long rope—actually it's nylon webbing—that they tie off securely to the trunk or a limb, or else to the risers of their parachute, if they're certain the chute will stay put.

"Don't tell me his line failed?"

"No, the line was sound. But Brian tied it off wrong. He secured it to his own harness instead of a riser, and he rappelled right off the end of it. Todd found him in the ashes at the bottom of the tree. His neck was broken."

"Oh, my God . . ."

"Some jumpers are more worried about falling from trees than they are about fires, but not Brian." B.J. drained her mug. "One night when we . . . one night he was talking about the training program, and he said letdown was a piece of cake. He was so cocky all the time, like he was invincible."

"Wait a minute, B.J., back up. What aren't you telling me? Were you involved with Brian?"

"No, I wasn't 'involved'!" She glared at me, tears welling in her eyes. "It was just—don't look at me like that! I should have known you wouldn't understand!"

The tears brimmed over and she left the table abruptly, shoving her way through the crowd toward the rest rooms. My own mug, still full, was tepid by now, and I curled my hands around the glass as I put the pieces together. "One night when we..." When we what? I thought I knew, and I wished that I didn't.

"Well, if it isn't long, tall Carnegie Kincaid."

I looked up into the face of a man I hadn't seen in years. I knew every feature by heart. The topaz eyes that met mine in a steady gaze, the narrow face whose high, hard cheekbones were burnished by wind and weather. The thin, mobile lips, as always, seemed to be smiling at some private joke. And the sinewy body, as always, showed a graceful economy of effort as he moved to sit across from me.

"Hello, Jack," I said serenely, and spilled Irish coffee all over the table.

Chapter Six

REDHEADS BLUSH AT THE DROP OF A HAT. OR A DRINK. BUT at least the fuss with the spill covered my reaction to Jack the Knack.

I jumped to my feet, apologizing, while he backed away from the flood. It spread swiftly to the table edge and cascaded to the floor in long brown streamers. Laughing faces turned toward us from other tables, and then the waitress appeared to mop up the mess with practiced nonchalance. The whole thing took only moments, but by the time she departed I had my face under control. Sort of.

"Think it's safe to sit down?"

The gold-brown eyes crinkled as he said it, and he slid his hands into the back pockets of his jeans. He wore his jeans snug beneath a blue denim shirt with the tails out and the cuffs rolled back. Both jeans and shirt were as pale and as sun-bleached as his tousled hair.

"Of course," I said, and sat myself. My cheeks were burning again, hotter than ever. *Dammit, he hasn't changed a bit.*

Jack, for his part, seemed untouched by thoughts of the past. But he was uncomfortable about something in the present. As he took B.J.'s seat, his face assumed a formal, almost embarrassed expression, and he tried to say something appropriate about Brian Thiel.

"I'm sorry about your cousin. He, uh, he was a good fire-fighter. Very strong. Looked like he was going to be a good jumper, too. I'm really sorry."

"Thanks, Jack, but you can relax. We weren't close. In fact, I hardly knew him."

"All right, then, I guess I've done my duty." He smiled his killer smile, one that came rarely but with devastating effect. He waved at the waitress for a beer, but after it came the smile faded. "There is one other thing, though. About Brian and B.J. It's none of my business if they were—"

"Old friends," I supplied hastily. "They dated once, re-member?"

"I remember. Carnegie, I don't know how to say this to B.J., but maybe you can." Jack winced. "She's been pestering people about the accident. Asking questions, calling atten-tion to herself. People are starting to wonder about her and Brian. She's a married woman, and this is a small town, you know?"

"I know. I'll...I'll talk to her." I made a last-ditch de-fense. "But surely everyone's upset about this?"

"Of course. All the jumpers are edgy, especially since we don't know exactly why he fell. That's why everyone's drink-ing so hard tonight, even though Thiel wasn't the most pop-ular guy." Jack's gaze dropped to the tabletop. "Everyone's thinking, sometimes Big Ernie just hands you a bad deal."

Big Ernie is the god of smoke jumpers, a twisted joke of a deity. He appears in costume at the initiation rites for new jumpers, and demands worship from the veterans in the form of prodigious beer consumption.

And yet he isn't quite a joke. Fate or luck or destiny, what-ever tips the delicate balance between life and death, that was Big Ernie, too. A faulty chute that unfurls at the last possible second, a flaming snag that falls a mortal moment too soon. Or a letdown rope knotted wrong, dead wrong.

Uneasy with these images, I tried to change the subject. "B.J. mentioned that she talked to you about Boot Creek. I thought you were retiring?"

"Oh, I am. But I've been hanging on since this heat came up so sudden and we had all these lightning fires. I promised Tracy I wouldn't jump after the wedding, though. And since we're all off the active list this week, that means I'm done jumping for good." Jack frowned at his beer bottle, then took a long pull and set it down. "Well, that was then, this is now, right? How are things with you, Carnegie? It's been a long time since you were here."

Since I was in your bed that night, I added silently. My blood was rushing around my body in objectionable ways. *Don't you even remember?*

But all I said was "Yes, a long time. Things are fine. Busy."

"Good." He nodded. "It's good to be busy."

A pause. A long one. We looked away from each other, and then straight into each other's eyes. *Oh,* I thought in sudden dismay. *Oh, dear. He remembers.*

"Carnegie—"

"Jack—"

On the very brink of madness, I came to my senses. "Jack, I haven't congratulated you yet! It's wonderful about you and Tracy. Just wonderful."

"Thanks." He shifted in his seat and blinked. "Thanks very much. I'm a lucky man."

If I held a different view on that point, I kept it to myself. But at least my blood was back where it belonged. "The wedding plans sound spectacular. I think I'll be helping out a little, but I'll have to talk with Cissy about that—"

"I knew it, I knew it, she's hitting on the groom!" B.J. was back, her tears scrubbed away and a manic note in her voice. "Girl, I can't leave you alone for a minute, can I? What's Tracy going to say?"

Jack rose at her approach. Back in the Muffy summer they had charmed me to pieces, these old-fashioned courtesies from lean, laconic Jack the Knack. B.J., less easily charmed, stayed standing and aimed a playful punch at his middle.

"You two taking up where you left off? Where is Tracy, anyway?"

Jack was unfazed. "Still in Portland. Gets back in the morning. How you doing, B.J.?"

"I'm fine, Jack." She fumbled for her wallet and dropped some bills on the table. "My treat. Hey, let's get over to the bar. They're starting the Talent Show!"

"Talent Show?" I had a momentary vision of karaoke, or worse, but B.J. bounded away before I could ask. As we followed her toward the boisterous crowd at the other end of the room, she sent me a look over her shoulder that said the rest of our conversation about Brian Thiel was going to come later—if it came at all.

"The Talent Show's a jumper thing, started last season." Jack grabbed a couple of beers from a passing tray and handed me one. I noticed the friendly wink he gave the young waitress, and the flustered smile she offered in return. The notorious Knack was still operational. "The Tyke takes on a guy at arm wrestling, and if he loses he has to perform. Watch."

Everyone in the place was watching, gathered in a tight, shifting semicircle around two stools at the bar. On one of them sat a woman in her twenties, stocky and suntanned in shorts and flip-flops, with a honey-brown ponytail pulled through the back of her red baseball cap. Her turned-up nose might have been cutesy on someone else, but on that broad-boned Nordic countenance it just looked cocky, ready for a fight. Her legs were muscled like a marathoner's, and her biceps were fit for a Nautilus ad.

Suddenly I felt pale and stringy, like spaghetti.

The Tyke said something to the brawny fellow on the second stool, and he nodded his blond crew-cut head. I couldn't see his face, but he was obviously another fire-fighter: the back of his T-shirt read "You Can't Send Us To Hell, We'd Put It Out!"

Slowly, deliberately, the two of them planted their right elbows on the bar, then locked fists. The crowd bellowed.

"Who's the challenger?" I asked Jack.

"Todd Gibson. We call him Odd Todd. He's a Ned."

Decades ago, "Ned Newboy" was the nickname for a first-season smoke jumper, and the "Ned" part stuck around as another word for "rookie." A second-year jumper was a "Sned" or a "Snookie." These guys loved nicknames.

It occurred to me that the Tyke and Odd Todd were two of the jumpers who found Brian's body. I looked around for the third, Danny Kane, but couldn't spot him.

"Tyke, Tyke, Tyke!" the crowd began chanting, with an occasional cry of "Yo, Toddy!"

The wrestlers' fists were trembling, but still upright. Seconds passed. The Tyke bared small, even teeth, and her opponent's arm inched back and downward ever so slightly. I found myself gulping beer just to break the tension.

Abruptly the Tyke grunted low in her throat, Todd's shoulders twisted in defeat, and his knuckles smacked the surface of the bar with a sound that was drowned by a new chant and a chorus of shouts.

"Talent Show, Talent Show, Talent Show!"

"Sing a song, Toddy!"

"No, dancing!"

"Yeah, belly dancing!"

But Todd, nursing his arm with a good-natured groan, deferred to the victor. The Tyke, it seemed, was the only one who could pronounce the loser's penalty. She hiked herself up to sit triumphantly on the bar and raised a mug, which trembled enough to slop beer down her arm.

"Todd Gibson," the Tyke declared, in a low but somehow girlish voice, "your best talent is . . . Shut *up*, you bastards! Todd, your best talent is . . . one-armed push-ups! Gimme ten!"

I couldn't do ten push-ups if I had three arms. But Todd Gibson just beamed all over his big, square, heavy-boned face. He was young, early twenties at most, and would have made a stereotypical farm boy if he'd had jug-handle ears to go with his lantern jaw. Instead his ears were small and delicate, and just now they were glowing cherry red, though with exertion or embarrassment I couldn't tell.

In either case, he dropped promptly to the floor and carried out his sentence, to the roaring approval of the onlookers counting him down.

"*Seven.* Come on, bro, you can do it!"

"*Eight.* Right on, Toddy!"

"*Nine!*"

"*Ten!*"

As Todd scrambled to his feet, Jack moved away from me to join his comrades in the last act of the Show: spraying beer over winner and loser alike. The Tyke shrieked and fired back at them, while Todd stood unmoving, exhausted but pleased, like a little boy who's finally been allowed to play with the big kids. I wondered if the beer shower was the usual Talent Show finale or something special for tonight, to take the edge off everyone's nerves.

I leaned down to B.J. "What happens if she loses?"

"She almost never does. She's strong as hell and she knows just how to brace herself on the bar. But if she does lose, that's the joke. Everybody tells the winner that the Tyke's best talent is arm wrestling, and she already did it. Then they all drink some more."

I chuckled. "Work hard, play hard?"

"You got it. Say, Muffy..." B.J. bit her lip. "Did I embarrass you with that crack about hitting on the groom? I mean, is it bothering you to see Jack after all this time?"

"Not at all," I said firmly. "Ancient history. But you look a little strung out. Maybe we should go home?"

"No way!" She turned in a slow, wobbly circle to survey the crowd. "You hardly ever come to Ketchum; you've got to meet all these terrific people. Hey, Tyke, meet a friend of mine!"

She grabbed the younger woman by the elbow—they were almost the same height—and tugged her away from the melee. The smoke jumper frowned at first, but shook hands like a gentleman.

"Pari Noskin Taichert," she announced. "And you are?"

"Carnegie...Kincaid," I replied, leaving out the Bernice. Her hand was wet with beer.

"You're Thiel's cousin," she said gruffly. "Sorry."

"We weren't close," I said again. "Actually, I'm an old friend of B.J.'s. We used to work together in Sun Valley, along with Tracy Kane."

"Oh. The actress." From her tone, she intended the word

"actress" to mean "despicable civilian who's making Jack Packard give up his job."

The crowd was shoulder-to-shoulder by now, and a couple of guys cut between us on their way to the bar. When they'd passed, the Tyke was already turning away.

"Am I imagining things," I asked B.J., "or does she hate Tracy's guts?"

B.J. laughed gleefully at that, too loud and too long, drunk on emotion as much as on beer.

"I think the Tyke used to have an eye on Jack herself," she said slyly. Or rather, she shouted. The noise level had risen to a dense, hammering clamor you could almost see in the air. "Maybe more than her eye, you know?"

"Interesting!" I shouted back. *This used to be so much fun,* I thought, my head throbbing and my throat raw. *Drink way too much, yell all evening, get up early for work, and then do it all over again. Was it really that much fun?*

But I was hot and thirsty, the beer was cold, and eventually the alcohol worked its tingling, numbing voodoo, even on me. The blur of voices and faces grew friendlier and more familiar, until I found myself wanting to stay all night in that golden glow.

At one point I was kidding around with a bunch of men, feeling like one of the guys, and soon after I was in the rest room with a cluster of women, all of them comforting me on the loss of my dear cousin. Pretty soon I was crying myself.

Another blur, time passing, and then we were back out in the crowd, B.J. laughing again and waving her beer bottle in the air. "Hey, there's Danny. Yo, Dan the Man! Here's your old pal Carnegie."

"Who? Oh, hello."

Danny Kane hadn't changed much, except for accelerating baldness. His dark eyes and narrow nose and mouth were small and bunched closely together, so that the space between them and his retreating hairline had a vacant, unoccupied look. Tonight the high curve of his forehead shone with sweat, and his eyes were stupefied.

Well, this was only Monday. Not forty-eight hours ago Danny had seen his comrade lying dead, in the kind of accident that could just as easily have happened to him. Big Ernie never rests, and we all drown our demons as best we can.

"I'm sorry about your cousin," he said mournfully.

"We weren't... I mean, thanks. It must have been hard for you guys."

He tried to reply and faltered, but B.J. interrupted him anyway. Her mood was flying higher and higher. "Carnegie's going to stay for Tracy's wedding. It's going to be absolutely fabulous!"

"Absolutely," Danny echoed, nodding. His head dropped lower with each nod, and we stood there, an awkward little island of silence in the beating, deafening surf of hilarity. The night's false euphoria was ebbing away. I could picture the guest bed in the loft of B.J.'s cabin, and I wanted to climb into the picture and sleep for a long, long time.

"B.J., why don't we get out of—h-hey, watch it!" Someone knocked me hard behind the knees, and I jostled into Danny. B.J.'s crowing laughter rose again, accompanied by... barking?

I turned around and saw that the intruder was none other than the troublemaker, Gorka. He stood there giving me a big drooling grin, and trying to give me something else, too. A red baseball cap, damp and mangled, hung from his crocodile jaws.

Gorka poked his treasure against my knees again, then laid it at my feet and barked merrily when I retrieved it. If the drinkers around us noticed all this, they didn't seem to care.

"Friend of yours?" said B.J., and hiccuped. Danny had wandered away.

"No, but he belongs to—Gorka, be quiet. No bark! *Sit*."

My new admirer sat, drumming his scarred tail against the floor, thoroughly pleased with himself. I rose on tiptoe to search for his owner and sure enough, Domaso Duarte was plowing toward us from the Pio's doorway. But the owner of the baseball cap got to me first.

"What do you think you're doing?" demanded the Tyke. Her honey-brown hair was loose around her face, strands sticking to her broad, damp cheekbones.

I realized that I was sweating myself. Between the hot night outside the building and the body heat inside, the air-conditioning didn't stand a chance.

"Don't yell at *me*," I bawled. "Yell at the damn dog. Here, take your hat."

"I don't want it now; it's all slimy. You should keep that mutt outside." She turned to B.J. "And you should quit asking stupid questions about the accident. Everyone feels bad enough already. You got that?"

The Tyke's voice gained an ugly note of menace with this last phrase. Gorka swung his muzzle toward her and lifted his lip, showing a fang or three. Not a snarl, really, just a pointed expression of disapproval. The Tyke backed up a pace, and I gave him a silent *Good dog*.

Gorka must have read my mind. He unfolded his back legs and stood, his massive head higher than the Tyke's waist. She swore, backing up farther, then turned and stamped away, her flip-flops flopping. *Good boy*.

"Hey, Carrie, this guy giving you trouble?" The voice came clearly through a sudden lull in the din, as a broad, black-furred hand grabbed Gorka by his brass-studded collar. "Sorry about that."

Domaso didn't look all that sorry. He looked like a cat who'd been sipping cream all afternoon. Through a straw. Even in this crowd of athletic types, his broad shoulders and rock-solid stance marked him out as a powerful man. I wondered how he would do in the Talent Show—and what his talent was.

B.J. nudged me. "Earth to Carnegie?"

"Oh, right. Brenda Jervis, Domaso Duarte. He's a friend of . . . he knows . . ."

"I work for Mrs. Kincaid in Boise," he said comfortably. "And I know Sam and Cissy here. In fact, I think I know you. B.J., right? Flower store? I picked up a load of topsoil for Cissy a while back."

"High Country Gardens," she said, pleased. "I remember now, you talked with Matt about kayaks. You didn't have the dog with you, though. What's his name?"

"Name's Gorka. Watch him for me for a minute, will you?"

Before B.J. could answer, Domaso scooped me into his arms. A slow, sultry number had arisen from the jukebox, and he danced me around for a few bars. And somehow I was just drunk enough to let him. He smelled like the sea, salty and dark. Then, as I began to protest, he deposited me back at B.J.'s side.

"I better get ol' Gorka out of here," he told her. "Be seeing you." Then he gave me a long look. "Be seeing *lots* of you."

I was about to make a rude retort—"In your dreams" came to mind—when I saw a new arrival standing in the open door behind him. I stared, speechless.

It wasn't Tracy's superstar, Oscar-night entrance that silenced me, as she paused in the doorway to shake back her long, lustrous hair. And it wasn't the way that all the men in the Pio, and half the women, swayed toward her like strands of seaweed in a tidal surge of admiration.

What struck me dumb was the fact that Tracy Kane, the blonde Muffy, was now a flaming, flaunting, flamboyant redhead. And damn her, she looked absolutely fabulous.

Chapter Seven

"SHE DYED IT AGES AGO! IN THE EPISODE WITH THE PRIVATE eye and the poodle?"

"I must have missed that one." I adjusted the cold washcloth draped over my face. "Please don't talk so loud."

B.J. dropped a decibel or two. "But her hair's been red for *weeks*."

"I don't watch much television. Forget it, OK? All I said was, I'm not sure red hair suits Tracy's complexion. No big deal."

It was Tuesday morning, and the washcloth was meant to defend my addled brain from the bands of sunlight slashing through the loft of B.J.'s cabin. But nothing could defend me from her voice as she sat on the edge of my bed giving me a hard time. As usual. She hadn't said another word about Brian, and I couldn't decide what words to say, so I hadn't, either.

"No big deal, huh?" I felt the mattress bounce as she leaned forward to lift a corner of the washcloth. "Look me in the eye and tell me it doesn't bother you that Jack the Knack's got himself a redhead who isn't you."

"The only thing bothering me is the firecracker going off behind my eyes. I cannot believe that you're up and around. You drank more than I did!"

"Like I said, you're a wimp. Want some coffee?"

I raised my head, an inch at a time. It didn't fall off. "Muffy, I would love you forever."

"Promises, promises!" she called, pounding down the broad open staircase to the kitchen. "Cream?"

"Please."

I subsided into the pillows, beneath the gentle stir of the overhead fan, and gazed around. B.J. and Matt had designed this big cozy A-frame of peeled logs set in an aspen grove on the edge of town. The loft was Matt's office as well as the guest room, so minimountains of folders and journals and technical-looking notebooks rose up from every horizontal surface.

Downstairs was a cheerful chaos of houseplants, Navajo rugs, and Pueblo pottery, all B.J.'s passions, along with overflowing shelves of horticultural books and magazines. The mess would have made me insane, but she seemed to thrive on it.

"Here we go." B.J. reappeared with a tray and set it on the nightstand, newly cleared for my arrival. "This should help."

I levered myself to a sitting position, ever so cautiously. The room was no longer whirling, as it had last night, but I wasn't going to push my luck. At least I wasn't nauseous anymore. The tray held two coffee mugs, steaming and fragrant, along with a plate of buttered scones and a bowl of grapes.

"I do love you, Muffy," I said, sipping and munching. "I do, I do, I do."

"Well, you should," she answered around a mouthful of scone. "I had to drive you back here last night, in case you don't remember."

I closed my eyes. "I do now. Sorry."

"No big deal. I wasn't planning to work today, but we can swing by the nursery later and get my car."

"Sure."

As we finished the scones, an awkward silence fell. It was time to get serious.

"B.J., you said you needed help. I can't help if you won't tell me what's going on."

She took a swallow of coffee, wiped her mouth on a napkin, and looked down at her hands. Her wedding ring threw back a tiny chip of sunlight.

"I'm in trouble, Muffy," she murmured. "You won't—?"

"Of course not. Not a word, not to anybody."

She heaved a sigh that came all the way up from her toes, and began.

"Matt and I have been having problems for a while now, with him traveling so much and me working so hard at the nursery, and other things. Being married is more complicated than you'd think."

I thought about Aaron and myself and smiled wryly. "I'll bet."

"Then Brian turned up in town to start training at the jump base. He kept hanging around the nursery, dropping hints about picking up where we left off years ago."

B.J. turned the ring on her finger around and around. "I shut him down, I really did. But then last week Matt and I had a fight on the phone, and that night I went out with some friends and had too much to drink. I didn't want to drive, so I let Brian take me home and . . . one thing led to another. It was a stupid, stupid thing to do. I must have been out of my mind. I've never cheated on Matt before, never. You've got to believe me!"

"I do, B.J. Go on."

"Well, I was wearing this silver necklace, and when Brian pulled my shirt off—"

I held up a hand. "I don't need the details."

"No, of course not. Sorry. Anyway, when I woke up Brian was gone and so was my necklace. I called him and asked for it back, but he teased me about it, the bastard." She stood up and began to pace, her bare feet silent on the loft's braided rugs. "Jeez, I shouldn't talk about him like that now that he's dead. You must think I'm horrible."

"B.J., sit down. I don't think you're horrible, I think you're upset. So what happened with the necklace?"

"He threatened to keep it." She sank into a chair and laced her fingers together, tight. "I was afraid someone would see it, like the guy who shared his apartment, but Brian laughed and said no problem, he was keeping it close to his heart as a souvenir. I was frantic! I called him again and again, but I think he enjoyed it."

"That *bastard.*"

"Oh, don't say that, Carnegie. I mean, Bri shouldn't have acted that way, but he wasn't a bad person at heart."

And now he's dead. I relented. "Sorry. Go on, what happened next?"

"I threatened to call the police, not that I really would have, and he gave in. He said I could come by the jump base and get the necklace, but before I got there he was called out for the Boot Creek fire. And now he's gone, and I don't know where it is."

"I take it this necklace is really valuable?"

"That's not the point! Matt had it made for me. Look."

She plucked a framed photograph from Matt's desk and held it out. It showed the two of them, arms entwined, smiling for the camera. Matt wore a jacket and tie; B.J., a low-necked dress of black velvet. The necklace was a twisted skein of silver, from which dangled a large silver charm in the shape of a four-petaled blossom.

"That's the flower on your nursery logo," I said. "Mock orange?"

"Yeah, the Idaho state flower and all that. Carnegie, I wear that necklace almost every day. If anybody local saw it, they'd recognize it and they'd figure out . . . what happened."

"So you think it hasn't been found yet? Or maybe it was found, but they sent it off to his family with his personal effects?"

"I don't know!" She sat beside me on the bed, angrily scraping tears from her face. "It's driving me crazy, trying to find out."

"That's what the Tyke meant about your asking questions."

She nodded miserably. "I can't come right out and mention the necklace, can I? So I've been asking about the accident in general, hoping someone would tell me what was in his PG bag—"

"His what?"

"Personal gear bag. It's sort of a knapsack that they jump with, with some standard gear and then anything personal they want to bring. Cookies or chewing tobacco or a camera or whatever. I know that Brian's PG bag was brought back, but I don't know if anyone's gone through it. I have to find out before Matt comes back. He thinks I'm going to wear the necklace to Tracy's wedding. I even tried it on with the dress I'm wearing and showed it to him. He'll be back Friday night and it's already Tuesday!" Her voice wobbled like a child's. "What am I going to *do*?"

"Calm down, Muffy." I handed her the tissue box. "Calm

down and let's think. You could always tell Matt you lost the necklace."

"But I never lose anything, and I certainly wouldn't lose that. Besides, what if I told him it was lost and then it turned up later and he found out Brian had it? Matt was really jealous of Brian that summer and didn't like it that he was back in town now. He'd know that I lied to him and he'd know why!"

"Not necessarily. The necklace could have slipped off somehow, and Brian found it and kept it..." That sounded pretty lame, even to me. "OK, the first thing is to find out for sure if anyone at the jump base has seen it. If not, then you're going to have to say you lost it and go from there. Agreed?"

She nodded again, her eyes woeful over the wad of tissues.

"But there's got to be a better way to go about this than interrogating people."

"There is!" The warm purple eyes lit up in a way that used to mean trouble. Usually for someone else. "It came to me last night when you said you'd work on Tracy's wedding."

"I said *what*?"

"Well, didn't you? She fussed over you about Brian, and then she launched into wedding stuff. She kept talking about it and you kept nodding."

"Oh, hell." *I should never drink beer. I hate beer.*

"Anyway," B.J. continued, "you're Brian's cousin, so *you* could ask about his personal effects. Help me out here, Muffy. Please?"

What could I say? B.J. was way past being rational about this necklace business. But if a few harmless questions on my part could protect her marriage, I didn't have the heart to refuse. Besides, I had the sense that she needed the necklace back for a deeper reason than placating Matt. She needed to erase, if only symbolically, a deed that she fervently wished undone. I'd made enough mistakes in own my life to appreciate how she felt.

"OK, I'll call his folks and—"

"No! God, Carnegie, don't do that. Their son is dead. I don't want them bothered about his trashy little one-night stand."

"But they wouldn't know that, they'd think he had a girlfriend . . ." I trailed off as I saw her point. If Brian's parents did find the necklace, without knowing how it came into his possession, they'd assume there had been a woman in his life. Then they might try to communicate with her, and that would be disastrous.

"So what do you want me to do?"

"Just ask around, but casually, and find out if Brian's stuff is still at the base. Then we can figure out the next step."

"All right, I'll ask around." I didn't plan on taking any next step, but I didn't say that. I just accepted her grateful embrace and sank back onto the sheets. "Now, let me close my eyes for a minute—"

But no, I was doomed to consciousness; an insistent rapping sounded at the front door. As B.J. went to answer it, I slowly got myself vertical and pulled on shorts and a tank top. The day was heating up already, in more ways than one.

"Sleeping?" pealed a well-known voice from beneath the loft. "I've done six miles along the river already. Carnegie, get yourself down here! You said to drop by this morning, and it's morning."

As I transported my aching head carefully down the stairs, I could see that Tracy had indeed been out along the river.

She lounged against the kitchen counter, water bottle in hand, breathing hard and happily. Her satin running shorts, neon yellow and ever so brief, rippled against the cutest butt in the business, and her yellow halter top revealed a deep cleavage that gleamed with healthy, photogenic perspiration.

Even her navel was cute, and who has a cute navel? Her eye makeup was light but skillful, and her hair, her gorgeous red hair, hung in a thick braid between smoothly muscled shoulders. Even in youth, Sam Kane's scarecrow physique could have been nothing like this. Tracy got her fair coloring from her mother, but where she got her long, languid beauty was a mystery.

I, on the other hand, felt like a train wreck. "I said to drop by?"

"Of course you did! Oh, it's *marvelous* to see you," said the sitcom star. She had acquired a trick of widening her pale blue eyes in feigned innocence as she emphasized certain words. The effect, both comic and sexy, was quite charming—or at least it would be to someone not screamingly hung over. "You don't look very well, though. I won't hug you; I can't afford to catch anything."

"I'm fine. Just feeling the effects of last night."

"You don't still drink *alcohol,* do you? Can't you see what it's doing to your complexion?" Tracy tilted her lovely chin to chug from the bottle. "I told John I'll hold a glass of champagne at the wedding, just for the video, but I'm certainly not going to *drink* it."

"John?"

"She means Jack," B.J. explained helpfully. She was stuffing various items into a canvas tote bag. "I guess the notorious Knack is reinventing himself, huh, Muffy?"

"He prefers John," she insisted. For an actress, she didn't

lie all that well. "And I prefer Tracy. Your bathroom is down this way?"

"First door on the left." B.J. hefted the bag, which read "Gardeners Do It Dirty" in faded letters. "Well, I'm off to work. You two have fun talking weddings."

"I thought you didn't have to work today," I said, following her to the front door. "You're deserting me."

"You bet I am. I went to the bridal shower last week, now it's your turn to play audience." Her nose wrinkled. "I'm still fond of her, for old times' sake, but she can be a pain in the ass. Here's a key for you. Call me later, OK?"

"OK." I closed the door and tried to gather my wits. *What exactly did I agree to last night? And did I say anything dopey to Jack?*

I hadn't gathered all that many wits when Tracy sailed back into the room. She paused fleetingly, as if for the camera to find her, then drew me onto an overstuffed couch. I flicked a glance at her left hand, where a cushion-cut diamond, three carats at least, sparkled from a platinum band.

"Alone at last!" The bride laughed an adorable laugh. "I still love B.J. to death, for old times' sake, but she can be—"

"A pain in the ass?" I offered.

She blinked. "Well, yes. But I won't tell her you said so."

"Thanks."

"You're welcome. It is just so *sweet* of you to help me and John like this."

"You probably don't need much help at this point," I ventured. "I mean, you already have Beau Paliere and his—"

"But I *don't* have him, that's the problem!" She twitched her head in irritation. "He brings you flowers and kisses your hand and practically makes *love* to you, and then when it's showtime, he sends some snotty underling to take over! It's ridiculous, like a P.A. trying to be a show runner."

"Want to translate that?"

"P.A.'s are production assistants," she said kindly, indulging my ignorance. "The show runner is what ordinary people would call an executive producer."

Ordinary people? I bit back an irate comment. I liked being ordinary. "So who did Beau send, and why isn't he here himself?"

She related the tragic tale. Beautiful Beau was pinned down in Venice by a crisis that concerned the daughter of the Italian finance minister and the closing of various canals for her waterborne bridal procession. So he'd dispatched one of his "Girls," Shara Mortimer, to Sun Valley in his stead. This woman was a witch, a vampire, a monstrous control freak who was thwarting both the bride and her mother at every turn.

"She contradicts everything!" Tracy wailed. "I changed my mind about the tiniest detail, white roses instead of red in the chair garlands, and she just refused! I mean, who's in charge here?"

"Your ceremony is outdoors?"

"Yes. So?"

Ah-ha. I began to feel some camaraderie with Ms. Mortimer.

"Tracy, there's a heat wave going on. White roses wilt in the heat, they turn brown and ugly. Your new wedding planner is only—"

"But *you're* my new wedding planner! Cissy is just thrilled." I couldn't imagine calling my own mother by her first name, but Cissy Kane, ever girlish, insisted on it. "I don't care if this Mortimer person wants to stick around, as long as you'll be here to keep her in line."

"Um, that's not quite the situation. Your contract is with Beau Paliere, I can't just barge in—"

"Whatever." Tracy bounced to her feet and began to jog in place. "We'll figure it out at lunch. Are you sure you want to wear that? I'm going to change when we get there."

"Lunch?"

She rolled her eyes and sighed, also adorably. No wonder the camera loved her. "Lunch at the lodge, with Cissy and Danny, remember? So hurry up and change if you're going to. Cissy hates waiting for her food."

"Oh, right." I sighed and started for the stairs. Despite B.J.'s ministrations, it still hurt to move quickly. *What's today, Tuesday? The wedding is Saturday. I can do this, if I just stay away from the beer. . . .*

As I climbed to the loft, the phone rang. From the machine on Matt's desk I heard a hum, a click, and then a familiar voice, speaking in an unfamiliar, businesslike tone.

"Hello, this is Aaron Gold. I'm trying to reach Carnegie Kincaid. If you could ask her to call me back, my number is—"

I grabbed the phone. "Aaron, hi!"

"There you are, Stretch," he said happily, and I felt a wave of guilt for lusting after Jack the Knack, however briefly. "You weren't answering your cell, so I called Eddie and he told me what happened. Sorry about your cousin."

"We weren't close," I said automatically. "But thanks."

"So how long are you staying?"

"Through the weekend." I lowered my voice. "Somehow I got stuck with—"

Footsteps thudded loudly on the stairs and rebounded inside my head. Tracy, keeping her lovely muscles warm, jogged up to the landing, made a show of pointing at her watch, and jogged down again.

"I'm helping with Tracy's wedding," I said more decorously. "I'll tell you about it when I get back. Unless you've changed your mind about coming?" The days ahead without him suddenly seemed very long. "You could fly straight to Hailey on Saturday—"

"I thought we settled that." Aaron sounded peeved, the way he often did these days. I heard voices at his end, and a distant phone ringing. "Look, I'm at work. I just wanted to see if you were OK."

"Why shouldn't I be?" Between the headache and the noise of Tracy's workout, I may have come across a little peevish myself. *Don't do me any favors, Aaron.* "The sun is shining; I'm seeing all my old friends; I'm having a great time here by myself."

"Well, good," he said stiffly. "Have fun."

"I intend to." And then, because I couldn't resist and because I'm an idiot, I said, "How's it going with the cigarettes?"

" 'How's it going'?" Aaron's voice went cold and flat. "Well, in the one whole day since you asked me that before, I guess it's going fine. Maybe you could give me two days next time. I've got to go now. Bye."

And that was that. I slapped open my suitcase and pulled on a loose dress of flowered cotton, the one I'd been considering and then returning to my closet in Seattle for the last two weeks. Downstairs Tracy was doing hamstring stretches in the open doorway, outlined by the brilliant sun. I winced and groped for my sunglasses and car keys. Then I remembered.

"I'll have to ride with you," I said. "B.J. has my car. Or we could go find her at the nursery—"

"Ride?" Tracy did the eye roll again. I was getting tired of the eye roll. "I'm on foot, silly. Don't be a wuss, it's barely half a mile."

Chapter Eight

IT WAS A LONG, LONG HALF MILE.

Tracy set a brisk pace, pumping her fists in time with her stride, and still had energy left over to talk about the wedding. Not the breathless gushings of a typical young bride, but a crisp, efficient run-through of her latest production. We might be old friends, but suddenly I was the staff and she was the star.

"You'll have to come up to speed fast. Tomorrow guests are arriving, and I've got my bachelorette party in the afternoon. B.J.'s invited, so I guess you can come if you want."

"How nice," I said dryly, but my tone was lost on her.

"Then Thursday afternoon there's a picnic and baseball game at the jump base. I offered the caterer for that, I thought a Wild West kind of barbecue would be cute, with a chuck wagon and cowboy hats and all?"

Baseball seemed an odd choice of activity—Sun Valley is golf and tennis territory—but then I remembered that Jack was quite the fastball pitcher in college. He'd even been scouted by a major-league team, he told me once, and when they didn't make him an offer it broke his heart. I wondered if Tracy knew that.

"John would look fabulous in a cowboy hat," she prattled on, "and Daddy has dozens of them. But the jumpers said no, it's just a casual bachelor party and all they want is beer and burgers. So I just need you to stop by there and coordinate with the caterer . . ."

I trudged along beside my new client, cowering from the glare behind my sunglasses. I would have been sweating, but the air was too dry. My tongue felt like cotton and my eyelids like sand. Had Ketchum been this hot back in the Muffy summer? *If only I'd brought a water bottle with me. Where the hell is the lodge?*

A remarkable sight along the roadside brought me to a halt. In a broad mown pasture, two bulls dozed contentedly in the grass. But these bulls were enormous, easily double life size, and made of bronze, with a small plaque bearing the name of a world-famous sculptor. Only in Sun Valley.

My good humor somewhat restored, I took a stab at sounding enthusiastic and professional.

"So, how many guests are we expecting?"

"Two hundred, two fifty, it's flexible." Tracy shrugged. "I told Bob, he's the caterer, just to have extra of everything."

Flexible. I thought about the very first wedding I'd done, figured down to the dollar for a bride with a modest budget, where two extra dinner guests would have been a problem. Money may not buy happiness, but it sure buys flexibility.

"Friday, people are on their own, for tennis or golf or whatever," she continued, "and Friday night is the rehearsal dinner on the terrace and the big skating party. We took the whole lodge for the weekend, so the rink will be open all evening. You have to be sure no one gets trash on the ice. . . ."

The details were slipping past me, but Shara Mortimer would have it all on paper anyway. Finding a way to work with her, while placating Tracy and Cissy, was going to be a tightrope walk with flaming hoops every few steps. But now

that I'd taken on this job, I was going to do it right. No way
was Beau Paliere—or any of Cissy's wealthy friends—going
to hear a word of criticism about the assistant from Seattle.
Better than that, I was determined to dazzle the whole
crowd.

A woman went by laden with shopping bags, which
prompted me to ask Tracy about her wedding gown.

"To die for," she pronounced. "To. Die. For. I was going to
go strapless, but I'm bored to tears with that after all the
award shows. So I'm doing the princess thing, but with a
twist. I'll wear my hair loose, with a pearled Juliet cap, and
the dress has long fitted sleeves and a million tiny buttons
down the back, and a chapel-length train from the waist. But
the neckline is draped low, just barely legal. And I mean
barely. The designer says it's all about contrast."

"Wow." It sounded all about mishmash to me, but then,
no one had asked me. When you're an on-the-day wedding
coordinator, you don't make things better. You make them
work. "What's the fabric?"

"It's slipper satin, very shiny, in a pale, pale coral to go
with the new hair. And the train is featherweight chiffon, so it
flutters down from the waist and sweeps along the ground in
back. The whole package photographs like a dream."

"I can't wait to see it. Maybe after lunch today?"

"Oh, it's not here. I changed my mind. I want pearl buttons instead of cloth-covered, to go with the cap, so I sent
it back. There's this Under Five on the show, Tessa, she's flying up from L.A. on Friday in her dad's jet. She'll bring it
with her."

"Under Five?"

"An actor with five lines or less. A nobody." She winked at
me. "But I needed the dress, so I invited her."

I got back to business. "Friday is cutting it awfully close for alterations."

"Alterations?" Tracy stopped in her tracks and turned on me in amazement, the sun flashing off her designer shades. "Like if I gained weight? Carnegie, I'm in television. I don't *eat*. I did a photo shoot in that gown for a wedding magazine two months ago, and I guarantee you, my waistline hasn't grown an eighth of an inch."

"It's just good to be certain—"

"I mean, if anything, it's smaller, because I've been working out like *crazy*. Elliptical trainer, spinning, upper-body lifting. My coach has me on free weights and machines both, especially the upper-bod stuff. I'm really afraid of saggy triceps, aren't you?"

"Terrified."

I glanced at her figure as we went on walking. She wasn't tough-looking like the Tyke, but her triceps were firmly sculpted, and her waistline was certainly taut and narrow beneath that remarkable bosom. Come to think of it, I didn't recall the bodice of her waitress uniform jutting out quite so boldly years ago. . . .

"What did you think?" said Tracy archly, noting the direction of my gaze. "Of *course* I've had them done. Frankly, I'm surprised that you haven't. You of all people."

I folded my arms across my chest and changed the subject. "Um . . . tell me about your trip to Portland. I haven't been there in months. Did you see the Vermeer show at the art museum?"

"Of course we did. Do you always walk this slow?" She stepped out a little faster. "Let's get back to the wedding. Beau hired Valerie Cox to do the flowers. She's good, isn't she?"

"She's the best." Valerie Cox of San Francisco was renowned in wedding circles for her exotic, extravagant creations—and notorious for carrying her creations in her head instead of committing them to paper. "A little eccentric, but—"

"Fine. And Bob I already know, I've been to his parties before."

"Were they open-air parties? Because it's a whole different ball game, serving outdoors."

"I guess so. I don't remember." She seemed to lose interest in her vendors—or maybe she was just working her way around to the real issue. "Listen, I need you to help me with something. It's this nonsense about John's best man."

I almost said "John who?" then caught myself. "What nonsense? Who's it going to be?"

More eye rolling, accompanied by a camera-worthy sigh. "He asked Pari Taichert, of all people!"

"Well, it's unusual to have a woman as best man, but it's not unheard of." Nor was it unheard of to have the best man loathe the bride, though of course I didn't say that. "And if they're longtime friends, it can be a really meaningful choice."

"Oh, screw meaningful! How is it going to look in the pictures, to have this little dyke standing there? And she wants to wear a *tuxedo.*"

I stopped dead. "Tracy, listen to me. The fact that a dear friend of Jack's—I mean, John's—is a lesbian is completely irrelevant here."

"Oh, she isn't really," Tracy admitted grudgingly. "She's got a boyfriend in the Air Force, but he can't make it to the wedding. What do you suppose *he* would think of her in a tuxedo? I swear, she's just doing it to get back at me for taking Jack away."

Personally, I thought the Tyke would look spiffy in a tux,

but my job was to soothe the bride, not torment her. "We'll worry about clothing later. Right now it's important to make John feel that this is his wedding, too. Years from now you'll look back on this and—"

"Yo, girls! Want a ride?" A dull red convertible screeched over to the curb and Domaso Duarte, looking anything but dull, leaned an elbow out. Beside him in the passenger seat, Gorka barked a deep-throated greeting, his extravagant pink tongue lolling and drooling. "Looks hot on that pavement."

"You're going the wrong way," I pointed out, amused despite myself, and thinking that a ride would be welcome.

"For you I'll hang a U-turn anytime." Domaso grinned at me, then cocked his head at Tracy. "Besides, I was only running into town for something, then I'm coming back. What about it, blondie?"

The former blond was indignant. "I don't *think* so."

"Just trying to be nice to your friend here—"

"Leave us alone, for God's sake!" She marched away, her braid swinging like a glossy copper pendulum.

Domaso laughed and roared off, and I hurried to catch up with Tracy.

"What was that about?"

"Nothing. He's just a jerk sometimes."

"You didn't have to be rude."

"What do you care?" she snapped. "Just because Dom was all over you at the bar last night."

"We were only dancing—"

"Oh, never mind. Let's cross over."

Well, brides do get temperamental, after all. I followed Tracy across the road and up the drive to the grand fieldstone façade of the Sun Valley Lodge. The glass-and-timber double doors were embellished with the face of Old Sol, Sun Valley's emblem since the early years. Back when Sonja Henie was cutting figure eights on the ice rink, and later on when Hemingway was upstairs typing *For Whom the Bell Tolls*. Quite a place.

"There she is!" The high-ceilinged lobby echoed with high-spirited voices as a gaggle of pretty people in swimsuits and robes rushed toward us from the hallway that led to the swimming pool. "Tracy, darling!"

Celebrities are de rigueur at the lodge, whose walls are studded with black-and-white photos of Lucille Ball and Leonard Bernstein and Clark Gable and the like, all smiling on the ski slopes. I didn't recognize the faces of these present-day celebrities, but they had to be actors. They had that beautifully groomed, larger than life air, as if ready to strike a pose or sign an autograph at a moment's notice.

Around the lobby the other lodge guests, mere civilians, murmured and stared at the glamorous group. Most of Tracy's friends had fabulous skin, and right now most of it was showing.

"Here comes the bride," warbled a bronzed fellow in a Speedo. "Isn't she too gorgeous?"

"Sweetie, *look* at your deltoids!" A luscious blonde, her thong bikini accentuated rather than obscured by a diaphanous little wrap, embraced the bride like a long-lost sister. "That trainer of yours is a genius, sweetie. A genius!"

"Olivia!" trilled Tracy, "Carnegie, this is Olivia, my maid of honor. You must recognize her, she plays the dog groomer."

She rattled off a string of other introductions, which in my overheated state I didn't quite follow. The pretty people were indeed actors, but there were some normal-looking types, as well, whom she referred to by first name and title.

"Susie is Makeup and Marjorie's Hair, Peter is Props . . ."

Tracy's agent had come, too, along with her manager, her lawyer, her business manager, her masseuse, and someone called D.P., though whether that was his title or his name wasn't clear. I tried to keep the names and functions straight—Marjorie Hair, Peter Props—but there were just too many.

My own function wasn't explained at all, but from the treatment I was getting from the bride it was clearly on the level of production assistant, not show runner. As the swimmers dispersed upstairs to change and she trotted along with them, Tracy tossed me a brief directive over her shoulder, to "go find Cissy." So I crossed the lobby, passing an espresso bar that was new since my day, and stepped through the grand double doors.

The scene before me could have graced a tourist brochure. On the flower-decked brick terrace, well-dressed and vivacious diners crowded the tables beneath a roof of stretched white canvas. Beyond them, past a lawn of emerald grass, lay Sun Valley's famous year-round ice rink, shaded by a black fabric awning that snapped and rippled in the blazing high-altitude sun.

Beneath the awning, skaters in summer clothes swooped and pivoted along the rail. Out in the center, their little faces solemn with concentration, a gaggle of eight-year-old Olympic hopefuls attempted toe loops and double Salchows to the applause of an imaginary audience. That's Sun Valley for you.

I found Cissy Kane sitting by herself in the bright and flattering shade of the white roof, stirring a snow drift of sugar into a tumbler of iced tea. She was gazing around happily, accepting a wave here and throwing an air kiss there.

Just like her daughter, Cissy was in her element in public view, and being mother of the famous bride was just frosting on her already-delectable cake. Some women in this role

struggle with jealousy, but she had long been convinced, in a
silly but rather charming way, that she was just as young and
pretty as her daughter.

I hadn't seen Cissy in years. She was plumper than ever,
her double chin tripled if not quadrupled, but her creamy
skin was still flawless and her baby-fine hair was still res-
olutely blonde. Only the subtlest of dye jobs would do for
our Cissy. She was always exquisitely turned out.

Today her dress, a ruffled lilac silk, was precisely matched
to her faultless manicure, her kitten-heel sandals, and her
fancy little purse. Not to mention her jewelry. An amethyst
the size of a walnut flashed and sparkled as she blinked her
ice-blue eyes and beckoned to me, twiddling the delicate fingers of one chubby hand.

"Carrie! Here I am, sweetie!"

I threaded through the tables and bent to kiss her cheek.
It was soft as an infant's, and I caught a whiff of her signature
perfume. Like Cissy, the perfume was flowery and girlish and
a bit too much, but so sweet that you liked it anyway. She
beamed up at me, then pursed her lips like a petulant child
as she caught sight of someone over my shoulder.

"Danny, you look dreadful! What on earth is wrong?"

"Late night," her stepson croaked. Danny Kane was truly
in hangover hell, I realized. I was merely in purgatory. His
skin was pallid, almost greenish, and his eyes looked like
poached eggs. But still, he made an admirable attempt to be
social. "Hi, Carnegie. You having a good visit with B.J.?"

"I always do," I said. "She's such a character."

"You can say that again. She was flying high last night."
He turned his head slowly, as if it pained him. "Listen, Cissy,
I'm not really up for lunch—"

"Of course you are, sweetie, you just need to sit down and

have something to drink first." As Danny sank into a chair, she went back to fussing over the menu. "I've ordered an appetizer already, but I can't decide between the Cobb salad and the club sandwich. I had the club yesterday and they didn't put enough bacon on it. I hate that, don't you? Where is Tracy? That girl is always late."

Cissy herself was famous for her last-minute arrivals, so I smiled at Danny over the rim of my water glass, and he smiled weakly back. It wasn't the most diplomatic moment to ask questions on B.J.'s behalf, but I had to start somewhere.

"Danny," I said quietly, remembering the effect of B.J.'s braying on my own painful head, "I was wondering about Brian's personal effects. Have they been sent back to his family already?"

"I don't know." He sipped some water. "You'd have to ask the L.O. The logistics officer."

"What about Brian's PG bag? Jumpers keep mementos and things in their bags, don't they?"

I waited nervously for Danny to ask why I was being so nosy. I had a cover story ready, but I didn't get a chance to use it, because just then the waiter brought Cissy's appetizer: smoked trout on toast, its pungent aroma rising distinctly in the heat of the day. Danny gazed at the plate in horror and turned a whiter shade of pale.

"Excuse me," he mumbled, rising from his chair. "Tell Tracy... 'scuse me."

He fled, jostling the waiter in his haste and nearly colliding with a woman clad in chic but unsummery black. She sidestepped him with a scowl and kept coming, bearing down on our table like the wedding planner of the apocalypse.

"Oh, bad to worse," muttered Cissy. Then she turned up a smile, like turning up a dimmer switch. "Over here, sweetie! Sit down and say hello to Carnegie Kincaid, your new assistant."

Shara Mortimer was a surprise. Beau Paliere was known for his coterie of female staffers, each one prettier than the next. But "Beau's Girls" tended to the blonde and willowy, while this one was olive-skinned and strong-featured, with thick black hair in a severe chignon. Her shoes were small, her earrings large, her briefcase sleek and expensive.

The whole look screamed Manhattan. Here was a woman who made maître d's grovel and cabbies quake. *Be afraid.*

"I'm *so* pleased to meet you," I said, baring my throat to the alpha female. "Shara, that's an interesting name."

I waited for her to make a similar comment about my name, but she just stared at me. I fumbled onward. "I, um, met Beau in Seattle last Christmas—"

"I know all about *that*," said Shara in an unmistakable New York accent. She sniffed indignantly and reached into her briefcase, drawing out a sheaf of papers with a red-taloned hand. "Monsieur Paliere contacted me this morning from Italy. If Ms. Kane chooses to employ an on-site wedding coordinator in addition to myself, that person must be a temporary employee of Paliere Productions. Otherwise we will not be held liable for the success of the event. Sign at the X and initial each page."

She offered me the papers, a fancy fountain pen, and a look that said the success of the event was a long shot at best, but she herself no longer gave a rip. Here was a woman who wanted to get Tracy Kane married and then get the hell out of Idaho.

"This is awfully formal," I protested. "I was just going to help out."

"That is what you're doing, sweetie, helping us out." Cissy barely glanced up from her inspection of the menu. "Just sign so we can eat, all right?"

"Give me a minute." I scanned the document. Other than stipulating a remarkably generous payment for me, it was vague about my responsibilities, lumping them under "Duties As Assigned." I hated the idea of working for Beau Paliere, but since he wasn't actually going to be here in person, and since Eddie and I were in serious need of the revenue ... "Well, it looks pretty straightforward, Cissy, if you're sure this is what you and Tracy want."

"Of course we do," she said absently. "Or maybe the crab cakes. What are you having, sweetie?"

"Not sure." As I initialed, I asked Shara Mortimer, "Are you joining us for lunch?"

"No." She closed her briefcase with a vicious snap and rose to her feet. But she must have heard how rude she sounded, because she unbent just a little. "I've already eaten. I'm meeting the photographer for a drink by the pool. You and I can get together later."

"Sure. Where? ..."

But the New Yorker, finished unbending, was already striding away.

"She's staying here at the lodge," Cissy said. "I lined up this gorgeous suite for Beau, and now it's going to waste on *her*. I'm going to try the Cobb salad. Or maybe the Asian orange duck salad. Do you suppose those are mandarin oranges? Because I'm not sure I like mandarin oranges ..."

I saw Shara pass Tracy on the terrace steps; the two women exchanged distant nods but didn't speak. *What have I gotten myself into?* Well, I'd just keep everything smooth and cooperative with Ms. Mortimer, win her over with my professionalism, and I'd be fine.

Meanwhile, I watched Tracy as she sailed across the terrace like a breeze across a wheat field, leaving a murmuring stir in her wake. Her layered ensemble was a mix of textures, fluttery silk and nubbly cotton and airy chiffon, that also mixed shades of white, from ivory to cream to champagne. Very feminine, very aristocratic, very *wow*. I made a mental note to put together a white-on-white outfit for myself, next time I had the funds to go clothes shopping.

As Tracy took her seat, excuses were made for Danny and air kisses were exchanged, then we ordered Cobb salads all around. The bride, perhaps mindful of her waistline, indulged in three or four bites, and given my condition, I didn't exceed her by much. But Cissy cleared her plate gallantly, sopping up the dressing with a roll, then ordered raisin rice pudding and coffee, extra cream.

And all the while, she talked. The rosebud lips managed to have food going in and words coming out, simultaneously, for every minute of the next three-quarters of an hour.

"I was going to stay with purple, Carrie, you know how that's my special color, but then I saw this dress in pink, not pink-pink, you know, but more shell pink . . ."

Tracy, having heard all this before, sat gazing at the skaters without much interest, waving vaguely at a friend or two, and autographing napkins for the waiter, the busboy, and four tittering women at the next table. I found myself watching her: the way she didn't fidget with her hair, not even once, the way she drank her coffee with a straw to preserve her lipstick. Always onstage, always perfect.

The few times Tracy took her shades off, her eyes were distant and preoccupied. Or was that just boredom?

" . . . but then when I had my pumps dyed they came out more of a rum pink, so I had to find new ones, which took even *more* time, and I'm already as busy as a cat in a room full of rocking chairs . . ."

I was starting to glaze over myself when a shriek from inside the lobby cut Cissy short. All the conversations around us halted as all eyes turned to view Domaso Duarte dashing out among the tables, swearing and shouting, with Shara Mortimer hot on his heels. He looked flustered enough, but she was soaked to the skin and apparently homicidal. *Be very afraid.*

"What on *earth*?" squeaked Cissy.

I was just as astounded as she was, until the object of the pursuit appeared right under my nose. Gorka, his tail beating the air triumphantly, flung his front paws onto our table and lovingly placed Shara Mortimer's dripping wet briefcase onto my lap.

Chapter Nine

"YOU *LAUGHED*, I SAW YOU. YOU WERE LAUGHING ALONG with the rest of them. You call yourself a professional?"

Shara Mortimer was beautiful when she was angry, and just now she was spitting mad. She stalked around the luxurious suite, spreading the contents of her briefcase to dry on every available surface and snarling at me. With her black hair swinging loose around her shoulders and her slim, tanned legs flashing beneath a white terry-cloth robe, she truly looked like one of Beau's Girls.

"I couldn't help it," I said meekly, peeling apart yet another vendor contract. "But you have to admit—"

"I don't have to admit anything. Hand me my cell phone. It's probably ruined."

I complied in silence. I had already apologized once, as a courtesy, and I was damned if I'd do so again. Domaso Duarte had been profuse in his regrets, and Gorka, unrepentant, had been banished from the premises. He was probably lolling in Domaso's front seat, having a little doggy chuckle over his delightful game of tug-of-war, which had ended with Shara toppling into the swimming pool, and Gorka plunging in after her to retrieve the briefcase and leave its owner floundering.

I secretly wished I'd been there to see it. If Shara didn't

simmer down soon, I might just banish myself from this wedding altogether. *Except that I already signed the damn contract, and if I broke it, Beau Paliere would probably sue me—.*

A bold knocking sounded from the corridor. Shara waved at me to answer it and whisked into the bedroom, pulling the double doors shut behind her.

"Hey, Red! Look at you, girl, pretty as ever!"

Sam Kane, father of the bride, shambled into the suite with his Stetson in his hand and a big grin on his homely old face. Sam was a cartoonist's dream, a walking caricature, all bulbous nose and flapping ears and oversized hands and feet, with long scrawny limbs in between. He'd lost some hair since I'd seen him last, just like his son Danny, and gained a bit of a paunch, but he still wore his trademark brown suede sports coat with the elbow patches and an enormous brass belt buckle with his initials on it. There was nothing small, subdued, or modest about Sam Kane.

"But what am I saying?" He gave me a long, fatherly hug. "My deepest sympathies, truly, on the loss of your cousin."

"Good to see you, Sam," I said. I was tired of explaining my nonrelationship with Brian, so I didn't. "Congratulations about Tracy."

It really was good to see him. I had fond memories of Sam teasing the Muffies about their boyfriends that summer, flirting with us himself with clumsy gallantry, and taking us out for the occasional sumptuous dinner. Tracy had plenty of spending money back then, but B.J. and I were counting pennies, and Sam always picked up the whole tab on the pretext of treating his darling daughter. Everybody in the Wood River Valley liked Sam, even his business rivals, and I was no exception.

"Thank you kindly, Red. I don't know which one of 'em's

luckier, her or Jack." He glanced around the sitting room at the papers that lay curling on desk, chairs, and coffee table, and shook his head. "Cissy told me what happened. I swear, that New York girl has been nothing but trouble."

I was about to counter this unfair assessment when Shara appeared. She had repaired her makeup, put on a tailored blouse and slacks, and knotted her hair in place, all in a few minutes. She was bitchy, but she was good.

"Mr. Kane," she said sternly. I'd never heard anyone call him that. "Mr. Kane, I was going to review some contractual details with you this afternoon, but as you can see, that will have to wait. However, I do need your approval to hire more waitstaff for the reception, now that the head count is increasing, and to hire a second truck to carry the sound system and dance floor up to White Pine."

"You do whatever you need to," said Sam grandly. I suspected he was showing off for me. Sam Kane didn't get rich by overlooking details. "With Carnegie here to keep you on track, this whole thing should go real slick."

I winced inwardly, and Shara bristled like a cat.

"Things were going perfectly smoothly already," she said in a tight, dangerous voice. "As I told Mrs. Kane, with the catering manager's assistant at my disposal, it's quite unnecessary to have a second coordinator here this week. I agreed to take her on as a favor to Tracy—"

"Whoa, you're doing *us* favors now?" Sam squared his bony shoulders and hitched his thumbs into his belt. "Seems to me we're the ones who have to keep on accommodating you and your almighty checklists."

Shara backpedaled just a little. "You have to understand, an event of this scope takes a great deal of organization."

"That's exactly why you need Carnegie." He grinned and dropped his arm around my shoulders. "Ain't it?"

"I *don't* need her." The cat was hissing now. "Now that all the planning is in place, a single on-site coordinator is perfectly sufficient. I keep explaining that to your wife."

Her voice held just the faintest hint of disdain when she referred to Cissy. And that was Shara Mortimer's undoing, because Sam Kane, who was utterly unemotional when it came to business, utterly adored his wife.

"Well, I'll explain something to you, missy," he drawled. Sam only drawled when he meant to. "You are absolutely right. We only need one coordinator, and we got 'er." He gave my shoulders a little shake. "So you can just pack up your bags and go back where you came from. Come on, Red, I'll buy you a drink."

And with that he marched me out of the suite and kicked the door shut behind us.

"Sam, wait—" I began. I followed him, protesting. "Let's take a minute. You really need to talk with Tracy and Cissy before you make a change like this."

"Oh, she's been rubbing them raw ever since she got here. It's not just me." The drawl was gone and the businessman was back, the man with his finger on the pulse of the Wood River Valley. "You run your own wedding business in Seattle, don't you? You're bonded and so forth?"

"Well, yes, but—"

"But nothing! You're the only man for the job, pardon the expression, and that is that." He paused on the step below me, and turned to look me straight in the eye. Unlike Tracy's big blue eyes, Sam's brown ones were small and watery, and rather tired. "Please, Red, as a favor to me and my women-folk?"

"Oh, all right." As we continued down, a thought occurred to me. *His finger on the pulse*...I'd promised B.J. to ask around, but I'd felt like a ghoul grilling Danny about his dead crewmate. Sam, on the other hand, wasn't traumatized by this death, and he might very well be able to help me. Or direct me to someone who could. "Sam, tell me something. Was there an investigation into Brian's accident?"

"Of course," he said promptly. We were crossing the lobby, where guests relaxed and tourists wandered, checking out the famous lodge. None of them was within earshot, so Sam paused to answer me in a serious tone. "A smoke-jumper fatality is extremely rare, thank God. This is a BLM base, so they looked into it, plus the local police had to sign off, that kind of thing. It's not a fire-management issue, since the accident was unrelated to the Boot Creek fire itself, or there would have been a whole task force here. But still, there were all kinds of experts swarming around by the next day, going over the safety procedures inch by inch. It's funny, though..."

"What's funny?"

He lowered his voice even further. "I heard there were some closed-door meetings, and some higher-ups flown in for them. The official report is going to be delayed, but they won't say why, which is kind of unusual. Julie Nothstine was consulting with them for a while, and she told me about it. She's a local gal who used to be a safety-and-health officer for the BLM. Retired now, but sharp as a razor. She can be something of a handful, though, and after a while the NIFC fellows shut her out of the investigation."

He pronounced it *niff-cee*, and it took a moment to register that he meant the National Interagency Fire Center, the big administrative operation located at the Boise airport.

"So you think they're covering something up?"

"Oh, nothing that dramatic. Prob'ly just some lawyer somewhere, afraid NIFC will get sued or something. The investigators have all gone back to Boise, but Julie's an old friend of mine. I could ask her more about it, if you want."

"I do, Sam, thanks. You see, I was just curious—"

"Of course you are, him being your cousin."

"—and I was also wondering what's been done with his personal effects."

I tried to make it sound casual, hoping he wouldn't ask me why I didn't just call Brian's parents. To my relief, Sam Kane was used to being considered the authority in all questions.

"Now, that I don't know," he said, "but I'll betcha we can find out. Hey, Al, got a question for you."

The man who looked up from his armchair in the lobby was dark and lean, with lively brown eyes and crooked teeth.

"This here's Carnegie Kincaid, Brian Thiel's cousin," said Sam. "Al Soriano. He's a jumper."

"I'm sorry about Brian," said Al, rising and extending his hand. "He was a good guy."

Sam cut right to the chase. "Carnegie's wondering what happened to her cousin's belongings, his PG bag and so on. Any ideas?"

Al shook his head. "I think they sent it all to his parents."

"Already?" I spoke sharply, making Sam frown, so I softened my tone and brought out my cover story. "The reason I'm asking is that I gave Brian a little, um, keychain once, when we were kids. He kept it as kind of a souvenir, and I was hoping to get it back. Did anyone find any jewelry or anything?"

"Not that I heard of. But Dr. Nothstine might know."

"I was thinking that, too," said Sam. "Thanks, Al. We'll see you later."

And if asking this Nothstine person doesn't pan out, I vowed, *I'm calling it quits. B.J. can just tell Matt she lost the damn necklace, and leave it at that. I've got a wedding to run.*

"Excuse me," came a voice from behind us. Shara Mortimer, a carry-on bag over one shoulder, held out a manila file. "Here are my notes and your copy of the contract. As long as you're an employee of Paliere Productions—that is, until this coming Sunday—you're to call in at least daily and report on the status of your event. Is that clear?"

"Perfectly." I tucked the file into my tote bag. Should I try to make peace? It's always worth trying. "Shara, I'm sorry things didn't work out."

"Better you than me," she muttered, for my ears only. Then, louder, "The rest of the paperwork is upstairs in the suite. Here's the key. You have a vendor meeting there tomorrow morning at eight, so you'd better prepare. Good luck, and good-bye."

"I hate to say it, but good riddance," said Sam, watching her go. "Now—"

"Sam, you've given me a big job, so I'd better start doing it. I'll call you after I've gone over the contracts and—"

"Hold on there," he said. "I'm heading up to White Pine for a coupla hours. Before you go fussing with the details, why don't you come up there with me and get the big picture? Got to start at the top, Red!"

He had a point. The paperwork would make more sense to me if I knew the layout of the ceremony site. And maybe the wide-open spaces would clear my head, so I agreed.

Soon Sam and I were climbing into his mammoth SUV, its air conditioner already set to blasting by the uniformed bellman who drove it up to the lodge entrance. I must admit, when the temperature's pushing a hundred, valet parking has its appeal.

I looked around the vehicle's interior, wide-eyed. I expected leather upholstery, of course, but not separate DVD screens for each rear passenger, or more cup holders than I own cups.

"Like it?" asked Sam. It was a rhetorical question. "Nice and roomy."

"I've had smaller apartments," I observed, and he laughed. I was tempted to ask about gas mileage and pollution and petty details like that, but there was no point. In Sam Kane's world, if you could afford it, you deserved it, and that settled it. I tried a safer query. "No bucket seats?"

"That was Cissy's idea," he told me, patting the bench seat between us. "She likes to cuddle, even when we're on the road. What a woman. Hey, there's Jack." He braked and opened his window. "Howdy, son-in-law!"

I craned around him to see Jack Packard approaching from the parking lot. He wore light khakis and a blue-on-blue Hawaiian shirt that hung straight down from his muscular chest and blew in the breeze against his flat, tight torso. *Oh, my.* Good thing I'd be keeping my distance from him this week. *Look but don't touch, that's the ticket.*

"Hi," said Jack, leaning into Sam's window. He slid his sunglasses up on his fair hair, and his golden eyes found me. "Afternoon, Carnegie. Where's this old devil taking you?"

"Up the hill to check out Wedding Central," said Sam. "Red's replacing the New York girl. That OK with you?"

"You're asking me for an opinion?" Jack retorted, and cocked his head at me. "Nobody asks the groom anything, do they?"

"You get your say," I said weakly. At this point I was melting, and it wasn't from the temperature.

"Well, I say it's a fine replacement." He slapped the edge of the door lightly. "In fact, I'll ride up there with you and give you the groom's-eye-view of the whole plan."

"Oh, that's not necess—"

"Climb in!" crowed Sam, and I was on my way to the White Pine Inn, hip-to-hip with Jack the Knack.

Chapter Ten

OUR DRIVE BEGAN ON ASPHALT, BUT ONCE OFF THE SUN Valley road we hit gravel. The private route wound for miles up a dry creek bed between wooded, steeply tilted slopes, crossing rocky little ravines that once carried tributary creeks into the main channel. But these, too, were dry in this extraordinarily hot June. Even in the SUV we bounced and jostled over the deep ruts, which left a dust cloud hanging behind us and made Sam grumble.

"Blasted delivery trucks. Cissy's got them coming and going every two minutes with something new for the inn." He swerved around a pothole. "I swear, they tear up the road worse than my construction equipment. I wanted to pave the whole goddamn thing before the wedding but the county's still processing my goddamn permits. I've got half a mind to do it anyway. What do you say, Red, shall we break the law and pave the road?"

"We've only got—*ow!*—we've only got three days," I said, grabbing the dashboard to steady myself. It was either that or grab Jack, and the dashboard was safer. I kept sliding toward him, his thigh warm against mine. He smelled, quite pleasantly, of soap. "If they didn't finish the job on time, we'd have to fly the guests in."

"Don't think I haven't thought about it," said Sam. I knew

he was quite the small-plane aficionado, so his next remark didn't surprise me. "I'm gonna build a little airstrip up there, you know. Once the wedding tents are cleared off, I'll have the meadow leveled and take a bunch of trees down, then Cissy can have her lampshades brought in by helicopter."

Sam went on describing his ambitious plans, the dozens of minimansions he would build and sell, each with its own minikingdom of acreage, though none as fine as the White Pine Inn itself. I tried to listen, to break my fevered awareness of Jack's body, his muscles moving under the thin shirt, the sun gilding his hair.

It didn't work—real-estate development not being a big interest of mine—so instead I gazed out the windshield and tried to concentrate on the non-Jack scenery.

The scenery was pure Idaho. Unlike the dark and dripping hemlocks of Seattle, the ponderosa pines around us stood bright green and glossy, in calendar-photo contrast to the hard and cloudless blue of the afternoon sky. As we passed one of Sam's construction sites, a 180-degree vista wheeled before us like a panning shot in a movie, with a view down to the Wood River Valley and out to the high, jagged skyline beyond. There wasn't a freeway or a shopping mall or a skyscraper in sight, just open country and open sky.

I felt my headache dissolving into the limitless distance. *Oh, Aaron should see this.*

Aaron? Wait a minute, why was I thinking about Aaron Gold when Jack the Knack was mere inches away? Aaron was hundreds of miles away, and besides that, he was irritable and uncommitted and he'd refused to come with me on this trip. How dare he invade my present thoughts while I was re-connecting with my past?

Sam startled me out of these reflections by taking the next

hairpin turn at a hair-raising speed. Presumably, since he was still alive, he was a better airplane pilot than he was a driver. He overcorrected and we fishtailed a little, sending a spurt of gravel into the ravine below.

"Careful, there," said Jack, amused and unflappable. "If I'm not in one piece to say 'I do' on Saturday, you'll have to answer to Tracy."

Tracy. The bride. Jack's wife. The mention of her name was a slosh of cold water on my overheated state. *This is a married man you're drooling over,* said my better self. Of course, my worse self chimed in *Not yet he isn't,* but I told her to shut up.

"Aw, shut up," said Sam. To Jack, not to me. "You're lucky to be in one piece to begin with. Like I keep telling Danny, anybody who goes jumping out of a perfectly good airplane should have his head examined."

"So I've heard," Jack answered, but absently. He was staring at the western horizon, where a gunmetal-gray mountain of thunderheads had begun to dwarf the green mountains below. "Here we go again. We've had enough lightning strikes for a whole season already, and it looks like more coming. These woods are like kindling."

Sam chuckled. "You itching for a Pulaski? You should be thinking about your honeymoon. Cissy's got the cottage all done up."

"Cottage?" I asked. "B.J. told me the honeymoon was in Costa Rica."

"It is," said Jack. "A spa for Tracy and after that an eco-tour in the rain forest for me. But she's got a huge fan club down there, and her manager has her doing interviews the minute we touch down. I wanted some peace and quiet first, so we're staying at White Pine for a few days."

"Sounds nice."

"Nice!" said Sam, gunning the engine up a final incline. "Heaven on earth. You can see for yourself, 'cause we're here."

B.J. was right: White Pine was spectacular. The three-storied inn, a tiered affair of log and shingle, thrust out from the crest of the ridge like the prow of a ship, its myriad skylights and bay windows glinting in the sun.

The inn's deep eaves and fancy woodwork suggested a Swiss chalet, but with none of the flimsy alpine kitsch you sometimes see in high-country motels. Here everything was richly substantial, with sure-handed design and gracefully executed details. From the massive fieldstone foundation to the tiny brass latches on the casement windows, Sam Kane bought only the best.

The road continued past a long, narrow parking area—crowded by pine trees and as yet unpaved—and disappeared into the woods. Somewhere farther, I assumed, the road led to the resort's condominiums and the other private houses still under construction. The construction site we had passed must be almost straight below us, judging by the way the road had doubled back on itself, but it was out of view below the treetops.

We alighted from the SUV. The landscaping around the half-circle drive was still sketchy, but with a million-dollar view of mountains and forests, who misses a few shrubs? As I took in the view, I took in a deep, contented breath. The air up here was almost as hot as in the valley, but the teasing breeze that trailed across my skin bore the clean, exciting scent of sun-warmed pines. Heaven.

"Heaven must smell like this," I said.

Jack smiled at me, the killer smile, but Sam was already throwing open the front door of his castle.

"Come on in!" he called, and waved an arm proudly. "Ain't this grand?"

Grandiose was more like it. The main room of the inn was vast, its western wall all windows under the soaring, open-beamed ceiling, with a generous flagstone veranda hanging out over that fabulous view. It was the kind of space that's called a "great room," and with good reason.

I glimpsed a gleaming kitchen down a hallway to the right, and on the left a wide staircase led up to a sort of mezzanine level with its own sitting areas among the corridors and doors.

"Sleeps sixty, including the staff, or it will once I hire 'em," said Sam. "Kitchen could feed an army. It's not all done yet, of course, but Cissy's been working on the decorating in the rooms we're using for the wedding."

"I can tell." I made a careful attempt to sound enthusiastic. The furnishings were mostly oak and leather, millionaire cowboy stuff, which suited the building and its rugged location. But overlaid on this masculine foundation were layers upon layers of ruffly pillows and cutesy whatnots and flowery curtains, most of them purple. Lots of purple. "She certainly has . . . a special touch."

I was saved from further fibs when Sam's pocket crackled and squawked. He pulled out a walkie-talkie and barked into it.

"What? No! No, no, no! Dammit, just stop what you're doing and wait for me." He switched off and turned to us with a preoccupied frown. "I've got a new foreman pouring foundations out there along the ridge, and if he doesn't straighten out, he won't be foreman long. Jack, you show Red around the place, would you? I shouldn't be long."

Jack barely had time to agree before Sam was out the door and gone in a rooster tail of dust. I listened to his engine fade in the distance, leaving us alone. Alone with Jack Packard in a building full of beds . . .

But some daydreams don't hold up in the harsh light of reality. *What exactly were you planning to do?* I asked myself. *Drag him down onto one of Cissy's purple bedspreads? What on earth would he think of you then?*

"You OK?" Jack touched my arm. "You look a little carsick."

"I'm fine." I moved away and raked a hand through my hair. "Just a bit queasy. Let's start in the kitchen, shall we? I could use some cold water."

As I stood at the polished granite counter, sipping from the glass Jack handed me, I took refuge in Shara Mortimer's paperwork. The general outline of the wedding was clear enough: an outdoor ceremony, champagne and a grilled supper back at the inn, and dancing under the stars. Very festive, very lavish, and, as I'd expect from Paliere Productions, very efficiently documented.

I put on a businesslike air, nodding gravely and making notes in the margins, until I regained my composure. Jack waited patiently, his arms folded, leaning against the stove. It was a restaurant-style range, double wide, with all the latest bells and whistles. He looked good there.

Though he'd look better naked. Maybe I should have poured cold water over my head. *Down, girl.*

"Right!" I said briskly, wrenching my gaze away from Jack to survey the rest of the kitchen. Strictly speaking, this was the catering manager's domain, but taking over the Kane/

Packard nuptials at the last minute put me in a tricky position. If I was to command the respect and confidence of my vendors at tomorrow morning's meeting, I needed to arm myself with the details of the venue.

So I checked on refrigerator and freezer space, extra sinks, power supply, the servers' access route from kitchen to veranda, all the while scribbling away in the fat spiral notebook I always have at hand. Eddie keeps nagging me about upgrading to something electronic, but I like paper. You would think he'd be the old-fashioned one, at his age, but—

"Eddie!" I said aloud.

Jack tilted his head. "Eddie?"

"My partner back in Seattle." I fumbled in my tote bag for my cell phone. "I can't take on a new client without letting him know. I should call B.J., too, and tell her where I am."

"No cell service up here, not until Sam builds his tower," said Jack. "That's why he uses walkie-talkies."

"Of course." I put the useless phone away and scribbled another note. "Well, let's keep going. Do you know where Tracy and the bridesmaids plan to dress?"

"Yeah, the master bedroom. Follow me."

The master bedroom was directly above the great room and shared the same breathtaking view of the western skyline. I crossed the bedroom—sure enough, the bedspread was strewn with icky pink and purple roses—and looked out the picture window. The drapes were purple, too, tied back with pink cord, and they clashed horribly with the blue sky and green forest scenery.

But I was thinking of photography, not scenery, because the veranda was straight below the window. Along with the classic shots of the bride checking her makeup and arranging her veil, the photographer might want to catch some candids

of the proud papa or the nervous groom pacing the veranda.
Nice.

A well-worn path led down the slope beneath the veranda
into a grove of aspens. The hot spring? I leaned to see, resting
my forehead against the window. As I did, I recalled standing
in the houseboat looking out at the rain, and then the warmth
of Aaron's arms around me.

The thought of him there in my Seattle home was comforting, and I suddenly felt much steadier. Of course I was at-
tracted to Jack—what female wasn't?—but I could handle
that. And I could handle this wedding, too. Like the man
said, that was then, this is now. I was a professional woman,
not the infatuated girl I'd been back in the Muffy summer. I
squared my shoulders and stepped away from the window.

And right into Jack. He had come up close behind me and
now he moved even closer, sliding one swift hand around my
waist and the other behind my head, to lift my face to his
kiss. It was a warm, confident kiss, and I confess I melted
into it. But only for a moment, I swear, and then I pulled
away.

"What do you think you're—"

"You can't pretend you—"

"Well, well, *well!*"

At the sound of this third voice, Jack and I whipped our
heads around to stare. Standing straddle-legged in the bedroom doorway, grinning a big white sharky grin, was Domaso
Duarte.

Chapter Eleven

TESTOSTERONE HAS ITS ADVANTAGES. OF THE THREE OF US, I was the innocent party; Jack was guilty of making an uninvited pass, and Domaso had barged into a private encounter. So why was I the one turning scarlet and groping for words?

Jack and Domaso, meanwhile, went straight into bull elk mode, pawing the earth with their metaphorical hooves and tossing their invisible antlers.

"What the hell are you doing here?"

Jack took an angry stride forward, his fists clenched, but Domaso stood his ground in the doorway and lifted his formidable chin.

"Hey, man, I work here. I'm looking for Sam." His dark eyes slid over to me and then returned to Jack. "I don't have to ask you what *you're* doing."

Thoughts and emotions tumbled through my mind, but words continued to fail me.

"Sam's at the construction site," said Jack. His teeth were clenched, too. "Couldn't you see his car isn't here?"

"Just checking."

"Well, go check at the site."

Domaso shrugged and retreated down the stairs, but it was a victorious retreat. Halfway down he called over his shoulder, "You two have fun!"

Jack waited for the front door to slam, then blew out a long breath. "I swear, that guy is always underfoot and he's always smirking. What is it with him?"

"Never mind *him*," I said, finding my voice at last. "You're the one getting married in a few days."

I'm not sure what I expected from Jack—guilt or defiance or even some attempt to pass the incident off as a joke. I didn't expect the tone of genuine dismay in his voice.

"I know. I know!" He sat on the edge of the bed and stared down at the carpet with a puzzled frown. "I love Tracy, I really do. My days of catting around are over and that's *fine* with me. I guess seeing you again got me thinking about that night, and acting like I used to."

He didn't say which night. We both knew he didn't have to.

"That was a long time ago," I began.

"Doesn't matter how long ago. I behaved pretty badly, didn't I?" He lifted his eyes to me, those topaz eyes. "I'm sorry, Carnegie. I should have at least talked to you afterward and made sure you were OK."

"I was OK. Eventually. But now—"

"Now I'm out of line."

"Absolutely." I felt like a hypocrite saying it, but it had to be said. Later on we could laugh off any gossip that Domaso might start, but right now I needed this settled, for my own peace of mind. "I'm sure you didn't . . . I mean, I'm sure it was just a momentary impulse. . . ."

"An impulse?" The killer smile had reappeared. He joined me by the window again, keeping his distance and narrowing his eyes against the afternoon sun. "I guess you could call it that, just an impulse to kiss a pretty woman. And we can call it momentary if you want."

"That's what I want," I said firmly, and strode to the door. "And the moment's over, all right? Let's finish our tour. How about showing me the meadow?"

What I really wanted, of course, was to jump Jack's bones right then and there. But I also wanted my self-respect, and the ability to look my latest bride in the eye before I sent her down the aisle.

I felt a bit wistful on the way downstairs, but as we left the inn for the sunshine outside, my heart grew lighter with every step. And the meadow was a mess, which helped ease us back into the prosaic task at hand. Nothing like piles of deer scat to alter the mood.

Not that it wasn't a lovely spot, a grassy acre or so with three tall ponderosa pines in the center where the ceremony would take place. The cinnamon-colored trunks were as broad as church columns, their green tops as lofty as a steeple. But the narrow skirt of open space surrounding them, which must have been lush and almost level back in May, now lay lumpy and parched.

"Could have sworn this grass used to be green," said Jack, nudging a dried-out clump of weeds with his toe. "I don't remember all these holes, either, or the rocks."

"There's a landscaping team lined up," I assured him. "And if we need to, we'll bring in rolls of carpeting. It never fails, the women know it's an outdoor ceremony and they still wear stiletto heels."

"Especially Tracy's girlfriends from the show." He chuckled. "I don't understand how some of them manage to walk. They sure look good, though."

"It's nice that you're getting to know her friends," I said primly, wondering if he hit on them, too.

"Hell, I was dating one of her friends, that's how I got to know her."

"Here in Idaho?" I was confused.

"No, down in Sonoma. I own a little property there that I'm working as a vineyard. Lots of L.A. people come for wine tours in the Napa Valley. I got involved with this one actress, and then she brought some of her friends for a weekend. I was just blown away when I realized that the star on her program was that gawky teenager from way back in Ketchum."

I bet the actress was blown away when Tracy stole you from her, I thought. But all I said was "You own a vineyard?"

"Just a small place. Bought it years ago, so I'm just now getting a decent harvest. Carpeting, huh?"

This was more like it. We paced out the space, laughing and chatting, while I scribbled notes about questions to ask my vendors in the morning. If the laughter was a little forced, so what? By Saturday night Jack would be a married man, and by Monday I'd be back in Seattle, getting down to business.

Then Jack inquired how B.J. was doing after our raucous night at the Pio, and I recalled my unfinished business for her.

"She's fine," I told him. "And she's especially happy that Matt is getting home in time to come to the wedding with her."

Jack nodded in satisfaction, knowing that I had delivered his friendly warning. B.J. wouldn't be asking any more awkward questions about Brian Thiel. I would, of course, but he didn't need to know that.

"Pari Taichert seemed especially distressed about the accident," I said. "Were she and Brian particular friends?"

"Not that I heard about," he said, shrugging. "I think I

would have heard, too. The Tyke's a good buddy. She's going to stand up for me, you know. You got a problem with that?"

"Of course not! The best man, or woman, should always be someone especially close to the groom. I think she's the perfect choice."

We were on our way back to the house by then. I looked around for Sam, but he hadn't returned. Just as well; in my reaction to Domaso's sudden appearance, I hadn't really checked out the house properly.

Back inside, I took a look in the bathrooms—you'd be surprised at how many weddings run out of toilet paper— and at the closets and other storage space. Then in the great room I surveyed the various surfaces where flower arrangements and candlesticks could go.

Candlelight is flattering in more ways than one. There's the soft quality of the light itself, but also the fact that a dim environment makes your pupils dilate. And dilated pupils send an unconscious signal to the human brain, a signal of emotional warmth, attentiveness, and even sexual arousal. Hence the romance of dining by candlelight.

I love knowing this stuff.

"It's interesting—" I began, about to relate my bit of candle trivia to Jack. Then I caught myself. This was hardly the time to talk about romance.

"What's interesting?"

He was standing by the empty fireplace, and a photo on the broad mantelpiece behind him helped me to improvise. It showed Sam and Cissy at a construction site, presumably for the inn, her tiny hands joined to his big ones on a shovel with a big bow on its handle.

"Um, it's interesting to think about earlier generations'

wedding ceremonies. I'd love to see a picture of Tracy's parents as bride and groom. Or your parents. Are they coming, by the way?"

He shook his head. "Long gone. The jumpers, that's my family. There's a picture of Sam and Cissy's wedding in that album over there, though. I saw it when they were looking for the groundbreaking picture to frame."

We sat on a couch with the album before us. Jack turned back the oversized pages, turning back the years, until he came to a set of wavy-edged snapshots. I recognized Sam's jug ears and gangly frame at once, even with the 1970's sideburns, but could that sleek little long-haired blonde in the shirtwaist dress really be Cissy?

Jack noticed my surprise. "Kind of different, wasn't she? I guess it was a quickie wedding, just a justice-of-the-peace sort of thing, on account of Sam's divorce."

"From Danny's mother?"

"Yeah. Sam doesn't like to talk about his first marriage. Danny, either. He was just a kid at the time, and it hit him hard, everyone talking about this gorgeous little gold digger who got hold of Sam Kane. Danny's kind of a melancholy guy. Maybe that's why."

"Thanks for the tip," I said. "I'll keep off the subject. What about aunts and uncles? Any special family members that Tracy wants to acknowledge in the toasts?"

I could have waited to ask Tracy herself, or dug out the information from Shara's notes, but we had to talk about something while we waited for Sam. And besides, I liked the sound of Jack's voice, and I didn't want to get off the couch. So sue me.

"Not really," he was saying. "Cissy doesn't seem to have

any family, and Sam's only brother died before Tracy was born. Big hero in the Korean war."

"Killed in action?"

He shook his head again. "Suicide. Drowned himself in the lake where he used to go fishing. They didn't call it post-traumatic stress syndrome back then, but I guess that's what it was."

"What a shame. Did Danny know his uncle?"

"Oh, more than that. He adored him. Wait, there must be a picture . . ."

There were several pictures, of a sweet, small-featured boy and a tall, broad-shouldered young man who looked a little like Sam and a lot like a vintage movie star.

In one picture, Roy Kane held a pair of fishing poles while little Danny hoisted a string of trout. In another, uncle and nephew were bundled in scarves and mittens, their cheeks rosy and their dark clothes starred with white blotches from a vigorous snowball fight. The affection on their faces made them seem like father and son.

"Tracy remembers Danny talking about this wonderful uncle that she'd never met," said Jack. "How Roy would tell him stories about Korea, and let him play with his dog tags. Real hero worship. Then the suicide and the divorce happened right around the same time."

"He must have been devastated."

"I guess so. I heard all this from Tracy, you understand. Danny never talks about it himself." Jack tipped his wrist to check his watch. "Sam might be a while yet. Probably still reaming out that foreman. Want to go look at the hot spring?"

"Good idea," I said, coming back to the workaday present. "Not to borrow trouble, but there's always a liability issue when you serve alcohol near open water."

I was right about the flagstone path that I'd seen from the bedroom. Jack led me along it, past clusters of pine trees and stretches of heavy brush. As we crossed a little meadow, thick with tall grasses and spangled with bachelor's buttons, he paused and scowled.

"Dammit, Sam told me he'd get all this cut back."

"But why? It's so pretty."

"Fire," said Jack. "Everybody wants to build up high where there's a view, but that puts you uphill of the fuel supply, and fire moves faster uphill. I'll talk to him about it. Come on, we're close."

The hot spring wasn't at all what I expected. Knowing Sam's taste for the grand effect, I had pictured a cement construction built around the water source, and maybe even a small bathhouse. Instead we came to a series of natural pools and cascades, stair-stepped down the slope among the boulders and trees. The slender, white-barked aspens made a shivering green roof above us, and cast kaleidoscopic shade over the smooth stone faces and the milky, faintly bubbling water.

"This is charming!"

"Sam's going to dam it later on," said Jack. "He's got plans for a poolside bar and everything. Completely illegal, interfering with a natural watercourse up here, but he'll probably get away with it."

"That's too bad. It's so nice just as it is."

I perched on a boulder and slipped off my sandals to dip my toes in the largest pool. It was roughly oval, not too deep, and big enough to hold three or four partygoers, or maybe six intimate friends. Very intimate.

The water was barely hotter than the air this afternoon, but by nightfall it would feel delicious. Jack leaned against an aspen trunk, watching me. He leaned very well, and the dappled sunlight glinted on his hair. *If Domaso hadn't interrupted us . . . No. Absolutely not.*

Just to drive the point home, I stood up and made myself ask, "So where's the honeymoon cottage?"

"Farther down this path. To get there by car, you curve around past the garage for about a quarter mile, but on foot it's only a hundred yards or so from here. Want to see it?"

His expression was bland, but I caught a sly glint in his eyes. "Come on, it will just take a minute. It's a pretty little place."

Suddenly, and finally, the light dawned. Jack's apology might have been sincere, but it was also a ploy. He was playing me like a trout, paying out a little more line, subtly reeling it in again, until he had me where he wanted me—like, in a bed. Three days before his wedding! Caution: Jack the Knack at Work.

"Thanks," I said coldly, "but I think I hear Sam coming back."

"Suit yourself," he said innocently, and led the way back up the path.

The sun struck hard after the shade of the trees. We ascended in silence, keeping our thoughts to ourselves, until the father of the bride called down to us from the veranda railing.

"You two been soaking?"

"Too hot," Jack called back up. "Are you minus a foreman?"

But the foreman, as we learned on the drive down the mountain, would keep his job for the time being. We also learned about the exact stage of construction each new unit had reached, the vagaries of the county's permitting process,

and the general dunderheadedness of any and all petty officials who came between Sam Kane and his vision of empire.

Jack said very little as Sam ranted on, and I said even less,
my headache having returned with a vengeance as we bounced
down the gravel road. It was a relief when we turned onto the
Sun Valley Road at last, and a real temptation when Sam offered to drive me all the way to B.J.'s house. I was yearning for
a cool shower, an early supper, and a long, long sleep. But
duty called.

"Just drop me at the lodge, please," I told him. "I want to
read through the vendor contracts and look over the setup
for the rehearsal dinner and the skating party."

"You're the boss, Red, but I'll be around for a little if you
change your mind. You can sleep in that suite if you want,
you know. Make yourself at home."

"Thanks, I might just do that after Matt gets back."
Though B.J. may want me around as a buffer. "Thanks for the
tour, Jack."

Sam waited behind the wheel for the valet, but Jack
walked me up to the lodge entrance.

"No hard feelings?" he murmured.

"Of course not," I lied. "See you later."

Once inside the lobby I made a beeline for the stairs,
thinking hard about Jack and Tracy. Should I warn her about
what he was up to? Surely she knew his reputation. For that
matter, she surely knew him better than I did, so maybe I
should mind my own business. But I always feel responsible
for my brides—

"Ms. Kincaid?" The reception clerk who approached me
was a rosy young brunette whose name badge said she was
from Austria. The lodge had quite an international staff these

days. "You are Ms. Kincaid? I was told, 'tall with red hair, but not the TV star.'"

I sighed. "That would be me."

"*Gut.* You are using the Paliere suite this week?"

"Yes. In fact, I'm holding a meeting there early tomorrow. Would you make a note to just send people up?"

"Very well. But now I have a message for you. Urgent."

The square of paper she handed me bore a misspelling of my name, with a question mark in parentheses, but there was no question about the urgency.

"Call Julie Nothstine," it read. A phone number followed, and two more words, heavily underlined. "Very important."

Chapter Twelve

JULIE NOTHSTINE WAS A CAT LADY. NOT THAT I HAVE ANY-thing against cat ladies. But I have to admit, when the trailer's screen door swung open and I took in the lopsided coil of gray hair, the Coke-bottle glasses and cardigan sweater, backed up by six or seven felines draped over the furniture and braiding themselves around her ankles, well, certain stereotypes came to mind.

"Ms. Nothstine?" I inquired, with the courtesy due to age and possible loopiness.

"*Doctor* Nothstine." Her voice was low, with a warm, rich timbre like a cello, surprising in someone so small and so ap-parently frail. "I didn't get a PhD all the way back in 1959 just to be called *Mizz* now. You took your time getting here."

"Sorry," I said meekly, and followed her inside the large but dilapidated mobile home, obviously immobile for years. "I had to go pick up my car."

Why am I apologizing? She was the one who had issued the urgent but cryptic summons for me to come see her. I had caught Sam in the parking lot and hitched a ride back to B.J.'s, though I hadn't been able to reach B.J. herself at the nursery. Gone out for a couple of hours, her assistant told me, so I left a message saying not to wait dinner, in case I was late getting back.

I'd called Eddie, too, to explain my temporary job with Paliere Productions. He was not pleased.

"You're working for *him*?" he had sputtered. "Are you out of your mind?"

"I'll explain later. But it'll do us some good, you'll see. Right now I've got to hit the road."

The long and winding road. Julie Nothstine's place turned out to be halfway to Hailey on an unsigned and deeply dusty track through miles of hot, unstirring pine trees. By the time I reached her door, the afternoon felt close to its conclusion, and I felt like four of the Seven Dwarfs: Sleepy, Dopey, Hungry, and their new pal, Dehydrated.

So, no more apologies. I cut to the chase. "Dr. Nothstine, you said you had something to tell me about my cousin."

I expected to be urged to call her Julie, but apparently that privilege was reserved for old friends like Sam Kane.

"Your cousin, yes. I suppose condolences are in order." She peered at me warily. Magnified by the glasses, her eyes were a bleached-out blue, with wide black pupils and a narrow black ring around the iris. The bull's-eye effect was disconcerting. "You don't seem very bereaved."

"That's because I'm not." What the hell, I could be blunt, too. "Brian and I weren't close."

"And yet he carried your . . . keychain, was it? I spoke with Al Soriano earlier, and he told me." She shuffled into the narrow living room, lined with bookcases on all sides, and tossed a couple of cats off the threadbare, claw-marked sofa. "Sit. Drink?"

The cats seemed used to this treatment. One of them disappeared under a chair and the other, sporting a black-and-white tuxedo coat and a spray of white whiskers, betook himself to the windowsill with a great show of dignity. He stared at me hypnotically, and I found myself staring back.

"I said, would you like a drink?"

"Um, some water would be good, thank you."

This earned me another suspicious look. "Mormon?"

"Me? No. No, I'm just thirsty."

There are plenty of Mormons in Idaho, of course, so I suppose the question was logical, if impolite. Dr. Nothstine made her way into the kitchen and returned with a small bottle of spring water in one hand and a tall glass of ice and fizzing liquid in the other. She tossed me the bottle, then settled onto the sofa beside me.

"I can't seem to get warm these days," she said, but it was an observation, not a complaint. "And yet I still appreciate my gin and tonic."

She sipped her drink with relish, and took a moment to size me up over the rim. I returned the favor, and it was then that the shuffling-plus-tossing business began to make sense. Julie Nothstine wasn't entirely frail; in fact, her hands and shoulders looked quite sinewy and strong. But one leg was twisted, and below the cuffs of her slacks her bare ankles were seamed with scars.

"Rock-climbing accident," she said, noting my gaze. "Ten years ago. I still lift weights, but I can't walk worth a damn. I use a cane when I go out."

So much for stereotypes. I had no idea what to say in reply, but she didn't give me a chance to say it.

"This keychain of yours," she said briskly, now that hospitality had been dispensed with. "Is it true that Thiel always carried it with him?"

"Well, maybe not always." I swigged gratefully at my water. This could get complicated. "How did you hear about it?"

"I keep in touch with the boys, especially Al," she said. "Though I suppose I shouldn't call them that; there have been women smoke jumpers for, oh, twenty years now. Good ones, too. They have to be, don't they? No separate physical requirements for females, you know." She looked at me wryly. "I don't suppose *you* could carry a hundred pounds for three miles. In any case, Al dropped off my groceries, and he told me you had come to Ketchum for Tracy's wedding. Was it valuable?"

"Was what valuable?"

"The keychain! Was it worth stealing?"

My hostess didn't suffer fools gladly, and I was beginning to feel like one. But I was also beginning to see where this was going.

"Are you saying that some of Brian's belongings were stolen?" I had an unpleasant vision of B.J.'s necklace displayed in a pawnshop window—and Matt discovering it there.

"I'm saying nothing of the sort. Not officially." Dr. Nothstine set down her drink and removed her glasses to squeeze the bridge of her long, narrow nose between thumb and forefinger. "Miss Kincaid...Carnegie is rather a silly name, isn't it? Miss Kincaid, what I'm about to tell you is under investigation by the National Interagency Fire Center, but it is not public knowledge yet, for reasons that will quickly be obvious. This conversation is absolutely confidential, is that clear?"

"Of course, but—*ow!*" From the tall bookcase behind me, yet another cat had plummeted onto my lap like a cougar onto an unwary lamb. I yelped, half rising, and received an affronted glare from a pair of lime-green eyes before the cat launched itself away again.

"None of this is clear!" I was feeling just a tad affronted myself. "Dr. Nothstine, would you please tell me what's going on? You obviously have something to say about my cousin, and I wish you would say it."

So she did. "The evidence suggests that Brian Thiel's death was not accidental."

"*What?*"

As I sat gaping, she went on in a detached, lecturing way, without much interest in my reaction.

"I was unable to visit the scene in person, but I did examine the photographs, and it is quite improbable that the mishap with the letdown line caused his death. Brian fell, yes, but it appears that he was able to break his fall and reach the ground alive."

"What? How do you know?"

"I don't *know*," she said reprovingly. "Only an eyewitness could make that claim. I am convinced, however, by the face-down position of the body and by the appearance of the largest wound, that death was caused by a single blow to the back of the head and not by a fall to the ground."

"But . . . but if the fall didn't kill him—"

"Exactly. If Brian Thiel's fall was not fatal, the question becomes what happened to him after he fell, and who else was present? Who tampered with the body before the initiation of standard accident reporting procedures? I presented all of these questions to the official investigators."

"And what did they say?"

She sniffed. "They refused to listen! 'Accidental death' was a much easier and more acceptable conclusion. They shut me out of any further discussion, and they have made it clear that they don't wish to hear from me again. But you see, the fact that this keychain is missing is a very strong argument in my favor. Please describe it for me, and be precise."

"Wait just a minute, please." I was still catching up. "What exactly do you mean, tampered with the body?"

She paused judiciously, then went on, "Not so much the body itself, as the burned-over ground around it, which looked quite disturbed, and Thiel's equipment, specifically his PG bag. The bag had been unclipped from his harness, but none of the other jumpers recall having done so. Or *admits* to having done so. Now, if you can say for a certainty that Thiel always carried this family memento with him, and we can determine that it was not recovered, then theft is a possibility. Theft, and possibly homicide. Are you sure you won't have a drink? You look pale."

I accepted the drink—she made a mean gin and tonic—and then the phone rang, which bought me a little time to think. As the good doctor shuffled into the kitchen to answer it, I absently stroked the bookcase cat, a heavy marmalade beast who had returned to my lap and was now purring like an outboard motor with his lime-green eyes squeezed shut.

I had plenty to think about. Maybe Dr. Nothstine was loopy after all. I hoped she was. But what if she wasn't? If Brian's death wasn't accidental . . . Why not use the word? If Brian was murdered, then one of the smoke jumpers murdered him.

But which one? The Tyke had jumped along with Brian, with Danny Kane and Todd Gibson coming soon after. Todd supposedly found the body first, but in the smoke and rough ground, one of the others could have arrived before him. Or did Todd himself report the "accident" after arranging the scene to his own advantage?

Motive was the other big question. Brian was new to this

crew, but he must have trained with Todd and the other Neds for weeks. Was that time enough to provoke a comrade to murder? My cousin was no Boy Scout, as B.J. could attest, but that was quite a feat, even for him. Unless the comrade in question had a murderous bent to start with. And if that was the case, we had a dangerous individual among us.

Mentally, I reviewed each of the personalities: Danny's moodiness, the Tyke's hostility, and Todd's . . . well, I hadn't noticed much about Todd Gibson except for his remarkable show of strength at the Talent Show. Any one of them could be the guilty party. For that matter, more than one. But what could Brian have done to turn a comrade in to a killer?

I must have stroked too hard, because the cat gave a sharp little yowl and hopped to the floor. I barely noticed. Here we all were, socializing with these three, inviting them to weddings—putting one of them in the wedding party!—when one or more of them might be homicidal.

You can't lock people up on so little evidence, of course, but I was sure as hell going to steer clear of all three. No dark alleys, and no one-on-one meetings without witnesses around. But then, what about my responsibility to Tracy and her guests? If I kept silent, would I be endangering them?

"How very nice of you," I heard Dr. Nothstine saying into the phone. "Danny Kane offered to bring it tomorrow but . . . Well, if you really don't mind. I can drive, you know, but it's quite tiring, so that would be most helpful. Good-bye."

She hung up and rejoined me on the couch, moving so slowly that I had time to make my decision.

"Dr. Nothstine, I have something absolutely confidential to tell *you*. There is no keychain. I invented it."

"Why on earth—?"

I rushed on before I lost my nerve. "But there is a necklace. You see, I have this friend . . ."

I related B.J.'s story, minus the specifics of what she was doing with Brian that night. Dr. Nothstine listened intently, nodding from time to time, and then sliced right to the heart of the matter.

"You wish to suppress any mention of this necklace, for your friend's sake."

"Exactly."

"And yet, if its absence might help to make the case that this is a suspicious death—"

"But it doesn't, don't you see? We don't know for sure that Brian had the necklace with him when he jumped at Boot Creek. He told B.J. he wouldn't leave it at his apartment, but it could be somewhere else, like in his car."

"Thiel sold his car last month," she said. "That came up in the investigation. But he had a locker at the jump base, and it still contains some personal effects, to be shipped to the family once his landlord gathers the rest of his belongings. I saw it being padlocked."

"Really. I don't suppose they'd let me open it in private?"

"No, I don't suppose they would."

I sighed. B.J.'s necklace had shrunk in importance, but it was still important to her, and I didn't dare draw attention to it by asking someone in authority to look for it in the locker. And besides, maybe Brian's things would hold a clue to his murder.

If it really was murder. The jury was still out on the loopiness verdict, after all, and Dr. Nothstine's next remarks didn't help.

"But it's a combination padlock," she said in a conspiratorial whisper. "An old one that's been in the office for years.

And I know the combination." She was leaning close to me, her blue eyes bulging, and when someone knocked on the front door she didn't blink. "That's him! This should be most interesting."

She levered herself up and trundled away, leaving me with goose bumps. They got bumpier once she opened the door to her new visitor.

At first all I could see was a pair of man's legs, extending below an enormous sack of cat food. But when Dr. Nothstine directed the legs into the kitchen, and the man bent to set down the sack, I saw the familiar burly shoulders and blond crew cut that belonged to Todd Gibson.

Chapter Thirteen

THE MESSAGE I'D LEFT FOR B.J. WAS *GO AHEAD WITHOUT ME,*
I can eat later. It should have been *Go ahead without me, I'm*
having roasted garlic fettuccine with a possible murderer.

"Most interesting" was putting it mildly.

Todd was clearly startled to see me, but Dr. Nothstine
rode right over his discomfort—and mine—by making much
of his kindness in bringing the cat food, and insisting that we
both stay for dinner.

"It's tiresome, always cooking for one," she said, slamming pans around in her shipshape little kitchen. "No, Todd,
I do not need any assistance. Make yourself a drink and sit
down there with Carnegie."

The young smoke jumper complied reluctantly and perched
on the edge of the sofa cushion, rattling the ice in his glass
and looking anywhere but at me. I bent down and busied myself inviting the marmalade cat to return to my lap, all the
while speculating furiously.

Was Todd merely doing a good deed in coming here? It
seemed unlikely. Al Soriano probably told the other jumpers
I was asking about Brian's belongings, and probably mentioned Julie Nothstine as someone who could help. Did that
mention prompt this sudden desire to visit an old woman

living alone on a back road out in the woods? If Odd Todd was up to no good, he wouldn't even need a dark alley.

My cell phone's in my tote bag in the car, I thought with a prickle of tension. *Should I go out and get it? That might tip him off. Besides, there's a phone right here in the living room. Calm down. Act natural.*

The cat cold-shouldered my advances in favor of scaling the bookcases again, so I sat up and said brightly, "It's nice of you guys to help out Dr. Nothstine. I guess she goes way back with the smoke jumpers, huh?"

"Yeah." Long pause. More rattling ice.

"It must be exciting, starting your first season."

The look on his big, square face darkened, and I winced. Todd's first season as a smoke jumper had started with a death, and if he wasn't the killer, then he was grieving a comrade. So much for small talk.

I was groping for a more diplomatic remark when the marmalade cougar made another leap, this time plunging claws first from a high shelf onto Todd's left shoulder.

"God *dammit!*"

Todd sprang to his feet and ripped the cat away from him. His face was almost purple, and when he raised one arm as if to strike the animal, I cried out in alarm. He stopped, but didn't turn to face me, and then the silent tension was broken by the sound of Dr. Nothstine's voice.

"Dinner is served!" she called. "I hope you both like garlic."

We did, and we liked the red wine she served even better. By the second glass I had relaxed a little, and Todd was positively animated. He focused mainly on "Dr. J.," as he called her, which befit her special status as a friend and confidante to the Ketchum smoke jumpers. But that gave me a chance to observe him closely, and to decide that my sense of him from the night before, of a small boy allowed into the charmed circle of the bigger kids, still rang true. But even small boys can be cruel.

Todd didn't swagger, as Brian would have done, because his admiration was all for his compatriots, not for himself. My unease about his show of temper faded a little as he told story after idolizing story about the other jumpers, their close calls and practical jokes and, most of all, their toughness.

Dr. Nothstine had stories to tell as well. She spoke of legendary jumpers from the past, men with nicknames like Paperlegs and Shish Kebab and Catfish, who had survived horrendous injuries and epic fires and parties of mythic proportion.

Todd drank in every word, his eyes shining. To him, every injury was heroic, every prank was sidesplitting, every beer bash a fabulous bacchanal. And most of all, every wildfire contained a victory for the warriors of fire. Todd Gibson might be a cat-hater, but he was head over heels in love with smoke jumping.

By the time we asked for seconds on the pasta, I was ready to join up myself. Of course, there was that little matter of physical fitness, and my lack thereof, not to mention the inconvenient detail that I'd be terrified out of my mind. But in telling his smoke-jumper stories, and attending to Dr. Nothstine's, Todd made it seem like the only job in the world worth doing.

The one story that both Todd and Dr. Nothstine knew, involved "Bambi buckets," collapsible hoppers slung from helicopters, which are used to dump hundreds or even thousands of gallons of water directly onto wildland fires.

"So where do they get the water?" I asked, still scarfing down fettuccine.

"Mostly lakes and rivers in the area," said Todd. He had plowed through two helpings and was working on a third. "Sometimes reservoirs, if they have to go farther away, or even the ocean."

"Tell her about that dreadful incident in California," said Dr. Nothstine, turning aside to refill his glass.

"Oh yeah, that." Todd's ears were reddening, no doubt from the wine. Beer must be his usual drink.

"What happened in California?" I prompted.

"Um, there was a big fire in the Sierras, and when they went in afterward to mop up, they found a corpse. Up in a tree."

"In a *tree*?"

"Quite a bizarre case, and very sad," said Dr. Nothstine. She blinked owlishly. "He was dressed in a wet suit, with fins and air tank. The poor man had been scuba diving in the ocean when he was scooped up in a Bambi bucket and dropped into the flames."

"Oh my God!" I imagined the diver's panic, the endless fall, the nightmare of the flames . . . then I heard a snicker from across the table. The two of them exploded into laughter, and after a moment I joined in. I'd been had.

"A marvelous tall tale, marvelous." Dr. Nothstine removed her glasses to dab her eyes with a napkin. "I'm told that scuba divers repeat that story even more often than firefighters do."

We all loosened up after that. The stories continued, and then circled back to the most recent one: the death of Brian Thiel.

If this starstruck young man had actually killed my

cousin, I'd have expected a well-rehearsed story about discovering him there in the ashes, already dead. So I nudged the conversation in that direction.

But Todd had no story at all. He spoke readily enough about the tragedy of losing a good man like Brian—or Bri, as he called him. But he shied away from my queries about the accident scene itself like a skittish horse refusing a jump.

"It must have been an awful shock, finding Brian's body like that," I said at one point, when our hostess had stepped into the kitchen. "You were by yourself?"

Todd simply nodded in silence and kept eating.

"I suppose there are procedures—"

"Of course there are! And I followed them." His voice was loud, almost anguished. Guilty or innocent, I was causing him pain. "Can we talk about something else?"

"Brownies!" Dr. Nothstine set a white cardboard box on the table and fussed around with it. "Store-bought, I'm afraid. I used to bake, but when my oven broke I took the door off so John Muir could sleep in it."

That threw me, but a glance into the kitchen identified John Muir as the tuxedo cat from the windowsill, whose tail was indeed dangling out of the stove front. It twitched like a rattlesnake as I watched, then unfurled itself in a languid arc. *Good night, John.*

"Hey, thanks," said Todd, grateful for both the sweets and the interruption. He polished off a brownie in three eager bites and reached for another while still licking chocolate from his lips. "Everything was great, Dr. J., but I should get going. If you need anything else and you can't find Al, just call me, OK?"

"I'll be sure to do that." She walked him to the door, watched him drive away, then returned to me. "Well?"

I listened to the engine fading. "Well, he seemed more embarrassed than guilty. I do think he's hiding something, but I'm not sure that it's murder."

"I'm inclined to agree. Leave the dishes, please. I prefer to do them myself." She settled on the sofa and was instantly bracketed by felines. "If not murder, then what?"

"Theft?" I sat beside the outer cat. "Todd could have stolen something of Brian's, the necklace or—"

"Nonsense. Can you imagine that gallant child plundering a corpse?"

That gallant child was ready to strangle your marmalade cat, I thought. But that one incident didn't really prove anything, and I let it go.

"No, I guess not. So where does that leave us?"

Her disconcerting black-ringed eyes held mine. "It leaves us to continue investigating. You'll have to question the other two, the Taichert girl and Danny Kane. Though he seems an improbable killer."

I'd almost forgotten, Sam had called Dr. Nothstine his old friend. A family friend, it seemed. "Do you know Danny well?"

"Since birth." She pointed a stern finger. "But don't imagine my judgment is clouded on that account."

"I wouldn't dream of it." She had me talking like her now. "So do you think Danny's capable of killing someone?"

"*I'm* capable of killing someone," she said dryly. "Presumably you are, too, given the right circumstances. But Danny has always been . . . weak. Not physically, of course, but there's something in his character that isn't quite sound. He's rather passive, despite his occupation."

I thought of what Jack had said, about Danny's parents'

divorce and his beloved uncle's suicide. "Did you know Roy Kane?"

"Of course! Everyone in Ketchum knew Roy." Her eyes grew distant. "He was a brilliant student, a natural athlete, everything a young man should be. We were all so proud to see him in his uniform. The Marines, you know. Danny absolutely idolized his Uncle Roy."

I suspected he wasn't the only one. I had a sudden vision of this formidable old lady as a girl, a tomboy, perhaps. And perhaps in love?

"I understand Roy was a hero," I said. "What a shame, the way things turned out."

"Those charges were dropped!" she snapped.

"What?" I said, taken aback. "I meant his suicide."

"Oh. Yes, of course. Although I've always wondered how someone as courageous as Roy could take his own life. It seems such an admission of defeat."

I couldn't help being curious. "What charges? Did he have something hanging over him that might have driven him to—"

"Nonsense. There were irresponsible accusations about looting, but Roy was entirely exonerated. He *was* a hero, in a brutal and unappreciated war." She shook her head impatiently and returned to the matter at hand. "Never mind, you young people don't even read history anymore. What about Pari Taichert? Is it true that she's acting as Jack's best man?"

"That's right." I waited for her disapproval of this modern notion, but I should have known better.

"Excellent. You'll have an opportunity to question her as you oversee the wedding."

If I ever get time for the wedding, I thought, with a glance at my watch. "Maybe. But I don't intend to question anyone without witnesses around. It could be dangerous. Are you sure you don't want to take this to the police?"

"I told you, the BLM authorities rejected my hypothesis. The police would hardly favor my opinion over theirs." She penciled the combination to Brian's locker on a scrap of paper and handed it to me with a bitter smile. "Never get old, Miss Kincaid. It plays hell with your credibility."

I pondered that and a lot more as I drove back out to the highway and north into Ketchum. The summer dusk hadn't yet relinquished the last of the light, and the mountains on either side of the road crouched darkly against the luminous, silver-violet sky.

B.J.'s car wasn't out front. When I let myself into the cabin, I found the fluorescent tube over the kitchen sink casting its cold flat light, but all the other rooms were in shadow. She had eaten dinner; a microwave lasagna box sat on the counter, its congealing scraps of long-frozen cheese still reeking of long-dead oregano. I slid the box into the garbage. How deflating, to have the combination to Brian's locker and no one to share it with.

Though to be honest, the one I really wanted to share my news with was Aaron. I relied on him to help me sort through my mental tangles; he had a knack for organizing information. That's why he made such a good reporter. That, and his flair for language, and his uncanny ability to ask the most awkward questions.

Suddenly I missed the sound of his annoying, wonderful voice. But our last conversation had ended on such a sour note . . . *No, I'll figure this out myself. I don't need him.* I was still telling myself that as I took a stool at the counter and tapped in his home number on my cell phone.

"Hello—"

"Aaron, it's me!"

"—you've reached Aaron Gold. Leave me a message and I'll get back to you. My number at the *Seattle Sentinel*—"

I sighed and turned off the phone. Then I turned it on again, berating myself for not checking it earlier. Sure enough, I had four messages waiting. To my disappointment, but not my surprise, none of them were from Aaron.

The first voice that played back was B.J.'s, keyed up as usual. "Hey, guess what? I just found out Brian had a locker at the jump base! Call me right away, OK?"

The next message was from Tracy's carterer, confirming for tomorrow's meeting, but after that it was B.J. again.

"Carnegie, where the hell are you? I can't wait all night, this is making me crazy!" A pause, and then, "Oh, someone called from San Francisco looking for you. They said that Valerie Cox got stung by a bee and isn't coming. Does that make sense? Anyway, call me."

I groaned. This couldn't be happening. Without Valerie Cox and her brilliant, undocumented floral designs, what was I supposed to do with two truckloads of blooms and greens when they arrived on Thursday? Stick them in mayonnaise jars? It didn't make sense, it made a disaster. A *bee*?

In my dismay over Valerie, I missed the final message and had to play it again.

"Look, Muffy, I'm going out to the base and sneak a peek at that locker. Don't worry, I'll be discreet. I bet there's nobody around this late, anyway."

I clutched the phone in vexation, as if clutching B.J. to give her a good shake. There was bound to be someone around this late, a dispatcher or a security guard or . . . a murderer?

I stood up, hearing my own gasp in the silence. Never

mind flowers. B.J. had no idea that Brian's death was anything but accidental. She didn't know that somewhere in the Valley tonight, someone was at large with murder on his mind. Or hers? In either case, the someone could very well be at the smoke-jumper base.

I knocked over the stool on my way out the door.

Chapter Fourteen

"HELLO?" EVEN MY HALF WHISPER SOUNDED LOUD. "HELLO?"

B.J. had been right after all. There seemed to be no one around, although a couple of cars, including hers, were still out in front of the ready shack. Out past the grassy field where the baseball game would be, a Douglas D3 and a Twin Otter, the jump planes, stood silent and unattended.

I passed the office and pushed open the front door of the ready shack, flinching as it squeaked. Most of the lights were off, and I left them that way. Once my eyes adjusted, I could get by on the faint glow coming through the uncurtained windows.

I'd already decided what to say if I ran into anyone: I was checking out the facilities for the bachelor party. True, eleven P.M. was an odd time to be doing so. And the game wasn't until Thursday, so this inspection could easily have waited for the light of day. But I'd bluff my way through that if I had to.

And what if I ran into Danny or the Tyke? Could I bluff them? *Don't think about it. Just get B.J., get the necklace, and get out.* I took a few reluctant steps into the ready room, the dispatch area where the jumpers meet for briefings and suit up for fires.

"B.J.?"

To my right, behind the dispatcher's desk, a large white-
board gleamed ghostly pale in the dimness. It was marked up
with names and notes, all circled and arrowed into hiero-
glyphic columns that I couldn't quite read. Facing the desk
were a few disorderly rows of plank benches, and beyond
them stood a metal rack with a row of helmets making bulbous silhouettes along the top. Below the helmets I could see
four Kevlar flight suits with high Elvis collars, waiting on the
speed racks for jumpers to step into them and race out to
the planes.

But I didn't see B.J., and I didn't see any lockers. Why on
earth hadn't I asked Dr. Nothstine exactly where they were? I
tried to reconstruct the one base I had visited, in Boise.
Office, ready shack, parachute loft, computer center, gym . . .

The gym! Physical conditioning was so vital to the job
that each smoke-jumper base had its own workout facilities, with weight-lifting machines, cardio trainers like bikes
and rowing machines, and showers. Surely showers meant
lockers?

I cut behind the dispatch desk and through to the next
area, which turned out to be the sewing room. It housed a
central row of tables, their surfaces littered with fabric and
yardsticks, tangles of strapping, piles of buckles. Along the
sides were ranks of ironing boards and heavy-duty sewing
machines, each with its own work light, swivel chair, and
wall bracket holding oversized spools of thread.

Smoke jumpers have time on their hands between fires
and they employ it well, making almost all their own gear except the parachutes themselves. And they repair all the gear,
chutes included. Besides being brave and strong, the warriors of fire are excellent seamstresses.

With the work lights off and the equipment idle, this site

of industrious activity felt eerie and abandoned. The heat of the day still hung in the air but I shivered anyway, and stood motionless a moment to listen. Silence. Then I hurried past the sewing machines into the next area—and stopped in my tracks to gaze around in wonder.

In the dusky gloom, the space before me seemed to be hung with vast filmy curtains. Suspended parallel to one another, they made wide aisleways along the floor. Even before I looked upward, the vault of open space high above my head made itself felt on my oversensitive skin.

I was in the parachute loft, where the chutes are spread on long rods and winched up for inspection. Forest Service parachutes are round, with the classic dome-shaped canopy. But I knew that the BLM used these "square" chutes, which aren't square at all but rectangular, like hang gliders.

What I didn't know was how huge a parachute is, close-up. As I made my way cautiously down one of the aisles, the silken rectangles created walls on either side of me, soft walls that swayed and billowed gently. In the hush they made a faint whisper, even fainter than my own.

"Hello?" A noise, sudden and furtive, came from nearby. Very nearby. "Who's there?"

Somewhere to my left, screened from my sight, a soft object dropped to the floor and was snatched up again. Someone was in the loft with me, and I was dead certain it wasn't B.J. Time slowed. I drew a guarded breath.

If I can't see him, then he can't see me. For a long moment I strained to listen, hearing nothing but the hollow thudding of my own heart. I turned to retreat, taking one stealthy step and then another, trying not to run.

Then I heard rushing footsteps, and I ran. Ahead of me, a bulge in the silken wall thrust into my path. I dodged around it, but a veiled hand caught at my shoulder. I wrenched away, lost my bearings, and when my sandal caught in the lower edge of a parachute I stumbled and lurched forward.

As I fell, my foot came out of the sandal and my fingers scrabbled in vain down the smooth fabric to the floor. I found myself on hands and knees, gasping and winded, shrinking away from the expected blow.

It never came. The footsteps hesitated, moved away. I slumped there in relief. *Thank heaven.* But then relief gave way to a reckless determination to learn the identity of my attacker. I guess adrenaline makes you stupid.

"Hey!" I yelled angrily, clambering to my feet. "Hey, stop!"

I'd barely gotten the words out when the walls came tumbling down. A creak of pulleys, a hissing slither of rope, and I was shrouded in what seemed like acres of thin, tough fabric. The more I flailed about, blind and panicky, the more I felt myself entangled like a doomed fly in a spiderweb.

And then I stopped flailing as fear coursed under my skin like a hot, prickly fluid. The footsteps were coming back. From a different direction? Hands grabbed at me, I struggled in darkness, the darkness parted as the fabric lifted and I saw...

"B.J.? What do you think you're doing?"

"What do you mean, what am I doing?" Her eyes were round. "I was just coming up from the gym. Who were you hollering at?"

"Brian's killer. Come on!" I rushed for the building's exit, but the intruder had vanished into the warm, still night. I heard a car moving away in the distance.

Swearing in frustration, I turned around, thinking B.J. was right behind me. But she wasn't there, and I heard her voice, quavering oddly, from back inside the loft.

"C-Carnegie? W-what? . . ."

I was at her side in seconds. She stood with a fold of the fallen parachute in her hand, gaping down at the floor. A humped form lay at her feet, half concealed by swaths of fabric. I gaped at it myself, and a roaring darkness filled my eyes and ears. My thoughts slowed to a crawl and then ceased altogether.

The form was a man, a heavyset man in a gray uniform with a shield-shaped badge sewn to the front pocket. I studied the badge in numb detachment. It said "Wood River Security Services," but as I watched, the W and the S were obscured by a liquid stain creeping slowly across the man's chest. The stain showed black, but in brighter light it would be red, the unmistakable red of fresh blood. I took a long, shaky breath and forced my gaze to the other side of his chest.

The man was dead, of course. How could he be otherwise, with the ax head of a Pulaski biting deep into his heart?

Shock plays tricks with the memory. The main thing I would remember about the next few hours was Howard Larabee's left eye. Larabee was the city of Ketchum's chief of police—"The assistant chief's on maternity leave, if you can believe such a thing"—and he seemed to be one of those people who are born indignant and never find reason to change.

Larabee's posture was rigid, his voice was grating, and his wiry gray hair seemed to coil furiously above his pinched and resentful face. As B.J. and I sat in his office, I noticed a photo on the desk of a high-school boy posing proudly with a cello, apparently at a recital. He was slim and blond, and very handsome in an elfin sort of way. *Must take after his mother.*

There was nothing elfin about the chief's left eye, which

blinked and jumped and quivered to a hypnotic degree. It was difficult not to stare, especially while I was busy lying. But even in shock, even in a police station in the middle of the night, I knew enough to trot out my story about scouting for the bachelor party. And to keep mum about Julie Nothstine's theory that Brian Thiel was murdered. Partly because I'd promised her I would, but mostly because I knew how bizarre it would sound.

And Dr. Nothstine might be wrong, anyway. Once in the past I'd told the police more than I meant to, thus putting an innocent man and his family through hell, and I had no desire to repeat the experience. But I didn't think she was wrong.

"A *bachelor* party?" grated Larabee. He said it as though he'd never heard anything so outrageous in his life, but apparently that's how he said almost everything. "Why on God's green earth would you have a bachelor party at the smoke-jumper base?"

"Because Sam Kane's son-in-law is a smoke jumper," said B.J. easily. B.J. is a beautiful liar, and she drops names with the best of them. "The wedding's Saturday up at White Pine—you know, Sam's new resort? But maybe you haven't heard about it."

"Of course I have!" Larabee sat up even straighter, if that was possible. "So the two of you heard someone moving around in the parachute loft, but you didn't see them? What about voices? Could you tell how many there were, men or women, anything?"

I shook my head. "Just footsteps, but it sounded like a single person."

"Doubtful," he huffed. "These junkies are different than most, they're working as a gang."

"Junkies in Ketchum?" I said. Larabee and B.J. both stared at me, the naïve city slicker. "I mean, it's such a small town, somehow I thought—"

"Drugs are a serious problem in rural areas," said Larabee, his eye shimmying double time. "Mostly heroin and methamphetamines, though we don't see a lot of meth labs in Blaine County. It's usually imported. We've had a string of robberies lately, addicts looking for cash and goods they can pawn for cash. Last week a computer-store guard in Hailey was severely beaten, almost died. Lots of computers at the smoke-jumper base."

Aha. No wonder he accepted my story, with a crime wave already in progress. This homicidal assault fit right in with it. Larabee had us sign our statements and then informed us that our vehicles had been ferried into town by a patrolman. The clear implication was that we should get into said vehicles and go away. So we did.

Back at the house, B.J. erupted out of her car and slammed the door. "Carnegie, what the hell is going on? Did you say Brian's *killer*? I didn't mention that to Howard, but—"

"Good," I said, fumbling with my key, irrationally anxious to get inside. The lasagna smell still hung in the air, domestic and comforting. "Because I don't want to tell them, not yet."

B.J. was right on my heels. "But why—?"

"Long story. Hang on." I made straight for the kitchen, picked up the stool I'd knocked over, and tugged open the fridge. As I did so I observed, as if from a long, muffled distance, that my hands were trembling. In fact, all of me was trembling. *Delayed reaction. Interesting.* I scanned the shelves. Beer, two-percent milk, beer, V8, beer. "Don't you have any wine?"

"In the door. Here, let me get it. You go sit down."

B.J. produced a bottle and a couple of mismatched glasses, and soon I was curled in a corner of her couch, swigging cheap Chardonnay and breathing deeply. She waited a few moments, topping me up, before she spoke.

"Better now?"

I swallowed and nodded. "Much."

"Good. Now tell me everything, right from the beginning. What have you been doing all day?"

So I told her, touching lightly on Cissy's lunch and Shara Mortimer's dismissal, and even more lightly on Jack's behavior up at White Pine. What I related at length was Dr. Nothstine's theory about Brian's murder, the impromptu dinner party at her trailer, and my indecision about Todd Gibson as a possible suspect.

"He's such a likable guy, but you should have seen his face when he screamed at the cat. And if he didn't do it, then either Danny or the Tyke—"

"For God's sake, Carnegie!" B.J. broke in. "These people are *smoke jumpers*. They're bonded together like family. You've heard them; they call each other 'bro,' the men and women both. 'Bro' as in 'brother.' For one jumper to kill another is just unbelievable."

"Dr. Nothstine believes it. And if Brian's death was an accident, then who killed that guard?" I realized, with a sick twist of guilt, that I hadn't even asked the man's name. "And might have killed me if you hadn't come up the stairs when you did."

We looked at each other wordlessly, then B.J. topped up both our glasses.

"Cheers, Muffy," she said weakly.

"Cheers." We sipped in silence for a while, and my mind

strayed, irrelevantly, to her original quest. "Did you find Brian's locker?"

"Yeah, but there's a big old padlock on it."

"I know. I've got the combination."

"You do? Why didn't you tell me? We could go back and . . ." Her face changed comically as she realized what she was saying, and why we weren't going anywhere near the jumper base tonight. "I guess that's not such a good idea."

"Not so good, no." I swigged more wine. I like wine much better than beer. "Actually, it's a dreadful idea."

Her snort turned into a giggle. "Horrible."

"Appalling."

"Atrocious."

We were both giggling now, then laughing, uncontrollably, deliriously. I slumped farther into the couch and sloshed some wine on the cushions. B.J. relieved me of my glass and we both slumped over, cackling like madwomen. By the time we subsided I was half asleep. Talk about a long, strange trip. I heard B.J. getting up, then felt a blanket settle over me, light and soft.

Within seconds I was dead to the world. So to speak.

Chapter Fifteen

THAT WAS TUESDAY NIGHT. WITHIN HOURS—NOT NEARLY enough hours—it was Wednesday morning and I was at the Sun Valley Lodge, unlocking the Paliere suite and throwing a fit.

"A bee!" I stomped inside and whirled to face the remorseful young man who'd been drooping out in the hallway. "A *bee*?"

I heard myself sounding hysterical, but I couldn't help it. I was a mess. I'd slept right through the alarm B.J. set for me when she left for work, and woke up on her couch in a panic less than half an hour before my big vendor meeting. No breakfast, no shower, and no time to react to the events of the night before. Which possibly wasn't a bad thing. I had to think weddings, not murders, and I had to think fast.

A heavy foot on the gas brought me to the lodge with three minutes to spare—just enough to blow up.

"Valerie Cox is bailing out on this wedding because she got stung by a goddamn bee?"

"*Please* let me finish." The remorseful young man was Wallace Waggoner, the tallest, thinnest, droopiest person I'd ever met. He looked even sleepier than I did, if that was possible. "Val is allergic to beestings. She went into anaphylactic shock, which brought on a minor heart attack. She's still in the hospital."

"Oh." My fury collapsed like a leaking balloon. "Oh. So they sent you."

"On the red-eye." He dropped his carry-on bag off one skinny shoulder and onto the floor as if he wanted to join it there. "Could I please make some coffee? I came straight from the airport."

"Of course. Make the whole pot, would you? There'll be eight of us."

The suite was set up for business, with a small conference table, a coffee urn, and a drawer full of pens and such bearing the lodge's sunburst logo. As Wallace fussed with the coffee, I arranged a pad and pen at each place, along with my business card and a copy of the wedding-events timetable.

We'd need the air-conditioning later, but just now the room felt cool and a little stuffy. I pushed open a window and stood staring out at the terrace and the ice rink, blinking in the early sunshine and trying to get my head in the game.

Who was coming this morning, and what did I need to discuss with each one? Caterer, photographer, videographer, floral designer, the tent-and-rental man, the entertainment director. I was eager to confer with the latter, because Shara Mortimer's paperwork contained not a single detail about music, as if a file had gone missing from the bundle she'd handed me.

Who else? Oh, the stylist, a woman from the studio who was apparently senior to both Hair and Makeup. Tracy had insisted on her presence today, since film and photos of the bridal party would be so widely distributed. Between the glare of publicity for my bride and the nightmarish scene last night, this was feeling less like a wedding and more like a made-for-TV movie.

I went on trying to focus on the meeting's agenda, but my thoughts kept straying back to Brian. I was convinced now that Dr. Nothstine's theory had merit. But why was he killed, and which of the three smoke jumpers had last seen him alive? Who had stalked me in the parachute loft, behind those silken walls?

Whoever it was, if I went to the police with my suspicions and the killer heard about it, I might be triggering even more violence. I felt dazed and paralyzed, and I wished I could talk to Aaron.

A knock on the door brought me up short. Wallace handed me a steaming mug and went to answer it. *Good man.* The rest of the vendors arrived all at once, increasing my sense of confusion. The well-groomed Englishwoman I pegged as the stylist turned out to be Joan, the tent-and-rental "man," while the caterer and videographer were both stout, mustachioed men named Bob. At least I recognized the D. P., whose name was actually Evan. He was Tracy's own director of photography from the TV show, and seemed to rank senior to Bob. Photo Bob, not Food Bob.

Well, I'd sort that out later. For now I took my place at the head of the table and addressed them as if everything were normal. I was shooting for friendly but confident, but it came out stiff and officious, at least at first.

"I'm Carnegie Kincaid, of Made in Heaven Wedding Design in Seattle, subcontracted for the moment to Paliere Productions. I'm an old friend of the bride's, and as some of you may know, Shara Mortimer has handed over coordination of the Kane/Packard nuptials to me."

By the looks exchanged across the table, no one was lamenting the change.

"I know you're all busy," I went on, "so thank you for taking the time to come this morning. We're in the homestretch now, with the baseball game and bachelor party tomorrow, the rehearsal dinner and ice skating Friday night, and the ceremony itself on Saturday."

"Don't forget the bachelorette party," said the stylist. She was a tiny but imperious Scandinavian named Ilsa, with a harsh throaty voice and a youthful, unlined face that contrasted with the silver of her geometrically cut hair. Either Ilsa was prematurely gray by a couple of decades, or she'd had some serious work done. Her smooth, blank expression reminded me of a beach after the tide has receded. "We need to talk about that after the meeting."

"Fine," I said. "Now, let's take it from the top."

As we worked our way through the timetable, I began to breathe easier. Some of these people had worked together before, and all of them knew what they were doing. As we reviewed the photography schedule, a businesslike but amiable spirit emerged, with suggestions offered and accepted, accommodations made for each vendor's requirements, and a general understanding that with a TV star for a bride, this wedding had to be picture-perfect.

As Tracy had already told me, the smoke jumpers were keeping the bachelor party casual. So Food Bob would grill burgers and tap beer kegs, and Evan would take some candid photos. Shara had planned to supervise the setup and the cleanup, but that was all.

"Unless your friend the bride is including you in the baseball game," said Joan, the tent-and-rental, in her plummy British accent. "I understand those gorgeous gentlemen from

Los Angeles are in need of players. I wouldn't mind joining *that* team."

"I didn't know the game was coed," I said. Then I realized that the smoke-jumper team would include women, so the California contingent might also. "Is Tracy playing?"

"You're *joking*," intoned Ilsa, horrified. "She could break a nail, or receive a bruise, or—"

"Of course," I said soothingly. "Silly question. Let's move on to the menus, shall we?"

Food Bob smacked his lips in anticipation. He had a genial, folksy manner, and I scribbled myself a crib note that his mustache was brown and bushy, while Photo Bob's was flat and black. Bad form to tell the photographer the sauce was too salty, or ask the chef for a shot of the bride's uncle.

"The rehearsal dinner's our really fancy meal," said Bob. "We'll have just a grill-to-order buffet kinda thing up at White Pine after the ceremony, and of course the wedding cake. Two of 'em, actually. Orange tiramisu with butter-cream frosting, and then a chocolate-chestnut groom's cake with sugar-dipped champagne grapes and laurel leaves. They'll be real good. 'Course, we'll use powdered egg whites in the butter cream, to stabilize it in the heat."

Real good? But any fears that maybe Bob wasn't real sophisticated quickly vanished as he led us through his fancy meal. From the seared pheasant breast with wild cherry conserve, through the lamb chops in phyllo, to the roasted pears with pecorino cheese and the chocolate-chestnut mousse, we were in the hands of a master. I began to regret, bitterly, my lack of breakfast.

"What about the vegetarian guests?" I asked, to cover the rumbling of my stomach.

"Pepper-crusted salmon on a bed of leeks."

"But that's not vegetarian."

"It ain't meat!" he protested, all innocence.

I felt my blood pressure rising. "Bob, a lot of vegetarians don't eat fish, either. In fact, vegans don't—"

"Take it easy!" The bushy mustache stretched over a broad smile. "I was just jerking your chain. We got a strictly non-flesh, nondairy wild mushroom ragout with roasted asparagus and carved potatoes. It's a beaut on the plate, you'll see."

Next up, among the general chuckles at Bob's joke, was Sebastian, the entertainment director, an *uber*-hip and supercilious southern California type with thick black glasses and thin blond hair. He filled us in about the big-deal rock group he'd hired for the reception, tossing off the famous name as if it were routine.

"And for the ceremony, of course, we have the quartet."

"What kind of instruments?" I asked, scribbling notes.

"What kind?" His eyes glittered behind the geeky glasses. "The Ladislaus Quartet plays string instruments. I thought everyone knew that, but apparently I was wrong. Dear me."

"You've got the *Ladislaus*?" My favorite recordings in the world were the Ladislaus renditions of the Beethoven middle quartets. The prospect of hearing those celestial strings attending Tracy down the aisle was . . . a problem. "That's wonderful, but if the wind comes up, those big pine trees in the meadow are going to generate a lot of noise."

Noise is a tricky issue at an outdoor event. I'd learned that the hard way at a seashore wedding, and again at a ceremony in a Seattle park that turned out to be under a flight path for SeaTac Airport. But today my fears were groundless. This was show biz, and not only had Sebastian arranged to fly the quartet in from their world tour, he'd also made detailed arrangements for mikes, amps, cables, power supply, and even backup power.

"Satisfied?" he asked airily. "Once we're done here I'm off to Cabo San Lucas for a client's birthday gala, but I'll be back on Friday afternoon. If you can spare me?"

"We'll get by. No problem."

There seemed to be no problems at all, in fact, except the one created by Valerie Cox's bloody bee. Wallace Waggoner, poor fellow, was the weak link at this wedding. He had the facts and figures down pat about the refrigerated semi-truck trailer full of cut flowers and the rental of nursery stock in tubs. But when it came to artistic vision, he was a washout.

The more I asked about decorating the tents and tables, the bridal arch and the guest chairs, the railings at the lodge and the porta-potties at the White Pine Inn, the clearer it became that Wallace was a born follower. He kept clutching his paperwork, stammering out broken phrases, and looking around as if Valerie would magically appear and save him from making decisions.

"We'll discuss the flowers in more detail later," I said at last, to put him out of his misery. *And even later than that,* I told myself, *I'll be back in Seattle telling Eddie funny stories about all this. Hold that thought.*

As the meeting broke up, the thought of Seattle brought on thoughts of Aaron. I yearned to call him, just to talk through this tangle, but would he think Dr. Nothstine was nuts and I was overdramatizing? Still, a corpse is a corpse, and at the very least I deserved some sympathy for the shock I had suffered. Not that Aaron was all that good at sympathy. He'd probably just tease me about—

"Well?" Ilsa had bustled up to me, but I'd been staring vacantly over her head. "Well, what shall I put you down for?"

"What? Sorry, I was just . . . put me down for what?"

"For injections at the bachelorette party."

"Injections?" I squeaked. Needles are not my friends. "What kind of party is it?"

"An afternoon at Peak of Pleasure," she said impatiently. At least I assumed she was impatient, from her tone of voice. I couldn't quite tell from her face. "The spa. Didn't you get the invitation?"

"No." I gestured her to join me in the suite's sitting area, where I wouldn't tower quite so far over her. "No, I'm a late addition to the guest list."

"Well, you're in for a treat." Perched on the needlepoint love seat, she still had to look up at me, but at least she smiled. It was nice to know that she could. "Heated stone massage, full-body sugar-scrub exfoliation, tanning, hot-oil scalp massage, French manicure, herbal pedicure, and your choice of Botox or collagen. What shall I put you down for?"

"Um, now that I think about it, I'm going to be awfully busy today. I'm not sure I can make it."

She lifted her hand to my face. You know how in the movies, the guy is always reaching out tenderly to trace his fingertips along the girl's cheek? I don't like it when guys do that, and I sure didn't like it when Ilsa did it.

"What are you?" she said, tracing away. "Thirty-four, thirty-five? You don't want to neglect yourself. And that's quite a frown line between your brows."

I jerked my head aside. "Barely thirty-two. And I'm not neglected, just busy."

"Well, it's too bad. All the bridesmaids will be there, and even"—she sniffed in disapproval—"even the best 'man.' "

"The Tyke's going to be there? I mean, Pari Taichert?" I

made a show of looking at the timetable again. "You know, I think I could fit in the time this afternoon. Yes, definitely."

"Excellent. And you know to wear red, of course."

I nodded without thinking, preoccupied as I was with the idea of scoping out the Tyke's alibi for last night. By the time her last remark registered, Ilsa was bustling toward the door.

"Wait a minute," I called after her. "Red? I don't usually wear—"

But she was already out the door. I sighed and reached for my phone. B.J. could explain it to me. I needed to confer with her anyway, and with Dr. Nothstine, too. Between the three of us, surely we could find out where the Tyke, Danny Kane, and even Todd Gibson had been last night around eleven P.M.

I carried the phone to the suite's king bed, yanked the covers down, and flopped onto my back amid the cool, clean sheets and brocaded throw pillows. No point letting this luxury go to waste, and I was bone tired. Might as well confer with my feet up.

But before I called either B.J. or Dr. Nothstine, I tapped in a Seattle number that I knew by heart. I was in serious trouble here, and only one man could get me out of it.

Boris Nevsky.

Chapter Sixteen

"SO WHO'S BORIS NEVSKY?" ASKED B.J. "PASS THE WASABI."

"My very best floral designer. Best in Seattle, in my opinion. He's on vacation this week, so thank goodness Eddie was able to track him down and talk him into coming. Here, I'll trade you for the gari."

"The what?"

I pointed. "The pickled ginger."

"Well, aren't we too, too Pacific Rim today, Muffy."

"Well, shut up, Muffy."

B.J. and I, a bit giddy after our bizarre night, were lunching at a Ketchum treasure called Sushi on Second. A tatami room, a comfortable bar, and paradise on a plate. It felt better not to be around meat today.

I'd asked Dr. Nothstine to join us—in fact, I offered to bring lunch out to her—but she was already on her way to the smoke-jumper base. The Wood River grapevine was very efficient, and once Dr. Nothstine heard about this second homicide, she had demanded a meeting with BLM officials in order to press her case about the first one.

"They'll have to listen to me now," she'd told me when I phoned. "If they don't, I shall go to the police. I intend to resolve this matter if I have to resort to a citizen's arrest!"

Something of a handful, Sam had called her. No kidding.

"Promise me you won't do anything risky," I pleaded. "Why don't B.J. and I join you at the base and—"

"Absolutely not. Part of NIFC's resistance to my interpretation of your cousin's death was their reluctance to make false accusations against a smoke jumper. The presence of outsiders like yourselves would only hinder my efforts. And by the way, young woman, you have no standing whatsoever to extract promises from me. Don't do so again."

"My apologies," I said stiffly.

"Accepted. But thank you for your concern. It's rather sweet. I shall contact you later."

With that she had hung up, and I'd gone into Ketchum to meet B.J. for lunch and strategy. But since our strategy was short and simple—check alibis as best we could and wait to hear from Dr. Nothstine—we had moved on to less serious topics. Though they seemed serious enough at the moment. I had far too many wedding details to attend to, and far too little time.

"I don't suppose Boris will get a flight till tomorrow," I mused, sipping at my green tea. "But he'll be on the phone with Wallace today, so I can leave the flowers to them for now. The food is under control and so's the music, but I've got to check the weather forecast and then talk to Joan about the tents."

"Aren't you forgetting something?" asked B.J.

"Hmm?"

"My necklace!"

"Muffy, listen to me." I clicked down my porcelain cup and fixed her with the steady glare that I reserve for especially frenzied mothers of the bride. "You have to give up on the necklace."

"But—"

"But *nothing*. The ready shack is a crime scene, for heaven's sake. Dr. Nothstine is over there right now telling the people in charge that Brian's death is connected to that security guard's. You think they'll let us waltz into that locker room and start digging around in Brian's belongings? Not to mention the fact that we might draw the murderer's attention. Remember that Pulaski."

"Like I'm ever going to forget it," she said with a shiver. "But what'll I say to Matt?"

"You say 'Welcome home, take off your pants.' Then later on you can tell him you lost the necklace and leave it at that. There's soy sauce on your chin."

She dabbed it off and sighed. "All right. But I'm still afraid Matt will hear about it somehow. I feel like Brian is cursing me. I guess I deserve it, don't I?"

"Cut it out," I told her briskly, but not without sympathy. "What's done is done. Forget it, and just be good to that man of yours from now on, OK?"

"OK." She waved for the check. "So, how should we tackle the Tyke? Maybe we can get her drunk at the bachelorette party."

"That woman could drink all the bachelors under the table, let alone us," I retorted. "I'm not sure what we should do, except be there and wait for the right moment. What's this business about wearing red?"

"Didn't Tracy tell you? She's invited a photographer from some wedding magazine. She wants a bunch of cute, unposed pictures of us looking exactly like she tells us to, including all of us wearing a red dress to the spa. Heart Health for Women Awareness Week, something like that. Makes her look like a do-gooder. What kind of dress did you bring?"

"I didn't! Nobody said anything about a red dress." I

pushed open the door of the restaurant and stepped into the blast furnace of midday. "Tracy will have to get over it."

"Yeah, that'll happen." B.J. slipped on her sunglasses. "We've got two hours. You want to watch her throw a fit, or you want to go shopping?"

So we shopped. It was like old times, but with more disposable income, and it made a soothing antidote to that nightmare in the parachute loft. We strolled through the downtown boutiques, sighing over the clothes we liked and making faces about the ones we didn't. There were plenty of both, Ketchum having its fair share of women with more money than taste.

"Six hundred bucks!" B.J. hissed at me from behind a rack of scarves. "For a shirt with holes in it!"

"Those aren't holes," I murmured. "They're artful slashes. It's probably conceptual or something. Come on, let's go somewhere with real clothes."

Too late. The owner, a handsome and fearsome personage, descended upon us.

"A casual ensemble, perhaps, for each of you?" she inquired, and flicked her long fingers. Instantly, two handmaidens produced an array of shorts, slacks, and tops, all of which she pronounced perfect for either one of us. Considering the difference in our coloring and figures, I had to wonder what the personage had been smoking lately.

"Nothing for me," said B.J. cheerily. "She needs a red dress, though."

Another flick, and I was whisked into a changing room while various scarlet frocks were whisked off their hangers and presented to me. Some of them cost more than a car, and all of them were outlandishly fashionable. Still, it might be fun to try one on. I slipped into a tight, low-cut number with a poufy skirt, and twirled in front of the three-way mirror.

"What do you think, is it me?"

The personage said, "Delightful."

The handmaidens said, "Charming."

B.J. said, "Ballerina slut."

So I said thanks anyway, and got us out of there.

The next shop we tried was more our speed: consignment clothing, upscale stuff at medium-scale prices. I love consignment shops, and this one was tended by a shy little salesgirl who left us to our search while she chatted on the phone. She had a low, melodious voice and a heavy accent of some Eastern European sort, which made it hard to tell if she was even speaking English. I thought I heard the name Vermeer, but I wasn't sure. *Funny coincidence,* I thought idly.

"How about this one?" asked B.J. after a few minutes, hoisting a hanger.

"Mmm, I've got a dress like that at home. No long sleeves, anyway, it's too hot."

The salesgirl ended her conversation and joined us, gesturing toward a circular rack of sundresses. "These are best for hot weather. The ones with noodles."

"Noodles?"

We looked at her blankly, and she tapped herself on one shoulder. "Noodle straps?"

"Spaghetti straps!" said B.J. The girl laughed along with us. "That would be fine, but it has to be red."

"Oh, there is a pretty one in the back."

She fetched the dress, which was indeed pretty, a simple sheath in a muted terra-cotta tone that would pass for red without clashing too badly with my hair. I bought it, along with a wide belt to break up my beanpole silhouette. I don't have much of a waist, so I had to emphasize its presence.

I didn't say that out loud, though. B.J. and I had a long-standing pact not to complain about our figures, and thus avoid the slippery slope of self-loathing that traps far too many women. Early on we agreed that I wasn't scrawny, I was slim, and that B.J., whatever her current weight, was voluptuous. It worked for us.

On our way out of the shop, some odd impulse made me pause and ask the salesgirl, "Were you talking about the Vermeer exhibit in Portland?"

She nodded sadly. "I want to see it, but it is gone two weeks now."

"Really? I thought . . . Never mind. Thanks for your help."

"What was that about Portland?" asked B.J., as we changed clothes at her place. Her red dress was a jaunty cherry-colored knit that set off her dark hair.

"Oh, nothing." I must have misunderstood what Tracy had said about her visit to the art museum. Why would she lie about a thing like that? "Come on, we'd better hurry."

All my wedding paperwork was still at the lodge, so we took separate cars. The Peak of Pleasure Spa and Salon turned out to be an intensely southwestern-style building, all cactus plants and faux adobe, just north of town. Tracy, deliciously draped in silk the color of rubies, stood posing in the main entrance while a photographer fussed with lights and reflectors.

"Use the side door," she called out. "I'll be there in a minute."

"No rush," said B.J. Then she muttered to me, "What do you bet the whole red thing was just so she could outshine us?"

It was half an hour before the bride joined the laughing, chattering flock of red-clad women in the main lounge. The flock consisted of Olivia the maid of honor, Ilsa the stylist, three bridesmaids who were also actresses, and the spa novices: the Tyke, B.J., and me. We lolled on our bandanna-patterned chaises around the coyote-shaped fountain, sipping champagne and prickly pear cocktails and nibbling chipotle cheese biscuits. All except Ilsa, who had probably never lolled in her life.

We also smiled every time the photographer's assistant told us to, which was tediously often. Olivia and Tracy, I noticed, managed to be in the foreground of every shot, while we three civilians kept being arranged in the background like furniture.

Still, spas are not a routine part of my life, and I must admit I was enjoying myself. When else would a motherly white-coated lady present me with an entire tray of nail polish colors to choose from? Should I go with the pale sparkle of "Durango Dawn," or the dark shimmer of "Sedona Sundown"? Decisions, decisions.

During the manicure I cast an eye over her motherly shoulder to watch B.J. Once her nails were done she wandered across to chat with Tracy and the Tyke, who stood beside a rather bizarre metal sculpture of Kokopelli, the hump-backed flute player of Anasazi legend. Or rather, B.J. and Tracy were chatting. The smoke jumper, her nails unpolished, was eating hors d'oeuvres and looking uncomfortable.

I felt an unexpected pang of sympathy for the awkward duckling next to Tracy's swan. She'd worn red, all right: a red T-shirt with a BLM smoke-jumper emblem, shorts, and red Converse high-tops. I thought the high-tops were a nice touch.

"Kokopelli was a fertility figure," said Mrs. White Coat in a cozy tone, buffing my final pinky. "Is the bride hoping for a big family?"

"Good question. Excuse me."

But just as I joined the group at the sculpture, a distinguished-looking fellow arrived bearing a steel tray of syringes in his rubber-gloved hands. Botox time. The women gathered around him, twittering with either nerves or excitement, and I saw Ilsa heading for me with a crusading look in her eye. I took a hasty step backward and bumped into the Tyke, who was also retreating.

"None for you?" I asked her.

"Right, like I'm going to shoot poison into my face. I only came today because Jack asked me to."

"I'm glad you did." Which was true, though it felt weird to say so to someone who might have killed my cousin. But then the champagne was going to my head, so everything felt a little weird. Especially the sight of syringes. "Sometimes the best man has to make sacrifices, so you're doing your job."

"He told me you were OK about that. 'Perfect choice' and all." The warmth in her voice surprised me. "So, thanks."

"You're welcome."

She smiled. "Tracy hates it, big time."

"She'll live." We both smiled, and I took a chance. Surely this was the right moment to tackle the Tyke. "You know, I have *really* got to get away from those needles. Want to step outside?"

We retreated out the side door and around the corner to a shady little area overgrown with tamarisk and Russian olive trees. I checked around, but we were alone except for a mourning dove hidden somewhere in the leaves. In the afternoon stillness, the dove sounded four soft, owl-like notes, again and again.

Once we'd settled onto a bench, the Tyke surprised me again—by reaching into her back pocket and producing a joint. She lit up nonchalantly, sucked in a hit, and offered it to me.

I had two simultaneous thoughts: *I can't get stoned, I've got work to do!* and *What an opportunity.* So I accepted the joint, faked a quick inhale, and handed it back. We sat in companionable silence for a few minutes. When she toked up a second time I declined, wondering how exactly to ask about her whereabouts last night.

More silence, then she said in a dreamy voice, "Jack's a great guy."

I examined my glossy new nails. "Yes, he's—"

"Bastard with women, though."

"Well, he's—"

"But a great guy." This might not be the Tyke's first joint of the day. The prospect of doing the spa thing with Tracy must have required some sedation. The brown eyes drifted shut and she hummed a little. "He was telling me about you, last night at the Pio."

"Really. What time last night?"

She frowned. "Why?"

"Just that I was there myself," I lied. She couldn't know that I'd been in the parachute loft instead—unless she'd been there, too, wielding a Pulaski. "It must have been around eleven o'clock. I didn't see you and Jack, though."

I waited, hoping for a nice clear alibi. I didn't want her to be guilty. *But face it,* I thought, *I don't want any of the three smoke jumpers to be guilty, and one of them must be.*

After a long moment, she shrugged. "We were at the bar till closing. You didn't hear us singing?"

"Oh yeah, I guess I did." I let out my breath. Nice and clear, and easy to verify. "Were Todd and Danny there, too?"

"I think Danny was," she said vaguely. "Yeah, Danny was. And maybe Toddy. Or not. Don't remember."

That didn't help much, but whether or not the Tyke was a suspect, I could still use her as a source of further information. She might have lost track of some facts while under the influence, but maybe she'd be more forthcoming about relationships.

"Tell me," I said, "how did Brian get along with the rest of the crew? I only knew him as family, but how was he to work with? Did you hear anything about arguments, or that he rubbed anybody the wrong way?"

"No!" she said quickly. Defensively? She went on to explain, "Brian wasn't here long enough to get on anybody's nerves, really. And when you're jumping, you don't let shit like that get in the way. You've got work to do, you do it. He was a good jumper, that's all that mattered."

"Of course." She was covering something, I was sure of it, but I didn't want to press her. I'd just have to ask Jack instead. There was another question, though, that I didn't want to ask him. Not that I really cared about the answer, but . . . "So, what did Jack say about me?"

The Tyke gave me a look I couldn't interpret. "He said you were the one who got away. The one who—"

"Ladies, ladies!" Mrs. White Coat had tracked us down. "You're going to miss the sugar scrub!"

The scrub was interesting, if scratchy, and I tried to slough off the thought of Jack along with my skin cells. That was ancient history, after all. Then the hot stone massage gave me time to mull over the alibi question. Alibi and motive.

If the Tyke really was at the Pio last night, that would clear her of the security guard's death, and therefore Brian's, as well. That left Todd or Danny. But if neither of them knew Brian on a personal level, what could possibly be the motive for his death? And whatever the motive, why risk killing him on a fire, when suspicion would fall on so few people?

Beyond that, why kill the security guard at all? Unless Larabee was right, and that death was part of a bungled robbery. In which case, maybe Dr. Nothstine was wrong, and Brian's death was accidental ... it was all too complicated to think about.

The final spa treatment made it hard to think at all. I knew that Tracy wanted her bridesmaids to present a uniform glow, so when Ilsa mentioned tanning I assumed she meant frying under bright lights. I planned to skip the redhead fricassee, but when I brought up the whole skin-cancer issue, Mrs. White Coat simply laughed.

"We don't do that sort of thing *here*," she said complacently, as if tanning booths were on par with scuzzy tattoo parlors. "We offer an airbrushed self-tanning micro-fine mist, administered by a licensed aesthetician, which guarantees against streaking or missed spots."

"Sort of like spray-painting cars?"

She smiled vaguely. "Something like that. You'll be a soft golden shade within four to six hours. Won't that be nice? Just step in here."

"Here" was a spartan little space like a massage cubicle, but with nowhere to lie down. Soon a matter-of-fact woman with a spray apparatus was doing her number on me,

oblivious to my nakedness and vigilant about every little
pulse of her micro-mist. Too, too weird.

The Tyke was gone by the time I emerged, so B.J. and I
compared notes in the parking lot. I told her about the alibi,
and she told me she'd gone with Sedona Sundown. She also
showed me that her frown lines had disappeared.

"But I *liked* your frown lines."

"Killjoy. Are we having dinner?"

"Maybe a late one, but I'm not sure," I said, climbing into
my rental car. "I've got a lot of work to do."

"Suit yourself. But let me know if Dr. J. lynches anybody
in the meantime."

Once at the lodge I stopped at the espresso bar to get myself a double cappuccino. You can take the girl out of Seattle,
but you have to keep the caffeine in the girl. The lobby was
crowded, not a chair to be had, so I pressed on upstairs to
the Paliere suite.

Between wondering about Dr. Nothstine and worrying
about the wedding, I was thoroughly preoccupied, and if
there were footsteps behind me in the carpeted hallway I
didn't hear them. Not even as they came closer. I just stood
with my back turned, engrossed in digging out my room key.

What I did hear, at last, was the rush of movement as
someone clamped my arms to my sides and lifted me half off
my feet, his breath hot on my neck. My scream was muted by
a gasp of fear, but I managed to squirm sideways and stamp
on his instep. Then I flung the contents of my paper cup in
his face, partly by design, partly because I was flailing in
panic.

Instantly his arms fell away, and a bellowing roar revealed
the identity of my assailant.

"Kharr-negie, are you *insane*?"

Chapter Seventeen

GETTING WARM MILK OUT OF BORIS NEVSKY'S BEARD WAS NO easy task. He ended up taking a shower in the suite's bathroom, while I sponged away at his spattered clothes and hunted in vain for an iron.

I felt like a fool. Boris couldn't have known why I was so jumpy, but I didn't intend to tell him. The fewer people who knew about this whole business, the better.

"Your slacks are OK," I called when I heard the water stop. "But your shirt will need pressing. Honestly, I am *so* sorry."

"No more apology!" Boris declared, emerging in a cloud of steam with a lodge towel knotted around his waist. Knowing him, I figured he wanted to show off his burly brown torso and the curly pelt of black hair on his chest. "You are woman, you are frightened. I forgive you."

"And I appreciate that," I said, suppressing any hint of sarcasm. He was the one bailing me out in a crisis, after all. "There's an ironing board here but no iron, so I called Housekeeping. That must be them now."

A brief rap had sounded at the door. Boris, who was closer, and who was perfectly willing to share his manly beauty with the maid, strode over and flung it open. But it wasn't a maid he found standing there. It was a scandalously handsome Frenchman.

"*Excusez-moi!*" said Beau Paliere. "It appears I have the wrong room . . ."

His voice trailed away as he took it all in. The half-naked stranger. The still-rumpled bed. And the tall skinny redhead, last seen in Seattle at Christmas, now seen clutching a man's shirt and staring at him in mute astonishment. The redhead who knew about his secret toupee.

Beau did a classic double take, first at the room number on the door and then back at me, before flinging up his arms and letting loose a tumbling flood of French and English. I couldn't follow it all, but the import was plain, and the few words I caught didn't bode well for Paliere employee relations. "Outrageous," for example, and "impudence."

I was just inquiring, rather weakly, whether Beau had heard from Shara Mortimer lately, when he used a French phrase that made Boris gasp, and set fire to the notoriously short Nevsky fuse.

"How dare you say such thing to Kharnegie!" bellowed the Mad Russian. "Who are you, to come and insult my friend? Get out!"

"*Get out*?" echoed Beau, as if he didn't recognize the phrase. "I am to 'get out' of my own suite? *Incroyable!*"

Boris replied in his own flood of French, and the two of them proceeded to insult each other at a rising volume and in escalating detail. At least that's what I assumed they were doing, because at that moment a pretty young woman in uniform arrived with an iron, Boris's towel began to give way, and I opted for the better part of valor by snatching up my tote bag and getting the hell out of Dodge.

Down in the lobby, I wove my way through the lounging guests and the milling tourists to secure myself another cappuccino, which I carried to a brocaded armchair in a quiet corner. There I sat, trying to put my thoughts in order before returning upstairs to explain the situation to this second set of bull elk. I was getting tired of testosterone.

So, would Beau banish me from the wedding? Not if I could help it. We had a contract, after all, and I was doing a damn good job to earn my remarkably high fee. Most of all, though, my official role gave me behind-the-scenes access to the smoke-jumper base, even if I'd just be tagging along behind Beau. I was determined to find out what had really happened to Brian, and maybe help B.J. with her necklace after all, and definitely prove to myself that I could watch Jack Packard get married without a pang. . . .

First things first, I told myself sternly. *Old flames are not the top priority here.*

The Tyke appeared to have an alibi for last night, one that I could easily check out with Jack. If he could confirm that Danny was at the Pioneer with them, as the Tyke had said, that would shorten the suspect list, at least for the guard's death, to a single name: Todd Gibson.

It looked like my indecision about Odd Todd might be decided after all. But if so, if Todd didn't have an alibi for the guard's death, then what? Then Dr. Nothstine and I would have to persuade the authorities to take over. Hopefully before the wedding, which was now less than three days away.

It's funny how your own name will reach you, right through a babble of voices that you think you're ignoring. At this point in my ponderings someone spoke my first name, and I looked around to see who.

Over near the main entrance, silhouetted by the bright afternoon, Sam Kane stood talking with his son. Talking at him, rather. Their body language was revealing. Sam was leaning forward with his Stetson tipped back, gesturing sharply, authoritative and angry. Danny's shoulders were hunched in stubborn defiance, hands jammed in his pockets as he stared at the floor and muttered some reply.

Apparently the Tyke was right about Danny being at the bar last night, because he looked just as hung over as yesterday. Sam turned his head away as if in disgust, then spotted me and waved me over. I complied, more than willing to postpone Beau for a few minutes.

"Hey there, Red," said Sam. "Talk some sense into this pigheaded boy of mine, would you? He says he doesn't want to be an usher after all, says we should get someone else!"

"I'm sorry to hear that." I tried to keep a neutral tone. No sense antagonizing the "boy" any further. "Tracy must be disappointed."

"She hasn't heard yet." Sam snatched off his hat and rubbed the back of his neck with a gusty sigh. "But she won't be happy, and her mother'll be mad as dammit."

"You don't have to make a big deal out of it," said Danny sullenly. He certainly was acting adolescent. "I just don't want to put on a monkey suit and get stared at, that's all. Why is that such a big deal?"

"It isn't, not really," I said, feeling my way along. "Though I'm sure you look fine in your tux."

I had no business doing this, now that Beau was on the scene, but I didn't care. Wedding diplomacy is a specialty of mine. I've learned that last-minute jitters, not uncommon in the wedding party, can often be soothed away. Although if they can't, it's best not to push.

"Of course he looks fine!" said Sam. "We all do. We got fitted up and tailored last week. Damn nonsense."

Danny clamped his mouth shut. I know a collision course when I see one, so I made a quick judgment call and slipped a hand under Sam's elbow to draw him aside. Technically, I was still running this wedding.

"You know, Sam, since you'll be busy walking Tracy down the aisle, Danny could just escort Cissy and then sit with her. We could ask one of the other jumpers to usher."

"You sure that's according to Hoyle, Red? The womenfolk are worked up enough already, and if this sets them off—"

"It won't," I promised. "They have plenty of other things to think about."

"Well, I guess you know best. But you better be the one to break it to them."

"Sure. Unless Danny wants to . . . Danny?"

But the grand doors of the lodge were swinging shut, and Danny was gone. It looked like I would have to break the news to them—and find another opportunity to ask him about the songfest at the Pio last night.

"Damn the boy," Sam fumed. "I know he's not all that keen on Tracy, but wouldn't you think he'd take her wedding seriously, just out of respect for me? Been drinking like a fish on a hot day, too."

"All the jumpers are having a hard time right now," I said, remembering the Tyke and her joint. "They've lost one of their own, Sam. It's only natural that . . . Good lord! I don't believe it."

"Believe what?"

Sam turned to follow my astonished stare. Beau Paliere and Boris Nevsky were descending the main staircase, not quite arm-in-arm, but deep in cordial conversation. They were still speaking French, but it hardly smacked of horse-whips and pistols at dawn. If anything, they sounded like a couple of men-about-Paris reminiscing over last night's spree.

"My dear Carnegie, there you are!" Beau approached us with outstretched arms. "We must discuss our plans. And my most esteemed *Monsieur* Kane! You see, I have left Venice behind to be here once again in your most glorious Idaho."

He swooped in for an embrace and a Gallic double-cheek kiss, but the lucky recipient was Sam, not me. And if I expected *Monsieur* Kane to give the Frenchman a Shara Mortimer-style heave-ho, I was sadly mistaken, because Sam lit up like a Christmas tree.

"Bo, you dog! Look at that, Red, we got Bo back. Now we'll get this show on the road!"

And here I'd thought the show was well on the road already. But the father of the bride, it seemed, was wholly in thrall to the Paliere magic, and I was suddenly demoted to sorcerer's apprentice. Especially when Beau brought Boris forward and gave me a quick master-level class in one-upmanship.

"*Monsieur* Kane," said Beau gravely, one hand on the Russian's shoulder, "I have fabulous news for you. Fabulous. This man is Boris Nevsky. This man is the *premier* floral designer of the West. He has agreed to design Tracy's flowers as a favor, a personal favor, to me."

Oh, gag me with a gladiola, I thought. But Sam bought it.

"Pleased to meet you," he said, pumping Boris's hand. "I thought we had that woman, Valerie something, but if Bo says you're the best, why, that's good enough for me and my girl."

Boris, the modest mastermind, inclined his shaggy head. "Very generous, my friend Beau. We make magnificent wedding for your daughter."

"I bet you will," said Sam. "I'll just bet you will. Wait'll Cissy hears this. Say, you and Bo should come to dinner at our house tonight. I got the caterer staying there; he'll do us up something special. You, too, Red."

"Alas, Carnegie will be busy here, will you not, *ma belle*?" Beau turned his bedroom eyes to me with an unmistakable message in their dark blue depths: *If you want the job, you play along. And not one word about my hair.*

"Terribly busy," I said, giving in. Then I decided on a lesson of my own. "What with the contracts and the timetables and that letter you asked me to draft for you. You remember, Beau, the letter of recommendation about all my fine work for Paliere Productions?"

"Good man," said Sam. "Damn nice of you."

I could have kissed him. Beau hesitated just a fraction and then said, "But of course, the letter. By all means."

"Good night, then," I said gaily. "Be sure and let me know when you're coming back tonight, so I can clear out of the suite."

"Hey, that's right," said Sam. "Red's been bunking here at the lodge. Tell you what, why don't both you fellas stay at our place for the duration? We got plenty of room, and then Red won't have to move. How's that?"

"Perfect," said Beau. The invitation seemed to soothe his pride. "My luggage is at the bellman's desk. I will see you tomorrow, *ma belle,* shall we say ten o'clock? Sweet dreams."

He followed Sam to the desk, his very shoulder blades expressing suave superiority. Boris lingered behind.

"What the hell is this?" I hissed, controlling my voice, if not my temper. "I thought he couldn't make it?"

"In Venice, it rains," said Boris, as if this explained everything. "The women, they are in raincoats, they are cold and disagreeable. Paliere, he wishes sunshine. And actresses, I think."

"Your old friend Paliere, you mean. The one you're doing personal favors for. You've never even met the man!"

The Mad Russian shuffled his feet. "Do not be angry. It is for Bill Gates and cruise."

"What?"

"Paliere and me, we stop shouting, we talk. I tell him why you are here, I tell him Valerie Cox cannot come. But I say now I, too, am leaving, because he insults my Kharnegie. Then he says he is director of summer cruise for Bill Gates, and if I help him now, I will come and do flowers for ship." Boris gave a large and eloquent shurg. "Is big contract, my Kharnegie. And I like to cruise."

I gaped in indignation. "Did you at least explain what you were doing in my shower?"

"Not exactly..." More shuffling, like a grizzly bear coming all over bashful. So *that's* what the men-about-Paris were smirking over.

"Oh, never mind." Beau's misapprehensions about my love life were the least of my worries. "Go eat your damn dinner."

The suite felt almost homey by now. I changed from the red dress into shorts, spread out my paperwork on the conference table, and labored away at my temporary office for the next few hours. At first I checked the clock every few minutes, impatient for Dr. Nothstine's call. But it was so long in coming, and I was so deep in wedding details, that when the phone finally rang it startled me.

"Did the BLM people listen?" I asked her. "Are they going to investigate?"

"They did not, and they will not." Julie Nothstine sounded tired and old. "The official finding still stands. Brian Thiel died as the result of an accident during his letdown."

"But what about the security guard?" I protested.

"Unrelated. They suggested that I take the matter to the police."

"And did you?"

"I did indeed." The familiar acerbic bite returned to her voice. "A dreadful person named Larabee. Quite obtuse. I had to raise my voice to him, which I dislike doing, and he still failed to understand. In the end he called me a hysterical woman and had me escorted from the building. I shall file a complaint, of course."

I grimaced, thinking, *I should have gone with her after all.* But I didn't say it aloud. Too patronizing, and maybe not even true. Would Larabee have taken me any more seriously? I could just hear him asking that if I really thought my cousin was murdered by a smoke jumper, why on God's green earth had I gone wandering around the base after dark? And I wouldn't have had much of an answer.

"I'm so sorry," I said lamely. "What should we do now?"

"I intend to return to the smoke-jumper base tomorrow and try again," said Dr. Nothstine. Her voice was dwindling. "For the moment, however, I plan to lie down and rest. I find the heat rather fatiguing."

"Of course. Please, take it easy. I'll talk to you tomorrow."

Discouraged and depressed, I returned to my paperwork,

but my heart wasn't in it. So I brewed some coffee and took a cup out to the balcony, hoping to distract myself with the lodge's late-afternoon scene.

My private little perch was almost as high as the surrounding evergreen trees, so I could look straight down into the terrace restaurant and beyond it to the skating rink. The restaurant was closed, but waiters were moving briskly about, laying the tables for dinner and setting up a buffet. Their occasional voices carried through the hot still air, punctuated by the clink of plates and the rattle of silverware.

Out on the rink, a polo-shirted man steered his little Zamboni machine back and forth, polishing the glistening white ice. I stood quietly, lulled by its whirring hum, and gazed east to the horizon. There, in a composition worthy of Georgia O'Keeffe, the high empty ridges rose in curves like the backs of whales against a fading, empty sky of silvery blue. Lovely, but somehow melancholy . . .

The hiss of ice skates drew my attention back to the rink. The Zamboni was gone, and a single skater in shirtsleeves and khakis was slicing expertly across the rink, faster and faster. He reached the railing, skidded to a showy stop—and fell right on his butt.

I chuckled, expecting curses, but instead the skater laughed aloud and scrambled to his feet, quite unselfconsciously, to try again. I caught my breath and leaned out from the balcony.

His next attempt was faster yet, but it wasn't his style I was watching. *I know that laugh.* This time he halted skillfully at the rail, his blades spraying ice crystals in a glittering fan. Then, satisfied with his performance, he began to circle the rink in long easy glides. As he rounded the far corner his face turned toward me, and I felt a sudden surge like a motorcycle being kick-started.

Aaron. With a private smile I bore my coffee inside, poured it out, and called B.J. to tell her I'd be spending the night in the suite after all.

Chapter Eighteen

"STRETCH, CAN I ASK YOU A PERSONAL QUESTION?"

"Of course." Seeing as how Aaron and I were lying naked in bed by the dawn's early light, with our pulse rates only now reentering the earth's atmosphere, his delicacy was touching. "Wait, though, what time is it?"

Aaron dragged the clock around to face us. Seven-thirty. Plenty of time before Beau descended. Had we slept much at all? I couldn't remember. Absence may not make the heart grow fonder, but it sure does wonders for the rest of the body. Too bad it didn't magically solve Commitment Issues.

I sat up and pulled a fold of sheet across my chest, the way girls do in the movies. Though I suspect they use duct tape. "OK, what's the question?"

Now that I was all the way awake, I wasn't sure I wanted to hear it. According to Aaron, he had flown in because the *Sentinel* assigned him a story on regional population shifts, and Sun Valley was a good place to start his research. Yeah, sure. Dollars to demographics he'd shown up because he was worried about Jack Packard.

Of course, he had nothing to worry about, and I was delighted to see him, but I didn't feel like discussing Jack. Not naked, not the way I blush.

"I was just wondering," said Aaron, drawing his forefinger

along the folded sheet in a way that sent tremors down to my toes. "Since when do you sunbathe in the nude? I'm not seeing any tan lines here."

"Oh. *Oh.*" I swung my legs out of bed and looked down. What was it Mrs. White Coat said, "a soft golden shade"? Yes, indeed. I could have 'fessed up about the spa, but why spoil a good illusion? "Well, Idaho can be kind of informal. The great outdoors, hot springs, that kind of thing."

"I think I'm going to like it here." Aaron's finger drifted lower, but I left the bed and pulled on my terry-cloth robe.

"I'm wondering something myself," I said, yanking the belt into a decisive knot. "How come you took the time to go ice skating yesterday instead of rushing right up here to find me?"

He leaned back on the pillows and grinned, a swift white lopsided grin that I'd had trouble resisting right from the start. "Stretch, did I ever tell you I once worked at Boston Garden?"

I shook my head, suppressing a smile. Aaron's employment history was rich and strange.

"Telephone ticket sales, a really cruddy job. But when the Bruins set up for hockey, they let us skate during our lunch breaks. Man, I loved to skate. So when I got here and saw that awesome ice in the middle of summer, well . . ."

"You chose ice over me?"

Aaron threw a pillow in my direction, so I gave up the woman-scorned act. I'm not good at it, anyway, and we had more important matters to consider. I sat back on the bed and reached for his hand.

"Seriously, now that you're here, I could use your help with something. It's about my cousin . . ."

In the clear light of morning, talking to a skeptic like

Aaron, the notion of murder sounded worse than far-fetched. I half expected him to dismiss my suspicions as paranoia, but he listened without interruption—another one of his skills. When I got to the bloody scene in the parachute loft, he made a sharp sound of distress and squeezed my fingers hard enough to hurt.

"Jesus, Carnegie, why didn't you call and tell me? I would have flown over that night."

"Would you really?" That sounded remarkably like commitment to me. "That's so sweet . . ."

My thoughts must have shown in my eyes, because Aaron dropped my hand like a snake about to bite and glanced across the room at the dresser. I recognized his expression immediately: he was longing for a smoke. On top of the dresser were his watch and wallet and the spare keycard to the suite that I'd given him. But in the top drawer, I knew, was a package of cigarettes.

I had pretended not to see Aaron slip the pack out of sight, and I kept pretending now as I watched him waver. But his resolve held, and I was proud of him for that. He folded his arms across his bare chest, and some part of my mind noted that he'd been working out at the gym lately. Maybe testosterone wasn't so bad after all.

"So," he said briskly, "what were the local cops up to while all this was going down?"

With a rueful sigh, I recounted Chief Larabee's theory about the guard's death. I also explained how the BLM managers had refused to take Dr. Nothstine seriously.

"If we could discover a motive," I said, "maybe they'd listen. Even better, if we could figure out the connection between the two murders. That's the real question."

"No, it isn't." His left eyebrow quirked. "The real question is, why are you getting mixed up in this?"

"What do you mean? Brian was my cousin!"

"Who you weren't crazy about, right? I seem to remember you calling him a jerk."

"So what?" I strode to the window and looked out at the hills that Brian Thiel was never going to see again. "He was family. Someone killed him and I'm going to find out who, whether you help me or not."

Aaron hesitated, but not for long, and then threw back the sheets. He'd been working out a *lot*. "You win, Stretch. Let me grab a shower and then we'll put our heads together."

"Thanks." I closed my eyes, aware that my own head was aching, though not from beer this time. "You know, I never ate dinner last night and I'm ready to faint. Let's have breakfast first and then talk. Unless you're going to be too busy with your research?"

Another quick grin. "I believe I can spare you the time. Where shall we eat?"

"I'll take you to the Kneadery, a Ketchum institution. Maybe B.J. can join us."

B.J. did join us, as I knew she would. She was intensely curious about my new man, and quite willing to leave me in peace with my trout and scrambled eggs while she peppered Aaron with questions. Where he was from and what school he went to, what made him choose journalism and how he liked Seattle. She kept it light, but she kept it up, all through the meal.

As Aaron's replies grew shorter and less enthusiastic, I found myself noticing just how loud B.J.'s voice could be. Then she went one question too far.

"So, Carnegie says you just got divorced," she said archly. "How's that playing out for you?"

Ouch. Over the rim of my coffee mug, I watched Aaron's eyes go flat. He was still smiling, but only with his mouth.

"Excuse me?" he said.

B.J. glanced at me for support, but I concentrated on huckleberry-jamming my toast. Something had just dawned on me. I'd taken it for granted that Aaron and B.J. would like each other right off the bat. But I loved B.J. for our history together. If I met her for the first time today, I might find her pushy manner a little tiresome myself.

"I just meant, how's the single life?" she said uneasily. "Um, dating and all that?"

"Fine. Just fine." Aaron took a long look around at the packed tables and the Kneadery's woodsy, old-barn interior. "I guess this place is nonsmoking. Back in a minute."

B.J. reddened as he walked away, but her best defense had always been a quick offense. "Your man's a little touchy, isn't he? Is that some kind of Napoleon complex?"

"Oh, don't be stupid," I said, mad at her, mad at Aaron for backsliding with his cigarettes, and just mad in general. I clenched my teeth and took a time-out while the waitress brought our check, but it didn't help. I was still mad.

"Just because a guy isn't big and beefy like Matt," I told her, "doesn't mean you can be rude to him. How's divorce *playing out*? For heaven's sake, B.J., would you have said that to a woman friend of mine the minute you met her?"

"Maybe," she grumbled. "OK, maybe not. But—"

"Look, Aaron is really important to me. I trust him, and he's the smartest person I know. I've asked him to help me think this through, so behave yourself. All right, Muffy?"

"All right, Muffy."

Aaron returned to the table then, calmer after his smoke. B.J. didn't apologize to him directly, but she did offer to pick up the check, and he accepted with constrained but courteous thanks. *That's right, kids,* I thought. *Learn to play nice.*

Then both of them kept quiet as I laid out everything we knew or guessed about the grim events of the last week. Aaron even pulled out his ubiquitous notebook and scribbled in it as I talked.

When I was done, he riffled backward a few pages. "Tell me again why Dr. Nothstine is so sure that your cousin was murdered?"

"She studied the photographs from the scene," I said. "At least, she did until the BLM investigators shut her out. She says the body was facedown, with a wound on the back of the head that she's convinced came from a blow, not a fall."

"And you believe her?"

"Yes. Yes, I do."

He flipped the notebook closed. "OK, then. Assuming it's murder, the killer had to be either Todd Gibson, Danny Kane, or this Tyke woman. Or some combination of two, or even all three, of them together."

"Right," I said. "And once the wedding is over and the crew goes back on the active list, the three of them could be sent anywhere in the West, for any length of time. If we're going to find out enough about this to make the police take us seriously, so they'll start a real investigation, we have to do it by Saturday."

"And it's already Thursday. Not much time." Aaron frowned, considering. "OK, where do we start? Thiel was a recent arrival, so the others didn't know him well. We can probably rule out a personal motive."

"We can ask around about their relationships," I said.

"Get other people's impressions, maybe pick up some gossip."

"We could. But first let's see who we can eliminate, by checking on their alibis for Tuesday night. Anyone who's cleared of the guard's murder is probably clear of Thiel's."

"According to the Tyke," I mused, "Brian didn't really have a relationship with Danny or Todd. And she's in the clear for Tuesday, because she was at the Pioneer all evening with Jack."

"*Claims* she was," retorted Aaron. "That's different. We need to interview someone who wasn't drinking that night, like the bartender."

"I could handle that," said B.J., being extracooperative to make up for her rudeness. "I know most of the staff at the Pio."

"Good," he said approvingly. "We have to keep in mind that someone could have slipped out of the Pioneer and back in again without being noticed, but we've got to start somewhere. So you do that, B.J., and Stretch, you talk to Jack Whatsis again."

"You won't have to twist her arm," B.J. murmured, reverting for a moment to her usual troublemaking self.

Aaron looked at her quizzically, so I hastened to say, "She just means I have wedding business to talk over with him."

"Well, while you're doing that, get his recollection of who was at the tavern when, and we'll cross-check it with the bartender's. Meanwhile, I'll try to interview the police chief, in case there's anything else we should know, and I'll take a look at the local newspaper's archives. I always do that anyway when I'm in a new—"

"Wait just a minute," I said, nettled by all these marching

orders. I wanted Aaron to help me think, not tell me what to do. "Let's go back to motive. It seems to me—"

"More coffee?" The waitress was back. When we declined, her eyes slid pointedly to the people standing in line for tables. "You folks all set, then?"

We took the hint, and tried to take our conversation outside. But it was too hot, even this early in the morning, and far too public anyway. So B.J. led us back to her house and I took up where I'd left off.

"It seems to me," I said, "that if the key to all this isn't a long-standing relationship, it might be a single incident. Something that happened on the morning of the Boot Creek fire, or even at the fire itself."

"Could be." B.J. waved us to the couch. "Maybe we should talk to the spotter on that flight. I think it was Al."

"What's a spotter?" Aaron took a seat right where I'd fallen asleep Tuesday night. It seemed like a long time ago.

"The one who sends each jumper out of the plane," she told him. "He, or she, drops streamers to gauge the wind, then coordinates with the pilot and picks the jump spot and so on. But the spotter's also kind of the baby-sitter for the crew, so if Brian was having trouble with one of the others, Al might have picked up on it."

"You mean Al Soriano?" I asked. "Sam introduced us. I could talk to him at the bachelor party this afternoon. It would seem natural for me to ask about my cousin's last flight."

"If you want," said Aaron dubiously. "But I still think the alibis are the critical point."

"And *I* disagree," I insisted. It was just like Aaron to be so contrary. The more I leaned one way, the more he tilted the other. Why did things get so complicated once we got out of bed? "You said yourself, someone could have slipped out of the Pioneer without being noticed."

"It's still worth checking," he said stubbornly. "Besides, even if this spotter did notice bad blood between Thiel and the other jumpers, how would that explain killing the security guard?"

But I'd been considering that very question. "Maybe Brian's murder wasn't personal. We keep hearing that no one knew him very well. And why choose such a risky moment for a murder? Maybe he saw something there in the woods, or—"

Aaron snorted. "What's there to see in the middle of a fire?"

Now I was really peeved. "They don't jump into the flames, idiot. I'll ask Al about the Boot Creek area, along with Brian's relations with the rest of the crew. I have to talk with him anyway, he's on my list of substitute ushers. Danny doesn't want to do it now."

"Oh?" Aaron looked up sharply. "That's odd behavior, ducking out of your own sister's wedding."

"Half sister," I corrected, and explained about Sam's notorious divorce. "No one's really behaving normally right now, but I suppose Danny could be the killer and that's why he can't face being in public. Sam said he's been drinking a lot since Brian died."

We talked about Danny, his past troubles and his present behavior, though neither B.J. nor I could picture that subdued, passive man as a murderer. Then I told Aaron about my dinner at Dr. Nothstine's with Todd Gibson.

"Todd refused to talk about finding the body, but if he was the killer, surely he would have rehearsed something? I think he was hiding something, but I just don't think it was murder. I mean, you can tell he loves smoke jumping. To hear his stories—"

"So he's innocent because he's a young hunk who tells good stories?" said Aaron in that snide tone he uses sometimes. I hate that tone. "Sounds to me like he was trying too hard to be charming. Not that you're hard to charm."

I bristled. "Meaning what?"

"Oh, nothing, just that—"

"The Tyke's been acting weird lately, too," said B.J. abruptly. I could see she was trying to head off our quarrel. "Look at how she yelled at us after the Talent Show."

"What Talent Show?" asked Aaron.

"I'll tell you on the way back to the lodge," I told him. "It must be getting late." I checked my watch. "Damn, it really is late. Come on, I don't want Beau complaining about me."

"I'd better get to work myself," said B.J. "I'll stop in the Pio at lunch, and Carnegie can talk to Al at the bachelor party."

"Wait, one last question." Aaron looked from her to me and back again. "After you two figured out that one of the smoke jumpers was a killer, why did you go out to the smoke-jumper base late at night? That was pretty chancy."

"Oh," I said, stalling. "Oh, that."

B.J. eyed me uneasily, afraid that I'd tell him about her and Brian. She needn't have worried. Even though I knew Aaron wasn't the type to sit in judgment, I'd sworn to keep her secret. And secrets are sacred in matters of the heart. Or the bed. No, I was stalling because I'd drawn a sudden blank about our excuse for being at the base.

What the hell did I tell Larabee, anyway? Something about . . . oh, right, the party.

"Well, you see, I had to scope things out for the bachelor party, and I was too busy to go there the next day—"

B.J. and I had delivered the tale so smoothly at the police station, but this time we stumbled all over ourselves.

"Yeah," she chimed in, "and I had to go with her to, uh, to help scope . . ."

It was a sorry performance, and Aaron looked unimpressed.

"Whatever," he said, "but try to be more careful, would you? No more sneaking around in the dark?"

"Absolutely not," I promised.

"No way," vowed B.J., as she snagged her tote bag and led us outside. But once Aaron was beyond earshot she murmured to me, "Try and get the necklace this afternoon, OK?"

"With all those bachelors around?"

"Come on, Muffy, I don't have much time before Matt gets back. Please?"

"OK, I'll try."

After all, I hadn't promised not to sneak around in the daylight.

Chapter Nineteen

WE HAD TAKEN AARON'S RENTAL CAR TO BREAKFAST, SO I navigated us back to the lodge. The short drive was just long enough for a bang-up fight.

"I appreciate your help with this," I said. I was still ticked off at him for being so bossy, but fair is fair. "Take the next left."

"I keep telling you, Stretch, I'm a helpful guy. Helpful, witty, handsome, modest..."

"How about honest? Tell me honestly, did the *Sentinel* really give you that story assignment?"

He cocked his head. "Well, maybe I pitched them the story. And maybe I took a few days off."

"I knew it!" I said gleefully. Maybe too gleefully. "Are you staying for the wedding? I'm going to be awfully busy, but—"

"Busy with Boris?" Aaron blurted, as if in spite of himself.

"How'd you know Boris was here? Did Eddie tell you?"

"Wasn't that the idea?" He looked over at me, his eyes invisible behind his sunglasses. Talk about a poker face. "Interesting that your friend doesn't have her own florist."

"As a matter of fact, she did." I would have explained about Valerie Cox, but I didn't care for Aaron's tone. "What do you mean, wasn't that the idea? What idea?"

He stared at the road. "Come on, Stretch, you be honest.

I turned you down about coming to this wedding, so you called your old boyfriend and got him to come instead. Eddie made a big deal about it. Don't tell me you didn't put him up to it."

"Aaron!"

"Look, it's fine. I should have come with you in the first place, I admit it. But I'm here now, we're having a good time, and we've got this business about your cousin to deal with. So forget it."

"I will *not* forget it. I can't . . . You . . . Pull over. Pull over right now!" He complied, and before the car stopped rolling I had my door open. "I cannot *believe* that you think I would play games like that. I have never been so—oh, *shut* up!"

This last was directed at the driver behind us, who had honked his horn. I climbed out, slammed the door with such violence that it popped open again, and marched off to the lodge.

My father used to kid me about smoke coming out of my ears when I got angry. I was still smoking as I entered the lobby, and painfully aware of my tardiness, as well. But when the rosy young Austrian girl beckoned to me from the front desk, I calmed myself and went over. I always hate it when people take out bad temper on employees who can't fight back.

"What is it?" I asked, forcing a polite smile.

"Herr Paliere asked me to watch for you," she said, growing rosier. "He is even more handsome than in the magazines!"

"Isn't he, though. Did he leave a message?"

"Oh, of course. He asked for a keycard to the suite, and when he did not find you in the suite, he was . . . not pleased.

He wishes you to know that he is waiting for you at the swimming pool."

I looked at her silently, breathing through my nose and counting down from ten. Then I pulled out my own keycard and slapped it on the counter.

"Change it," I said. "Please."

"Change your suite?"

"No, just reprogram it. I want one, and *only* one, keycard programmed for that suite, and I will pick it up myself, in person, in ten minutes. Me, not Herr Paliere, and not . . . anyone else. Especially anyone else. Is that clear?"

"Of course," she said. "But I must ask the manager—"

"You do that." I turned toward the hallway to the pool. "I'll be back."

The lodge's swimming pool was a perfect circle, its turquoise-blue surface reflecting a ring of white lattice fence and a surrounding stand of lofty pine trees. In my day the pool was strictly off-limits to staff—a rule that was deliberately and frequently flouted. Oh, the midnight swims, the damp husky shoulders of the boys, the chlorine-flavored kisses . . .

In a somewhat better frame of mind, I emerged into the dazzling sunlight and looked around for Beau. I was expecting an impatient but elegant figure, perhaps clad in an Italian summer suit, seated in the shade with a pile of papers and a laptop.

But the only laptops I saw were smeared with cocoa butter. As I scanned the dozens of suntanned and bikinied figures that reclined on lounge chairs or stood waist-deep in the pool, I was painfully aware that my face was flushed, my hair was frizzy, and I was the only one out here with clothes on.

Then I heard Beau's unmistakable voice, deep and smooth,

like audible cognac. It came from the far side of the pool, where a pair of lounges were drawn cozily together, well placed for the occupants to see and be seen. The occupants were Beau and Olivia, Tracy's maid of honor, lying facedown and murmuring to each other across their folded arms.

Olivia's sarong was absent today, but it wasn't her unveiled derriere that arrested my attention. It was Beautiful Beau's. You don't get many men in thong bikinis in Seattle, which is not a bad thing. The spectacle before me was like a bakery's display case, four round brown buttered buns in a nice neat row.

"You're late, *ma belle*." Beau broke up the display by rolling onto one elbow. "I expect promptness from my Girls."

The sight of Beau's generous assets took the wind from my sails, but only for a moment. I wrenched myself into a more businesslike frame of mind.

"Sorry. Shall I wait for you upstairs?"

He waved a languid hand. "*Non, non.* As you can see, I am engaged in discussing the wedding with this exquisite *mademoiselle.*"

Olivia trilled with laughter, and I waited for Beau to introduce me, or sit up, or ask me to sit down, or *something* besides leaving me standing there in the hot sun like a lackey. Fat chance.

"You," he continued, "may proceed with your work. Go and find Nevsky, review his plans for the flowers."

"What about the bachelor party?"

"The game of base ball?" Beau spoke the two words separately, pursing his lips in distaste. "A schoolchild's game at a gala affair . . . *Eh bien,* I bow to the wishes of the groom."

"That's big of you. What I meant was, when are we going out to the smoke-jumper base? The party starts soon."

"You will see to it on my behalf." He was already turning back to Olivia. "As I was saying, *mademoiselle*..."

I left them to it. I didn't object to going solo to the smoke-jumper base, given the snooping around I had in mind. In fact, the crumpled bit of paper with the padlock combination was already nestled in my pocket.

But as I reentered the lodge I marveled at Beau's laissez-faire attitude. Did he always let his assistants do the work while he got the glory, or was he just coasting on this particular wedding to take advantage of me? If I ever met another of Beau's Girls, I'd have to ask her.

When I picked up my recoded keycard, the young desk clerk gave me an appraising look, one female to another, and handed me a folded note. It bore my name in Aaron's slanted, angular handwriting.

"Another gentleman asking for you," said the clerk.

"Let me guess. He also was not pleased."

She dimpled. "No. But also handsome!"

I unfolded the note. *This is crazy, Stretch,* it read. *Can we talk? I'll be in the bar—love, A.*

Love, huh? I walked over and peeked through the door of the Duchin Lounge. Sure enough, there was the back of Aaron's undeniably handsome head. His hair was black as crow feathers, but fine and silky to the touch. My fingertips still kept the feel of it...

Maybe I overreacted, just a little? I told myself that it couldn't hurt to talk, though I really should be working. I reached for the door handle—and saw Aaron take a deep drag on a cigarette. *To hell with it.* I shoved my hands in my pockets and turned away. Let him cool his heels and work on his apology while I went looking for Boris.

Sun Valley Village is a pleasant pedestrian complex, with

restaurants and shops scattered among the lawns and the duck ponds. I cut through them at a rapid clip toward the tennis court parking lot, where I knew that a refrigerated trailer full of flowers had been trucked in last night. But I was waylaid by two people I couldn't turn away from: the mother of the bride and my own mother.

"Oh, there you are, dear," said Mom. "Are you having fun?"

She and Cissy, along with three other ladies, were just emerging from the Chocolate Foundry. As the door closed behind them I caught a heady draft of fudge perfume. The Foundry stocks a dizzying array of candies, but the real treat is watching them sculpt molten chocolate into truffles on the marble countertop. Cissy, I noticed, carried a bulging paper sack.

"Carnegie's not supposed to have fun," she said with a droll little finger wag at me. "She's working. Beau says you're wonderful, you know. A real fast learner."

"Golly. How sweet of him."

I tried to press on, but Cissy insisted on introducing her companions. And when I heard their names I was glad she did. Two of the ladies, sisters with long horsey faces, were well known for their wealth, and the third was the governor of Idaho's wife. Even better, all three of them seemed to have marriageable daughters or nieces or both, and I had a sudden vision of opening a Made in Heaven branch office in Boise.

"Let me give you my business card and—ack!"

Domaso's dog Gorka, tail wagging and drool flying, burst out of some nearby shrubbery and into our little group. The sisters whinnied in terror, and the governor's wife was nearly upended. Gorka wasn't barking, but only because his mouth was full of a length of black fabric, which whipped through the air as he snapped his massive head playfully back and forth.

"Get away!" yelped Cissy, her bonbons ascatter. "Carnegie, can't you stop him?"

"That's your dog?" one sister inquired from behind the safety of the Foundry's porch railing. "I hardly think . . ."

"He's not mine," I protested. "Gorka, down! I'm not playing tug-of-war with you, so don't— Hey, drop that. *No!*" Gorka had abandoned his toy to lunge for Cissy's chocolates. I kicked one out of his way and hauled at his collar before he reached the others. "Cissy, pick those up. Hurry, I don't think I can hold him."

"Pick them up?" Cissy was incensed. "Don't go telling me what to do, sweetie, especially when it's your fault—"

"Oh, for heaven's sake!" said my mother, bless her. "Chocolate is poisonous to dogs, don't you know that?"

Mom recovered the paper sack and began to collect the toxic goodies from the grass. One of the sisters helped, but the other women just stared spellbound at Gorka, who favored them with his biggest, toothiest grin, like a mouthful of steak knives. Then he let loose a bark, bunched his muscles, and bounded away, breaking my grip without even trying.

I let him go, figuring he'd make his way back to Domaso or to a dogcatcher, and serve them both right.

"I'm sorry," I said, "but he's really not my dog. Now if you'll excuse me, I've got to go or I'll be late."

As I stepped away the tangle of fabric caught at my feet, so I picked it up. One of the ladies tittered. It was a bra. A lacy, capacious, shredded black bra.

"Is that yours, dear?" asked my mother, damn her.

"No, it is *not*."

I dropped the thing in a wastebasket on the porch, and when I turned back Cissy was herding the ladies away. Mom, lingering behind, had a twinkling, girlish look on her face that should have tipped me off.

"Poor Carrie, still so irritable. You miss him, don't you?"

"Miss who?"

"Your new friend, silly." More twinkling. "But I've got a feeling that you'll have a date for the wedding after all."

"Mom," I said, a horrid suspicion dawning, "what exactly are you talking about?"

"Oh, I hate to spoil the surprise, but I'm dying to tell you! And anyway, I'm afraid you might be up at White Pine when Aaron gets here. You see, I had a little talk with Eddie and—"

"You *what*?"

"Don't shout, dear," she said mildly.

But I was smoking again, and flaming, too. "You put Eddie up to it, didn't you? *You* had him tell Aaron all that nonsense about me and Boris! How could you?"

She was entirely unfazed. "Is your friend here already? How nice. He must care for you a great deal to hurry like that. I can't wait to meet him."

"Mom, Aaron thinks I set this up. He thinks I'm playing some stupid little game with him!"

"Oh, I'm sure he doesn't think that. And if he does, I bet he finds it flattering. Men are like that. Now, Cissy's taking us to lunch, so you run along. Bye!"

Between the summer heat and the sheer indignation, I reached the parking lot barely able to breathe. The sun burned down on me and the black asphalt bounced it back up, unrelieved by any breeze. I headed for the canvas awning along the side of the trailer, but its breathless shade was scant relief.

"Boris? Anybody home?"

By tomorrow a line of work tables would be set up beneath the awning, and the floral crew would be working furiously at Boris's direction. But for now there was only the hot asphalt and the grinding rumble of the trailer's refrigeration unit as it kept the cargo of blossoms nice and cool.

Nice and cool. If Boris didn't show up soon I'd have to leave for the bachelor party, but I didn't have to broil while I waited. Why not meet him inside? I went around back, mounted three steps to the double door, and slipped into heaven.

Ahhh...After the furnace outside, the trailer was positively arctic. But the Arctic never smelled this good. The long narrow space was jammed with flat boxes and plastic water tubs, and they in turn were jammed with many-colored roses and midnight-blue delphinium and the tightly furled spears of irises in white and plum and gold.

The flowers nearly hid the corrugated steel floor, except for an aisle down the middle that led past a heap of canvas sacks and a tower of crates. The crates must hold vases and bowls for arrangements, and I could see wands of curly willow poking out of the sacks. Boris would have a field day.

Breathing in all this cold floral glory, I began to cool off. And not just physically. *I shouldn't have yelled at Mom,* I thought, *or Aaron either. No wonder he thought what he did, after Eddie laid it on thick about Boris. And his note did say "love"* ...

I pictured Aaron slouched at the bar, gloomily checking his watch, wondering if and when I'd come. Then I pictured myself with a peace offering, one of those lush apricot-colored roses from the tub at the far end of the trailer.

Smiling at the thought of his face when I handed it to him, I moved forward.

That's when I saw something protruding from beyond the stack of crates. It made a small, pale shape against the gray floor. Very pale, and very still. My mouth went dry, and I heard the same dark roaring that had filled my ears in the parachute loft.

The shape was a naked foot.

Chapter Twenty

I BEGAN TO SHUDDER, BUT NOT FROM THE COLD. SWALLOW-
ing bile, palms clammy, heart slamming like a fist inside my
chest, I forced myself forward, step by step, along the aisle
between the tubs of flowers. I wasn't thinking, not in words,
but my mind's eye filled with images of horror upon blood-
spattered horror.

The pale, still foot led to an ankle, to a bare calf, to the
back of a knee . . .

"Do you *mind*?"

Foot, leg and all, jerked and withdrew in a thrashing of
limbs. And not just one leg. Four. Tracy's, of course—for the
voice was hers—but also someone else's.

"Oh, shit!" I stumbled back among the flowers, averting
my eyes from the spectacle of my buck-naked bride surrounded by her flung-about clothing, and her snatched-up
blanket, and her half-empty bottle of tequila. Not to mention
the stunned but sated face of Domaso Duarte.

I could have fled the trailer, to complete this scene of utter
farce, but at first I was too shocked to move, and then I was
too angry.

"Tracy?" I said finally. "Tracy, I think I know what happened to your bra."

I heard a bumping and muttering and shuffling, then the

bride appeared around the corner of the crates. Her perfect tresses were tangled, her perfect makeup was a smeary mess, and she'd pulled on an oversized T-shirt that was clearly Domaso's. She smelled like a double margarita with a chaser of sweat.

One might have expected confusion or embarrassment or even apology, but only if one didn't know Tracy Kane. She merely offered me a photogenic smile and that adorable widening of the eyes. And Domaso kept out sight entirely— no doubt, the way Tracy had kept out of sight when I pulled over near Domaso's Cadillac on the roadside Monday. At least that time he'd put his pants back on.

"Carnegie!" said the bride, in a sort of breathy purr. "Thank goodness it's only you! You'll understand."

"Understand?" The shock was back. "Tracy, are you going to tell me that this isn't what it looks like? I may be ordinary, but I'm not stupid, and if you think—"

"Of course you're not!" She turned away with a petulant scowl and plucked up one of the apricot roses, pulling the petals from it one by one. "But you've been around, you know what it's like."

"What what is like? Cheating on Jack?"

"Oh, as if you're so pure," she retorted, and flung the half-denuded flower right at me. "Dom told me what was going on with you and John up at White Pine, you bitch!"

The rose slapped against my bare arm, and a stray thorn drew a thread of blood from my skin.

"Hey, that hurt! Dammit, Tracy, if you want a flower fight, you're going to get a willow wand up your nose. Grow up would you?"

Show business is tough, but the wedding business is tougher. Tracy caved.

"I'm sorry," she whimpered. Make that a triple margarita. Tracy Kane never apologized. "I don't blame you, Muffy, really I don't. But I'm just doing the same thing you did with him, saying good-bye to . . . to an old friend. There's no crime in saying good-bye, is there?"

I opened my mouth, but so many things were trying to get out that they jammed in the door. An explanation that Jack's kissing me at White Pine wasn't my idea. Indignation at Domaso for telling her otherwise. And amused vexation that Tracy had chosen this of all moments to call me Muffy for the first time in years.

"You know what?" I said at last. "I'm going to a baseball game. And as far as I know Boris Nevsky is on his way here right now, so you and your old friend better say good-bye for real."

I was almost back to the lodge before I realized that I hadn't taken a rose for Aaron. Well, he'd get a kiss instead. A big old kiss and an apology, because however skeptical and annoying Aaron could be, he was one of the ordinary people, too. And we were at least attempting to be honest with each other, unlike Tracy and Jack . . .

But no, I didn't want to think about them right now. How was I supposed to give my all to this wedding with the groom coming on to me and the bride behaving like a cross between a soap-opera tramp and a two-year-old?

I arrived at the lodge by the back way, past the ice rink and across the terrace, but I barely noticed the skaters and diners in my eagerness to see Aaron. I pushed open the door to the Duchin Lounge, squinting in the dimness after the glare outside, and hurried up to his bar stool.

The trouble was, the stool was now occupied by a woman

in golf clothes. She frowned at me over her martini as I stood there, nonplussed.

"Help you?" said the bartender.

"I was looking for a friend . . ." I glanced around. Aaron wasn't at any of the tables, either. "Never mind."

Feeling a little foolish, and a lot let down, I retreated to the lobby to ask at the front desk for messages. None. Checked my cell for missed calls. Also none. And finally, though I really wanted to apologize in person, I tried Aaron's cell phone. When his recorded voice invited me to leave my name, I disconnected.

Damn the man, why couldn't he stay put so we could kiss and make up?

I tried his phone again when I got out to my rental car, and once more after the short drive to the smoke-jumper base. Still no answer, so I grabbed my notes about the barbecue arrangements and climbed out to survey the scene.

The scene differed considerably from the eerie darkness of Tuesday night. A row of picnic tables was set up in the shade of the ready shack, their red-checkered cloths fluttering in the breeze, and the same breeze carried the tantalizing summer smell of hot charcoal.

I didn't see Food Bob, but one of his staff was busily filling tall red cups from a beer keg, while others tended the barbecue grills and set out generous bowls of potato salad and whole cherry pies. Lines of party guests in T-shirts and shorts were eagerly awaiting the food and drink.

Most of the partygoers were men, with a few women, but all of them were laughing and talking and no doubt telling each other outrageous stories. I was pleased at that. The bride and groom could misbehave all they wanted, but I still felt a duty to the guests.

Across from the feast, the grassy field beside the airstrip had been marked out as a baseball diamond. Various smoke jumpers and visitors were scattered across it, warming up for the game and exchanging good-natured taunts with the spectators.

The jumpers were mostly clowning around, but not the L.A. people. I recalled Sam's comment that the studio boasted a real team, and that's exactly what these guys looked like. While some of them stretched and jogged in place, the others formed a widening circle and snapped a ball from player to player with nonchalant precision.

But one of the players was a ringer from Seattle. And was he gloomy, was he sighing and consulting his watch and wondering where I was? Hell, no. He was out in the sunshine in his Red Sox cap playing catch and grinning like a kid, the bum.

I slammed the car door and marched over to Aaron. The grass was cooler than the parking lot back at the lodge, but I was still steamed.

"I thought you were waiting in the bar?"

"I was." Aaron made a long throw to a husky blond fellow I recognized as Peter Props. Then he turned to me and the grin disappeared. "I waited quite a while, Stretch, and the longer I waited the madder I got about you locking me out. Then I started talking to these guys, and it turned out they were short an outfielder. I have to enjoy my vacation somehow, right?"

"Right." *And I was going to apologize to this man? Please.* Still, I couldn't help relenting just a little. "You can come back tonight, you know."

"Maybe."

There was an unpleasant pause, and then he made a show of looking back at my car. "Where's your friend?"

"Which one?" I asked coldly. "I have a lot of friends here."

"I meant Boris, but maybe you mean this guy Jack, the one you don't need your arm twisted to talk to?" Again Aaron's eyes were hidden by sunglasses, but I could imagine the look in them. "Is that why you were here the other night, to visit your friend Jack?"

"Of course not!"

"Then what were you and B.J. hemming and hawing about when I asked why you came?"

"Nothing," I said huffily. "Not a damn thing. Not that it's any of your business, but Jack and I are just—"

"Hey, Gold!" Peter Props gave me an amiable nod as he approached. He wore a "Tails of the City" tank top stretched across his beefy torso, and his broad nose was sunburned already. "Center field OK with you? I've got a camera guy who wants left and I usually play deep right."

As Aaron replied, someone tapped my shoulder. It was Food Bob, wearing a "Kiss the Cook" apron around his broad middle and nibbling absently on his bushy brown mustache. He looked like a preoccupied walrus.

"Sorry I'm late," I began. *And sorry I'm burning up work time with lovers' quarrels.*

"No, no, you're fine," he said, folksy as ever. "There's not hardly anything for you to do. Though I have got a question or three about the rehearsal dinner tomorrow . . ."

He began to move away, clearly expecting me to come along. Behind me, Aaron and his teammates were deep in conversation about defense strategy. I sighed and followed Bob. *Business before pleasure,* I told myself virtuously. *Not that I'd call this pleasure.*

Over at the picnic tables my virtue was rewarded by the sight of Al Soriano, the very man I wanted to question about Brian's last hours. Let Aaron obsess about alibis. I wanted to understand Brian's relationships with our three suspects.

Al was sitting by himself with his ball cap pushed back on his dark curly hair, nursing a beer and excavating his way into a minor mountain of potato chips. I concluded my business with Bob as fast as I decently could, then snagged a beer of my own and sat next to him.

"Hi, I'm Carnegie Kincaid. We met the other day?"

"Sure," said Al. "Brian's cousin."

"That's right. I didn't get a chance to ask you, did you know him very well?"

Al shook his head. "Not really. I would have, as the season went on."

"But I suppose he got along well with the rest of the jumpers. Danny and the Tyke, for instance, and Todd Gibson?"

"Oh, everybody gets on with Danny. The Tyke kind of picks and chooses her friends, you have to let her make the call. But Toddy's a Ned, you know, so he and Brian trained together. You could talk to him."

"Of course." I could see Al wondering where these questions were going, so I shifted my ground. "But I heard you flew as spotter on the Boot Creek fire, so I was wondering if you could tell me about that flight. About whether Brian was"—I wasn't sure how to phrase this—"if he was distracted or anything."

Al wiped the crumbs from his mouth with the back of his hand and sat up straighter, donning an air of responsibility like an invisible uniform. His tone was serious, but not unkind. "You mean, did I observe some sign that Brian Thiel might fail to execute his safety procedures? No ma'am, no way. I'm the spotter. Anybody isn't a hundred percent on the ball, I don't send them out the door. Period."

"Sorry, I didn't mean to suggest.... So, nothing unusual was going on that day?"

"Well, it's not exactly usual to hang up in a tree," he said, unbending a little. "It just happens sometimes when you get these squirrelly little wind shifts. I saw Brian's canopy clear the plane, then he caught some down air that took him away from the jump spot. But he drifted into the black zone, so I thought he'd be OK, just get a little sooty ahead of time. I even laughed."

Al scooped another handful of chips and crunched on them thoughtfully. "Then I got distracted, thinking I saw a tent down there, and when I looked back he was hung up in this big stand of pondos. You want to land in lodgepole pine or Doug fir, because they're softer and the canopy's sturdy enough to hold you, but he didn't have a choice."

" 'Pondos'? Oh, ponderosa pines." The three tall evergreens in the White Pine meadow were ponderosas. "So then Brian—wait a minute, a *tent*? Someone was camping that close to a fire?"

"Well, this particular fire blew up so fast, and people can be so damn foolhardy. But it was just a glimpse through the smoke. The Boot Creek drainage is pretty country, but kind of inaccessible, and we never got a report on any campers in the vicinity. So I must have been wrong."

Or else you were right, and the camper kept his presence quiet for a reason. The idea was dizzying, and I barely noticed when Al excused himself to go claim his hamburger. All of us, Dr. Nothstine and B.J. and Aaron and I, we'd all been so focused on the three smoke jumpers who had parachuted down with Brian. But what if a fourth person had been on the ground already?

For one smoke jumper to kill another had seemed inconceivable, and maybe it was. Maybe Todd's evasions and Danny's moodiness and the Tyke's belligerence had nothing to do with Brian, and we had to look at his death from another angle altogether. Maybe—

"Hey, Carnegie." Into this maelstrom of uncertainty came Jack the Knack, star pitcher. He was slapping a ball into his glove and scanning the picnic area anxiously. "Have you seen the Tyke? She's late."

"Sorry, no. Can't you start without her?"

"Not really. We made a big deal about allowing two women on each team so Annie and the Tyke could play, and now these guys are saying that two women are required. Tracy told me they're serious players, but this is ridiculous. Still..."

He gave me a speculative look, nose to toes. "You used to play a little ball, didn't you? I don't suppose you could cover first base for a few minutes, just till the Tyke gets here? Everybody's waiting."

I looked over to the diamond, where most of the players were watching Jack talk to me. The smoke jumpers had taken the field, including a lanky dark-haired woman, presumably Annie, at third base. One of the L.A. visitors, the bronzed man I'd last seen in a Speedo, stood at home plate taking practice swings with an aluminum bat that glinted in the sun.

"Come on," coaxed Jack. "I promise, if we have to throw to you we'll toss it real gentle."

I wavered. My mind was on Boot Creek, not baseball. Then I spotted Aaron at the visitors' bench with the rest of the California contingent, and when he saw me looking he turned his back. That tore it.

"Never mind the tossing." I stood up. "I can't hit for beans, but I'm not afraid of the ball. You can throw to me."

"Good woman!"

Jack draped an arm on my shoulders, and I checked for Aaron again. He was watching, so I threw back my head and gave a loud, merry laugh.

"Happy to help. Where's my mitt?"

Jack was right, these friends of Tracy's were serious players. Jack's vaunted pitching was rusty, and all I did for the first half of the inning was scoot out of the way as they sprinted past my base. California five, Idaho zero.

Leading off the second half, Jack redeemed himself with a home run, but it was downhill from there for the smoke jumpers. A strike is a strike whether you can do one-armed push-ups or not.

I struck out myself—no surprise—and then it was time for our side to take the field again. The Tyke still hadn't shown, so I checked in with Bob, gulped some beer, and went back to first base. This was fun. And if I made certain that Aaron saw me having fun without him, well, it served him right.

The second inning took an interesting turn. Peter Props was first to bat, hitting a high fly that was caught for the first out. Then one of their two token women, a giggling script girl named Ramona, flailed the bat around for number two. Things were looking up for the home team.

"Don't worry about it," Aaron called to the visitors as he strutted up to the plate with his Red Sox cap turned backward. "These guys are going down, and they won't need parachutes."

That raised a laugh, and Aaron smiled as he took his stance at the plate. Then he brought the bat to his shoulder, tightened his jaw, and stared hard at Jack the Knack. Jack stared back for what felt like a long time. I realized I was holding my breath.

An eternal moment passed, and then everything happened at once. Jack fired off a high-speed pitch and Aaron smashed it right back at him, dropped his bat, and came pounding down the baseline toward me like a locomotive. The crack of the bat was still sounding as Jack snatched at the ground, pivoted, and drilled the ball straight at my sternum and hard enough to restart my heart, which seemed to have quit beating.

With Aaron bearing down on me, instinct took over. My glove at my chest, I planted my left foot on the base and lunged to the right. I didn't so much catch the ball as let it strike me, like an arrow striking a target. But I closed the glove tight, and though I staggered with the force of Jack's throw, I didn't take my foot off the base. *Yes.*

When I opened my eyes the smoke jumpers were cheering uproariously and Aaron was walking away without a backward glance. His shoulders were slumped, and my petty triumph began to feel sour. All this bickering was getting out of hand.

"Aaron? Wait a minute." He kept going.

"What a play, what a woman!"

Jack rushed over to embrace me, but I held him off, and then I heard a familiar tomboy voice.

"Not bad, Kincaid, not bad at all."

The Tyke was advancing across the grass. Time to quit while I was ahead. I tossed the Tyke her mitt, waved to my teammates, and rejoined the boisterous crowd at the picnic tables.

A few of the guys commented on my catch, but most of them were busy with their burgers. Someone handed me a beer, and I poured half of it down my throat as the adrenaline drained from my system. I headed for the grill as I drank, feeling suddenly ravenous.

Food Bob greeted me with a flourish of his long-handled spatula. "I bet you're a medium-rare lady."

"Medium-well," I told him. "And I'll take two."

I polished off both burgers and was seriously contemplating the cherry pie before I remembered B.J.'s necklace. I glanced around. With everybody playing ball or chowing down, and with Aaron busy in the outfield, this was just the right moment to search through Brian's belongings. I felt in my pocket for the padlock combination, took a fortifying swallow of beer, and wandered casually inside.

Chapter Twenty-One

BESIDES HAVING DAYLIGHT TO SEE BY, ON THIS SECOND FORAY into the ready shack I knew my way around. I slipped through the dispatch room and past the sewing machines, then instead of continuing on to the parachute loft I followed B.J.'s instructions and took the stairwell down to the lower level.

As I descended, my footsteps on the concrete stairs grew louder than the party noise filtering in from outside. The base office was staffed today, but this main building seemed to be empty.

B.J. had told me that the jumpers' personal lockers were down on the lower level, but in a corridor on the way to the gym, not inside the shower room itself. Good thing, too. Empty building or not, I had no intention of invading the smoke-jumpers' showers. I'd had enough naked bodies for one day.

Except maybe Aaron's, and something told me that putting him out at first base had probably killed my chance to get lucky tonight. Men take sports so seriously.

I emerged from the stairwell into a wide hallway. The air down here was tinged with that sweat-and-disinfectant aroma that signals a weight room nearby. Beyond a pair of rest rooms stretched a long row of lockers, their slatted metal doors illuminated by the windows high on the opposite wall.

I walked along the row with the padlock combination in my hand.

Each locker was marked with the owner's surname, and most of them were decorated with funny magnets and goofy stickers and snapshots of little kids and pretty girls. I saw a lot of smoke-jumper emblems, along with "Everybody Out of the Gene Pool!" and "Keep Honking, I'm Reloading" and a death's-head logo that said "Vomit Shop," which I hoped was a band and not a retail establishment.

Some of the jumpers' names were familiar: Packard, of course, and Taichert, Kane, Soriano, Gibson. But there were plenty of others: Schorzmann, Uehling, Fox . . . *Thiel.*

My stomach knotted around Bob's burgers. The door that said "Thiel" was hanging open, and the locker was empty. Cleared out. Absolutely bare, save for a few curling scraps of Scotch tape left clinging to its metal insides.

Damn. B.J. would have to lie to Matt after all. And after that, she'd have to live with the possibility of the necklace resurfacing and giving rise to awkward questions. Poor B.J. I spared a moment to be grateful for the anonymity of a big city like Seattle. But only a moment, because at that point I heard footsteps in the stairwell, and then men's voices.

Adrenaline surged again, spreading like a hot, prickly fluid under my skin. I told myself the men were probably just guests looking for the rest rooms—which wasn't a bad excuse for me to be down here myself. I hurried back up the corridor into the women's room and waited for the men to pass. But instead they halted at the foot of the stairs and continued what seemed to be an argument.

"So let's hear it," demanded a low, menacing voice that I recognized as Danny Kane's. "You and the Tyke have been sitting on something about Thiel and I want to know what it is."

"Dunno what you're talking about."

The other voice was a sullen mumble, hard to make out, but I thought it belonged to Todd Gibson. Danny's next words confirmed my guess.

"Sure you do, Ned," he prodded. "I saw the official findings. You radioed in when you spotted his chute, but you didn't report the accident until seventeen minutes later. What the fuck were you and Taichert doing for seventeen minutes?"

"I told you, she wasn't there!" Todd sounded frightened. "She didn't get there till after I called in. It just took me some time to get to . . . to find the . . ."

I leaned my ear closer to the crack in the door.

"The body," said Danny. "The dead man. The corpse. Say it!"

I cringed, as Todd must be cringing, from the cruel words.

"OK!" he said. "I found the corpse, and I radioed in right away. The Tyke showed up a couple of minutes later, and then you came, and that's all."

"That *better* be all."

I heard a thump and a clanging noise, as if Danny had shoved the younger man against the lockers. He said something more, but I lost it in a burst of laughter from above. Someone else had entered the building.

The two men fell silent, then one of them went rapidly up the stairwell. After a moment the other followed, his footsteps slow and uneven. I waited long enough for them to get clear and then went upstairs myself, past a trio of carefree guests looking for the rest rooms, and stepped out into the bright, innocent world of sunshine and baseball.

The game was still in progress, of course, and the tables were still crowded, though I felt like I'd been in the basement for hours. Todd had taken a seat by himself, but Danny was already in the parking lot getting into his car. I went around the corner of the building and leaned against the wall, thinking hard.

So Danny Kane suspects foul play, too. No wonder I'd observed him drinking so much and acting so temperamental. He was a smoke jumper, and right now he believed that one of his comrades, or maybe two of them, had murdered another. *No wonder.*

Was Danny's only clue the time discrepancy in the radio calls, I mused, or had he noticed something out of order at the accident scene itself? Dr. Nothstine said the photographs showed Brian's PG bag unclipped from his harness, and a suspicious wound on the back of his head. Danny could have seen all that in person, and followed up by examining the official report.

It would be simple enough to ask him, but I wasn't sure that would be wise. Danny had been drinking a lot since Brian's death, and down in the basement just now he'd sounded almost violent, like a man in a nightmare. "Something weak in his character," who had told me that?

In any case, I didn't want to fuel Danny's suspicions with my own, for fear that he'd do something rash. Especially now with this new information—if it was fact and not illusion—about a campsite near the Boot Creek fire. If Al Soriano really did see a tent down there, then the field of suspects for murder went far beyond Todd Gibson and Pari Taichert, and Danny could awake from his nightmare of murder within the brotherhood.

But he's convinced that those two were hiding something, and

I thought that, too. In fact, I still do. I shook my head in frustration. My thoughts were spinning in circles, and I needed someone to help me straighten them out. But my first choice of someone was busy playing center field. Maybe he could take a time-out . . . I stepped away from the wall and scanned the baseball diamond. Aaron wasn't anywhere in sight. Had he left early?

Maybe that was just as well. I still hadn't decided whether I owed him an apology, or vice versa. So I dug out my cell phone—it showed a couple of missed calls—and reached B.J. at work.

"Finally!" she said. "I've been chewing my nails to the elbows. Did you find it?"

"Sorry. The locker's been cleared out." I gave her a moment for this to sink in. "I'll help you explain things to Matt, OK? But listen, I heard something new about Boot Creek that I need to talk over with you. Can I come by the nursery after I'm done working here?"

"Fine," she said dully. "Whatever."

"I'll get there as soon as I can. Hang in there."

The bachelor party was going well, but the number of guests had swelled far beyond expectations. I offered my services to Bob, who allowed as how he could use an extra pair of hands slicing pie. So I pitched in for a while, and even made a beer run back into town.

Finally, in late afternoon, I checked in with him one last time, and he waved me away with a smile. "Everything's under control now, m'dear. You get on with your other business. Oh, by the by, any idea where Beau's at this afternoon? His office just called me looking for him, and then Cissy did the same thing."

I couldn't very well say that Beautiful Beau was probably

in a shower somewhere with Overripe Olivia. So I promised to keep an eye out for him and headed for my car, listening to my messages on the way.

One was Paliere Productions in New York, asking for Beau, and the other was Dr. Nothstine, asking me to call. She didn't answer, so I left her my own message. I think that's why cell phones were invented, to increase the amount of telephone tag in our lives.

I didn't call New York, though. The office was probably closed by now, with the time difference, but that wasn't the reason. I decided to let Beau make his own explanations, whenever he finally surfaced. I was the assistant planner here, not his personal secretary.

I found B.J. out back of the nursery, sitting on an up-ended wheelbarrow among the tubs of aspen saplings and baby crabapple trees. A roof of shade cloth dimmed the sunlight here, but I could see the tear tracks on her face.

"I'm so sorry, Muffy." I laid a hand on the shoulder of her High Country Gardens T-shirt. "Matt will believe you about the necklace being lost, you'll see. It'll be all right."

"I guess. I'm just so mad at myself for having to lie to him in the first place. And all for a roll in the hay with a bastard like Brian Thiel. You know what Steve told me?"

"Who's Steve?"

"The bartender at the Pio. I was fishing around about people's alibis for Tuesday night, like I said I would, and he went off on this rant about smoke jumpers. He told me that one night he saw Brian in a corner, making out with the Tyke!"

"*What?* She told me she hardly knew him."

"That's not what Steve said. He said they were going at it like crazy. He was all disgusted because he knows the Tyke's got a boyfriend." She lifted her tearstained face. "What if people knew about Brian and *me*? What would they say then? What's Matt going to say?"

I was startled—no, shocked—to hear about Brian and the Tyke, but I didn't have time to think about it. B.J. was beginning to cry again, and I sat beside her.

"Matt's never going to know, Muffy. And you're going to forget about Brian and concentrate on improving your marriage. Come on, chin up."

B.J. sniffled into a tissue, and then sat up straight and squared her shoulders. "Well, like you said, what's done is done."

"There you go. Now tell me, what did you find out about Tuesday night?"

"Nothing definite. People were coming and going all night."

"Well, that may not matter anymore. Listen to this . . ."

I was just finishing my story about the campsite that Al Soriano had spotted, when B.J.'s assistant, a bright-eyed college girl named Liz, called to her from the door of the garden store.

"Someone to see you, boss. I'll be out front watering the hanging baskets."

"Why not send them back here, then?" B.J. groused.

But she headed inside, with me following, and we soon saw why not. The visitor was Dr. Nothstine, ensconced in a white wicker peacock chair that B.J. had for sale among the pots and the patio furniture. She looked drawn and tired, and her twisted leg lay limply to one side. But she sat her throne with dignity, like an aristocrat about to issue orders to the servants.

"I apologize for interrupting you at work," she began, with an intriguing little smile.

"No problem," said B.J. "In fact, you should hear this. Carnegie says there might have been somebody camping at Boot Creek at the time of the fire."

The doctor's smile froze in place, and I could see the brisk intelligence working behind her faded blue eyes. "So the killer might not have been a smoke jumper at all. This changes everything. We shall have to—"

"Hey, hey, guess who came back early?" A grinning Liz pulled open the front door, sloshing water from her sprinkler can, and stepped aside to reveal a good-looking wide-shouldered fellow holding a suitcase.

"Matt? Oh, *Matt.*"

B.J. flew into her husband's arms, and his embrace lifted her right off the floor. A charming moment, but all I could think was: *What is she going to tell him?*

Then Dr. Nothstine beckoned me to her side with a stealthy little movement of one hand. As B.J. and Matt went on smooching, she dipped the hand in her purse, fished something out, and dropped it quickly into my palm. I caught a glitter of metal and closed my fingers over the cool silver coils of B.J.'s necklace.

No time for questions. I stashed the necklace in my pocket and mouthed a silent "thank you" just as Matt came up for air.

"Carnegie, hello!" he said heartily. "We haven't seen you for way too long."

I'd always liked Matt, and now I could give him my usual hug and kiss without reservation. "It's good to be here. This is Dr. Julie Nothstine. I don't know if you've met?"

Matt greeted her with a courteous handshake, and th

canny old lady held onto his hand and his attention just long enough for me to slip the necklace to B.J. Her face sagged for a moment in astonishment and relief, then she whipped it out of sight and held up her beaming face for another kiss from her man.

"Young lady," Dr. Nothstine said to me as she rose from her throne, "I believe our presence is no longer required. Perhaps you could walk me to my car."

She filled me in along the way. "I returned to the base this morning, as I told you I would. The gentlemen there refused to meet with me, but as luck would have it, a box containing your cousin's effects was brought into the office just as I was leaving. I asked the secretary to fetch me a glass of water, and while she was gone—"

"You swiped the necklace!"

"I wouldn't put it quite like that. But I'm pleased to have returned it to the rightful owner. A good morning's work, and now I'm in need of my afternoon's rest. Perhaps we can discuss your new discovery later on."

"Of course." I opened the car door for her. "Dr. Nothstine, can I hug you?"

She lifted her chin. "Certainly not. But you may call me Julie."

My cell phone sounded as she drove off. This time it was Cissy Kane, mother of the bride, calling to pay her respects to tradition. She was performing a special ritual, a wedding custom that's been cherished and nurtured by mothers of the bride for centuries, perhaps millennia.

Cissy was going ballistic.

Chapter Twenty-Two

"WHAT DO YOU MEAN, YOU DON'T KNOW WHERE HE IS? What kind of wedding planner are you? He's chasing after one of those actresses, isn't he?"

Cissy was stalking angrily up and down the Paliere suite—if a short lady with a figure like a balloon can be said to stalk. It was more of an infuriated bounce, exaggerated by the fluttery sleeves of her pale purple sundress.

"How could he disappear like this?" she moaned. "Even Shara Mortimer used to answer her phone. And why won't Sam answer his? He's off at some construction site, but don't they have phones? This is all his fault!"

"Cissy, please sit down." I shut the door behind me with a sigh. Who wants to be closeted with a madwoman?

I had driven back to the lodge at top speed to find Cissy in the lobby, red-faced and quivering, having a full-blown meltdown. I've seen some amazing temper tantrums in my business, but this was off the charts. Various members of the staff were hovering around her like zookeepers around a rogue rhino, and the other guests were trying hard not to stare.

Herding Cissy upstairs to the suite had at least removed us from the public eye, but despite her ravings, I still didn't know what had set her off—except that at some point she'd noticed Beau Paliere flirting with someone besides herself. A least she didn't know which specific actress he was chasing. We didn't need a blowup between the mother of the bride and the maid of honor.

"This is a disaster," Cissy said, her voice breaking. "A *catastrophe!*"

She was working herself into a frenzy. Time for sterner measures. I slapped the back of the needlepoint love seat— in lieu of her face—and raised my own voice.

"Cissy, sit down. Right here, right now. Sit!"

She bridled, but she sat.

"All right, deep breath. In, out. That's good. One more. In, out. Good." She coughed a little, having ranted herself hoarse, so I got her a glass of water from the carafe on the conference table. She sipped at it, then shook a couple of round white pills from a bottle in her purse and gulped them down.

"Tranquilizer," she said with a dramatic sigh. "Sam says I take too many, but how else can I manage all this stress? I'm a very sensitive person."

"Of course you are," I said, with a serious effort not to sound sarcastic. "Now, tell me what's wrong."

I was expecting either a major calamity—the wedding was off—or a minor hitch, like another mismatched pair of shoes. Mothers of the bride can go either way. What I got was somewhere in between, but edging toward calamity.

"It's the Ladislaus Quartet," she said venomously, as if laying a curse on all four of them. "Their manager called. They've cancelled."

"But they can't," I said, taken aback. "Did he say why?"

"Something stupid about a coup," she said. "They're in Java or Jakarta or someplace stupid like that, and there's been a coup or an uprising or something and they can't travel. How could they do this to me?"

I let that one go. I was busy calling Beau's cell phone, but he didn't answer, and I couldn't wait for him. Did I have a number for Sebastian in Mexico? He was the entertainment director, so this was technically his problem, not mine or Beau's. But someone had to reach him as soon as possible. Wedding ensembles aren't available at a moment's notice.

"Cissy, we'll work something out, but I need to make some more calls. Why don't you—"

"I want Beau." Amazing, how dangerous those little rose-bud lips could look. She got to her feet again, ready to rejoin the battle. "He should be handling this, not you. We're paying him a fortune, and where is he?"

"I'll find him," I promised. I would, too, if I had to search Olivia's sheets to do it. "But meanwhile, why don't you go home and look over your outfit for the rehearsal dinner to-morrow? Or you and Sam can—"

"Sam is *working*," she said, waving the tumbler and sending droplets flying. "As if I'm not! He leaves all the real work to me, all these details about the wedding, hundreds of deci-sions. He goes off to work and Tracy goes off to play and no-body appreciates what I do, *damn* them all!"

I wouldn't have guessed such a chubby little arm could heave a water glass that far or that hard. At least she didn't throw it at me. The tumbler hit the minibar refrigerator and burst like a small bomb, spraying glass shards everywhere.

I yelped in alarm. Cissy broke into sobs. And someone rapped a jaunty shave-and-a-haircut on the suite's door. Given the alternatives, I answered the door.

"Aaron!" I practically dragged him inside. If anything could calm Cissy, it was an attractive new man. And even if Aaron was still mad at me, surely he'd rise to a crisis?

"Listen—" he began, but I cut him off.

"In a minute." I was whispering, though Cissy probably couldn't hear us above her own wailing. "I've got an emergency here. Help me out, OK?"

"What do you need?"

"Just be charming. *Major* charm."

Then I raised my voice to say brightly, "Cissy, here's my good friend Aaron Gold. This is Cissy Kane, Tracy's mother."

My hero. Without another word of explanation, Aaron came on like Cary Grant.

"You mean sister, don't you?" He set down the laptop he was carrying and took her hand in both of his. "Or else you had Tracy very young. Tell me all about the wedding, Cissy. Sun Valley seems like a perfect spot . . ."

He led her to the love seat and she followed like a lamb, leaving me with the mess. *Probably a lifelong pattern of hers,* I thought sourly, as I phoned Housekeeping for a vacuum.

I considered calling Olivia's room as well, to begin the hunt for Beau, but opted to wait till Cissy was out of the way. So I disposed of the bigger bits of glass and shook the slivers off my paperwork as Cissy prattled happily away at her new admirer.

The next knock on the door wasn't Housekeeping. It was my mother. She took in the broken glass, gave a knowing nod when I rolled my eyes at Cissy, and then joined us in the sitting area. I made introductions, we all sat down, and there was an expectant pause.

"So you're Aaron Gold," said Mom. "I thought you'd be taller."

"*Mom!*" Strange but truthful, that's Louise Kincaid.

Aaron just leaned back and laughed. "And I thought you'd have red hair."

"That was my late husband," she said, not quite hiding a smile. "Carrie has his temper, too."

"Does she have a temper? I hadn't noticed."

"Lucky you. Give her time."

As we went on chatting. I watched these two faces, so dear to me in their different ways. I could tell that Mom and Aaron approved of each other, and somewhere inside me a little knot of tension untied itself. I was surprised at how good that felt.

Cissy certainly approved of Aaron. She laid a coy hand on his arm and said, "I'm hungry, sweetie. Why don't we all go downstairs for a little bite to eat?"

"I would just love to, Cissy, but I can't." He gestured toward the laptop with a convincing show of regret. "I'm on a working vacation, and I have to get back to it. But I'll see both of you tomorrow, won't I?"

I begged off as well, and when Housekeeping came, the ladies got up to leave.

"You'll take care of the music, won't you?" Cissy asked me in parting.

"I'm not sure—" I began, but then I saw Mom beaming at me confidently, and I couldn't resist showing off for her. "I'm not sure who it will be, but I promise, Tracy will have her string quartet."

Once the glass was cleared away and I was alone with Aaron, I dropped into the love seat and blew out a sigh of relief. "Thanks a million."

"You're welcome a million. Is Cissy your usual kind of client? Your job's harder than I thought." He flipped opened his laptop on the conference table and jacked into the

Internet connection. "I like your mom, though. She's got you and your temper pegged."

I blushed, remembering my show of temper in his car earlier. "Aaron, I owe you an apology. But you have to understand, Eddie and Mom cooked up that whole story about Boris."

"Apology accepted," he said without even looking up from the keyboard. "But I'm still going to get you back for locking me out. Now, take a look at this."

"Why?" This was hardly the kiss-and-make-up scene I'd imagined. "I have calls to make, I really don't have time for—"

"Yes, you really do. Trust me. I left the ball game early when this guy in Seattle returned my call. Big expert on the Korean War."

Intrigued, I joined him at the table. "What's that got to do—"

"Cardinal rule of reporting, Stretch. Follow all your leads, especially with history buffs and old guys in newspaper offices." He went on tapping as he talked. "While I waited for you in the bar I got busy on the phone, including a call to the local paper here. Didn't find much about our three smoke jumpers, but I got an earful about Danny Kane's Uncle Roy. Then I put together everything I'd heard, and look."

He angled the glowing screen toward me. It showed a full-color picture of an exotic, ancient-looking headdress, fashioned all in gold and adorned with glass beads and bits of carved jade. Golden chains with links like leaves dangled down from the circular headband, and tall golden branches rose up from it. Their antlerlike shapes gave the piece a wild, barbaric air.

"Magnificent," I said. "What is it?"

"This, my dear Dr. Watson, is a Crown of Silla, a priceless

sixth-century Korean artifact. There was more than one, back then, but damn few are still in existence."

"And?"

He struck a key and the screen darkened. "And this one is identical, or near enough, to the one Roy Kane was accused of stealing from the Toksu Palace in Seoul in 1952."

"Oh my God." I sat down. "Julie Nothstine said something about an accusation of looting, but she insisted that Roy was cleared."

"Not according to rumor, Stretch," he said, taking a seat beside me. "According to rumor, Roy Kane brought his golden treasure back with him, and buried it somewhere near his fishing cabin at Tamarack Lake, which is where he committed suicide. And guess what Tamarack Lake is very close to?"

"Boot Creek?"

"Bingo. Supposing the spot where he buried the crown was burned over in the fire, and when your cousin climbed out of that tree he found it. And supposing one of the other smoke jumpers..." Aaron hesitated, frowning. "OK, this is the part I have trouble with. One of the smoke jumpers hikes over to Brian, sees him with the crown, and kills him for it? Doesn't seem very likely."

"It doesn't have to! You haven't heard *my* piece of news. Actually, there's two."

I told him both, first about Al Soriano glimpsing a tent amid the smoke, and second about how Danny Kane suspected Todd and the Tyke of murdering Brian. There was actually a third item, the tidbit about the Tyke fooling around with Brian at the Pioneer. But somehow I forgot about that one as Aaron leaned closer, listening keenly, until I could feel the warmth of his body in the air-conditioned room. The excitement of all this investigating was sparking a certain, well, excitement.

"So I suppose we could join forces with Danny," I said, trying to stick to business, "but he's so volatile right now, I'm afraid of setting him off. And anyway, he's on the wrong track. I'm sure Brian was killed by someone else, not a smoke jumper at all. Someone who knew about the Crown of Silla and . . . That doesn't work, does it?"

"Nope. Thiel finding Roy Kane's buried treasure would have been a completely random event. No one could have anticipated that, so our mysterious camper was at Boot Creek for some other reason." He made a face. "Why do people go camping anyway, don't they have beds at home? I've never understood that."

Aaron was being facetious, but I considered the question seriously. "Al said the Boot Creek area is hard to get to, so the killer must have been physically fit enough to hike in there."

"That sounds like half the guys in this town. At least it's a small town, so we can ask around. The bachelor party is adjourning to someplace called the Casino Club after the game. It's supposed to be a local hangout, so why don't we start there?"

"Good idea."

"I'm full of good ideas, Stretch," he said, and leaned forward to kiss me. I wasn't the only one feeling distracted here. "Mostly about you . . ."

I leaned away. "My dear Sherlock, can you play Mozart's 'Eine Kleine Nachtmusik' on the cello?"

"Huh? No."

"I didn't think so. That means you have to go away while I find somebody who can."

"It's always something with you, isn't it? Can you join the party later?"

"I'll try. Now go."

So he went—after a kiss or two, or six. When it came to kissing, I thought dreamily as the door closed behind him, Aaron Gold was the winner and still champion.

With that point settled I got back to work, trying Beau again and then sifting my files for Sebastian's number. Nothing. I even phoned the Paliere office in New York, but with the time difference they were already closed. So I bit the bullet and called Olivia's room.

At first she affected not to know where Beau might be. She was an actress, after all.

"Beau Paliere? Why, I can't imagine. We were chatting by the pool earlier but—"

I didn't have time to play along. "Save it, Olivia, I know the man. Is he still there with you or has he left? Come on, this is important."

"He left for the White Pine Inn half an hour ago," she said flatly. "He wanted to look over the wedding site. You know, I would really prefer that you didn't—"

"Not a word. But he wasn't answering his cell."

"Oh, he left it here." She giggled. "It rang at the worst possible moment, so he turned it off and then it fell under the bed. Do you need it?"

"No, I need *him*," I snapped. "And there's no cell service at White Pine, anyway. I suppose I could drive up there after him . . ."

And have him snub me again? Forget it. I said good-bye to Olivia and sat pondering. After all, what could Beau do that I couldn't? He wasn't the only wedding planner around here. I had my own contacts. Surely I could come up with some musicians on short notice. I'd made a promise, and I didn't need him to fulfill it.

An hour later, I wasn't so sure. And neither was Eddie Breen, when I called him at home in Seattle and asked him to help me out. I'm supposedly Eddie's boss, but you would never know it, to hear him.

"It's Thursday night, for chrissakes! You never did call me back to explain what the hell you think you're doing over there, and now you want me to find you a classical quartet for Saturday afternoon in Idaho?"

"Eddie, please, I've made a commitment to this wedding. I need to show them what I can do, but I can't find anyone in Ketchum, or even in Boise, who's not already booked. Please?"

"All right, already. I'll call around."

We both called around, but to no avail. I'd almost given up and resigned myself to turning the problem over to Beau after all, when a brilliant idea came to me. Goofy, but brilliant. I called Chief of Police Larabee, and the problem was solved.

Now I just needed the bride to sign off on my solution before her mother had a chance to throw another fit. Tracy had skipped the softball game, but with any luck she'd be at the postgame party. I was on my way out the door when B.J. called.

"Muffy, I will love you forever," she said, her voice low and surreptitious. "Matt's in the bathroom. How'd you do it?"

"I didn't." It was good to hear her so happy. "You can thank Julie Nothstine. She found the necklace in—"

"Isn't that nice," said B.J., much louder, and I knew her

husband was back in the room. "Matt and I are going out for
a late supper. Want to come?"

"I'm still full of hamburger," I told her. "And anyway, I'm
going to the Casino Club. I bet I can find a nice Jewish guy
there who'll buy me a drink."

Chapter Twenty-Three

THE CASINO CLUB HASN'T BEEN A REAL CASINO FOR FIFTY years, although illegal poker games persisted there for some decades after that. These days the only games happen at the pool tables, but a framed sketch of some Ketchum residents bent over their cards still hangs in the front hall of the Casino for old times' sake.

I passed the sketch on my way in, and stood for a moment adjusting to the noise level and taking in the scene. Especially the scene at the bar, where most of the bachelor party crowd, home team and visitors alike, had gathered to raise their voices in song.

They were belting out a lewd and lengthy ditty, inventing verses as they went and capping every chorus with a generous glugging of beer. Terrible singers, but excellent drinkers.

Well, well, I thought. *Who knew?* Who knew that a citified reporter out of Boston would get along so well with a bunch of ballplayers from L.A., not to mention a swarm of smoke jumpers from Idaho? Of course, the jumpers hailed from all over the country, but I was still surprised to see Aaron bellied up to the bar with Todd Gibson's arm draped over his shoulders and Al Soriano lighting all three of their cigars.

I didn't want to barge in, so I slipped into a seat at the back and bought my own drink. For that matter, I mused as the waitress left me, who knew that a smoke jumper's bachelor party could be such a good-natured, almost wholesome, affair? The song was more lusty than nasty, and the choir included both female jumpers and many of their comrades' girlfriends.

I guess if you're tough enough to leap from a plane and battle a fire—and if you're pushing forty, as Jack was—you don't feel obliged to ogle strippers and drink till you vomit. How refreshing.

Not that this crowd wasn't having a good time. As I listened to the high-spirited laughter at the song's conclusion, and the volley of wisecracks over at the pool tables, I compared the mood tonight with Sunday's strained gaiety at the Pioneer. No one had forgotten Brian, but tonight the celebration of life, in the form of Jack's wedding, had pushed death into the background.

But not for me, not yet. Realistically, I had to admit that the nameless camper might be impossible to identify. But was I willing to let Brian's death be written off as an accident, one that the victim brought on himself?

No. I didn't care for my cousin, and he treated B.J. badly, but no. I couldn't collar his killer myself, but surely I could stir up enough information to make the police take notice. That was the least I could do, and I was determined to do it. When my wine came—I'd had enough beer for the year—I raised my glass in a private farewell to Brian Thiel.

"Look, it's the star of first base!" Jack stopped on his way past my table with Tracy hanging on his arm, looking for all the world like a fond and faithful fiancée. He was freshly showered and glowing with vigor, but she was pretty green around the gills. Tequila is tough stuff. "Trace, you should have seen this catch she made."

The bride gave me a deer-in-the-headlights stare. "Oh! I . . . I didn't know you'd be here."

That much was clear, but it was also clear that Tracy had come to her senses. The bitchy arrogance of this afternoon was gone, replaced by a contrite and even anxious smile. She must be wondering if I planned to spill the beans about her and Domaso.

Serve her right if I did, I thought, but I knew I wouldn't have the heart. Or the inclination, given the groom's recent behavior. At times like this, a wise wedding planner stays out of the crossfire. So I turned my farewell into a salute.

"Cheers, you two. Quite a party."

"Oh, we're just getting started," said Jack, and gave me a mischievous wink. You almost had to admire his gall. Then someone waved from across the room and he gave them the finger, but in an amiable way. "Hey, the guys from Montana showed up! Come on, sweetheart, you'll love these guys."

As he towed Tracy away she said over her shoulder, "I need to talk with you tonight, OK?"

"Sure. I've got something to ask you about, too. Come find me."

As they disappeared into the crowd, Aaron emerged from it, his face flushed and his eyes shining. He smelled like tobacco, but he looked handsome as hell.

"Glad you made it, Stretch." He dropped into a chair. "God, these smoke jumpers are great people. I'm having a great time."

"I can tell."

He rolled his eyes. "Give me a break, would you? The groom gave out cigars. What was I supposed to do, throw it away?"

"I didn't mean that, honestly. I just meant I can tell you're enjoying yourself. Aaron, am I that much of a nag?"

He was suddenly serious. "You can be, Carnegie. Sometimes you really can be a nag."

I blinked rapidly against the stinging in my eyes. *Must be the smoke.* "I'm only thinking about your health, you know."

"I know that, Stretch. Never mind, I shouldn't have said it." He took my hand and gave it a little shake, side to side. "Let's change the subject. Before I joined the choir, I was asking some locals about Boot Creek."

"Did you find out who went camping there?"

"Well, no. But I did find out why somebody might have been. Turns out it's a primo trout stream, so fishermen hike in there from time to time. Not often, because it's hard to get to. And one guy told me about an old hermit who supposedly lives up there and runs people off."

"A hermit? Maybe he was the killer!"

"I thought about that, too, but then the bartender told me it's just a story the fishermen tell to keep other fishermen away. Pretty soon we'll be pinning the murder on Sasquatch."

"But it's worth checking out, don't you think? Julie Nothstine might know if there's any truth to the story. She's lived around here forever."

"Maybe." Aaron waved for the waitress. "Excuse me, miss?"

She came over and he ordered Scotch rocks. It wasn't his first one, or even his second, as I could tell by the way he suddenly shifted to yet another subject.

"This smoke-jumping business, it's really something. One of the guys here is a cardiologist, did you know that? He's been back every summer for ten years now, just to keep jumping fire. Isn't that amazing? I mean, dirty, dangerous work that doesn't pay all that well, and a doctor can't wait to spend his summer doing it? They get sent all over the west, too, Alaska to Arizona, anywhere there's a fire. You should hear the stories these guys tell. . . ."

Aaron, I realized, had caught the bug. He was falling in love with smoke jumping. I watched him fondly as the words came tumbling forth about the camaraderie and the courage and the exploits. It was Todd Gibson all over again. Not the hero worship, exactly—Aaron was older than Todd, and more sophisticated—but enthusiasm, admiration, and even envy.

"It's like war," he said at one point. "Izzy, my grandfather, he was at Pearl Harbor. All that death and destruction, but he calls World War Two the best years of his life. You don't get that intensity working in an office, you know? Fighting wildfires is like war, but you're saving lives instead of taking them. Danny Kane was saying—"

"Danny's here?" I stood up and gazed around. Most of the revelers had gathered around one of the pool tables, and through a gap in the bodies I could see that Danny was playing Peter Props. I sat down again and said quietly, "I'm still wondering if we should tell him what we've found out, and ask him why he suspects Todd and the Tyke of killing Brian. Maybe he can help us."

"I don't know, Stretch. I've been keeping an eye on old Danny, and I think your first impression was right. He's awfully jumpy. I vote we wait till we know more."

"I guess. Let's go watch them, anyway."

I've always wished I could shoot pool. Not enough to actually learn the game and practice, but it isn't the skill I want anyway. It's the attitude. Pool players always look so cool.

Aaron and I found a place among the jammed-in spectators. Even Danny Kane, unprepossessing as he was, looked

cool as he bent over the table with brooding intensity to cal-
culate his shot. There were only two balls left on the deep
green felt, a solid and a stripe. The game was down to the
wire, and the crowd was keyed up high.

"You can do it, Kane, just take it easy."

"Aw, he's gonna blow it for sure."

Judging by the catcalls, this was a grudge match. Danny
was defending the honor of the smoke jumpers against the
Californians. Or at least defending their money. One of the
onlookers clutched a fistful of five- and ten-dollar bills.

"Piece of cake, Danny Boy."

"Shut up, you'll jinx him!"

Danny's expression never changed. He slowly drew back
his cue, deliberated for one last moment, and slammed the
cue ball hard at the far corner. Too hard. His target ball, the
solid, went spinning into the pocket and bounced right out
again, while the cue ball popped off the edge of the table and
onto the floor.

"I've got you now, sucker!" crowed Peter, over the tri-
umphant jeers of the L.A. crowd. "You're a dead man now. A
dead man!"

He didn't mean anything by it, of course. Why would he?
But I heard someone gasp, and saw the dismay on Todd
Gibson's face, and on others.

"Oh, brother," Aaron muttered, close at my side.

Danny went white. He opened his mouth to speak, then
seemed to realize how many people were watching his reaction. He bent abruptly to pick up the cue ball, and smacked
it down on the table even harder than he'd hit it in the first
place. Then he turned on his heel and left.

The silence that fell was not what you want to hear at a
party. I considered throwing myself into the breach with a

toast to the happy couple or something lame like that, but I couldn't see where Jack and Tracy had gone.

The Tyke had a better idea, anyway. From over at the bar she called out, "Hey, you bozos! Who wants to arm wrestle?"

"Her?" said Aaron. "That's ridiculous. I'm sure she's strong, but still—"

"Give it a try, then," I said. "I dare you."

His eyes narrowed. "Maybe I will. Hey, I think your bride wants you."

Tracy was gesturing to me from a small door beyond the bar. When I reached her she drew me outside to an alley behind the building. The night air was still warm, but it felt fresh after the fumes within, and I breathed it in gratefully.

In the faint light that reached us from the streetlamps, the television star looked positively scared of me. I must say, I enjoyed that just a bit.

I waited a moment but she didn't speak, so I went first. "Tracy, did Cissy tell you about the Ladislaus Quartet?"

She nodded indifferently. "Um, about this afternoon—"

"I'd prefer to forget all about that. Let's just forget it and get on with the wedding."

"Wait!" She clutched my arm. "Did you . . . are you going to . . ."

"I'm not saying a word. I only wish I didn't know, that's all. And I wish you didn't think there was anything between me and Jack except—"

"I don't think that. Dom told me later what really happened. I'm sorry."

And how the hell would he know what really happened? I asked myself. For all Domaso knew, Jack and I could have been carrying on at the hot spring for hours. Perish the thought.

"But I want to explain about me and Dom," Tracy was saying. "We fool around sometimes, that's all. We always do, when I'm in town. I'm not going to keep doing it, you know. It's just that, it's just . . ." I was startled to see that she was close to tears. "It's just that I'm scared."

"Scared? Of what?"

"Of getting married. Jack's wonderful, but he wants to have *children*."

"And you don't?"

"I don't know!" she moaned. "I guess so. I don't even know if I want to be married. I just got so excited about having a wedding and then . . ."

"Then it took on a life of its own?"

"Uh-huh."

I'd seen this before. And much as I dreaded the outcome, I gave Tracy Kane the same advice I'd given my other brides whose feet turned cold in their dyed-to-match pumps.

"Honey, listen to me. It's not easy to cancel a wedding, or even postpone one, but it's a lot easier than canceling a marriage. The wedding is just an event, just a ceremony and a party. The marriage is what's important. So you think this over carefully, and you talk it over with Jack, all right? And if you really do want to change your plans, I'll help you every step of the way."

"Oh, *Muffy*!" She was weeping now, so I hugged her and patted her shoulder and pulled out one of the spare handkerchiefs I always carry. I never get them back, so I buy boxes.

"But if you *do* proceed with the wedding," I said as she sniffled and dabbed, "I need your go-ahead about the music. I've found a string quartet of high-school students who play private parties in Ketchum. The cellist is the police chief's son."

She looked dazed. "High school?"

"I'm told they're pretty good, and the media will love it. Tracy Kane, big star, still a hometown girl at heart. So is that all right?"

"Anything you say, Carnegie."

"And you'll keep Cissy from fussing about it?"

"Absolutely." Tracy's composure was returning, and with it her confidence. She'd be bossing me around again in no time. "It's my wedding, not hers."

"That's the spirit. Now come inside, I think we might be missing something good."

Sure enough, the chanting hit us as we opened the door.

"Talent Show, Talent Show, Talent Show!"

Over the heads of the crowd I saw the Tyke perched up on the bar, her ponytail coming loose and a victorious grin on her face. I pushed my way through to the front. Aaron stood below her, flexing his aching hand and smiling ruefully. *Good man*, I thought. I'd been hoping he would take his defeat gracefully.

But then the Tyke raised her beer mug to pronounce sentence, and I was suddenly horrified at the thought of my deskbound guy being humiliated in front of all these other men. What if she said one-armed push-ups, or something even harder? What had I done?

"Aaron Gold," the Tyke declared, "your best talent is . . ."

She paused doubtfully, and into the hush that fell I piped up and said, "Kissing! He's talented at kissing."

Pandemonium. Everyone whooped and roared, and Aaron gave me a glittering look and laughed aloud.

"Excellent suggestion." The Tyke waved her mug, anointing him with a slosh of beer. "Go ahead, mister, give it your best shot."

I edged forward, blushing, and that was when Aaron Gold got me back for locking him out of the suite.

He slapped both hands on the bar, vaulted up next to the astonished Tyke, wrapped one arm around her shoulders and the other around her neck, and laid on a long, *long,* passionate kiss that brought down the house.

When he was finished, another hush descended as the crowd waited breathlessly for the Tyke's reaction. Would she laugh at Aaron, or swear at him, or clobber him senseless?

But the Tyke did exactly what I would have done. She ran her tongue slowly across her lips, looked Aaron up and down, and said, "Best two out of three?"

Chapter Twenty-Four

"AARON SEEMS NICE."

"He's very nice, Mom. Please don't touch anything."

My mother put down the pink gerbera daisy she'd been twirling between her fingers. It was Friday, the morning after the Talent Show and the day before the wedding, and we were visiting the floral workstation. Mom had never seen me on the job before, so she was tagging along as I did my rounds of checking on Food Bob and Photo Bob and Boris. I still hadn't heard from Beau, but given what I was dealing with, that was fine with me.

Having Mom along was a distraction, but hardly my only one. In addition to pondering Brian's death, I was wondering whether my bride was going to cancel her wedding. And on top of all that, I was half asleep. After Aaron's performance with the Tyke, I had vowed to lock him out again—then spent much of the night letting him change my mind.

Now Aaron was off somewhere consulting with Julie Nothstine about trout fishermen and hermits and the spoils of war, while I went through the motions of getting Tracy Kane married. At least the flowers seemed to be shaping up well.

The floral crew was appropriately busy as bees, chatting

gaily and zooming in and out of the refrigerated trailer as if it
were their hive. They buzzed industriously around the work
tables, gloved against the rose thorns and constantly misting
their materials from spray bottles to combat the rising heat.

As Mom and I watched, scissors snipped briskly, spools of
floral tape spun merrily around, and blocks of green foam
were carefully carved and soaked and fitted into white porcelain bowls and elegant silver epergnes for the rehearsal dinner tables. Our general themes were candlelight and lilies for
tonight, sunshine and roses for the ceremony tomorrow.

I snagged a worker bee as she zipped past. "Is Boris
around?"

"Can't you hear him?" She nodded toward the trailer. "Poor
Wallace."

Now that I listened for it, I could make out the disgrun-
tled rumbling of the Russian's voice. I told Mom to stay put
and entered the chilly atmosphere inside. The trailer was half
full of finished arrangements today, and I tried to thrust yesterday's image of Tracy and Domaso romping among the
tubs and sacks to the back of my mind.

"Then you must find space!" Boris bellowed, as Wallace
cringed. "Kharnegie, is no cold space for buddy flowers. I
cannot mek them all tomorrow, I must start today, but must
be cold space!"

"Buddy . . . oh, body flowers." Body flowers are bouquets,
boutonnieres and corsages, as opposed to tabletops and garlands and covered tent poles and such. Boris was an expert
at directing the adornment of spaces, but he liked to create
all the personal pieces with his own two gigantic hands.

I reviewed the possibilities. "The kitchen can't loan you
one of their coolers?"

"Full of food," said Boris, disgusted at the thought of protecting mere edibles instead of his creations. "All full."

"Well . . . I know, we'll crank up the air-conditioning in my suite, and you can store the dinner arrangements there for the afternoon." I couldn't get the suite down to forty degrees, the ideal temperature for flowers, but every little bit would help. "That will free up the trailer for tomorrow's flowers. How's that?"

"Brill-i-ant!" he bellowed, and engulfed me in a rib-crushing hug. Over his shoulder, I saw Wallace make a grateful thumbs-up and slip away. "Many thanks, my Kharnegie. Flowers will be magnificent for this wedding. Everything magnificent. You have talked to Beau today?"

"Not yet, but I need to tell him about a change in the music situation. He might not be too happy about it."

Boris tilted his shaggy head and pursed his lips lasciviously. "Beau is most happy with maid of honor. He will not mind about music, you will see."

"Let's hope. Come outside and say hello to my mother."

Mom had met Boris before, and she greeted him now with a wide smile and a shameless lack of concern for the fibs that she and Eddie had concocted about us. Boris surveyed the tables and his minions' work with satisfaction, then checked his watch.

"Beautiful ladies will have lunch with me, yes?"

But Mom, it seemed, had other plans. "I'm so sorry, Boris dear. I have a date already. Oh, there he is!"

She waved at someone approaching from the grassy lawn beside the parking lot: Sam Kane, shambling along with a companion by his side and his white Stetson bobbing in the sun. The other man, no doubt a wedding guest, looked to be in his early sixties, almost as tall as Sam but built much sturdier, with fair-haired, ruddy-cheeked good looks and a vigorous stride.

"You and Sam can join us, Mom," I said. "I need to speak with him, anyway. . . ."

I faded off here. While Sam was nodding genially at Boris, tipping his hat to me, and stooping to peer at the flowers, his companion marched right up to my mother and kissed her on the mouth. And she kissed him back. Hard.

"Carrie, dear," she said, and she was damn near glowing when she said it, "I'd like you to meet Owen Winter. Owen, my daughter Carnegie."

"Good to meet you," said this Owen person, his blue eyes twinkling. He had a thin tenor voice, the kind I dislike. "I feel like I know you already, from everything Lou's told me."

Lou? I didn't like that, either.

"We'll have to chat more later on, dear," Mom was saying. "Owen has promised me a wonderful afternoon on the Harriman Trail, a bicycle ride and a picnic, so we'd better be moving along."

They began to depart—holding hands, yet—when Mom paused and said, "Owen, did you ask Sam your fishing question? He wants to go trout fishing, Sam, but I told him I wouldn't have the faintest idea where. I thought you might know?"

"Nope, but I know who does," said Sam. "Domaso Duarte. He's around here this week. Duarte knows every secret trout stream in Blaine County. We'll get you fixed up, Owen."

Owen expressed his appreciation and escorted my mother away, leaving me standing there stupefied with startling thoughts flashing through my mind like heat lightning. *Mom and this new guy? Domaso and trout streams?*

"Your mouth's open, Red," said Sam. "That Winter's a handsome fella, isn't he? Good taste in women, too."

"I . . . yes, I can see that. Who is he, anyway?"

He chuckled. "Oh, I get it. Louise has been playing things close to the vest, huh? Winter just retired from Boeing. Pretty high up the food chain there, too."

"And he lives in Ketchum now?"

"Not yet, but he's thinking about it, and he's got the bucks to do it in style. I gave him a quote on one of my best view lots up at White Pine, and he didn't even blink. He'll be at the wedding and the dinner and all, though, so you can check him out yourself." Sam resettled his Stetson. "Now, Tracy told me about the switch in musicians."

"Right." I took a steadying breath and prepared to defend my unilateral decision. "I couldn't reach Beau last night, and I thought I'd better get on it right away. I really think this is the best solution—"

" 'Course it is!" He slapped me on the back and I staggered a little, not as steady as I thought. "It's just fine to have Larabee's kid playing his fiddle for us. No, it's the cello, isn't it, the big one? Anyhow, I heard them at a party last Christmas."

"How were they?" I asked, mental fingers crossed. The kids' references were good, but—

"Terrific! Practically professional. And I can always use a little extra support from our police force, if you know what I mean. Parking tickets and such. In fact, I invited the chief to the wedding so he can watch his boy perform."

"Good idea." I thought it over. "Actually, that's a very good idea."

The more I thought about it, the more certain I was that a police presence at White Pine was exactly what we needed. If Aaron and I could turn up enough information about Brian's death, or even stir up some kind of reaction from the killer, Chief Larabee would be on hand to take over from there.

I was less certain about the significance of Domaso's interest in trout. The Wood River Valley was teeming with fishermen, any one of whom could have been camping near the fire last Saturday, the day Brian died. *Although I did see fishing gear in Domaso's convertible on Monday. He could have been just coming back from Boot Creek—*

"Kharnegie!" Boris tapped my shoulder impatiently. "Do you take care of air-conditioning, or do I send someone?"

"Sorry, I'll go do it right now. I'll see you at dinner, Sam."

We weren't actually rehearsing the ceremony till tomorrow morning—it was too much trouble to transport everyone up to White Pine and down again—but then tonight's affair was less of a standard rehearsal dinner and more of a general bash. Between Tracy's photo ops and her father's business-related hospitality, this wedding wasn't standard at all.

I did my own mental rehearsal on the way to the lodge, running through the list of vendors I still had to check on. Beau may have planned this wedding, but he sure as hell wasn't directing it. I was.

As I crossed the lobby I glanced through the glass door of the Duchin Lounge. Speak of the French devil, there was Beau at a table for two, very much *tête-à-tête* with Olivia. They seemed to be arguing, but I pretended not to notice.

"Good morning," I said. "Beau, I've been trying to reach you since yesterday."

"And here you find me," he answered smoothly. But his tone carried a warning, from boss to underling. "As you see, however, I am engaged. Everything progresses well, *non*? You are capable of managing today's schedule without my direct supervision?"

"Of course I am," I snapped. "But there are some details we should—"

"You two go right ahead." The actress rose abruptly, her mouth tight and her considerable bosom lifting indignantly beneath a skimpy black crop top. "We're done talking. In fact, we're done altogether!"

Heads turned toward us from around the lounge. Beau captured one of Olivia's hands and drew her into her seat again, murmuring in French, pouring on the charm.

"*Ma chere,* in Paris one always flirts with the chambermaid. It meant nothing. . . ."

I thought I'd seen Beau in action before, but this was like watching a horse whisperer. Olivia's expression softened, her eyelids drooped and fluttered, and by the time I left the lounge he was nibbling on her fingertips and she was cooing like a contented dove. Amazing.

Back in the lobby, I heard a different kind of whispering. Staff and guests alike murmured and pointed, discreetly directing each others' attention to a side window that looked onto a private little alcove of the terrace outside.

At least, the man and the woman standing in the alcove must have thought it was private. On their side the sunlight would be bouncing off the white window curtain, making it look opaque. But the curtain was perfectly sheer from our side, affording us all a front-row seat for Tracy Kane's latest love scene.

And a charming scene it was, too. She was looking up into Jack's face, speaking rapidly, her palms on his chest and her lovely features set in earnest appeal. The words were inaudible but obviously persuasive, because Jack bent closer and closer, spoke a few words in reply, and enveloped her in a tender embrace.

Throughout the lobby, their unseen audience let out a single, satisfied sigh. Mine was especially sincere, being a sigh of profound relief, and I headed upstairs with a far lighter heart. The wedding was on.

I found Aaron and Julie—it was hard not to think of her as Dr. Nothstine—sitting on the love seat with the coffee table pulled close, surveying a room-service tray of sandwiches and iced tea. Her cane lay on the floor by their feet.

"Hey there, Stretch," said Aaron. "This seemed like the most private place for us to have lunch. Dr. Nothstine's been telling me something really interesting."

She frowned and set down her glass. "I simply don't agree that it's significant. As I've told you repeatedly, the charges of looting were dropped altogether. Therefore your theory is incorrect."

"Wait, back up." I joined them and appropriated the other half of Aaron's turkey on sourdough. "What's going on?"

"Nothing pertinent to your cousin's death," said Julie firmly. "People will always resurrect old rumors from time to time. I'm sure it was mere coincidence—"

"And I'm sure it wasn't." Aaron leaned toward me across the coffee table, and I could see the reporter's fire in his eyes. "Carnegie, the guy at the newspaper office said that somebody else called him recently to ask about back files from the 1950's. He couldn't remember the name, but now I've got a pretty good idea. Guess who chatted up Dr. Nothstine at the gas station a couple of weeks ago, and just happened to ask her about the Crown of Silla?"

The hair on the back of my neck stirred. I swallowed the bite I was chewing and said, "I don't have to guess. Domaso Duarte?"

"Exactly. What do you bet he was up at Boot Creek hunting for buried treasure?"

"It's possible," I said slowly, watching Julie's face. Aaron had her off to his side, but I was seeing her straight on, and I didn't like what I saw. She sat rigidly erect, as always, but her lips were quivering and her face was paling. "But Sam told me that Domaso's a big trout fisherman. Maybe he was just there fishing."

"And just happened to commit murder in between casts? And just happened to be curious about the Crown of Silla?"

"But then, what about the security guard? Why would Domaso—"

"The cops think that was a robbery, and maybe they're right." Aaron was on a roll. "No, I figure either your cousin was killed because he saw Duarte with the crown, or else he found the crown himself and Duarte killed him to get it. It all makes sense!"

I watched as a tear slipped from behind the thick glasses and ran down Julie's lean, lined cheek. She ignored it.

"On the contrary," she said, in a voice that came out quavering and a little too loud, "it makes no sense whatsoever. It is simply inconceivable that Roy Kane would have stolen something of such value and historical importance. Or stolen anything at all, for that matter. He was a decent, honorable man, a remarkable man. If you had heard the many, many tributes at his service—"

"I'm sure he was a fine man," I said, with a glare at Aaron. "I'm sure it was a hero's funeral."

"Not a funeral, a memorial service." Even in distress, she was precise and pedantic. "They were never able to retrieve his body from the lake. It was such a shock to everyone. We had no idea that Roy meant to take his life. If only he had confided in me, I might have helped him. . . ."

The tears were raining down now, and she turned her face away to hide them. Horrified, Aaron reached toward her to comfort, to apologize, but I grabbed his arm and towed him out to the hallway. If Julie Nothstine was going to break down, we'd let her do it in private.

"Jesus," he said as I closed the door behind us. "I didn't realize the guy meant that much to her."

"She was in love with him. I don't think she's ever recovered from his suicide, and here you are calling him a criminal."

"I didn't call him—"

"You implied it, though, didn't you? Aaron, maybe we're jumping the gun here. We're just blithely assuming that Roy Kane was a thief, but he's only a name to us, not a person. Julie actually knew him."

"Yeah, but did she really?" he said, the skeptic in him reasserting itself. "Love is blind, remember? Crooks sweep women off their feet every day. You are such a pushover for a romance, Stretch."

"Keep your voice down, she'll hear you!"

I was nearly in tears myself, for some reason. But no, if I was honest, I knew the reason: my mother's romance had me way off balance. And I felt dreadful for Julie Nothstine. To have someone you care about take his own life . . .

The door swung open behind us. Julie had wiped the

tears away, but her voice was still husky. "Thank you for lunch. I believe I'll go home and rest a bit. I hope you enjoy tonight's festivities."

"Aren't you coming?" I asked, but she shook her head.

"I generally prefer to be at home in the evening. I shall attend the wedding itself, however, with great pleasure." I had the sense she was talking to recover her composure.

"I'll walk you out to your car," Aaron offered, moving to take her arm. "I didn't mean to—"

"Nothing to be sorry about, young man," she said, and waved him off with one strong and sinewy hand. "You're simply mistaken. As I'm sure you'll come to admit, once this matter is resolved."

She held his gaze for a moment, unblinking and proud, then began to make her slow, laborious way down the corridor. She leaned heavily on her cane, and her twisted leg made a *shush*ing sound as it dragged along the carpet.

We stepped back inside, and Aaron leaned his hips against the conference table and folded his arms. "So what are you saying, Stretch? You think the buried crown is a myth, and we're back to suspecting the smoke jumpers again? Because now that I've spent time with them, I just can't buy that."

"It's not smoke jumpers in general we suspect," I pointed out. "It's Todd Gibson and the Tyke. Talk about a pushover. One kiss and you're ready to swear she's innocent."

"That really got to you, didn't it?" He chuckled in that infuriating way he has. "Like I told you last night, Stretch, it was just a little fun."

Fun. Just like Beau's fun with the chambermaid.

"No problem," I said, turning my back on him to crank up the air-conditioning. "You go have some more 'fun' and

I'm going back to work. It's going to be a crazy afternoon, so I'll see you at dinner. Scram."

Aaron shrugged. "Be that way. But I'm telling you, I can't wait to ask this guy Domaso some questions."

"Well, you won't have to wait long," I said. "Guess who's coming to dinner?"

Chapter Twenty-Five

THE REHEARSAL DINNER WAS A SMASH HIT—IN MORE WAYS than one, unfortunately.

It began graciously enough, in the golden glow of a high country summer evening. Under the canvas roof of the terrace, each table was a masterpiece of blush-pink linen and glittering crystal and the restrained but sensual curves of white lilies.

And that was just the tables. The mellow twilight laid a gloss of goodwill and good looks on all the faces, as well, from Sam's suited-up business friends to Tracy's fashion-forward crowd, to the casual vitality of the smoke jumpers.

I was heading into the kitchen to consult Food Bob about the dessert course when I ran into Sebastian the entertainment director, his ponytail bedraggled and his geeky glasses askew. He carried a suitcase and looked like a corpse.

"Montezuma's revenge," he said hollowly. "Don't ask, don't even ask. The flight from Cabo was ghastly, but I'm here. Everything copacetic?"

"Why, sure," I said. "Except for that little business about the Ladislaus Quartet canceling."

"*What?*"

"If you'd bothered to call in, you'd know that. But I took care of it. We're having the..." *Did the kids have a name?*

"...the Quartetto Polizia. You've heard their latest CD, of course?"

"Of course," he said nonchalantly. "Nowhere near the caliber of the Ladislaus, but—"

"But it's a done deal and that's that. Now if you'll excuse me—*agh!*" I wasn't *agh*ing at Sebastian, but at the drooled-over oven mitt that had just been dumped at my feet. "Bad dog, Gorka! Where did you get that?"

"Got it right off my goddamn hand," panted Food Bob, coming up to us with his eyes bulging and his mustache all aquiver. "Is that your dog? You ought to—"

"He's not mine!" I protested. "He just...brings me things."

Gorka let out a bark of agreement and beat his tail against the floor.

"Just get him out of here, would you? Doggone dog in my doggone kitchen..."

Bob bent to retrieve the mitt, but snatched his hand away when Gorka snarled low in his massive throat. Apparently this treasure was meant for me and me alone. I picked it up and handed it back to its owner.

"Sorry, Bob. As I was saying, Sebastian, if you'll excuse me, I've got work to do. Come on, Gorka."

But as I slipped my hand under the brass-studded collar, Gorka once again shook me off and bounded away, out of the lodge and into the night. Well, at least this meant that Domaso was around. Aaron was itching to talk with him.

When I returned to the terrace most people were digging into dinner, though a few continued to circulate, greeting friends or paying their respects to the bride and groom. The ceremony tomorrow would be videotaped, of course, but tonight the cameras flashed like summer lightning as Photo

Bob and his helpers recorded the occasion with posed shots and candids.

Satisfied that all was running smoothly, I made my way back to my own table, which was unoccupied except for Aaron. He was looking good—very good—in a pink shirt and the linen blazer he'd worn in Miami on New Year's Eve. Even as I smiled at him, I was cringing inside at the memory of that night, and my unfortunate remark about the nonexistent engagement ring. If I hadn't said that, how would things stand between us by now?

Let it go, I told myself. *The way Aaron and I rub each other wrong lately, it might be just as well.*

Oblivious to my inner turmoil, he smiled back and cut into his lamb chop in phyllo. "How's it going backstage?"

"Well enough, but Domaso's dog invaded the kitchen."

"So he is here tonight." Aaron drummed his fingertips on the table. "Once I find our Mr. Duarte, I'll drop a few hints about the crown and see how he reacts. That should give us something to go on. Is that him over there?"

I looked. "No, not hairy enough. I told you, Domaso's unmistakable, like a really tall wrestler with a broken nose. So when you do find him, be careful." I tried a forkful of salmon. Perfect. "Oh, there's Chief Larabee, with the blue jacket and the scowl. And that must be his wife, poor woman. Boy, Sam's invited half the town. I guess he can afford to—"

"Muffy!" B.J. appeared beside us and made a show of inspecting my dress. "My, my, look what they're wearing in the rainy city these days. Is it waterproof?"

She herself wore the same black velvet dress as in the photograph she'd shown me, with a black ribbon holding back her curls and the silver syringa blossom gleaming at her throat.

Aaron turned his head to find B.J.'s cleavage at eye level. "Hi, there. That's quite a ... necklace."

"Present from my husband," she told him, with a wink and a giggle for me. She took a seat. "What's up?"

"Plenty." I told her briefly about the Crown of Silla, and Aaron put in his two cents about Domaso as his prime suspect for murder.

"I suppose it's more likely to be him than one of the smoke jumpers," said B.J. thoughtfully. "And the way he's built, he's certainly strong enough. You know, guys, the sooner you turn this over to the police, the better."

"We will," I promised. "As soon as we get enough to convince them to investigate. We don't want Larabee throwing us out of his office like he did Dr. Nothstine."

"Gotcha." She shifted uneasily. "Listen, I'd offer to help some more with this, but..."

She trailed off, and I realized there was something that B.J. didn't want to say in front of Aaron. Something like "but I don't want my husband to think I have any interest whatsoever in Brian Thiel."

"But Matt's only home for a little while before his next trip," I filled in. "I understand. You stick with him and we'll work this out ourselves. Have fun tonight."

"No fear. We've got our ice skates in the car." She gave me a quick kiss on the cheek and went back to her table.

Quite a few guests had brought their skates, and something about playing on the ice in their good clothes brought out a childlike gaiety in them. As the long summer dusk faded to darkness, the lights came up on the ice rink, illuminating the artful spins of some guests and the clumsy lurching of others.

By the time we were served our white chocolate crème

brûlée with raspberry coulis, there were enough skaters out there to make entertaining viewing for the rest of us—especially when a woman in a red evening gown fell on her butt, and then joined in the laughter that spread across the terrace.

My date wasn't laughing, though. He was drumming on the table and jiggling one foot and generally being less-than-stellar company.

"Aaron, if you want to smoke, go ahead. At least we're outdoors."

"Where the hell is Duarte?" he said, as if he hadn't heard. He half stood to peer over the heads of the other diners. "I still don't see him."

"Maybe he's taking his dog home. Aren't you eating your dessert?"

"No. Listen, I'm going to wander around and look for him, and maybe do some skating. Want to come?"

"No, I need to keep an eye on things, but you go ahead."

As I watched Aaron move away between the tables, I wondered. Was he anxious about talking to Domaso, or looking forward to it? "You don't get that intensity working in an office," he had said. Maybe office work was hemming him in these days. Maybe all the smoke-jumpers' stories were making him restless.

Or maybe he was just a guy trying to quit smoking. I shrugged and ate my crème brûlée, and after a moment's hesitation, I ate his, too. Wondering is hungry work. Then I gulped my coffee and went looking for my mother and her date. Murder wasn't the only mystery on my mind tonight.

It took me a while to locate her, because Photo Bob had some questions about this evening's cast of characters. There always seems to be one self-effacing aunt who has to be roped into a picture, and one self-important acquaintance who has to be nudged away from appearing in all of them.

I also socialized a bit, with the smoke jumpers and the actors both. Between the masculine attention and the feminine appraisal that I got, the turquoise dress felt like a good idea after all.

Especially when I stopped by the head table to check in with Tracy. As I waited for her to finish speaking with an older couple, Jack raised his eyebrows at me and whistled. A little too enthusiastically, considering the occasion, but I can't say that I minded.

"Look at *you*," he said. "Look at the devil with the blue dress on. Hot, hot, hot."

"Thanks." I added, with a flicker of malice, "It's Aaron's favorite."

Jack laughed, and nodded as if to say "Touché." "I meant to tell you, by the way, I'm impressed with your guy Aaron."

"With the way he gets along with all kinds of people?"

Jack shrugged. "That, too, I guess, but what I meant was, he almost beat the Tyke at arm wrestling. Not bad for a desk jockey."

"What's not bad?" asked the bride, turning her big blue eyes to us. She looked even more absolutely fabulous tonight, in an emerald-green gown with a mermaid silhouette, and a spray of diamonds in her hair. She looked like a star.

"Nothing," I said. "I just wanted to make sure your wedding dress arrived all right, and that you've tried it on?"

"Oh, Tessa got it here, no problem, but I've been too busy. Anyway I told you already, I don't need to try it on. Don't you ever listen?" Tracy sounded like a spoiled child, and for once she seemed to notice the fact. "It'll be fine, Muffy, thanks for following up. In fact, thanks for all your help this week. You've been great, really."

You're damn right I have, I thought. But I just smiled and wished them well, and continued on my search for my mother.

I found her seated next to an empty chair with a man's jacket over the back, and her trusty Folger's jar right out there on the tablecloth next to her beaded evening bag. The bag was ruby and silver to go with her outfit, a soft tunic and skirt in a deep red that set off her feathery silver hair. I tried to see her as Owen might, and was startled when the words "classy" and "sexy" came to mind.

The other guests at her table were deep in conversation. I slid into Owen's chair and said, "How was the bike ride?"

"There you are, Carrie. Goodness, are you warm enough in that dress?"

"Mom, it must be eighty degrees still. If you don't like the dress, say so."

I tugged irritably at my short hem, and squared my shoulders to keep the neckline from gaping. This was not how I meant to begin the conversation.

"It's very nice, dear." She said it absently, and then hurried her next words. "It was a bit hot for the bicycles so we just had a picnic. Owen found the nicest salads at that little organic café—"

"Mom, what's going on?"

She bit her lip and looked away. Voices and laughter babbled all around us, but I swear I heard her sigh. "Oh, I'm going about this all wrong, aren't I?"

"You're not doing anything wrong, Mom. You've got a right to . . . to have a social life." *And to love someone who isn't Dad.* The unspoken thought was loud in both our minds.

"I'm not surprised that you're dating, I just don't understand why you haven't even mentioned Owen before. Actually, I don't understand what happened with you and Eddie."

"Eddie Breen?" She sounded shocked. "Eddie and I are friends, Carrie, we've always been friends. What made you think—"

"Well, what about that trip to the Oregon coast?"

"Friends go on trips," she said simply. "Goodness, Eddie is more than ten years older than I am. He wouldn't want to play tennis or go bike riding or"—here she blushed—"or anything. Owen and I are so compatible, I felt it right away. I didn't tell you about him at first because I was afraid to . . . well, to jinx things. I suppose you think that's silly."

"Not at all, Mom. I've done the same thing myself. But this isn't 'at first' anymore. How long have you been seeing him? And is he divorced, or still single? A man his age—"

I stopped short, dumbfounded at hearing myself ask exactly the sort of intrusive questions that I resented so much when she asked them of me. "I'm sorry, Mom. He seems really nice, and I'm glad you're happy."

She laughed. "Is that how I'm supposed to do it when you tell me you're seeing someone? You're going to make an excellent mother some day."

"I have an excellent role model."

We both teared up a little, but Owen returned before things got too mushy—and before Mom spoiled the moment by asking me whether Aaron liked children.

"Private conversation?" Sam was right, Owen Winter was a good-looking fellow. His cuffs were folded back on brawny forearms, and he had loosened the tie on his broad chest. His voice wasn't so bad, really. "I can come back."

"Not at all." I got up from his chair. "Actually, I should get back to work."

"Sorry to hear that. We haven't really had a chance to talk yet. Maybe tomorrow after the wedding, when you're not so busy?" He touched a hand to my mother's shoulder, and something in the nature of his touch caught at my heart. "Louise, they're loaning ice skates tonight, and I bet they have our sizes. What do you say?"

"Well, I—"

Mom's answer was lost in a sudden racket: shouts, thuds, a woman's startled scream. And then a confusion of alarmed and curious voices as we all converged on the skating rink to see what was causing the commotion.

Out on the ice, most of the skaters were backing away to the rails, some slipping and falling in their haste, while a few others stayed in the center, tangled together in a grunting, flailing knot. Then the knot resolved itself into two men, grappling feverishly, almost hidden from view by the four or five peacemakers trying to pull them apart.

Just what a wedding planner wants at the rehearsal dinner. A goddamn fistfight.

Hitting another person is unreasonable to begin with, in my book, but hitting someone with both of you on ice skates is entirely ludicrous. The laws of physics won't cooperate, it's the old equal and opposite reaction thing. The opponents have to cling fervently to each other with one arm, just to keep upright as they pummel away with the other, and the whole business looks like a slow dance gone wrong.

I shoved my way toward the railing, thinking that whoever these idiots were, they deserved every bruise they'd be left with in the morning. Then one peacemaker—it looked like Peter Props—swore and shoved another, who sadly for him happened to be the Tyke. She replied with an uppercut to his jaw, causing a third peacemaker to lunge to his defense, and the two-man fray escalated into a general brawl.

Casualties were limited, because most of the combatants immediately fell down, but the original pair was still grunting and grappling. I caught a glimpse of a swarthy face and then a flash of pink shirt.

One of the idiots was Domaso Duarte, and the other was Aaron Gold.

Furious, and also frightened, I yelled something regrettable and charged forward—right past the railing and onto the rink. You'd think stiletto heels would jab into the ice and give you some purchase, but you'd be quite, quite wrong. I went skidding toward the combatants at a dizzying speed, until my heels went north while my butt went south, and I ended up flat on my back, spinning like a boomerang away from the fight.

It must have looked comical, but it felt terrifying. I could easily have smashed my skull against the uprights of the rail. But at the last moment a pair of shovel-sized hands grasped my shoulders, and a pair of trunklike arms lifted me to safety and set me on my feet.

"Kharrnegie!" boomed my very favorite voice in the whole world, at least at the moment. "Kharnegie, you stay here. I was star of Red Army hockey team. I will fix."

Chapter Twenty-Six

"RED ARMY, MY ASS," AARON MUMBLED THROUGH SWOLLEN lips. "The guy played for the best team in the world and now he makes corsages?"

"You're just lucky that corsage maker can skate and fight at the same time." I lifted the ice pack away from his right cheekbone to survey the damage. Nasty. "I wonder how Domaso is looking this morning."

"Worse than me," he insisted, but he groaned pitifully as he sat up in bed.

It was Saturday, the day of the wedding, and the Idaho sky showed vibrantly blue outside the windows of the Paliere suite. The side of Aaron's face was vibrantly black and blue, but the rest of him seemed intact, and thanks to the Mad Russian, my own bruises were negligible.

Once Boris had cleared the ice, none too gently, I'd helped Aaron up to bed and then gone back down to oversee the remainder of the party. Luckily most of the older and more shockable guests had departed before the fight, and Beau had apparently slipped away with Olivia. Irresponsible on his part, but at least I didn't have to hear his snotty comments on my date's behavior.

As for the younger guests, most of them found the whole episode funny. Even Tracy shrugged it off, and Jack's only regret seemed to be that he hadn't participated. I didn't understand, but I couldn't complain.

So now I let Aaron do the complaining, as I disposed of the ice pack and carried two cups of coffee back to the bedside. Like most men, Aaron made a lousy patient.

"Needs more sugar," he grumbled.

I brought some over, then asked the question he'd been too dopey to answer last night.

"What on earth did you say to make Domaso hit you? You didn't come right out and accuse him of murder, did you?"

Aaron began to speak, then hissed in pain and gingerly touched one fingertip to the corner of his mouth. He tried again. " 'Course not."

I waited for further explanation, but he just sipped in silence. "Well?"

"Well, what?"

"What set him off? You must have said something to provoke him. Did you ask him if he was camping near the fire?"

Aaron hesitated, then said, "Can't remember. It hurts to talk, OK?"

"I'm sorry about that, but I need to know the details. Chief Larabee will be at the wedding, and if I'm going to persuade him to investigate Brian's death, I need a real eye-opener to get his attention, something he hasn't already heard about and dismissed. So come on, tell me why Domaso started the fight."

"Let it go," said Aaron sullenly. "Don't you have things to do today?"

"You mean, besides coddling you while you're being rude? Yeah, I sure do."

The strain of dealing with a murder, a wedding, and an ill-tempered man was suddenly too much. I yanked an outfit from the closet—the red sheath I'd worn to the spa and some nice flat nonskid shoes—and zipped them into a garment bag to change into later.

"The rehearsal's at White Pine in an hour," I said in my frostiest tone, "and the ceremony is this afternoon at five. I won't be back in between."

Then I stalked into the bathroom and slammed the door behind me, muttering to myself as I did my hair and makeup. Aaron was still in bed when I came out.

"Are you going to feel up to coming to the wedding?"

He didn't look at me. "If you want."

"Oh, don't do me any favors." I snatched up the garment bag and my purse, and when I stomped out the hallway door I slammed it, too.

The drive to White Pine didn't do much for my disposition. I took the first hairpin curve too fast and scared myself by skidding on the loose gravel. After that I slowed down, keeping in mind that this was my lightweight rental car and not Sam's tank.

But slowing down made for a longer drive, and the heat of the day was building up relentlessly. My next mistake was cranking the air conditioner to high as the car labored up the steep mountain road. I was only halfway to the inn when the air whistling from the dashboard vents went from cold to cool to warm, and the engine temperature gauge crept into the red zone.

"Bloody *hell.*"

I pulled off in a patch of shade, where I lowered all the windows before cutting the engine. The last thing I needed was an overheated car to go with my overheated temper. Being a wedding planner means never having to say "I'm sorry I missed the rehearsal."

I smiled a little at this thought, and smiled some more
when I remembered Mom's comment to Aaron about my
temper. I'm not sure redheads have a shorter fuse than anyone else, but people do seem to notice it more when you ex-
plode.

When I was a kid, Dad used to tell me to count to ten before I blew up—but to do it in seven languages. So I chal-
lenged him to teach me how, and we spent some giggly
afternoons at the library with a stack of foreign dictionaries. I
still missed my father, but I was so lucky to have had him.

Eventually the engine cooled off, and so did I. *Of course
Aaron was cranky this morning,* I told myself. *He was hurting,
poor guy.* I pictured us drinking champagne in perfect har-
mony on the terrace this afternoon, and by the time I got
to White Pine my spirits were rising. I do love weddings, after all.

Weddings, but not mothers of the bride. The moment I
entered the inn with my garment bag over my shoulder, I was
pounced upon by a caterwauling Cissy. She wore a purple
bathrobe and no makeup whatsoever, a condition I'd never
observed her in. Between her stark pallor and her heartrend-
ing tone of voice, you'd think someone had died.

"It's ruined! The wedding is ruined, *ruined*! Beau doesn't
even know yet, he's at the meadow with the carpet people,
but what could he do anyway? What are we going to *do*?"

"Cissy, deep breath, remember?" I was beginning to feel
like a Lamaze coach. "In . . . out. Again. Good. Now tell me
what's happened. Is it really that bad?"

"It's pretty bad." Olivia spoke from the top of the stairs,
with the oddest expression of amusement and distress on
her face. "You'd better come see this."

Cissy followed me up to the master bedroom. A jumble of

dresses and shoe boxes and lingerie obscured the icky purple bedspread, and a triple mirror stood near the picture window. The bridesmaids, along with Hair and Makeup—I couldn't recall their names—were clustered around it, staring in horror at the bride in her wedding gown.

"Oh," I said. "Oh, brother."

Tracy stood with her back to the glass, looking over one shoulder at her reflection. It was a classic pose for a prewedding photograph, but instead of girlish delight her eyes held only sick dismay.

I could see why. The coral satin gown was stunning, all right. But the long line of pearl buttons down the back was separated from the corresponding line of button loops by a long gap of Tracy's bare skin.

The gap started out narrow, just above the point where the chiffon train attached with snaps at her slim, trim waistline. But up at shoulder level it spread to a good two or three inches, making the buttons impossible to fasten. And with the back unsecured, the barely legal front of the gown would be noticeably illegal, especially in the state of Idaho.

"It's the upper-body workouts," said Olivia in a giddy whisper. "She's all bulked up. I mean, look at her trapezius muscles. And her deltoids—"

"Carnegie," wailed Tracy, "do something!"

The bridesmaids began to twitter like flustered sparrows, while Hair and Makeup chimed in with accusations, lamentations, and suggestions. The suggestions ranged from wearing a shawl—a shawl, for God's sake—to "running into town" for another dress, as if we could hop a bus and get off in Manhattan.

"Out!" I said. "Everybody out, now. You too, Cissy."

Alone with me, Tracy's Botoxed face attempted a petulant frown. "Go ahead, say it."

"Say what?" I asked absently. I was thinking, and thinking hard. *Ribbon . . . or some kind of cord, or even string . . .*

"Say that you told me so! I haven't gained an ounce, how was I supposed to know this would happen?"

"Mmm," I said, walking around her. "We'll do a Watteau train. . . ."

"What's that?"

"It's what you'll be wearing," I said briskly, as I unsnapped the chiffon train from her waist. "It fastens at the shoulders and flows to the hemline of the dress, sort of an Elizabethan look. Now, we need some narrow ribbon . . ."

Fate smiled on us then. As I laid the train carefully over a purple armchair, I spotted the cord that tied back Cissy's purple drapes. It was pink, not coral, but close enough. With a little cry of triumph I pulled the cord free and began lacing it in a zigzag pattern between the buttons and the loops.

"We do *this*," I said, finishing off with a tiny bow at the base of her neck, "and then we sew on some snaps and add *this*."

I held the train to Tracy's shoulders, to show her the effect, and waited for her reaction. *If she sulks about this*, I thought, *I'm driving right back down this mountain and getting on an airplane.*

"Oh, Muffy," she breathed, with tears in her eyes. "It's beautiful."

"Yeah, isn't it? I almost like it better this way. Don't cry, kiddo, you'll spoil the pictures."

"You saved the show," said Tracy, reverting to actress mode. "You absolutely saved the show. Thank you *so* much."

"You're welcome. Now let's get you back into your casual

clothes for the rehearsal. It's scorching out there, so dress cool."

As I busied myself with unlacing her, a devious idea occurred to me. If we couldn't ask Domaso about his whereabouts, why not ask his "old friend"?

I decided on a surprise attack, so right in the middle of Tracy's gushings about the dress I said, "Tell me, were you and Domaso camping near the Boot Creek fire?"

She frozen, and her eyes grew round. It was no cute little mannerism this time, but genuine alarm.

"He said not to—" She faked a little fit of coughing. As I said, for an actress she wasn't much of a liar. No script, I guess. "Um, no. No, I haven't been camping in ages. Why?"

"Oh, a friend of my mother's was asking about fishing at Boot Creek, and I wondered how much damage the fire did. Maybe someone else can tell him."

A lame explanation, but with any luck Tracy would be too busy getting married to think any more about it. As we gathered up the other women and she told them about the dress, I silently congratulated myself. Vermeer, my eye. Tracy was never in Portland, she was playing in the woods with her old friend Domaso. Which put Domaso near the scene of Brian's murder. I had found my eye-opener for Chief Larabee.

I figured if Dr. Nothstine could restate her belief that Brian's corpse had been tampered with, and then I could point to a shady character like Domaso covering up the fact that he'd been in the vicinity, surely Larabee would have to pay attention.

With that settled, I could bide my time until the chief arrived. So now, out on the sunny green meadow with its centerpiece of lofty pine trees, I concentrated on helping Beau direct the rehearsal. Now that the spotlight was on, Beau was front and center. But I must say he did it well, using his famous charm to smooth over the inevitable conflicts that arise when so many specialists are brought together.

The videographer, for example, wanted Tracy to approach the grove from a different direction, for the sake of shadows or backlighting or something. But the landscaping foreman refused to rearrange his carpeting and turf, and Joan, the tent-and-rental woman, needed a decision before she could unload her truckful of white folding chairs.

While they haggled that over with Beau, I tried to defuse the hissy fit that Sebastian threw once he got a look at the Quartetto Polizia.

"They play perfectly well," I told him as we stood in the shade of the pines watching the kids tune up.

"I don't *believe* this," said Sebastian darkly. "The viola has *acne.*"

"They'll be fine. And I was right about the publicity."

The reporter for *People* magazine, a jaded name-dropper who would have taken the Ladislaus Quartet for granted, was startled and enchanted by Tracy's novel choice of musicians. After doing a joint interview with the students, he arranged to photograph Tracy in T-shirt and shorts hanging out with her "young hometown pals." She'd never laid eyes on the kids before, of course, but who needs facts when you've got an angle?

So the quartet played, and the bride proceeded across the grass on the arm of her cowboy-hatted dad. Jack stood by the pine trees with the Tyke by his side as best woman, gazing at Tracy so lovingly that I could only pray he would never get wind of her "friendship" with Domaso. Especially if Domaso turned out to be involved in Brian's death.

But I was too busy to dwell on that, as Beau and I made

notes about timing and coached the participants through their roles. We had to send Sebastian back to Ketchum, since Montezuma was still having his revenge, and I wasn't surprised. I've never seen skin quite that green. What did surprise me, as the day wore on, was to find myself working with Beau in a reasonable spirit of professional cooperation.

"*C'est bon,*" he said grudgingly, as we watched Jack and Tracy lead the recessional. "You understand your work."

I considered jogging Beau's memory about that vastly successful Christmas wedding of mine, but I didn't want to awaken memories of the toupee incident. So I kept my mouth shut—something I thought I might try more often with Aaron in future.

We all finished up in reasonably good spirits, and adjourned to the inn for a sandwich lunch out on the grand veranda. Even the mother of the bride had calmed down, once Tracy reassured her about the dress and she pulled out her economy-size bottle of tranquilizers. I was happy to see those little white pills disappear past Cissy's rosebud lips, though it made me uneasy to see how much wine she chased them down with. But with any luck, the whole mix would keep her sensitive nature under wraps until after the ceremony.

I finished my BLT and went looking for the Red Army star, to thank him for his efforts on the ice. I found him upstairs, directing the placement of some daisy-filled buckets in the guest bathroom. With an unlimited budget for flowers, no space goes undecorated.

"Kharnegie, you are not hurt?"

"I am not hurt, and you are my hero."

I tried to deliver a kiss on the cheek, but Boris strong-armed me into something far more emphatic as Wallace Waggoner looked on openmouthed. No doubt Valerie Cox behaved with more decorum. I waved the two of them away, laughing, and stayed behind to wash up.

I took my time, and when I emerged the hallway was empty and the upper floor was quiet above the distant clamor rising from the veranda. It seemed like a good time to change into my red dress, so I headed for the master bedroom.

But as I passed one half-open doorway, a surreptitious murmur of voices stopped me cold. What were Todd Gibson and Pari Taichert doing up here away from the party?

"You promised you'd never say anything." Todd sounded angry, desperate. "You promised me."

"Well, I shouldn't have," said the Tyke. "But it's going to come out anyway. Dr. Nothstine's not going to let this alone, and now Danny's been asking me about it. He's creeping me out. You'll just have to—"

"You up here, Red?" The voices fell silent as Sam came clumping up the stairs and into view at the end of the hall. "Oh, there y'are. Bob wants to know if he can start bringing up his paraphernalia."

"Which Bob?" I said blankly.

He chuckled. "The photographer, of course. For the pictures of Tracy gettin' dressed and all."

"Of course, I knew that." I walked right past the half-open door, trying to sound casual. "Tell him to give me a minute to get changed myself, and then I'll round up the bridesmaids for him."

As Sam descended I went into the master bedroom and shut the door firmly behind me, to let the conspirators make their getaway. But conspiring about what? I had thought that Domaso's presence at the murder scene let the smoke jumpers off the hook, but did it really?

And did Todd and the Tyke know that I'd overheard part of their exchange—or more important, that I'd heard only part and not the whole? If the rest of their exchange had been incriminating, and if they assumed I'd heard all of it . . .

Normally I love helping the bride and her attendants to dress, but with a TV star for a bride I was superfluous. Hair and Makeup attended to all the ladies under Ilsa's vigilant eye, and I was reduced to holding hangers and handing out handkerchiefs.

Which was just as well, because paranoia is very distracting.

Chapter Twenty-Seven

THE MARRIAGE CEREMONY OF TRACY MARIE KANE AND JOHN Holland Packard III went flawlessly. Almost.

The event began as planned, with the string quartet pouring the joyful strains of Mozart into the summer air. As the first of the two hundred guests arrived to take their ribboned and garlanded seats, the groom and his best woman had already taken their places up front. Standing beside them, with the three ponderosa pines as backdrop, stood the presiding minister, a stout older gentleman who was a longtime family friend.

The Tyke had dropped her tuxedo idea—surely meant just to tease Tracy—and was looking smart in a navy-blue jacket and skirt with her hair combed loose on her shoulders. You'd never know she'd been brawling the night before. Or that she might have murdered one of her colleagues.

As the groom, Jack Packard wore a lightweight suit, a stephanotis boutonniere, and an unwontedly solemn expression. Could the Knack be nervous? In the Victorian language of flowers, a fragrant white stephanotis blossom is the emblem of marital happiness. *It might even come true for him,* I thought. *Stranger things have happened.*

But I couldn't spare more than a thought for Jack, because I was feeling pretty solemn myself. It had been easy enough to avoid being alone with the Tyke, but I wasn't sure where Todd was, and I jumped every time someone came up behind me. I'd feel a lot less anxious once Chief Larabee arrived, and I could turn my suspicions over to him.

Seeing B.J. was a nice diversion. She came across the grass holding Matt's hand, her dark curls bouncing and a wicked gleam in her eye. Once again, the silver necklace sparkled at her throat.

"I heard about the big battle last night," she teased. "You sure you haven't hooked up with Napoleon?"

"Oh, shut up and sit down, would you?"

She snickered and led Matt through the elaborate archway of roses, grapes, and aspen branches that marked the rear of the congregation. No telling what Valerie Cox had intended here, but Boris had worked wonders.

As more guests arrived, Beau stood languidly beneath the arch and beckoned one of the several photographers to get a picture. Theoretically he was stationed there to cue the bride and her attendants for their procession down the rose-petaled aisle, but he was also perfectly placed to lap up compliments. Some of the guests—ladies, of course—even asked for his autograph.

Meanwhile he sent me off to shuttle along the path through the trees between the meadow and the parking area, giving directions to the ushers and watching for last-minute glitches. I also watched for Aaron, but when he showed up at last, bruised but presentable, he was in the middle of a group of smoke jumpers. Al Soriano and the others greeted me with smiles, but Aaron looked the other way and took a drag on his cigarette.

As they walked off, one of the jumpers asked Aaron something that I didn't catch. They must have thought they were out of earshot, but I have excellent hearing. In a lull in the voices around me I heard Aaron say, "Nah, we're just dating. Nothing serious."

His next words were lost in the chattering approach of the two philanthropic ladies I'd met at the chocolate shop—and in the mortified pounding of my own pulse.

Just dating? Was that why Aaron had been so sullen this morning? Because he'd come all this way and gotten all roughed up for the sake of someone he was "just dating"?

Breathing hard and blinking back tears, I hurried along the path to the parking area, to keep an eye out for Chief Larabee. Between making my case to him and keeping the wedding on track, I couldn't spare the energy to worry about Aaron. Or so I told myself.

Larabee arrived by squad car, in uniform and armed, his heavy black belt laden with holster and radio and various leather pouches—not your typical wedding-guest attire. With his razor-creased shirt and his fixed pinched features and his tightly kinked gray hair, he looked like a caricature of the no-nonsense cop. The kind whose face would break if he smiled.

"Sorry about the get-up," he said, unsmiling, and slammed the car door. He had an instant camera in his hand, and I wondered how well he took pictures, given his twitchy eye. "Didn't expect to be on duty today, so I'll have to leave right after the I-Do's. How's my boy sounding?"

"Great. Listen, Chief, I only have a minute—"

I could see the bride and her attendants emerging from the inn. Hair and Makeup, having done their best, lingered behind in the doorway, while a squadron of photographers and videographers formed around Tracy and documented her every step. Beau would be walking up the path to meet them, so I hurried to say my piece before he arrived.

"Chief, please don't leave before I get a chance to talk with you. It's about Brian Thiel."

Larabee scowled. I could read his mind—something about hysterical females talking nonsense.

"Now look here," he said sourly, "I told that Nothstine woman, accidents happen, and this one's officially an accident. I know you're upset, miss, but—"

"Shoot it!" Beau must have sprinted from the meadow. His exquisite silk tie was crooked, and his face glistened with sweat. "Shoot it now!"

"Calm down there, mister," said Larabee. "Shoot what?"

"Come, hurry!"

In his agitation, Beau grabbed roughly at Larabee's arm. Bad move. The chief responded to this lapse in judgment by stubbornly planting his feet and demanding that Beau identify himself, but I didn't stay to hear the rest. Instead I did some sprinting myself, back to the meadow.

The proceedings had reached that pleased-and-eager hush before the bride's appearance, and a few guests peered over their shoulders at the sound of my coming. But everything seemed in order, and I couldn't imagine why Beau was so alarmed . . . until I looked down.

In the grass at my feet, a long sinuous form undulated forward, barely disturbing the scattered rose petals. It was slithering right for the archway and the unsuspecting congregation beyond.

Damn. Time slowed to a silent, surrealistic crawl as I took in every detail of the snake's appearance. Its four-foot length was dull yellow, with reddish brown blotches down the back and a band of bold dark rings around the tail. *Damn, damn, damn.*

Ilse the Stylist was sitting right at the back, ready to primp Tracy one more time before her big entrance. She spotted the snake and leapt to her feet, knocking over her chair, and the wicked little head reared up and back as if to strike. Ilse opened her mouth to scream.

I broke out of my trance and darted forward, snatching the snake at the base of its head and hauling it up off the ground. The tail whipped back and forth, rattling furiously, as I turned around and marched into the nearby trees.

Behind me I heard a babble of consternation, and then Sam's foghorn voice raised in reassurance. Through it all, the quartet kept playing and I kept marching, through the crackling-dry underbrush to the edge of a rocky gully. I heaved the snake into the gully and dusted off my hands with an exasperated sigh. *Never a dull moment.*

As I turned back to rejoin my wedding, Aaron came crashing through the bushes with Chief Larabee following at a brisk but less panicky pace.

"Carnegie!" Aaron grabbed my shoulders and shook me, his voice sliding up to a shout. "Are you insane? What did you think you were doing? You could have been bitten, poisoned—"

"No, she couldn't." Larabee's left eye winked and fluttered as he gave me a curt nod of approval. "That was a bull snake. Harmless. Looks like a rattler, though, don't it? Nice work there, miss."

"Thank you. Aaron, this is Chief Larabee. We'll be talking about Brian after the ceremony. Won't we, Chief?"

"Well, now," he said, considering the utterly nonhysterical female before him. "Well, now, I guess we will."

Bewildered and then embarrassed by his show of concern for my safety, Aaron wordlessly threw up his hands and returned to the meadow.

The rest of the ceremony really was flawless. Boris had worked his usual magic with body flowers, from the circlet of baby rosebuds in the flower girl's hair to the regal sweep of orchids and stephanotis vines that Tracy carried with her coral gown.

My makeshift lacing and Watteau train provoked nothing but gasps of admiration from the stylish Californians, and when at last the minister directed Jack to kiss his bride, the gasps were lost in a roaring, stamping ovation from the smoke jumpers.

The sight of the bride and groom's embrace is usually one of my favorite moments, but the longer I was single, the more wistfully I watched it. I was always happy for the new couple, of course, and basically happy myself. But still . . . I glanced around, hoping to catch Aaron's eye.

Instead I spotted my mother and Owen Winter, lost in a private moment among the crowd. He murmured to her, she dropped her eyes, he touched her cheek and kissed her gently. I looked away, feeling like an intruder, and went back to work.

My next task was to shepherd the guests over to the inn. There they could dip up chilly spoonfuls of lobster gazpacho, or nibble on scallop and jalapeno ceviche, as they contemplated the heartier fare of Food Bob's grilling buffet. I could smell the distinctive smoke of the grills already, which meant Bob was ahead of schedule, so I tried to move people along.

But some of them wouldn't be moved. They lingered to chat with one another, or even to compliment me if Beau was busy with someone else. Much to my amusement, Beau was now pretending to be quite blasé about the snake.

Beyond him, I noticed a pair of men standing out among the parked cars. They were too distant for me to hear, but judging by their contorted faces, Domaso Duarte and Danny Kane were arguing furiously. Danny kept pointing to the back of a pickup, which I assumed was his, while Domaso raised his shoulders and his upturned hands as if to say "What am I supposed to do about it?"

Then I caught a glimpse of the culprit who'd caused their conflict: Gorka, up to his usual tricks. Unseen by either man, the dog was galumphing away from the parking lot with something clamped in his jaws.

I shook my head ruefully. Whatever his trophy was, I just hoped Gorka wouldn't bestow it on me in the middle of the reception. Maybe I could persuade Larabee to escort Domaso away for questioning, and take the dog with him.

But meanwhile the mother of the bride, resplendent in her shell-pink ensemble, was making a citizen's arrest. Cissy must have come looking for her stepson, but she paused to watch Gorka disappear into the woods. She took a step as if to follow the dog, then made a beeline for the men, who were still arguing obliviously. Cissy wagged a playful finger to scold them, then took each one by the hand and tugged them away to the party, chattering nonstop the whole time.

You go, girl, I thought. *No more fistfights, please.*

Once the stragglers had gone off to the inn, I checked in with Joan and her crew about setting up the dance floor. A big wedding is like a Broadway show. It takes hardworking stagehands and scrupulous timing to create a seamless experience for the audience.

In this case, Act One was the ceremony and Act Two was

dinner on the veranda. For the big finish in Act Three, Tracy's guests would be led back to the meadow. There they'd behold a fairy-tale pavilion, strung with lights and banked with flowers, where they could dance the night away to Sebastian's big-name rock band. If all went well, the wedding of the season would get five-star reviews.

With the setup in progress, I looked around for Larabee. He was with his son's quartet, but they'd already packed up their instruments and were eagerly heading for the front of the inn and Bob's grill stations. Each station had its own gaily decorated sun umbrella and its own special menu item: tandoori chicken, pork satay, cilantro shrimp, and so forth. The Quartetto Polizia was charging us peanuts, compared to the Ladislaus, so I'd told them to eat all they wanted.

But the grills were only now being lit, so the hungry kids would have to wait. Bob wasn't ahead of schedule after all. That was fine with me, though, because I was determined to pin down the chief before he got away again. Having Aaron in on this might have bolstered my case, but I figured he'd be touchy after the snake incident. So I went ahead on my own.

"There's appetizers on the veranda," I told the students, and they perked up and left us in a hurry. *Alone at last.* I drew Larabee away from the food crew, to be as private as possible. He stood there, skeptical but patient, as I plunged in.

"Here's the thing, Chief. Did you know that Al Soriano saw a tent on the ground near the Boot Creek fire?"

"Wait," he ordered, and pulled a pencil and a spiral pad from his pocket. "Al who?"

I was beginning to spell it when the Tyke came striding toward us across the grass, her hair tied back in its usual ponytail and a determined set to her jaw.

"I'll tell him myself, Kincaid," she said. "I know you over-heard us, but you don't know everything."

"But that's not—"

Larabee held up a hand to stop me and looked at her woodenly. "Everything about what, Miss ... Taichert, isn't it?"

She nodded and licked her lips nervously. "About what happened with Thiel. It's my fault. I shouldn't have covered for Toddy, but I was trying to help him out. If we could keep this quiet—"

"It was Todd after all?" I exclaimed. "But—"

Larabee glared me to silence. "Miss Taichert, you want an attorney present for this?"

"I just want to tell you what really happened," said the Tyke, also glaring at me, "before you get it secondhand from some eavesdropping bitch."

Maybe I should have left then, but Larabee didn't order me away and the Tyke didn't stop talking. The words came rattling out of her, and fascinating words they were, too.

"Todd Gibson's just a Ned, a rookie. He knows his stuff, but he was all keyed up for his first fire, and when he found Brian dead under the tree there he just lost it. He freaked." She rubbed the back of her neck and frowned, remembering. "When I got to him he still hadn't radioed in, he was just kneeling there bawling. He'd puked all over, and some of it got on Brian's PG bag."

So Julie was right, I thought. *There was interference with the body.* But she, and Danny Kane, too, had been mistaken about its nature. I closed my eyes for a moment, imagining the scene of my cousin's death.

"I got him calmed down enough to call in his report," the Tyke continued. "Then I helped him unclip the bag and clean it off, but we didn't have time to clip it back before Danny showed up. We didn't tell Danny what happened. Todd made me promise not to tell anyone. He was afraid he'd never live it down, being the Ned who cried." She smiled a little. "He's got funny ideas about being a smoke jumper, you know? Heroes and all that shit."

"But what about you and Brian?" I blurted. "Steve the bartender saw you two, um, getting close."

The Tyke went scarlet.

"Once!" she said. "I let him grope me once when I was dead drunk, and the next day I told him if he ever touched me again I'd . . . I told him to lay off, and he did."

"So Brian Thiel was dead when you arrived," said Larabee, overlooking this detour. "And there's no question in your mind that he died as the result of an accident?"

The Tyke looked shocked. "What else would it be?"

"Well, Miss Kincaid here seems to think—"

"Yo, Tyke!"

The three of us looked up at the sound of Jack's voice. He'd come out to where the veranda wrapped around the side of the inn, and was waving an arm to summon us. I checked my watch, wondering if it was time for the toasts already.

"That can wait," I said, but the Tyke knew her comrade well, and she saw something in his bearing that I didn't see.

"No." She was already in motion. "No, it can't. Come on."

Out on the veranda we found an eerie tableau. All the trappings of a lively party were in place, from the bow-tied bartender to the rose-strewn and gauze-tented cake table. But instead of partying, everyone from the bride to the busboy was standing motionless and staring into the west.

Most of them had lifted one hand to shield their eyes, as if in salute to the lowering sun. Its golden rays gilded their faces as they searched among the countless forested ridges that rippled out to the horizon, and focused on a single point.

I followed their gaze, and stopped motionless myself. Thunderheads were building off to the west, as they did so often here on summer afternoons. But today there was a difference.

In the middle distance—no, nearer than that—rose the same kind of smudgy yellow-brown veil of smoke that I'd seen from the plane. The veil seemed to lean in our direction, and a breath of warm air brought the distinctive smell I had noticed before.

The smell of fire.

Chapter Twenty-Eight

NOBODY PANICKED, THOUGH FOR DIFFERENT REASONS. THE Idaho people, including the high-school musicians, were interested but hardly surprised, wildfires being a normal part of summer in the arid West. This particular fire was screened from us by an intervening ridge, but they gauged the distance of the smoke plume, and the relative calm of the wind, and went on eating their lobster gazpacho.

Some of the L.A. crowd were less relaxed, perhaps recalling the conflagrations that had ravaged southern California in recent years. They looked at the dry woods surrounding White Pine, and the grass-choked meadows on the slope below the inn, and began to talk about going home a little early.

But others seemed to view the smoke as part of the day's entertainment. Olivia, for example, handed Boris her camera and posed at the veranda rail with the gray plume in the background. She wore a painted-on plum-colored dress that was cut up to *here* and unzipped down to *there,* and everything in between had the Mad Russian's undivided attention. Floral directors aren't usually invited to the wedding itself, but somehow Boris always showed up, and how do you banish a good-natured grizzly bear?

For myself, I tried to read the smoke jumpers' faces. Tracy must be upstairs somewhere, perhaps with Cissy, but the groom was deep in conversation by the bar with his new father-in-law. Julie Nothstine stood beside them, leaning against the veranda railing to spare her legs, in loose cotton trousers and a blue blouse that echoed her eyes. All three of them held highball glasses.

Other jumpers began to join them, including Todd Gibson and Al Soriano, but so far nobody looked too worried, and at one point Al's narrow features even split into a snaggle-toothed grin.

So it's all right, I thought, taking my cue from them. *I don't have to close down the party.*

I'm so accustomed to taking charge at weddings, I had to remind myself that changing the program at this one would be Beau Paliere's call, not mine. I didn't see him at the moment, though, so I tagged along toward the bar with the Tyke and Chief Larabee.

"What have we got?" said the chief, addressing himself to Jack. He, too, recognized the authority here.

"Well, we're not sure," said Jack. "Sam's having a little problem with his radio."

Larabee glowered. "Damnation, Kane, you assured me you had proper emergency communications up here. It could be months before you get that cell tower approved."

"I know, I know," said Sam, looking chagrined. "If the county commissioners would quit fussing around about scenic values and just approve my permit—"

"Later," said Jack, and his tone made both the older men stop and listen. "Chief, could you help us out with the mobile in your squad car? Just check in with the jumper base, get a status report."

" 'Course I can. Be right back."

As Larabee walked off grumbling to himself, Jack gave the

rest of us a brief smile. "I think we're fine. The humidity should come up a couple points as the day goes on, which'll park that fire right where it is. It's just that if we start getting lightning strikes up here, it might be a different story."

Sam shook his head mournfully. "My womenfolk aren't gonna like it if you cut short their shindig. Let's give it some time if we can."

"I can talk to them if necessary," I offered. "Just keep me posted on the plans. Me and Beau, I mean."

The minutes seemed to drag before Larabee came back, but when he did the news was reassuring—although at first I didn't understand that.

"It's about a forty-acre fire, five miles from here," he told Jack. "They've got a hundred and twenty personnel on it, looking at containment by nightfall."

"No call for a Type One?"

"Nope."

The jumpers all nodded sagely, and the group began to break up. But I was still in suspense, so I appealed to Julie Nothstine.

"I don't get it. What's a Type One?"

"It's the level of Incident Management Team that NIFC assigns to major fires," she said.

"So we're OK?"

"I believe so, unless the weather pattern suddenly destabilizes." She tucked a wayward strand of gray hair back into place. "I notice that that obtuse police officer is here today. Have you been able to make him see reason?"

"Believe me, I'm working on it."

I caught up with the chief at the appetizer table, and resumed making my case. Aaron didn't seem to be around to chime in, and that was fine with me. I wanted to pull this off on my own.

"It wasn't Todd Gibson I was worried about," I explained, as Larabee gazed suspiciously at the gazpacho. "Well, maybe a little, but what I really wanted to tell you was about a man named Domaso Duarte. He does odd jobs—"

"I know who he is. Get to the point."

"The point is that Domaso was camping near the Boot Creek fire. He could have been there when Brian landed."

Larabee's left eye stopped twitching, just for a moment, and I could sense him going on the alert. "I never heard that."

"He's been keeping it secret! And he's also been asking about the old rumor that Roy Kane buried his war loot in that same area. What if Domaso dug it up..." As I related Aaron's theory about the Crown of Silla, I was dismayed to see Larabee's skepticism mounting to outright disbelief. "Look, I know it sounds far-fetched, but remember what Dr. Nothstine said, that the fall itself shouldn't have killed Brian."

"That crazy woman?" Larabee scoffed.

I stepped closer, wary of being overheard. "That crazy woman was right about Brian's PG bag being tampered with, so what if she's right about this, too? Shouldn't you at least question Domaso? He's here today, you know."

The chief pursed his lips, then nodded decisively. "All right, I'll talk to him. But if I'm satisfied that there's nothing more to go on, I'm dropping the matter. And I don't want to hear another word about it from you or Nothstine, is that clear?"

"Crystal."

As the chief strode away, scanning the crowd for his

quarry, I went so limp with relief that I swayed on my feet. There might be more thunderclouds heading our way, but it felt like clear skies to me. I snagged a glass of champagne from a passing tray and knocked back a celebratory slug. *I did it. I did right by Brian.*

I wanted to share my victory with Julie or B.J., or even Aaron. But none of them was tall enough to stand out above the press of bodies on the veranda, though I could see Boris hoisting a vodka glass aloft, and Sam's Stetson bobbing.

The party was reaching critical mass, that joyful condition where everyone's talking at once, strangers are becoming fast friends, and more than half the guests are convinced that they're sexy or brilliant or both. Beau and I had a hit on our hands.

I saw my mother talking with Julie Nothstine, and Owen Winter bringing them both drinks, maneuvering his way skillfully through the crowd. I hadn't yet made up my mind about Owen, but he did have good manners. *And Mom's got good judgment, after all. I should give him the benefit of—*

"Carnegie?"

Someone touched my arm, and I turned to find the Tyke looking at me with an oddly shy expression. She had shed her jacket, her sleeveless white blouse crumpling in the heat, and I noticed a nasty scrape on her elbow. So she hadn't escaped the fight unscathed after all.

"I, um, need to apologize," she said. "I guess if you thought Toddy and I were messing with your cousin's body, you had a right to . . . Look, we weren't disrespecting him."

"I know that."

"I mean, he was my bro, and—"

"I appreciate your saying so." I felt shabby, letting her apologize for disrespect when the real question was murder.

But I could hardly tell her that, so I tried to change the subject. Her scraped elbow suggested a way. "Tell me, are you OK after last night? That was quite a fight Domaso started."

"Are you kidding?" The Tyke was drinking beer from the bottle, and she took a swig now. "We're used to getting banged up. But he didn't start it, you know. Your friend from Seattle did."

"Aaron?"

"Oh yeah. Duarte said something to another guy about you and Jack, just being a jerk, you know? Then he called you a—" A camera flashed nearby, making us both blink, and during the interruption she reconsidered. "He called you something he shouldn't have, and Aaron heard him. I've never seen a man move so fast."

"Really?" I sipped thoughtfully at my champagne. "Huh. Have you seen Aaron out here, by any chance?"

She didn't reply, because a distant crack of thunder rumbled across the veranda and we both fell silent. The flash had been lightning, not a camera, from a mass of clouds approaching from the south. This was no Seattle sky, no uniform soft grayness. The air between the sharp-edged shapes was still a dazzling blue, but the clouds themselves were dark and menacing.

Another flash and another thunder crack, still distant but noticeably closer together. The gay babble of voices around us faltered, and then a questioning buzz arose. I cut to the outside edge of the crowd and made my way around the railing to find Chief Larabee.

Jack and Tracy were with him, along with Sam, all of them looking gravely at the clouds and then at the smoke plume in the distance. It was progressing northward, left to right from our viewpoint. But it was perceptibly bigger now, not a plume but a column, and it didn't feel so distant anymore.

"What's the verdict?" I said quietly.

"We're still fine," said the chief, equally quiet. "But that fire's getting away from them down there."

Sam gave a deep sigh and said, "How 'bout if we wrap things up in the next hour or so? Folks can leave earlier if they care to, just not all at once 'cause that road won't handle it. All right with you, son?"

"That would be best," said Jack. "And let's not let the people who stay wander off too far. We don't want people out in the woods somewhere if we have to clear out in a hurry."

"So, no dancing?" said Tracy.

"No." He put his arm around her shoulders. "Sorry, honey."

"It's all right," she said, and I could see from her face that it was. Tracy had grown up today, at least a little. "We're having a perfect, perfect wedding, aren't we, John? Carnegie, I'm not sure where Beau is, so could you—?"

"No problem." There was an empty chair by the railing, and I stepped up onto it. "Ladies and gentlemen! Listen, please . . . Can you all hear me?"

The faces turned toward me, some anxious, some still in party mode. But none panicky, and I was determined to keep it that way.

"Ladies and gentlemen, there may be some bad weather coming." Doubtful that anyone thought I meant rain, but "fire" is such a spooky word. "So we're going to change our schedule a bit, and do our dancing down in Ketchum tonight."

Heads nodded at that, and I continued. "Meantime, dinner is served! Please help yourselves at the grill stations out front. You can eat out here on the veranda or inside, we've got tables everywhere. But please—this is important—please stay in the immediate area of the inn, all right?"

Then I had a sudden idea, so I improvised. "If anyone needs to leave early, feel free, but there's no law against going straight from the appetizers to the dessert, is there? Please gather round, and let's toast the bride and groom as they cut their wedding cake."

Chapter Twenty-Nine

THE CAKE-CUTTING STRUCK JUST THE RIGHT NOTE, AND IT gave Tracy some lovely photographs for her album, no matter what happened later. All the cameras flashed and all the guests applauded as Tracy sliced deftly into the towering orange tiramisu confection. Then Jack made an amusing show of attacking the chocolate-chestnut groom's cake, and got a big laugh.

Both cakes were decadently rich, but most of the smoke jumpers—who still planned to eat dinner—managed a slice of each. The Quartetto Polizia accounted for eight more pieces, and Cissy showed up late but devoured three.

All in all, and just as I'd hoped, the cake made a festive finale for any guests who had decided on an early departure. That turned out to be almost everyone, but when they began to leave White Pine they did so in an orderly manner, and in an upbeat mood.

The few who were left loaded up their dinner plates and settled down to eat, savoring the spice of adrenaline along with their meal. I wanted to find Aaron, but first I had to stop in the kitchen to tell Food Bob the plan, and then go across to the meadow to discuss the dismantling of the dance floor and sound system with Joan.

After that I stood at the steps of the inn near Tracy and

Jack, as they bid farewell to their guests. Sam came out to join them at one point, but Cissy was still on the veranda drinking. I kept notes on a clipboard about who left, just in case we needed to know later. Somehow taking all the precautions for an emergency made it seem quite certain that no emergency would occur.

B.J. and Matt were among those who left early, not so much worried about fire as on fire for each other.

"You know how it is," smirked B.J. as Matt brought their car up. "You've got to make every minute count. Where's Aaron, by the way?"

"Around. Listen, I got Chief Larabee to listen to me about Brian."

"Wonderful!" she said. Matt honked his horn. "Oops, gotta go. Call me tomorrow?"

"Definitely," I said. "You two have a good night."

Various families left as well, to get the kids to bed, and seeing them go seemed to stir the television people into leaving. And after that Mom came out of the inn with Owen Winter. They congratulated the bridal pair and then came over to me.

"Wonderful party, Carrie," said Owen, pumping my hand. At some point I'd have to make him stop calling me that. "Can you join us for brunch in the morning? You and I need to get to know each other."

Do we really? I thought, as my mother blushed. *I suppose we do.* I waved good-bye as they drove off, then went back inside, wondering where the hell Beau was.

I was still wondering almost an hour later. I did have a suspicion, but I was dismissing it as unworthy when lo and behold, my suspicion was confirmed. I was coming out of the kitchen with more ice for the guests on the veranda—

having sent Bob and his staff back to Ketchum—when Olivia slipped hurriedly downstairs and across the great room. She was zipping her dress as she went.

I strolled over to the foot of the stairs. "Beau? Are you up there?"

The fabulous Frenchman descended with a masterful air of nonchalance. "You need to speak with me?"

"I've been needing for quite a while," I said sweetly.

As I filled him in about the fire situation, his beautiful face paled. "We are in danger?"

"No, of course not. Sam's just being extra prudent, that's all. I've been taking notes for you . . ." I offered him the clipboard. "Want to take over from here?"

"Mais . . . non," Beau said slowly. He consulted his Rolex with lowered eyes, and moved toward the front door as he spoke. "You will continue. I did not realize how late it has become, and I have many important calls to make. To New York. As there is no telephone here, I shall have to go."

"Go?" said Olivia's voice behind me. She'd come back into the great room for some reason, and she'd heard his every word. "Were you going to tell *me* you were going?"

"But of course," he crooned. The man was a master, all right. He barely missed a beat. "And you shall come with me, *ma chere*. But let us hurry, *non*?"

"No," she said flatly. "I don't think so. I think I'll go back out there where the men are."

Olivia was an actress, and she knew a terrific exit line when she had one. She stalked off to the veranda without another word. Beau said something under his breath in French, and made his own exit out the front door.

The Tyke passed him on the way, coming in from the grill

stations with a plate heaped high with food. "What's going on?"

"Nothing much," I said. It would be easier to work without him, anyway. "Beau had to leave, but I'll be here till the party's over."

She snorted. "I get the picture. You still looking for Aaron?"

"Yes!" Beau vanished from my mind. "I mean, I was just wondering where he was."

She grinned. "Yeah, like you hardly care. I asked around for you. He went down toward the hot spring a while ago."

"Thanks," I told her. "Thanks a lot."

I followed her out to the veranda to look for Sam or Jack, but when I couldn't find them I reported in to Larabee. I didn't bother to tell him about Beau.

"So far all the families with children have left," I said, running down the list on my clipboard. "Also the quartet and the dance band, and Boris Nevsky's flower crew. Bob will send his food servers down as soon as everyone's eaten, and most of the tent and dance-floor guys are on the road already."

"Good work," he said. "You seen Duarte anywhere?"

"No, haven't you found him yet? His car is still out there."

"I'll keep looking. Where will you be?"

"The hot spring," I told him. "I've got some business there."

Aaron wasn't all the way down at the spring. I found him just inside the aspen grove, seated on a low gray boulder in the dappled shade. He was gazing uphill through the screen of shivering branches, as if contemplating the inn and its inhabitants, and sipping from a highball glass.

"Room for one more?" I asked. He scooted over but didn't speak, so I sat beside him with my plate of wedding cake. I'd brought two pieces and a couple of forks. "Here, you can have either one, or half of both."

I could only see his unmarred profile, but his smile was still lopsided because of the swelling, and his voice was still a bit mumbly. "No, thanks. Not too hungry today."

"I guess it takes a lot out of you," I said, as I licked a smudge of chocolate-chestnut frosting off my thumb. "Starting fights and all."

He swirled the ice cubes around in his glass. They were small and rounded off, melting fast in the heat. "Who told you that?"

"Some people who were on the rink."

"Some people talk too much."

I took a big bite of orange tiramisu cake, for courage, and said, "Aaron, can we sort this out? We've been . . . We haven't been . . . Dammit, things have been weird ever since Miami, and I can't stand it anymore."

"Stand what?"

"The *confusion*. I mean, last night you tore into Domaso, which was very gallant but very dumb, so thank you kindly but please don't do things like that anymore. And then today—"

"Kharrnegie!" called a jaunty voice. We looked up to see Boris clomping heavily toward us along the path from the veranda with a pretty, giggly blonde close behind him. "Kharnegie, does anyone use the hot spring?"

The blonde giggled some more as the breeze whipped her hair around her face, and I remembered her as Ramona, the script girl who struck out at the baseball game. From the look she gave Boris, she wasn't going to strike out tonight.

"Dunno," said Aaron. "We haven't been there. But have fun."

"Don't go any farther than the spring, though," I cautioned. "And don't stay too long."

"Not too long, Kharnegie."

Boris dropped me a wink as they passed, and I waited for their footsteps to fade into the rustle of the leaves before speaking again. I kept my voice down, and I hurried. The breeze was becoming a wind.

"And then today you're telling people we're just dating, it's nothing serious. Could you please define 'serious' for me?"

The ice cubes stopped swirling. "You were eavesdropping?"

"I don't *eavesdrop*." I stabbed at my cake again, and the second fork bounced from the plate and pinged onto the stony ground. "I just hear things. And I heard you saying—"

"I said what guys say, that's all." Aaron slid off the boulder to retrieve the fork, then drained his glass and clattered the fork into it. He sniffed the air. "Does it seem smokier to you?"

"No. Maybe. But what do you mean, that's all? How could you—"

"Well, what did you want me to do?" he said plaintively. "Bare my soul to somebody I just met a couple of days ago, and tell him that I'm madly in love?"

"Is that what you'd tell someone?" I set down the cake plate. The surface of the rock was warm and smooth against my fingers. "I mean, if you bared your soul?"

Aaron looked at me with narrowed eyes, as if I had the sun behind me. He turned his free hand palm up, and drew a deep breath.

"Carnegie—"

A woman screamed. It was a high penetrating shriek, and she kept on shrieking as Aaron dropped his glass and I leapt from the boulder and we both raced down the path to the hot spring.

Boris was kneeling by the edge of the oval pool, reaching out his huge hand. Ramona was backing away from the water, her eyes round with horror. Her screams were unbearable, so I ran to take her by her shoulders.

The instant I touched her she fell silent, her mouth still wide. Behind me there were splashing sounds.

"This way," I heard Aaron telling Boris. "Here, I've got the . . . *Jesus.*"

Ramona screwed her eyes shut and averted her face, but I turned to look. Boris and Aaron were hauling a large, dark, sodden shape from the water. They manhandled it across the stones that ringed the pool, and laid it faceup on the ground.

The air was definitely smokier now, though I smelled something sweet, as well, like flowers. The sky above the wind-whipped aspens had darkened to the color of a bruise. But even in this dim and shifting light we could see that the face was Domaso Duarte's, and that he had a gaping wound in the center of his forehead.

Chapter Thirty

"HEY, WAIT!" I HURRIED AFTER LARABEE TO THE UNPAVED parking lot, wincing as the gusty wind flung a spray of grit into my eyes. "Wait up!"

The chief had given his orders with grim efficiency. Aaron and Boris were to stay with the body and prevent anyone else from approaching it. No one but Sam and Jack was to be told what had happened, until he said otherwise. And I was to convey Ramona back to the inn and "keep her from telling anybody anything, for God's sake," while Larabee radioed to Ketchum for reinforcements, an ambulance, and a status report on the fire.

But I had no intention of cooling my heels inside. If Domaso had been murdered, and he wasn't Brian's killer—I couldn't believe we had a second murderer on the scene— then maybe Danny Kane was right, and either Todd or the Tyke, or both, were involved in Brian's death. And now Domaso's, as well.

I'd stashed the now-tearful Ramona in an upstairs bedroom with Julie Nothstine, transferring my assignment to her, and then gone racing after Larabee. I caught him halfway to his squad car and trotted along beside him. I was winded, and it was hard to keep up.

"It was murder, wasn't it?" I demanded. "The rest of

Domaso's forehead didn't have a scratch on it. You don't believe he hit his head and drowned accidentally, do you?"

"Medical examiner decides that," he said curtly. "Not you and not me."

I grabbed his arm to halt him. "Then give me your opinion, Chief. Because I've got about thirty people up here who are my responsibility now, and—"

"Yours?" Larabee made an indignant sound in his throat, like the one Eddie Breen makes sometimes when we argue. "Seems to me this is Sam Kane's property."

"Well, it's my wedding, and I want to know if you think my guests and my staff are in danger."

"The answer's yes." Jack, coming up behind us, had misinterpreted my remark. He spoke calmly but urgently. "That fire's hooking. Get on the radio, Chief, and tell them we're evacuating. I'd like all the numbers and especially the weather data, but I can see enough now to want everybody out of here."

I was so focused on Domaso's death that my brain stalled. "Hooking?"

"Changing direction," he said, as the chief shook me off and continued to his car. "The wind's getting fluky, and now the fire's moving uphill toward us."

I looked at the sky to the west, into the wind, and saw instantly what he meant. No longer a plume or even a column, a broad wall of gray-brown smoke rose from the ridges below us. Near the top it blossomed and spread like the canopy of a jellyfish, making visible the invisible gradations in the movement and temperature of the upper air. It was actually quite beautiful, a vast sculpture forming itself before our eyes.

"Domaso's dead," I heard myself saying. "I think some-one killed him."

Then I dropped my gaze and observed Jack's reaction very carefully. Because if Jack Packard somehow found out what his fiancée had been doing with Domaso Duarte among the flowers just a few days ago, then I might be having a conver-sation with a murderer. Domaso was a big man, a powerful man, and it wouldn't be easy to fell him with a single blow. But Jack had a smoke jumper's strength. He would be up to the task.

"What?" Jack's face showed astonishment and then dis-may. "Oh, shit, does Tracy know? Is she all right?"

I was astonished myself. "Tracy?"

"Yeah, they're . . . close. They were close." He looked at me quizzically. "You knew, didn't you? You knew they were lovers."

"I . . ."

"Never mind. She told me it was over, and I believe her." A trace of the famous Jack the Knack smile showed briefly in his eyes. "Not like I've been a saint, right? But that was then, this is—"

A shout from the squad car stopped him. As we looked, Larabee stood up from the driver's seat in a spasm of anger, and clouted the roof of the car with his fist. We reached him in seconds. He was staring into the car, at the smashed-in wreckage that had been its radio.

I looked closer. Shards of plastic lay across the car seat, and among them rested a softball-sized stone. The stone had blood on it.

Larabee's struggle to compose himself was brief and effec-tive, but his left eye was vibrating so fast I thought he must have trouble seeing. "Miss Kincaid, you have a list of everyone who's here?"

"Not exactly. But I've got the guest list, and I asked the vendors for their staff names and—"

"Get it together for me while we get these people in their vehicles, all right? I'll need interviews with all of them, and I can't do it here"—he glanced up at the smoke—"but I'll want to start with you and your list. You drive straight to the police station when you get down there, no stops, understand? Packard, she tell you what happened?" When Jack nodded, he went on, "Get your jumpers together, would you? I'll deputize the bunch of you to help me secure the area around the spring."

"Is that where he died?"

"Looks like it." Larabee sighed heavily, a man with a lot of factors to prioritize. "Any of those photographers still around?"

"I think so," I said. "Why?"

"I need photos of the scene, the body, this mess here, everything." He spoke without looking at me, thinking aloud. "I'll have to leave the body where it is, and come back when the fire's contained. Packard, you organize the evacuation. How much time have we got?"

"I wish I could tell you," said Jack. "Depends on the wind. If the main fire reaches that slope below the inn, it's going to make an uphill run and we've got to be long gone by then. It might not get that far, of course, but—who the hell is that?"

A car was racing up the road toward us, the engine whining, a cloud of dust rising behind it only to be snatched away by gusts of acrid wind. It was a luxury sedan, a rental, and one front fender was newly crushed, its headlight gone. The car slewed to a stop and Beau Paliere scrambled out. His face was slack with terror.

"The road . . ." he said, and coughed harshly. "The road is *en feu,* the road burns. Smoke, everywhere smoke and fire!"

People were coming out of the inn now, voices were rising in alarm. Beau turned toward them and threw up his arms. He began to shout something in hysterical French but he didn't get far because Larabee strode to him, clamped his arms to his sides, and hustled him into the backseat of the squad car, which was screened off from the front seat by a serious-looking metal grille. Then he got in beside him and slammed the door, no doubt for a heart-to-heart talk about not spreading panic before panic was called for. Instinctively, Jack and I moved out of earshot.

"We'll be rescued, won't we?" I asked him. "They'll open the road, or send a helicopter, or—"

"First they'd have to figure out that we're up here, and that may take a while. The people who left first probably think that we got away, too." He glanced around. "And I don't know where you'd land a copter, anyway."

"They'll send smoke jumpers, then."

"Maybe. If resources aren't spread too thin, and if this is judged to be a defensible position." He saw the dismay on my face and backpedaled. "Sure they will. They'll drop jumpers and a mess of equipment. It'll be all right."

I didn't necessarily believe him, but I wanted to so badly that I kept my fears to myself.

"So what do we do in the meantime, Jack?"

"First thing is, you and Sam get those people back inside and get a head count. We need to keep everyone together." He looked up toward the veranda and signaled to someone.

"I'm going to take Al Soriano and drive down the road, see what the situation is. We'll be back as soon as we can."

They were back within the hour, and the situation was bad. Jack didn't have to tell the twenty-nine of us left at the inn that the fire was getting closer, because while he was gone we could see it happening. The column of smoke was a massive wall now, a wall with orange flames along its base that crept toward us along the valley. As we watched, the wall became a living beast. With a deep and constant roar, the beast clawed through the woods, creating gashes of black destruction in the green of the trees.

Jack called a council of war in the great room, standing in his shirtsleeves with his back to the windows, flanked by Chief Larabee and Sam Kane. These were our leaders now, and we looked to them to keep us safe. They remained calm, so we did, too.

"The road's a no-go," said Jack. "We have to work fast, but first we're going to take a minute to make a plan and make sure everyone understands it."

I looked around as he spoke, examining each face. No one had mentioned Domaso Duarte, but then most of these people either didn't know him or would assume he had left the party earlier. Larabee had allowed Sam and Jack to tell their wives about the murder, but in private, so that only we few knew that Domaso lay murdered at the hot spring. And only one of us in this room knew how—and why—he had come to die.

Aaron sat next to me in our chairs along the wall, serious and intent, taking notes for some future news story or maybe a book. I tried to imagine myself in Seattle one day in the future, relaxing somewhere safe and cool and reading Aaron's book about a forest fire. *Oh please, let that day come.*

On my other side, Julie Nothstine looked alert and intelligent as always, but tired, deeply tired. She should be lying down, and I made a mental note to get her settled in one of the bedrooms soon. I'd ask Cissy to stay with her, just to steady her and give her something to do. Cissy's plump pink face was trembling like a baby's about to bawl, and her eyes darted around the room like tiny creatures seeking safety.

Cissy's daughter was another matter. Still in her wedding gown, still lovely, Tracy sat on an ottoman with her coral-colored skirts tucked around her and attended to her new husband. Jack had told her about Domaso, overruling Larabee's objection, and she'd been very quiet and very calm ever since.

Ramona was quiet, too, having cried herself out, and sat limply on a sofa now in the circle of Boris's massive arm. Beau was beside them, apparently seeing Boris as an ally, and to my surprise he seemed calm and cooperative. Or perhaps he was still in shock. Or perhaps . . . No, Beau had never even met Domaso, as far as I knew. Why kill someone you've never met before?

Jack was explaining that we would create a fire line to protect the inn, and a safety zone at the parking area in case the fire line didn't hold. He was good at this, I realized, good at shaping a team.

"So I'll want everyone who thinks they can do some chopping to come with me now out on the veranda," Jack concluded. "We don't have a lot of tools, so we're going to work in shifts, and I want you to sack out in between. That's what jumpers do, you know. We take more naps than kindergartners."

That got him a little laugh and he flashed his special smile, nursing us along. "The rest of you stick with Carnegie there. She's going to organize the food and water situation. Like I said, we need every one of you to help, even if it's just carrying water bottles out to the people cutting line."

There were a dozen or so other guests in the room, of various ages and physical condition and stages of alarm, and also a handful of staffers whose job it would have been to clean up the inn after everyone left. Most of Jack's firefighter buddies had taken off earlier, to go partying elsewhere, but standing in the back of the room, ready for Jack to give the word, were the remaining four: Al Soriano, Danny Kane, the Tyke, and Todd Gibson.

These people are firefighters, not skydivers, I thought, suddenly seeing the obvious. The parachuting they did got all the attention, but it lasted mere moments. What they did for hour upon backbreaking hour, working through long days and then through the night when they had to, was dig fire line and fell trees and gouge hot embers out of the earth, robbing the fire beast of its food.

It was hard to believe that Todd or the Tyke could have harmed my cousin—and harder still not to be grateful for their presence anyway.

Outside the window, the beast went on roaring.

Chapter Thirty-One

POSTED AS A LOOKOUT IN THE MASTER BEDROOM, WAITING at the window for the fire, Julie Nothstine recalled some figure in a old poem. *The Lady of Shalott. Was that the name? And was it by Tennyson or Wordsworth? And why the hell am I thinking about poetry at a time like this?*

I must have made a sound from where I stood in the doorway, because she turned and blinked at me. "I beg your pardon?"

"Sorry. I just came to see if you needed anything."

We spoke in whispers. Far from tending Julie, the mother of the bride was sprawled on the purple bedspread, snoring. She must have taken another little white pill, but that was fine. We had more bodies than we needed downstairs, working on the fire line, and Cissy asleep in a crisis was probably preferable to Cissy awake.

I joined Julie at the window. In truth, I'd come upstairs to tell her about Domaso's murder—why not, if Jack could tell Tracy?—and ask her advice about keeping track of the possible suspects, given the bizarre situation we found ourselves in. But that was before I truly understood the situation.

I did begin to tell her, though. I described finding Domaso's body, skipping over the gory details, and told her my doubts about Todd and the Tyke.

"Her explanation was so convincing," I said, "about Todd freaking out when he first found Brian. I believed her, I really did. But maybe Danny was right to be suspicious of them."

Julie listened intently, though she kept up her watch out the window as she did, and I kept watching, too. The flames that flowered wildly in the forest were visible only in glimpses as the smoke swirled and parted.

"Domaso's death might have been an accident," said Julie. "People do fall—"

"I think the fire is slowing down!" I peered eagerly out at the creeping shape of our enemy. "Julie, I'm sure it is! I'll go tell them."

"No." She imprisoned my wrist with one powerful hand. "This could change in an instant, with a shift of wind or a piece of burning debris blowing ahead of the fire itself. It's essential that everyone stay calm. That's the real reason Jack has them working down there."

I looked down at the slope below the veranda, where half the stronger members of our group were hard at work while the other half rested inside. They hacked and chopped at every substance that could burn, from weedy meadow grass to landscaped shrubbery, making a band of bare dirt that followed the contours of the inn some yards out from its foundation. It looked woefully puny compared to the monstrous tongues of flame licking their way up the valley toward us.

One of the laborers was the bride. Tracy had changed out of her gown and was working shoulder to shoulder with Jack, while the less muscular individuals were fetching tools, dragging away the debris, and doing anything else they could think of to be useful. But without the brawn of the other smoke jumpers, the civilians hadn't gotten very far.

Especially with the disruptions like Ramona fainting from

the heat, and Chief Larabee turning white and clutching at his chest after a few minutes of digging. He had reluctantly admitted to heart trouble, and promised Al he would stay safely inside with Ramona.

Larabee was utterly phlegmatic about the fire in any case, seeming to view it mainly as an obstacle to his consideration of Domaso's murder. But the other civilians believed that their labor was necessary. That it could save us.

"What do you mean, the real reason?" I said. "Julie, is there something Jack isn't telling us?"

I could see the challenge in her strange blue eye. "Are you sure you want to know?"

"Of course I am. Tell me the truth. I mean it."

"Very well, I shall." She flung the truth at me as if it were too painful a burden to carry alone anymore. "A fire line of this sort might protect the inn, in calmer conditions and on flatter ground. But with these unstable winds and the steepness of the slope, it's unlikely to succeed. If the fire reaches this far, it will be as the result of an explosive run up the ridge, and that run will be unstoppable. Are you familiar with the size of a football field?"

I nodded. The question was surreal, but then so was this wedding day.

"For some reason," she said, with the puzzled frown of an academic deciphering a footnote, "these things are often explained in terms of football fields, even though some people, such as myself, have rarely visited one. I have never understood—"

"Julie, please!"

The blue eyes met mine straight on. "A fire making an explosive run can incinerate the length of a football field in one second."

"Minute, you mean?"

"I mean what I say. One second."

I felt dizzy. "Then why bother with the fire line?"

"Because it gives those people something to do before they are led to the safety zone and asked to remain there, possibly for a lengthy period of time, without panicking."

"Then is the safety zone going to work? Is that really our best hope?"

I didn't like the pause that followed.

"There is an unfortunate lack of large open spaces on this ridge," she said carefully, "and these woods are dry in the extreme. The heat of a forest fire can easily exceed two thousand degrees."

"But—"

"Our best hope is that the fire never reaches us at all."

It was as well for my composure that Cissy stirred just then. She sat partway up and looked around drowsily, then her face seemed to collapse as she realized where she was, and that the nightmare of fire was real.

"Two thousand degrees?" she cried. "Oh, God, we're all going to die!"

I rushed to sit beside her. "Shh, it's all right, Cissy. Everything's going to be fine. Are you thirsty, can I bring you something?"

She shook her head peevishly as she lay down again, and within seconds she was deep into her drugged sleep again. I wished I was, too. Julie didn't say a word as I left, simply turning to resume her bleak vigil. Yes, it was *The Lady of Shalott*, and in the poem she was waiting for her doom.

On my way down the stairs, I realized that I'd lost my train of thought about Domaso. But what did it matter now?

His body would be cremated where it lay, and his murderer's fate would be the same as mine, and Aaron's, and . . .

"Kharnegie?" My fears must have shown on my face, because Boris looked deeply concerned. He stood gazing up at me from the foot of the staircase, a water bottle in his hand and dark rivulets of sweat streaking the coat of dust on his bare chest. "Kharnegie, do not be afraid. I will protect you."

I laughed. A little wildly, but at least I laughed. "I'm sure you will, Boris."

He drained the water into his open mouth and sighed in satisfaction. "Come outside, my friend. Come see our good work."

As I began to go with him, I remembered Domaso draining that can of beer on the roadside a few eternal days ago. And I realized that while I adored Boris, and had felt considerable distaste for Domaso, the two men did have something in common. An uncomplicated passion for life, as pure and simple as a child's or a—

"A dog! Oh, my God, the dog!"

"What dog?" Startled, Boris stared around him. "Where is dog?"

"That's just it, I don't know. Domaso had a dog. I guess he'd only had him for a little while but still, poor Gorka's running loose in the woods somewhere by himself. Oh, Boris, he might get caught in the fire, we've got to go find him!"

The Mad Russian seemed to think I'd gone mad, and maybe he was right. But his words were lost in a new noise, one that cut through the distant monotone roar of the fire. This was a staccato bass-note throbbing that sent Boris and me, and everyone else in the great room, stampeding out to the front of the inn.

For a moment I was caught up in the euphoria, as the helicopter appeared in a gap above the trees. It bucked a little in the wind, appearing and disappearing in the clouds of smoke. All around me the civilians were leaping up and down ecstatically, waving their arms, and even Aaron, the skeptic, stood over on the other side of the group grinning.

But not the smoke jumpers. Weary and sweat-soaked from working nonstop on the safety zone, they turned their skeptical eyes to Jack, and I felt a sickening chill as I recalled what he'd said. Nowhere to land.

"That pilot's a nervy son of a bitch, coming out in these conditions," said Al Soriano beside me. "He can't hover properly to drop us a rescue line, but at least now they know we're here. That's something."

Suddenly the copter tilted and swerved, like a horse reined hard to one side, and just as suddenly it was gone from our view.

"They will be back?" asked Boris.

" 'Course they will," said Sam, raising his voice over the babble of questions and exclamations. "It might take a little while, though, so let's all get back to work. May as well get that fire line done, huh, gang? Then they'll whisk us down to Ketchum and I'll buy you all a drink for helping to save White Pine. Hell, you all get free rooms for life, how about that?"

Dear old Sam, ever the optimist, with his mansions in the sky and his grandiose plans and his . . . *Helicopter. Didn't Sam say something once about a helicopter?* It came back to me as I pushed through the milling people and grabbed Jack by the arm. *He said he'd build an airstrip and Cissy could get her lampshades by helicopter.*

"Jack, couldn't we make a place for them to land?" Even

as I said the words, I saw the futility of the idea. How could a few exhausted people make an airstrip? "I guess not . . ."

But Jack's face was lighting up like a sunrise. He suddenly embraced me and swung me around with a fervor that was worthy of Boris. "Of *course*! My God, girl, I've got to stop getting married, it's screwing with my brains."

I half smiled, bewildered but willing to hope. "Could we cut down that many trees?"

"We don't have to," he said, already forgetting me as he turned away. Love 'em and leave 'em, that was Jack. "We only have to cut down three. Yo, Al! You know the most about extractions. Could a copter drop into that meadow and take these people off if those pondos were down?"

The smoke jumpers huddled with Sam, talking low and rapidly, and we civilians knew enough to stay out of their way. I saw Aaron shaking his head doubtfully, and went over to him.

"You think the meadow's too small, don't you?" After listening to Julie, I was ready to be angry at any further pessimism. "Don't you?"

"How would I know, Stretch? I just don't see how we're going to chop down any trees that big. We've got landscaping tools, not lumbering stuff. We're barely getting out the bushes down there."

"Listen up," said Jack loudly. He mounted the inn's front steps and looked down into each of our faces. "We all know the fire's getting closer. It might slow down, but it might make a run up this ridge, so we've got to do everything we can to protect ourselves. The fire line teams should keep working, but once the safety zone is ready I want all of you in it, and the jumpers will finish the line. Is that clear? I'm putting Al Soriano here in charge, and what he says goes, no questions."

"And what shall you be doing?" asked Beau Paliere. He'd been thoroughly subdued since his talking-to from Larabee, but I had to admit he'd been working as hard as anyone.

"I'm going down the ridge to that construction site you probably saw on your way up here. There's some chain saws there, and I'll bring them back here so we can take down those ponderosa pines. I figure we can buck up the trunks and clear them out of the meadow in a couple of hours, so *if* the copter comes back and *if* it can land, that's one of our tickets out." He flashed his smile generously now, handing out hope. "That's a lot of ifs, so we've got to keep working as hard as we can, all right? And for your own safety, you have *got* to cooperate with Al."

Al stepped up beside him with his usual good-natured smile, but by the look in his eye, anyone who didn't cooperate was going to be sorry.

"One more thing," said Jack. "I'm taking my Jeep down the road after those chain saws, but I may have to do the last part on foot, and if that's the case I need a second pair of hands to help me carry them. Now that's downhill, toward the fire, which is not the safest direction in the world. My jumpers are pretty beat, but—"

"I'll go," said Aaron. He said it quietly, but he was close beside me and I felt the excitement running through him like an electrical charge. "I've been napping, like you said, so I'm rested."

"Good enough," said Jack, and headed for the Jeep with his arm around Tracy, murmuring to her as they went. What a start to a honeymoon.

As the group dispersed, with Al issuing curt but even-tempered orders, Aaron paused to give me a quick kiss. At least he meant it to be quick, but I held on to his arms. I didn't plan to let go.

"Are you *insane*?" I said, keeping my voice down. "Do you know how fast a fire can travel uphill? This is a crazy idea—"

"This was your idea, Stretch," he said mildly. "And I'm going."

"It's too dangerous," I pleaded. "Don't go. I mean it. Don't."

"Carnegie, listen." It struck me for the first time that Aaron only used my proper name during his rare solemn moments. "Remember what I told you before, that firefighting is like war? I've never been in a war, and nobody ever should, and I hope to God I never will be. But this is my chance, don't you see? My chance to do something, I don't know, something good. I have to do this."

"Your chance to get killed, you mean." I held on tighter. We were alone now by the steps, smoke stinging our eyes. "Don't be a fool, Aaron. Don't do this."

He cocked his head. Usually when he did that, a lock of black hair fell across his forehead. But now his hair was stiff with dried sweat, and his unbruised cheek was creased from sleeping against a sofa pillow. Aaron looked terrible, and I loved him terribly.

"So you don't mind if Jack Packard goes?" he said.

"Of course not! I mean, I do, but it's his job. It's not yours, and I want you safe."

"That's nice to hear." His smile was still lopsided. "Now let me go, Stretch. See you soon, I promise."

He got in the Jeep. Jack kissed Tracy through the window and drove them away. I watched them go, streaming with tears, until the road was empty.

And then, galumphing up the empty road toward me, came the only creature in the world who could end my weeping at a moment like this.

"Gorka! Oh, Gorka, you dear idiot. Come here, boy, come here."

And come he did, his rope leash flying as he tore up the hill at full speed. He had something clamped in his huge drooling jaws as usual, and as usual he dropped his trophy at my feet and barked in triumph.

I had to wipe the tears away to see properly, but even then I couldn't believe what I was seeing.

Gorka's trophy, covered in ashes and soot, was pale gray and roughly spherical, the size of a stone you could hold in your two cupped hands. But stones don't have eye sockets, or a gaping darkness where a nose had once been, or a few teeth still attached to what remained of the upper jaw. There was another, smaller hole on one side, and I thought I knew what had caused it. In fact the only thing that kept me from fainting in horror was curiosity about whether I was right.

If I was right, Gorka's trophy was a human skull with a bullet hole through the temple.

Chapter Thirty-Two

I WOULDN'T HAVE PEGGED THE CHIEF AS A SHAKESPEARE buff, but then, you never know. Sitting upstairs in the master bedroom, holding the skull in one hand, he rubbed his chin with the other and lifted his eyes to me wryly.

"I feel like Hamlet," he said. "Alas, poor Yorick."

I didn't answer. I was busy looking for somewhere to tie Gorka's leash, now that he'd slobbered all over me and Sam, and been ordered away from her pretty pink handbag and then off the pretty purple bed by an indignant Cissy. Pawprints on the bedspread seemed to bother her more than the skull. Julie Nothstine, the cat lady, was far more interested in the skull, but she kept her post at the window and kept well away from the dog. Everyone else was still at their labors down below.

I had taken the skull directly and discreetly to Larabee, and when he brought Sam and me upstairs that meant bringing Gorka. We needed a private place to confer without losing contact with a lookout, so we stayed in the master bedroom. But Gorka was clearly an outdoor dog.

"Just shut him in the bathroom and he'll settle down," said the chief. "Go on there, Max, good dog."

"Max?" I said, as I followed his advice and pulled the bathroom door closed. From behind it came the sounds of scratching, a whine or two, and then silence. "Domaso said his name was Gorka."

"Never heard of any Gorka," he said, "but I'm telling you, that's Edie Hammond's dog Max. She lost him from her place down in Hailey about a month ago. Come to think of it, she's a redhead, too, about your build."

"Let me guess. They play fetch a lot?"

But the chief had gone back to contemplating mortality, or at least the mortality of the owner of the skull.

"Wonder where Max found it," he said. "Looks like it's been in the woods a while. Sam, you know of any missing person cases up here, hunters or whatever?" Seeing Sam shake his head, he went on, "Not that this entry wound looks like any hunting accident. If that's not a small-caliber pistol, I'll eat my hat. No telling how old it is, though, not till I get it back to—"

A knock on the bedroom door interrupted him. He set the skull on the low vanity table and sat himself squarely in front of it, then nodded at me to answer.

Danny Kane stepped in, rank with sweat, and said, "Al wants a report on the fire from up here."

"It appears to be stationary at the moment," said Julie. "But the winds are still fitful."

"Check."

What happened next was all because of the three-way mirror in the corner where, incredibly enough, Tracy had tried on her wedding gown only this morning. As Danny turned back to the door, he happened to catch a glimpse of the skull behind Larabee's back—and I happened to be looking at him when he did.

Danny's small, bunched-together features went absolutely stiff with shock, and his eyelids fluttered like a man about to lose consciousness. He took a stumbling step forward, unspeaking, but no one else had noticed his expression. To them he must have seemed tired, nothing more.

"Do you recognize it?" I said sharply. Larabee frowned at me and Sam began to say something, but I ignored them. "Danny, was that skull in your truck? Was that why you were yelling at Domaso?"

He stood frozen, his fingers on the doorknob. I heard Cissy give a little gasp. Then he turned around to face his stepmother and his father. His eyes were haunted, and when he spoke, he spoke to Sam.

"He was going to report it," said Danny in a dull monotone. "I didn't mean to hit him so hard, but then he went down and it was too late. . . ."

His voice trailed off and he stood there swaying, a tree about to fall. Larabee got up slowly and took him by the arm. Danny let himself be led to a chair, moving like a sleepwalker, mumbling again, "Too late . . ."

"Sit down, son," said Larabee gently. Something in his manner warned us all to stay quiet, not to break the spell. "Now tell me, what was it that Duarte was going to report?"

"Duarte?"

"You said that Duarte was going to report something, that's why you hit him. Just tell me about it from the beginning, son. You saw Domaso Duarte at the hot spring, and then what?"

"I wasn't at the hot spring." The younger man scowled in confusion. "I never hit Duarte. I wanted to, after his dog got into my gear and ran off with . . . with . . ."

"We know what the dog ran off with," the chief said. "But then who are you talking about? Who did you hit?"

Danny turned his face away, and as he did, he saw me.

His eyes widened and then filled with tears. "God, Carnegie, I'm sorry. Forgive me?"

Larabee and I exchanged baffled glances, but Danny's next words brought everything into focus like the click of a kaleidoscope wheel.

"Bri was your cousin," he moaned, "and I killed him. I didn't mean to hit him so hard, I swear. I'm sorry!"

"I don't believe it." Sam strode over to his son. "*You* killed another smoke jumper? Why? How could you possibly—"

"I was protecting you!" Danny leapt to his feet, his lethargy burned away, his face dark with fury. "You thought I didn't know, you thought I was just a kid, but I saw you. I saw you getting out of your plane with blood on your hands, and I saw you that night getting rid of a gun."

Now we were the ones frozen with shock. Julie motionless at the window, Cissy still sitting on the bed, Sam and Larabee and me standing in the middle of the room. None of us moved as Danny's grimy hand dove into a pocket and pulled something out, flat pieces of metal that clicked against each other as they slid along a tarnished chain. Dog tags.

"I *was* just a kid," said Danny despairingly. "I thought I must have dreamed about the gun because everyone said that he drowned, but it's always been in the back of my mind, and then Brian found these and I knew!"

As he waved the chain at Sam his voice began rising, louder and higher. "Bri read me the name, he said Kane, Roy J., that's the same name as you. I told him to hand them over, I told him it was a secret, but he laughed and said what was it worth to me. I grabbed at them and we fought and I hit him with the handle of my Pulaski. I didn't mean to hit him so hard. I'm sorry. I'm so sorry . . ."

Danny was sobbing now. None of us moved.

"I brought the . . . I brought *that* back with me, but then I didn't know what to do with it. I didn't want anybody to see it, like that security guy did. But I couldn't just get rid of it, could I? It's all that's left of Roy, for God's sake. There should be a funeral, there should be some *respect*—"

Sam took a step toward his son, and Danny's face changed.

"It wasn't a dream, was it?" he snarled. "You shot your own brother, you son of a bitch, and you flew over Boot Creek and dumped his body out of the plane where no one would ever find it. You killed my Uncle Roy and I'm going to kill *you*!"

He sprang at Sam then, and that snapped us all out of our trance of disbelief. For a man with heart trouble, Larabee moved like a snake, pinning Danny facedown on the floor and snapping handcuffs on him while Sam was still backing away in horror.

"The boy's gone crazy," said Sam, in a shaky, old man's voice. His face was gray. "He's . . . I never . . ."

"Sit down, Sam," said Larabee. "Get him some water, please."

This request was directed at me, not at Sam's wife, because Cissy was sitting on the bed, wringing her pudgy hands and making tiny moaning sounds, the very picture of utter uselessness. Julie went to sit by her, and I went for the water.

The room had two sinks, one outside the bathroom proper, which was lucky because Gorka/Max was pawing at the door and barking. I kicked the door to silence him and brought Sam the glass. He accepted it with trembling hands and thanked me, and he didn't say another word as Larabee walked Danny out of the room.

Danny did, though, as he came past me.

"Bri *could* have died in that fall," he said. "He tied off wrong, you know. He had a lucky break coming down through the branches the way he did, but he could have died, even if I hadn't... It could have been an accidental death, just like it said in the official findings."

I couldn't find my voice, and then he was gone. And I don't know, to this day, what I would have said.

The chief came back looking grim. "I've locked him in the squad car. You want to tell me about this, Sam?"

"Not without my attorney." Sam smiled bleakly. "If I ever see him again. And a shrink for Danny, of course. Anybody with eyes in his head can see that he's disturbed, hallucinating even. You can't leave the boy cuffed, Howard, not if the fire comes."

"Well, I'm damned if I know what else to do," said Larabee. "He's killed three people, for God's sake, one of 'em right in the middle of this party. I've been asking questions. Somebody saw Duarte just before the cake cutting, and then the Russian fellow found his body right after. Danny must have sneaked down to the hot spring in between and—"

"No, he didn't." Julie spoke up from her place beside Cissy. "Danny was on the veranda with me throughout the party. He's always very attentive. He couldn't have gone to the hot spring."

"She's right. I saw him, too," I said. Then I spoke what was in all our minds. "But if Danny didn't kill Domaso, then who did?"

"What does it matter?" Cissy blurted. "We're all going to die anyway, why don't we just admit it?"

Julie glared at her in disapproval and Cissy fell silent, a scolded child.

"As I said before," said Julie sententiously, "it may have been an accident, after all. People do fall, especially when they have been drinking alcohol, or perhaps even using drugs."

"Duarte wasn't known as a user," the chief said, as if to himself, "but you never know. He might have been smoking dope, or popping some kind of pills."

Cissy made a small movement with her foot. She saw me looking and made a show of crossing her legs, but not before I saw her foot nudge something small and pink under the purple dust ruffle of the bed.

"You know," I said casually, "I'm feeling awfully upset about all this. Cissy, do you have any more of those tranquilizers?"

We had a bit of a scuffle over the pretty pink handbag, but in the end Julie clamped her long hands over Cissy's pudgy ones and prized it away from her.

The tranquilizer bottle, which I'd seen full only a few hours ago, was completely empty.

Chapter Thirty-Three

IT WAS THE WEIRDEST CONFESSION OF MURDER YOU CAN imagine—and not one that would ever stand up in court, because the defendant seemed to be stoned.

"If it wasn't for that awful dog..." said Cissy, her eyes glazed and her voice dreamy. "I saw it run off with *that*"—she nodded at the skull, still glaring at us blindly from the vanity table—"but of course I had no idea what it was until Danny told me."

"He *told* you?" I blurted, and someone else made a small sound of wonderment. Outside the picture window the light was dimming as the streamers of smoke became overlapping veils, but none of us really registered the fact. We were mesmerized by Cissy's high-pitched, little-girl voice.

"Oh yes, he told me on the way back to the party." She fluttered those curly eyelashes, inviting us to share a tidbit of gossip. "He hardly knew what he was saying, poor boy, just mumbling about dog tags. I pretended not to hear him, but then he said Roy's name and that's when I realized. And to think Danny knew about the gun all these years!"

Sam stirred. "Cissy, honey—"

"Oh, I know, we never talk about it, even in private." She giggled. "Never, never. That's why I had to make sure Domaso never talked about it either. I fixed him a little drink with my pills, and then I said, Sweetie, I've got something special to show you down at the honeymoon cottage. I said, You know that old crown you keep asking about? Well, you come down to the cottage with me. So he came."

Cissy gave a contented little sigh and looked blandly around, as if the story was done.

"And then what?" Larabee said it quietly, but his eye was twitching nonstop. "You got to the hot spring, and then what?"

"Well, what do you think?" she said petulantly. "He got sleepy and laid down on the ground by the water. I tried hitting him with a rock, but that was messy, so I just rolled him into the pool and left. Howard, sweetie, I'm sorry about your nice radio, but I didn't want you to tell anyone, you know? Never, never, never, that's what Sam says. But it doesn't matter now. We're all going to die."

Larabee was gentle but relentless. "You're saying that you killed Domaso Duarte to conceal the murder of Roy Kane."

"Oh, it wasn't murder," she pouted. "It was just—"

"That's enough," said Sam. He wasn't shaky anymore. He had control of himself, and he seemed to think he could control this situation, too. Old habits die hard, and Sam had a lifetime of being in charge. "She was protecting me, Howard, and that's all there is to it."

"But why, Sam?" said Julie. "What possible reason could you have for killing Roy?"

Sam refused to look at her, but addressed himself to Larabee. "Once we're back in town and I've got my attorney with me, I'll tell you all the details. But we're not going to talk about this anymore, understand?"

"Talk about what, Daddy?" Tracy stood in the doorway,

her bare arms dirty and her long hair in strings. "And why's Danny in the police car? What's going on?"

"Nothing to worry about. You go back downstairs," Sam told her. But first he crossed the room to embrace her, perhaps for the last time. Perhaps he was grateful that she'd never know the truth about him.

"Be brave, sugar," he murmured into her hair. "But you always are. I've always been so proud of you. You're the joy of my life, you know that, Tracy girl? The joy of my—"

"Oh, for heaven's sake," Cissy burst out. "She isn't even yours!"

Sam and Tracy turned to gape at her. With nothing left to lose, plump little Cissy shook herself like a hen settling her feathers, and triumphantly played her final card.

"That's why I had to shoot him, don't you see?"

"Shoot who?" said Tracy. But her mother didn't seem to notice. Cissy was far away, far in the past.

"We were on the way to Bitterroot Lake in the Twin Otter," she said. "Sam was piloting, and Roy and I were in back. I told Roy my news, about being pregnant, and I asked him to promise not to tell Sam. But he said no!"

She frowned to herself at the foolishness of men. "Roy said that Sam had to find out about us sooner or later, and that he'd marry me himself. I had my little gun that Sam got me for burglars, and I pulled it out and said, Listen to me, Roy Kane. I am going to marry the next governor of Idaho and that is that, so you keep quiet! He tried to take the gun away and so what else could I do?"

"You told me . . ." Sam's voice caught and choked. "You told me Roy molested you. I would never have—"

"You would never have staged your brother's suicide?" demanded Julie Nothstine. Her strange blue eyes burned from the pallor of her face. "You would never have blackened the memory of a fine man, a hero? How dare you, how could you—"

"People!" bellowed Boris from downstairs. "All people come to safety zone, now!"

We stood like statues, struck motionless by Cissy's revelations. Then a more pressing question came back to me, and I rushed out to the landing.

"Has Jack come back?" I called down, but of course I meant Aaron. "Did they bring the chain saws?"

I already knew the answer, because Tracy would have told us if her new husband had returned. But when Boris shook his head I felt a cold fist gripping at my heart.

"Let's go," said the chief behind me. He sounded calm and official, but urgent, not to be disobeyed. "Everybody downstairs, pronto."

I stepped aside as he led Cissy past, holding her by the elbow as though guiding a blind person. Sam followed, his long cheeks slack and ashen, with Tracy beside him looking like a lost child.

Julie Nothstine came last, blinking back tears. But when she stumbled a little on her twisted foot, Tracy returned to her and slipped a supportive arm around her waist. Julie leaned gratefully against Roy Kane's daughter, and they left the suite.

But I wasn't the last one left. I heard a faint scrabbling behind the bathroom door, and then an inquisitive whine. Gorka—Max—had been patient all this time, but he could tell that everyone was leaving and he didn't like it.

I opened the door carefully, ready to grab at the rope leash, but Max rocketed past me and made for the hallway, barking in excitement. When I caught up with him on the stairs, Sam had him by the collar.

"Thanks for remembering him," Sam said quietly. He looked old and defeated. "You're a good girl, Red."

I didn't reply, but wound the frayed end of Max's leash around my knuckles and followed Sam out the front door. And into a changed world.

While we'd been inside, a poisonous-smelling shroud of dense brown smoke had overtaken White Pine. Through the smoke came soft pale flakes of ash, sifting down in a constant shower like some surrealistic fall of snow. The heat in the air was a brutal assault to the senses, and I stopped for a moment to brace myself against it.

Out in the gloom and the falling ash, dim figures were shouting to each other over the distant deep roar of the fire. But the roar wasn't so distant anymore. The beast was approaching. Max stiffened all four legs, planting his paws and growling back at this invisible enemy.

"Come on, buddy," I coaxed. "Come on, stay by me."

I dragged at the leash and followed the shouts to the parking area. The once-narrow strip of weeds along the road had been scraped down to bare soil and widened several yards on either side. But this safety zone looked pitifully small with thirty people crowded into it, even with all the cars moved to a distance.

All the cars but one. Squinting through the murky air, I saw Chief Larabee and Al Soriano in private conference by the squad car. The chief still had Cissy by the elbow, but Al took over that duty as the chief unlocked the back door, helped Danny out, and removed his handcuffs.

Both Danny and his mother moved listlessly, like sleepwalkers, their eyes on the ground. I looked around for Sam but he was on the far side of the group, his arm around Tracy, keeping as distant from them as he could.

"Toddy!" Al shouted. "You want to move this vehicle for me?"

Todd emerged from the smoke and calmly took the keys that Larabee proffered. He slid behind the wheel and started the engine, and as the brake lights came on they made angry red embers in the smoke.

The Tyke appeared at my shoulder as the car rolled away. She had ashes in her hair, and her voice was a harsh croak.

"We don't want any gas tanks too close to us," she said grimly. "You OK? Larabee told us what went down with Danny and his mom. I can't believe it."

Neither could I, but I wasn't thinking about them anymore. I was thinking about Aaron, and trying so desperately to contain my dread that I couldn't say his name for fear of breaking down.

"No sign of them?" I asked her.

"No." The Tyke's eyes were blood-colored from working in the smoke, but I could see dread in them as well. "They could have gone the other way, you know. This is a fluky fire and we can't tell what it's doing. They could have gone downhill if they couldn't make it back up. They're probably down there someplace worrying about us."

She didn't believe that and neither did I, but it helped a little to pretend that we did. I nodded and bent down to stroke Max, and kept stroking him as the Tyke moved away.

Max was shuddering now, and whining like a puppy, so I knelt beside him in the dirt and put my arm around the heavy muscled neck. His coat was rough and bristly where I laid my cheek against it.

"It's all right," I murmured. "It's all right, Maxie. I'm right here."

"Is he OK?" asked Todd, squatting beside me. "You need help with him?"

Todd was clear-eyed and calm, as he'd been since the crisis started, the very model of the stoic smoke jumper that he'd always idolized.

"Thanks," I said. "We're taking care of each other."

"Listen up, everybody!" Al called out then. I grabbed the leash as we gathered around him, eager for leadership. Eager for a miracle. "Listen close, 'cause this is important. We could be here for a while. The head of the fire might not even come in our direction, but if it does, you're all gonna want to lie flat and keep your nose and mouth down on the ground."

"We are to put our faces into the dirt?" asked Beau Paliere, affronted. Which was ironic considering the amount of dirt already on his face. His elegant shirt and jacket were long gone, and his undershirt—the sexy tank top kind—was filthy.

"Is right!" Boris called from the back of the group. "Air is cooler at ground."

"Exactly," said Al. He, too, had ashes in his air, and his eyes were like wounds. "You want to scoop out a little hole for your mouth and nose and take shallow breaths, understand? But like I said, it might not come to that. The most important thing is to stay right here in the safety zone. Buddy up with the folks next to you, and help each other stay put. . . ."

There were nods and murmurs all around me. People were embracing now, and the roar of the fire from behind its curtain of smoke was a background to their weeping. I felt myself slipping into a sort of numbed trance.

This can't be happening. This is happening. Take care of Max. I stood quietly petting him, grateful to have someone who needed me to stay calm. The shuddering had stopped, but he was panting hard in the mounting heat and his eyes were blank and staring.

The rest of Al's words were lost in a sudden roar of the fire. It wasn't a roar, though, more of a drone. A motorized drone, growing louder...

A small plane burst into view between the smoke clouds, skimming perilously low over the treetops. A crate tumbled from the plane's belly and plummeted down like a stone, and then a parachute blossomed above the crate like a round white flower.

As we held our breaths, the crate jerked and swung and floated, to land heavily on the road just down the hill from us. We stood speechless for a moment, then Al let out a wild rejoicing whoop.

"What is it?" asked Boris. "What is in box?"

"Chain saws, man," Al crowed. "Freakin' chain saws!"

Chapter Thirty-Four

MAX DAMN NEAR DISLOCATED MY SHOULDER, LEAPING FORward and trying to dash after Al, Todd, and the Tyke as they trotted down the road to retrieve the precious equipment. He was desperate for an end to this ordeal, poor creature, and so were the rest of us.

As we shouted and laughed and waved, the plane circled away and came back for a second pass, much higher up. Two more parachutes blossomed in the air, rectangular this time, with human figures guiding them. We stood staring up at these new smoke jumpers, cheering, and then suddenly we had to clear aside to let them land in the safety zone.

The first jumper had barely tucked and rolled and removed his helmet before we swarmed all over him with questions.

"Are they sending helicopters?"

"Is White Pine going to burn?"

"How soon can we get out of here?"

Then Al came back with a chain saw in each hand, grinning his snaggle-toothed grin. "Took you long enough, you sons of bitches. Let's get going, Hardcase."

"Wait!" Tracy pushed her way to the front and asked the question I'd been afraid to voice. "Did you see any sign of

Jack Packard from up there? He drove down the ridge in a red Jeep, but he should have been back by now."

"We spotted the Jeep, all right, pulled over on the shoulder about halfway down the ridge." Hardcase—real name Buford Hart—was a dark-haired fellow, very young, sporting a neatly trimmed beard and a soft Southern accent. "This heah fire hooked over the road, so he couldn't have driven back up. But there's a hot-shot crew cutting line a little farther down, so my guess is he's with them."

"Thank goodness," said Tracy, swaying a little in her relief. "I knew he'd be all right, I just knew it."

"There was a second man," I ventured. "Did you see him?"

Hart shook his head. "No, ma'am, but like I said, they're probably with that crew. Al, we've got three helicopters on the way, and we brought—"

I clutched his arm. "Can't you radio the crew and find out?"

"Can't get through, the signals are interrupted up here." He said it patiently enough, but I suddenly saw myself in his eyes: a disheveled, nearly hysterical woman who was delaying his mission. "Now if you'll let me go, the sooner we clear that meadow for a helispot, the sooner we can get y'all home. Al, we brought a med kit, have you got casualties?"

"We're good," said Al. "Let's go cut down some trees."

With Al directing the smoke jumpers and the stronger civilians pitching in—and with Chief Larabee and Max standing guard over the prisoners—the ponderosa pines were felled, limbed, and sawed into sections with remarkable speed. It was hard, hot work, but no one faltered and no one complained, not with the smell of burning in our nostrils and the roar of the beast all around.

We knew that if the smoke closed in again the copters

couldn't land, so we worked like fiends. In little more than an hour we were dragging away the last of the debris, glancing up often to reassure ourselves that the trio of helicopters was still circling overhead. Staggering with exhaustion, I barely noticed that my lungs were raw and my hands were scraped and bleeding. I was even too tired to be afraid.

But finally it was done, we had cleared the meadow, and moments later the first helicopter lowered itself to the ground in a blinding cloud of dust and pine needles. The din of the rotors drowned out even the fire, so the evacuation took place in a weirdly deafened pantomime of shouts and hand signals.

"Come on, Chief!" Al bellowed, windmilling his arm and sprinting to the door of the helicopter in a crouching run. "Come on!"

Larabee hustled Cissy and Danny Kane inside, followed by as many of the civilians as could safely be jammed in with them—including Beau Paliere, who somehow managed to be first in line.

As the rotors whined and the copter lifted off, Al and his crew began to form up the remaining civilians, counting them off into groups to make the loading go as fast as possible.

Hart came over to where I sat drooping on the ground next to Julie Nothstine. Unable to help much with the physical work, Julie had been tending Max for me. He was calmer now, and had laid his huge head in her lap.

"You're next, ladies," Hart shouted, reaching to help Julie to her feet.

Sam and Tracy were nearby, and Tracy hurried over to support Julie as the three of them joined the group for the next helicopter. I wanted to tell Hart that I'd go later, but my voice was failing, so I shook my head and waved my hands to signal "No."

"Come on, ma'am! Nothing to be scared of!"

He grabbed my hand and I tore it away, furious and frustrated. The effort of explaining to him that this was my wedding, that I couldn't leave before my guests and my staff, was simply beyond me. Plus I hate being called "ma'am."

"No!" I hollered, and Max seconded the motion with a snarl and a show of teeth. "Take the others!"

The smoke jumper swore at Max and reached for me again, but the Tyke, who'd been watching, interceded.

"Back off, Hardcase. She knows what she's doing."

Muttering in anger, Hart threw up his hands and stomped away. The Tyke slapped me approvingly on the back—I nearly fell over—and went to round up load number three.

Thankfully, the smoke held off for loads three and four. And though we couldn't see the fire from here in the meadow, the roar of the beast seemed to be holding steady, or even retreating. We had our miracle.

The fifth batch, the last one, consisted of smoke jumpers, Boris Nevsky, Max, and me. Boris had worked like a fiend and a half, but he was still stoked on adrenaline.

"Is your dog?" he asked, as we waited for our helicopter to return. He extended grimy fingers, and I relaxed the leash to let Max sniff them.

"Only for now. Chief Larabee's going to return him to his real owner. Boris, you were a wonder today."

"*Da*, I was most wonderful. Is good to work hard. I think I will become smoke jumper, then my Kharnegie will admire me even more!"

I laughed for the first time in forever. "I don't how I could admire you any more than—Max! Max, come back here!"

Whether it was the clamor of the helicopter or just another mad whim, Max had torn the leash from my scraped-up hand and gone bounding across the meadow. I started after him, but my feet were leaden.

"Let's go," the Tyke yelled from the helicopter. "Everybody in, now!"

"Wait!" I shrieked. "Wait till I get him. Please?"

But the fire beast was roaring louder now. The smoke jumpers were dashing for the helicopter, which was rocking on its skids, barely staying earthbound in the rush to fetch us away. I tried to keep running, but then Boris had me by the left shoulder and the Tyke was at my right.

"We go *now*," she commanded. And then, in a different voice, she said, "Oh my God."

"I got him!" called a voice from the far edge of the meadow. There, coming out of the trees with a hand clamped on Max's collar, was Jack the Knack. He was hardly recognizable, his clothing scorched and his fair hair blackened with soot. I couldn't read his expression.

"Packard!" the Tyke called out, tears springing to her red-rimmed eyes. "Get your ass over here and get on this chopper! Where've you been?"

There were cries and shouts from behind us, but they faded into the distance as I forced my feet forward, one and then the other.

"Jack?" I heard myself saying as he trudged toward us. My voice was a stranger's, someone far away. "Where . . ."

Everything seemed to go silent and distant then, everything seemed to fall away from my vision except for Jack Packard's somber, stricken face.

I ran to him. "Where is he? Where's Aaron?"

Jack closed his arms around me.

"I'm sorry," he said roughly. "Bad news."

About the Author

DEBORAH DONNELLY is a sea captain's daughter who grew up in Panama, Cape Cod, and points in between. She's been an executive speechwriter, a university librarian, a science fiction writer, and a nanny. A longtime resident of Seattle and a bloomingly healthy breast cancer survivor, Donnelly now lives physically in Boise, Idaho, and virtually at www.deborahdonnelly.org.

Dear Reader:

Welcome to the Wedding Planner Mysteries!

You know, some of my best wedding anecdotes (like Tracy Kane's ill-fitting dress or the snake who slithered down the aisle) are inspired by absolutely true real-life stories. So if you have a wedding story of your own, why not share it with me?

Whether it's a disastrous bachelor party, an unusually charming bridal gown, or your suggestion for the perfect wedding venue, I'd love to hear all about it. Just visit www.deborahdonnelly.org and click on "Drop Me A Line."

I hope you enjoyed Death Takes a Honeymoon, and if you've missed any of Carnegie's other escapades, please read on for a special peek at each one.

Cheers,

Deborah Donnelly

Don't miss any of Deborah Donnelly's mysteries in
the coast-to-coast-adored series that's

"A DELIGHTFUL MIX OF BRIDES, BODIES AND
MAYHEM . . . A TREAT TO DEVOUR" (*Book Page*).

Available from Dell Books.

Read on for special excerpts of each—
and look for your copies at your favorite bookseller.

Veiled Threats

on sale now

When love is in the air, Carnegie Kincaid is not far behind. A wedding planner who works out of her Seattle houseboat, Carnegie makes magic—usually . . .

In Veiled Threats, *Carnegie agrees to plan a wedding for one of Seattle's most prominent families—who happen to be going through a high-stakes, headline-grabbing legal war. Before she can get her bride-to-be into just the right dress, a murder and a kidnapping plunge Carnegie into a mystery of extortion and violence . . .*

I LOVE THIS MOMENT. YOUNG AND TREMBLING OR calm and not-so-young, seed pearls or tie-dye, intimate ceremony or extravaganza, this first public appearance of the bride always makes me misty. There's all the romance that Western culture can bestow: the idea of the fairy princess, Cinderella, the one and only true love. Not to mention the sheer theater of making a solo entrance in a knockout costume. But it was the courage that caught at my never-married heart. To publicly say, He's the one; I pledge my life to his life. All the divorce statistics in the world can't tarnish that moment.

That's the real reason why I help people get married. I'm a sucker for romance.

So I lingered while Diane, bright as a sunrise, took her place beside her chosen man. The candlelight gleamed on her gown and in her eyes, and Jeffrey looked, as all bridegrooms should, like the luckiest fellow on earth. I sighed, dabbed at a tear, and slipped back through the fine old oak-floored dining room into the mansion's kitchen. I had to track down a pair of antique crystal goblets sent over by the groom's grandmother this morning, thus setting off the old lady's tantrum. And I had to ask Joe Solveto, the caterer, where the hell that third waiter was.

The kitchen was crammed with hors d'oeuvres but empty of Joe or anyone else. My stomach growled fiercely at the fans of prosciutto-wrapped asparagus, ranks of crisp snow pea pods piped with velvety salmon mousse, and clusters of green grapes rolled in Roquefort. The wedding cake, three tiers of chocolate hazelnut glory, was already in the dining room, but the old marble countertop along the kitchen wall held a parade of cut-glass dishes piled with petit fours and chocolate-dipped apricots. Surely I could pluck just one apricot from its dish, one tiny cream puff from its pyramid, one oyster from its bed of crushed ice, without disturbing Joe's fearful symmetry . . .

But no, first things first. I stepped out to the back porch and squinted into the drizzly night, hoping to see the waiter's headlights. Sercombe House sits high on a hill, with terraced flower beds stretching down the lawn. The parking lot behind the house had filled. Parked cars were now lined up nose-to-tail the whole length of the steep drive leading down to the highway, where a mossy old brick wall bordered the property. I could see my modest white van, nicknamed Vanna White, just uphill from Nickie Parry's candy-apple-red '66 Mustang.

The car had been a college graduation gift from Nickie's father. Douglas Parry owned several department stores, a few Alaskan fish canneries, and a good chunk of downtown Seattle. He was so very fond of Nickie that he'd said the three magic words about her wedding: Money No Object. Fifteen percent of Money No Object was going to put me firmly in the black, for the first time since I'd started Made in Heaven. I wondered idly if my parking brake was set—I'd hate to dent that Mustang—but I wasn't willing to brave the downpour to find out.

Someone else was out in the rain, though: a heavyset figure was striding downhill just beyond the Mustang. His long raincoat flapped as though he were shoving something into a pocket. Car keys, probably. But he was heading away from the house, not toward it, so he couldn't be my waiter. Well, we'd have to manage with only two. I turned my back on the hissing of the rain and went inside to find Grandmother's goblets.

I had better luck on this count. The crystal in question, facets winking in the light, had been unwrapped and set on a high shelf out of harm's way. Also out of reach, even for me, so I pulled over a wooden chair and stood on tiptoe. Just another inch...A startling blast of damp air lifted my skirt. Already off balance, I turned abruptly to see a handsome, frowning man enter through the porch door and shake the rain from his windbreaker. My third waiter. The chair wobbled, then tipped over with a clatter, sending me in a harmless but ungraceful leap to the checkerboard tile floor. I saved myself from sprawling flat at the cost of a cracked fingernail and my dignity.

He reached out a hand. "Are you all right?"

"Of course I am," I snapped, brushing off my dress. The broken nail launched a run in my left stocking. Damn, damn, damn. "But you just barely made it. Where's your tie?"

He looked down at his heathery sweater, and then down at me. I'm over six feet tall in dress shoes, but he was six four, with wavy chestnut hair and the most distinctive green eyes I'd ever seen on a waiter or anyone else, the glass green of a breaking wave.

"This was the best I could do," he said coolly. "I just came from the airport."

"The best you could do!" I kept my voice low, but green eyes or not I was angry. "Black slacks, white shirt, black bow tie. I was very specific! Look, I need those glasses up there."

"Yes, *ma'am*." He mounted the chair, reached up, and handed the goblets down to me. He had broad, tanned hands, still chilly from the rain where they brushed my fingers.

"Thanks," I said. "Now let's find the others."

"Right here, Carnegie." Joe Solveto's cunningly

mussed sandy hair and narrow, theatrical face appeared in the stairwell leading up from the basement-level pantry. He brandished an unopened champagne bottle. "We're popping the corks downstairs, but this is the special stuff for the happy pair. I see you found the goblets. Excuse me, sir."

Sir? Joe relieved me of the glasses and pressed on into the dining room, quickly followed by all three waiters, in their white shirts and black bow ties. Number Three must have arrived during Susie's sneezing attack. I felt a blush rising from the asymmetrical neckline of my jade silk dress. It was my one haute-couture rag, and my favorite outfit for weddings: gracefully appropriate for day or evening, generously cut to allow mad dashes to my van in case the best man forgot his tie or the maid of honor her lipstick, and equipped with pockets in which to thrust my hands when embarrassed. Which I was, and did.

"You're a guest. I'm very sorry. I—"

"My fault." He had a light tenor voice, surprising in such a large man, and slightly crooked front teeth that showed when he smiled and saved him from being male-model perfect. Not that one objects to perfect strangers. "Obviously I came in the wrong door," he was saying. "Have I missed everything?"

"Yes. No." Deep breath. "The ceremony is almost over, but you can slip in the back if you go through the dining room and to your right. I am sorry."

"No problem," he said, smiling as he walked by. "You can order me around anytime."

I stood bemused for a moment, muttering "Who *was* that masked man?"

Then I got back to work.

Died to Match

on sale now

Luke Skywalker was juggling martini glasses. Albert Einstein was dirty-dancing with Monica Lewinsky. And Zorro was arguing with Death himself. For wedding planner Carnegie Kincaid, it was just another night on the job: a coed bachelor party thrown by one of Seattle's hippest couples. But what started as the perfect evening ended in disaster: one beautiful bridesmaid was dead, and another had thrown herself into Elliot Bay.

With families to please, dresses to hem, and headlines to grab, Carnegie is discovering the dark side of love and marriage amid high and low Seattle society— and that while some passions may be forever, some are a motive for murder . . .

"WHAT EXACTLY DID YOU DO BETWEEN ELEVEN o'clock and the time you discovered the body?"

I described my circuit through the party, my dance with Zack, the people I recalled seeing on the dance floor, and then meeting Aaron on the stairs and going out on the pier with him. All the while, Officer Lee scribbled away. Graham seemed unsurprised by Corinne's fall into the harbor;

maybe it happened all the time at waterfront parties. I continued on, explaining about my final walk-through routine, and mentioning Aaron's departure. This time I managed to describe the corpse without tears.

I thought we were finally finished, but instead, the detective began to skip around in the chronology of the party, repeating questions he'd already asked, probing at my memory like a man with a poker stirring at a fire. It's surprising what you can remember if someone asks the right way. Graham coaxed out details I hadn't even registered at the time, like the triangular gap in the rocks near Mercedes' shoulder—the source of the murder weapon, I surmised, though he wouldn't say—and the damp patch of drool on Tommy's leprechaun jacket.

"Would you assume that Mr. Barry had been lying by the pillar for some time?"

"Well, long enough to sit down and then pass out, but it might not have taken long. I expect he was pretty well plowed when he first arrived. Marvin was at the front entrance, he could tell you."

"He already has. I'm double-checking. Mr. Breen gave us the guest list, and we'll be interviewing everyone on it, as well as the staff from Solveto's and the cleaning firm and so forth." The lieutenant smiled sorrowfully. "Too bad it wasn't a smaller party. Let's go back to your encounter with Ms. Montoya in the rest room. Was she taking drugs?"

"What?!"

"It's a simple question." Graham sat remarkably still and composed, as if he could do this all day. I suppose he often did. Outside, the rain went on raining, a muffled drumroll against the windows.

"I . . . didn't see her doing anything like that." Of course, I suspected that Mercedes blabbed about Talbot only because she was high. But suspicions aren't facts. "Why do you ask? Were there drugs in her system?"

As before, he ignored me. "You said the two of you talked a bit. What about, exactly?"

I was dreading this question. I'd deliberately glossed over the conversation in my step-by-step account. Mercedes had confided in me—I thought of her now as one of my brides—and it seemed cruel to expose her private life. But facts *are* facts. And murder is murder.

"She told me she was engaged to be married. To Roger Talbot."

Graham was startled, though he hid it well, merely elevating one eyebrow a millimeter or two. His voice stayed level. "That's . . . quite a piece of news."

"She said it was a secret, no one knew about it yet."

"Did you believe her?"

"Well, I didn't think she bought that ring herself."

"Which ring? She was wearing several."

"That was all costume jewelry. She had a diamond ring on a long chain around her neck. She waved it at me and then hid it down her blouse. . . ."

Lightning struck both of us at once. Graham

leaned forward. *"There was no diamond ring on the corpse."*

"Oh, my God." I pictured again the bloody rent in Mercedes' skull, the vulnerable nape of her neck. "No. No, it was gone. I should have realized that last night—"

"Never mind. Can you describe it?"

I closed my eyes and took a breath to steady myself. "A marquise diamond, between two and three-quarter and three carats. Six-prong setting. Pear-cut side stones. Platinum band engraved with leaves. I'm not sure of the size on the side stones, maybe half a carat apiece."

"Ginny, call that in. And find out if Talbot's in his office today." She went to the window and spoke quietly into her cell phone. Graham was looking at me curiously. "She *waved* it at you and you saw all that?"

I shrugged. "It's my business."

"Really. And you didn't see any sign of it when you found her? No ring, no gold chain?"

"No. But maybe if you search the exhibit—"

"Ms. Kincaid, we are sifting the goddamn *sand,* grain by grain. Excuse my French." He sighed heavily. "So she asked you to plan her wedding. Was she happy about this secret engagement? Any anger at Talbot for keeping it secret?"

"She seemed fine with it, as far as I could tell. She was kind of . . . excitable."

"Excitable. What was she excited about?" Graham's tired brown eyes were expressionless, but I could sense the active intelligence behind them as he weighed my words.

"Well, about Talbot's running for mayor, and about their wedding. She was very insistent that I agree to work for her. She even gave me some cash as a deposit."

This brought both eyebrows up. "Cash? How much cash?"

"I don't really know. I didn't want to take it out and count it during the party, and then after I found her I forgot all about it. It's still in the pocket of my costume."

Another sigh. First the ring, now this. I was definitely flunking Witness 101. "Ms. Kincaid, we'll need to take the money in as evidence. You'll be given a receipt. All right?"

"Of course." *But still, she meant to hire me. She meant to be my bride.*

"Let's go back to Mr. Barry. Tell me again what he said."

I shifted in my chair. Wicker's not that comfortable. "Tommy said 'Stop it.' I think he said that twice. And then he said 'You're killing her!'"

"So he believed that you had killed Ms. Montoya?"

"Is that what he told you? Lieutenant, Tommy couldn't even focus his eyes at that point, he was dead drunk! I think he must have been repeating something he'd said earlier, during the murder."

"And yet if he had spoken out earlier, the killer would hardly have left him alive as a witness."

"Well, maybe he didn't say it out loud, except later, to me, only he didn't know it was me, he was just raving! Look, I know you're supposed to be cagey about testimony, but *please* tell me, who did Tommy see? Did he recognize the murderer?"

Graham stood up. "We'd very much like to know that ourselves. Unfortunately, after leaving the crime scene, Mr. Barry drove his car into a concrete abutment under the Alaskan Way Viaduct. He's currently in intensive care at Harborview. In a coma."

May the Best Man Die

on sale now

Carnegie Kincaid plans weddings, not stag parties. When a client asks Carnegie to manage a pre-wedding blow-out—complete with a stripper—she tactfully refuses the job. So why is Carnegie peering through binoculars across the Seattle Ship Canal, watching a shapely Santa Claus turn naked inside a hip dockside bistro?

Because her own significant other—with whom she is having some significant differences—is at the party too. And so, it turns out, is a killer . . .

THE MINUTE I PUT DOWN THE PHONE, I GRABBED the binoculars and focused on the Hot Spot for a second look. Not that I cared whether Aaron was inside. Not that I cared about Aaron at all.

Not that I could see him, either. Santa had left the lighted window, and the revelers milled aimlessly inside, as if the party were winding down. I spotted Mr. Garlic, but no one else familiar—until a flurry of movement drew my attention to the grassy slope below the deck.

There in the silvery frost and the tilted shadows, two long-limbed figures were struggling together, dodging and flailing in clumsy counterpoint. I had no trouble recognizing them as the best man and Lily's baby brother. Jason Kraye was obviously drunk; maybe Darwin was the designated driver, trying to take his car keys away?

But you don't punch people to get their car keys, I thought. And then, *Maybe you do, if you're young and male.* It was hard to tell if this was a ritual scuffle—elk clashing their antlers—or a serious fight. Either way, I can't say it bothered me to see the supercilious Jason getting knocked around a little.

The third figure was less ambiguous: Frank Sanjek, the bridegroom, was kneeling on the grass near the two combatants and vomiting hideously, his head jerking and lolling. *Another male ritual.* I smiled ruefully. Time for me to go home.

But once I went downstairs and gathered up my things, a nagging doubt stopped me from walking out the door. I had assured Lily that her brother was fine, and now he was apparently in the middle of a fistfight. Shouldn't I check on the outcome?

For that matter, shouldn't I make sure that the amiable, sensible bridegroom wasn't unconscious and abandoned by his drunken friends, out in the freezing night? Eddie tells me I fuss too much about our clients, and maybe it's true. But I was eager to see Sally Tyler walk down the aisle and out of my life on New Year's Eve, and to that end, I needed Frank Sanjek safe and sound.

So I dashed up to the storeroom, hurried over

to the worktable, and raised the binoculars to my eyes for the third and last time.

There was even less to see than before. Some of the café's windows had gone dark, making it hard to get a clear view into the shrubbery. But at least Frank was on his feet; I watched him stagger to the sliding door and wrench it open. I didn't spot Darwin, or Jason either, but they might have already left.

The stripper was just leaving, striding briskly up the sidewalk, head up and shoulders back after a job well done. And someone else was working his way down through the bushes toward the bike path, but I couldn't make out his face, or whether he had a bicycle waiting for him. The guys were supposed to take cabs or buses home instead of driving, but even a bike could be dangerous—

"Bird-watching?"

I jumped, and Eddie's binoculars slipped from my suddenly clumsy fingers, to land in the silver punch bowl with an enormous and resounding *gonnng*.

I was shocked, and not just because a man had suddenly materialized in the doorway. I was shocked by who it was. Aaron Gold.

Unlike the younger party guests, Aaron wore a tie. But it hung loose from his collar and his crow-black hair was mussed. My former suitor's deep-set brown eyes gleamed glassily, and when he smiled, the familiar swift white grin came out lopsided. Even from where I stood, halfway across the room, I could smell the combination of cigar smoke and retsina.

So he was shooting pool in the other room. And then afterward, he must have been watching Santa...

"No birds at night," said Aaron, shaking his head sagely. A lock of hair flopped down into his eyes. "I know! S' Christmas. You're gonna find out who's naughty or nice. Merry Christmas, Stretch."

I stood with my back to the reverberating punch bowl and took a deep, shaky breath. I didn't know how long Aaron had been watching me, or whether he guessed that I'd been spying on Santa's striptease earlier. I also didn't know how I felt about him, after the last few weeks of angry silence and unwilling tears.

And what neither of us knew, and wouldn't learn until the next day, was this: of the three young men I had observed on the grass behind the Hot Spot Café, only two were still alive.